Kavan knelt beside the body and felt for a pulse. The trail of crimson on the pure white snow suggested the answer, but he still had to check. His perceptive eyes were immediately drawn to the growing blood stain in the middle of the boy's back. His muscles tensed under his loose-fitting jerkin. Kavan felt rage. Sickness swelled within him. A closer inspection of the corpse showed him what he both knew and dreaded: teeth and claw marks.

It had been the same for the previous four victims. Kavan instinctively glanced about. The gesture was futile; if the beast was still here, Kavan held little doubt it would already have attacked. Still, Kavan let a hand drop to the hilt of his short sword. Even a Gaimosian Knight could be caught unaware and killed. Kavan had no desire to fall into that category.

A cold wind blew across the open field. The tree line was a hundred meters in any direction. The beast had no fear; that much was obvious from the spot of the kill. Loose snow danced across the field, tickling Kavan's neck and face. Kavan removed a glove and gingerly placed his fingertips in the wound. The blood hadn't begun to dry yet. He smiled, cruel and wicked. The beast was close.

"I've got you," he whispered to the gathering dusk.

The Gaimosian looked around again, this time for a trail. Snow had been falling for the past few hours, but it was still loose enough for him to just make out a set of prints moving east. Kavan looked up towards the forest edge. He could barely distinguish a thin plume of blue smoke rising into the grey skies. With night falling, he knew his task had just gotten more treacherous. The beast was dangerous enough in daylight. Night made it particularly lethal. Kavan drew his sword and left the body behind. The hunt was on.

BEYOND THE EDGE OF DAWN

A History of Malweir Book III

Christian Warren Freed

Copyright © 2020 by Christian Warren Freed

Excerpt from *Hammers in the Wind* 2021 Christian Warren Freed
Cover design by Warren Design
Cover copyright 2021 by Warfighter Books
Author Photograph by Anicie Freed

Warfighter Books
Holly Springs, North Carolina 27540
https://www.christianwfreed.com

Second Edition: January 2021

Library of Congress Cataloging-in-Publication Data
Name: Freed, Christian Warren, 1973- author.
Title: Armies of the Silver Mage/ Christian Warren Freed
Description: Second Edition | Holly Springs, NC: Warfighter Books, 2021.
Identifiers: LCCN 2021930770 | ISBN 9781734907544 (trade paperback)
ISBN: 9781735700090 (eBook)
Subjects: Epic fantasy | Military fantasy | Paranormal

Printed in the United States of America

10 9 8 7 6 5 4 3 2 1

"Armies of the Silver Mage was a great read...any fan of Lord of the Rings or Game of Thrones will love this book. I'm looking forward to next book."

"The book is almost an homage to the great classics like Sword of Shanara and the Lord of the Rings. The author has cleverly used his past military and combat experience to make the battle scenes more realistic."

The Northern Crusade
Hammers in the Wind
Tides of Blood and Steel
A Whisper After Midnight
Empire of Bones
The Madness of Gods and Kings
Even Gods Must Fall

The Histories of Malweir
Armies of the Silver Mage
The Dragon Hunters
Beyond the Edge of Dawn

Forgotten Gods
Dreams of Winter
The Madman on the Rocks
Anguish Once Possessed
Through Darkness Besieged*

Where Have All the Elves Gone?
The Lazarus Men
Repercussions: A Lazarus Men Agenda*
Coward's Truth: A Novel of the Heart Eternal*
Tomorrow's Demise: The Extinction Campaign
Tomorrow's Demise: Paths of Salvation*

A Long Way From Home: Memories and
Observations From Iraq and Afghanistan+

Immortality Shattered
Law of the Heretic*
The Bitter War of Always*
Land of Wicked Shadows*
Storm Upon the Dawn*

War Priests of Andrak Saga
The Children of Never*

SO, You Want to Write a Book? +
SO, You Wrote a Book. Now What? +

*Forthcoming   + Nonfiction

Acknowledgements

This story was born over the course of my 3rd tour of duty in the War on Terror. I was stationed at Camp Victory, Baghdad- right beside Baghdad International Airport- in 2005. Each night (when I could) I got into my physical training uniform and ran around a small lake. Not much, just a few miles. In the center of the lake was a bombed out palace that Saddam and his sons used as a private resort. Fancy place with golden toilets. It just so happened that Saddam was being held prisoner within the palace during my time there. (I was in Mosul, Iraq when he was captured two years earlier.) I spent the better part of a year hoping to see a glimpse of the dictator, though I never did. What did happen was a name entered my head. That name evolved into a job, then a kingdom. His friends popped up along the way and I eventually arrived at what you see before you.

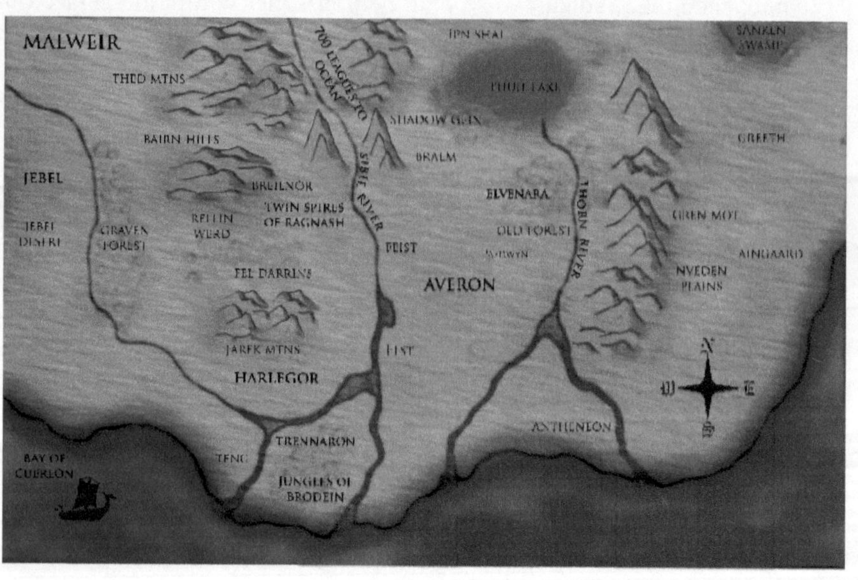

MALWEIR
THED MTNS
700 LEAGUES TO OCEAN
IPN SHAI
SANKEN SWAMP
THORL LAKE
SHADOW GLEN
GREETH
BAIRN HILLS
BRALM
JEBEL
BRELLNOR
TWIN SPIRES OF RAGNASH
SEBLE RIVER
ELVENARA
THORN RIVER
CIREN MOT
JEBEL DESERT
GRAVEN FOREST
RELLIN WERD
OLD FOREST
AINGAARD
MORWYN
PEIST
NVEDEN PLAINS
FEL DARRINS
AVERON
JAREK MTNS
FIST
HARLEGOR
ANTHENEON
TRENNARON
BAY OF CUERLON
TENG
JUNGLES OF BRODEIN
N
W
E
S

ONE

Kavan

Kavan knelt beside the body and felt for a pulse. The trail of crimson on the pure white snow suggested the answer, but he still had to check. His perceptive eyes were immediately drawn to the growing blood stain in the middle of the boy's back. His muscles tensed under his loose-fitting jerkin. Kavan felt rage. Sickness swelled within him. A closer inspection of the corpse showed him what he both knew and dreaded: teeth and claw marks.

It had been the same for the previous four victims. Kavan instinctively glanced about. The gesture was futile. If the beast was still here, Kavan held little doubt it would already have attacked. Still, he let a hand drop to the hilt of his short sword. Even a Gaimosian Knight could be caught unaware and slain. Kavan had no desire to fall into that category.

A cold wind blew across the open field. The tree line was a hundred meters in any direction. The beast had no fear. That much was obvious from the spot of the kill. Loose snow danced across the field, tickling Kavan's neck and face. Kavan removed a glove and gingerly placed his fingertips in the wound. The blood hadn't begun to dry yet. He smiled, cruel and wicked. The beast was close.

"I've got you," he whispered to the gathering dusk.

The Gaimosian looked around again, this time for a trail. Snow had been falling for the past few hours, but it was still loose enough for him to just make out a set of prints moving east. Kavan looked up towards the forest edge. He could barely distinguish a thin plume of blue smoke rising into the grey skies. With night falling, he knew his task had just gotten more treacherous. The beast was dangerous enough in daylight. Night made it particularly lethal. Kavan drew his sword and left the body behind. The hunt was on.

He moved swiftly and with purpose. Everything he owned was on his back. He was a man without home or family. Revenge drove him, keeping him warm at night when the harsh reality of the world threatened to claim him. He was a man lost, damned for the crimes of a kingdom that no longer existed. Hatred tainted his heart. He, and those few others remaining, roamed the lands eternally in the quest for vengeance. These were the Gaimosian Knights, travelling under the shroud of steel and mysticism. The world knew them as Vengeance Knights: the fallen sons and daughters of once proud Gaimos.

Now Kavan worked for money and the thrill of the hunt. A belief system instilled from birth bade him act in the sake of honor and righteousness. As such, he'd been hunting this beast for nearly a month. Every time he drew close, some form of devilry allowed the beast to escape. Kavan was determined not to let that happen again. He picked up the pace. What was left of the sun now dazzled a demonic red across the horizon.

Kavan viewed it as a good omen. Killing was always easier at night. The blood red sky felt right for the moment. He continued watching for signs of the beast as he got closer to the trees. His boots crunched softly on the under-layer of hardened snow. Stealth had never been his strong suit. He'd ever been one in favor of kicking in the front door and seeing how matters played out. Others of his kind had taken to the shadows and the lives of assassins since the fall of Gaimos. Kavan was better than that.

A howl rose from the mountains. Local wolf packs were on the hunt. Kavan smiled and entered the forest. It was a good night to kill. He paused beside an ancient oak tree and let his eyes adjust to the gloom. The heavy branches stretched far and covered large areas with darkness. He smelled the smoke now and knew he was close to the house, close to the beast and the end of the hunt. The twenty gold pieces promised by the villagers wasn't exactly a king's ransom, but they would more than satisfy his meager needs until something better came along. After chasing this beast for close to a month, Kavan was ready to kill it for free.

The sounds of the forest echoed hauntingly. Winds rustled rotted branches and dead leaves not yet covered by the quickly accumulating snow. Kavan wanted the beast to know he was coming. He wanted it to know death approached. After so long, Kavan needed a fight. Low branches reached out to lash at his exposed face and arms as he stalked towards the house.

The smells of roasting meat and burning wood grew stronger. He was close. Kavan felt the shadows creep in around him the deeper he went into the woods. He tilted back his head and sniffed the wind. Death had already beaten him here. The thatch-roofed home came into view. Kavan spied the broken-in front door and lamented for the family. What remained of the door left a gaping wound marred by the invitation of a subtle fire in the hearth. A blood-streaked hand curled up in the doorway. The fingers were broken and gripped a thick tuft of fur.

Kavan instantly decided against going through the front. The beast knew he was coming and would be lying in wait for him to make the fatal error of charging in blindly. A woodpile lay just off to the left of the house.

Snow powder covered the top rows. A crude bronze-edged axe rested deep in a large piece of oak nearby. Fresh snow partly covered dozens of tracks. Some were human; most weren't. Dog tracks intermingled with the rest.

It didn't take Kavan long to discover the fate of the rest of the family. A pair of corpses was stacked by the back door, both bodies savagely torn apart and callously dropped beside the carcasses of the dogs. They'd had their spines broken and throats torn out. Kavan swore under his breath. The dogs would have provided warning to the family, but it hadn't been enough. Only death and evil remained inside the meager cottage. Kavan crept to the back door and stopped to listen.

He knew from experience what was going to happen next. Kavan ducked under the windowsill and crept right. Using the shadows for cover, the Vengeance Knight rose slowly and peered inside. Only his right eye broke the silhouette of the stained window. He scanned the home for signs of his prey. The fire had burned low, offering just enough light for him to make out two more bodies. What he assumed was the father lay in the door while a child of five or six had been butchered beneath the table.

Enraged, Kavan resisted the urge to charge inside. He still didn't know where the beast was. The murder scene was one he'd witnessed a hundred times. Their ordeal was ended. Nothing could be done to assuage their suffering now. Kavan needed patience. He thoroughly searched the rest of the ruined home before his eyes settled on a partially hidden corner by the front door. A shadow stretched just enough past the edge of the light and moved with the gentle rhythm of slow breathing. Kavan narrowed his eyes.

"At last," he whispered.

Kavan was about to slip back to the rear door when a pair of frost blue eyes suddenly opened and fixed him with a baleful glare. Swearing, Kavan ducked as the beast launched at him. Only a lifetime of training saved his life. He dove left, narrowly avoiding the sudden explosion of glass and wood. He felt the rush of a large body pass overhead. The beast reeked, gagging him as he rolled and brought up his sword.

The beast crashed into a small tree. Snow fell from the impact. Kavan rose to one knee and got his first true look at his prey. Stark realization flooded his senses. This was no ordinary creature. He faced a werebeast! Kavan watched in shock as the beast shook off the effects of the collision and recoiled to strike again. Werebeasts hadn't been seen in this half of Malweir in decades. Battling one now didn't make sense. It shouldn't be alive. His chances of surviving were suddenly diminished.

The werebeast lowered its massive head and centered on Kavan. Sheer hatred blazed in those eyes. It was then Kavan noticed something startling. Many of the beast's features were those of a man. What foul arts had twisted this genetic nightmare, he'd never know. Kavan was certain of one fact: some dark evil had created this creature.

Heavily muscled, the beast had a mane of pure black running down its wide spine. Silver hair covered the rest. Hot spittle dripped from menacing fangs lining the mouth. Razor sharp claws dug into the ground. Easily five hundred pounds, the beast went on four legs and had a stubbed tail. Whatever magic was responsible for its creation, Kavan knew the beast was made for the sole purpose of killing. Only one of them would be walking away from this battle. He hoped it would be him.

The werebeast flexed, giving Kavan a split second to react before it attacked. Kavan knew he had but one chance to survive. He had to strike fast and sever the beast's head. The theory was untested, but Kavan was certain decapitation killed just about everything. He rolled to his right as the beast crashed into the ground where he'd just stood. Letting out a fierce roar, the Vengeance Knight swung with all his might at the exposed underbelly.

Sharpened steel ripped into the thick hide, tearing a great gash over the sternum and down the rib cage. Blood and fur splattered down. The beast let out a twisted scream as it crashed into the house. Glass burst as the werebeast tumbled through the cottage. Kavan rose in a fluid motion and ran at the dazed and wounded beast. He burst through the ruined front door and aimed his blade. Fast as he was, the werebeast recovered faster. It lashed backward with a hind leg, catching him in the stomach. The force of the blow sent Kavan flying across the family room.

Kavan slid across the already bloodstained floor. Glass and wood shards ripped into his back and neck until he crashed into the fireplace. Stunned, he struggled to rise. The back door exploded in a shower of splinters. The werebeast stalked inside, hungry for the kill. It knew it had the advantage and meant to toy with Kavan before killing him.

Kavan crawled up on his hands and knees. Pain lanced through his entire body. He guessed at least three of his ribs were broken, and he was cut in a dozen places. His vision swirled darkly. He cursed himself for underestimating his enemy. Kavan looked up through his pain and noticed the beast had a heavy limp. A trail of blood and gore followed it into the house.

The werebeast stopped a goodly distance from the stunned knight. As much fun as it had in inflicting suffering, the beast knew it was wounded and grew leery of tasting the bitter steel again. The clouds leaving his vision, Kavan grinned fiercely at the reluctant approach of the beast.

"Hurts, does it?" he asked and raised his sword in challenge.

The beast bellowed in response and attacked. A battle rage came over the Vengeance Knight, and he met the attack head on. They collided in a sickening crunch of bone and flesh. Kavan was driven to the floor. The beast fell on him with malice. Elongated claws snarled around Kavan's torso and squeezed. He felt the breath crushed out of him. He fought back the urge to cry out as the pressure on his ribs intensified.

He started hammering the pommel of his sword into the beast's side, striking just beneath the ear. The beast screamed, and Kavan could have sworn it was the sound of a man in pain. He hit harder despite his own growing agony. The pressure eased suddenly, if just a bit. Kavan turned his sword sideways and drove the wrist guard into the beast's ear canal.

The werebeast let him go and recoiled from intense pain. Kavan struggled to his feet. Brain matter dripped down the sword onto his hand and wrist. He looked down on his wounded enemy and felt…nothing. There was no hatred. No remorse. Pity was absent as well. At this one moment in time, Kavan wanted only to kill the beast and be done. He took an unsteady step forward and raised his sword one last time. The werebeast looked up at him with pleading eyes. Kavan understood it all then. The beast wanted to die.

He stood over his elusive quarry and hefted his mighty broadsword, making ready to strike. Another man might have paused to study the beast or learn from it. Kavan already knew what he wanted. The werebeast had run free and killed for far too long. It was only fitting to repay it in kind. He gathered what little remained of his full strength and brought the sword down with a mighty swing. The werebeast never took its eyes off its killer.

After a sickening crunch followed by brief resistance, the beast was dead. The body fell in a great heap of lifeless flesh as the head rolled to a stop at the foot of the slaughtered farmer's child. Kavan took neither satisfaction nor disgust from the task. He'd been paid to rid the land of a murdering creature and had done just that. He quickly searched the house for a towel and medical supplies before sitting down to clean his sword and dress the more major of his wounds.

Kavan then collected the severed head and wrapped it in a burlap sack. Once finished, he gathered the bodies of the family and set them in the center of the main room. He lacked the time or energy to give them a proper burial, instead choosing to enact an old Gaimosian tradition of burning the bodies. He left the beast where it had died. Some things didn't deserve the honor. Kavan spent a goodly portion of the next hour collecting fuel for the pyre. Setting the pyre to flame, he snatched the severed head and strode out the front door.

TWO

Revelations

Mun added another log to the fire and shivered against the growing cold. He wished he'd gone east to the Jebel Desert to wait out the winter. A hundred wishes later, here he was. Grumbling to himself, the old man gathered his patchwork blanket and went back to his desk. His teapot still hadn't whistled, and that only served to compound his frustrations. Winter hereabouts was cold and cruel, and, even after sixty years, he still hadn't left for warmer climes. So Mun sat in the constable's office waiting for something to happen and working for a man ten years his junior. Sometimes life was just cruel like that.

The door opened with a loud boom, causing Mun to startle and jump up. He eyed the newcomer with a wary gaze before sitting back down. "Hadn't expected to see you again."

Kavan offered a thinly veiled gaze of contempt. "Sorry to disappoint you, old timer. Where's Chardis?"

"Constable's out on his rounds. Just because we've had one of you mercenaries wandering about doesn't make the village safe," Mun scowled.

He clearly had no issues with his mistrust of Kavan being known. Mun spied the dripping sack in the Gaimosian's hand and let curiosity get the best of him. Perhaps this was the exciting something he'd been aching for. "Eh, what's that in the bag making all that mess? You'll be cleaning it up if you know what's good for you."

Kavan bit back a wild laugh. He'd grown accustomed to being treated this way, despite his normal good nature and willingness to help. Gaimosians were feared and reviled the world over ever since the war. "Care to see for yourself? It should make for quite the gossip once I'm gone."

Mun licked his lips tenderly as temptation reached out. "Constable'll be back soon. Feel free to sit over there 'til he does. And you'll be cleaning up that bloody mess afore you be leaving."

Kavan sat without saying a word. Mun's attitude was nothing new. He'd seen it in every little village and hamlet west of the Jebel Desert. Folk around Malweir eyed his kind with strong measure of mistrust. The pride of Gaimos was a scourge across the realm, and there were few old timers who had anything good to say about it. More times than not, Kavan ignored the stares and whispered conversations that went on behind his back.

There was no hiding who he was — what he was. Gaimosian Knights were world renowned as the very best swordsmen and warriors. None could stand against them in single combat. It had taken the combined might of seven kingdoms to defeat and destroy the kingdom of Gaimos. Those few hundred knights who survived the war now roamed Malweir in vain attempts at erasing the signs of their pride. It was thankless work.

The warmth of the fire felt good. He leaned back against the wall and let his eyes drift closed. Seeing the dance of the flames brought back those last few moments of his battle with the werebeast. Three days had gone by, and the memories continued to bother him. He hadn't been able to come up with any answers to the mounting riddles facing him. Beasts of legend held no human characteristics, or so he'd always been told. Yet the one he'd fought and killed had been more human than not. Foul thoughts nagged at the corner of his consciousness.

His first thoughts were of magic and wizards. But a wizard was rarer than a dragon these days. In fact, there hadn't been a wizard in western Malweir since the fall of Gaimos, some seventy odd years ago. Not that magic was a rarity. Several species carried the gift. The Elves were said to be the most powerful. Kavan left that to rumor, for he'd never seen an Elf.

The door opening suddenly broke his thoughts. Snow flurries hurried in before the gaunt frame of Constable Chardis. There was a surprised look on the man's face.

"Well, well," Chardis said. "Welcome back, lad."

Any misgivings he might have had about Kavan were wisely kept to himself. Having the knight in his village was a boon to his job and those he'd sworn an oath to protect. Mun grunted disaffectedly from the opposite side of the room.

Kavan grinned at being called a lad. Truth be told, he was already over one hundred years old. The bloodlines of fallen Gaimos were blessed with lifespans up to three times that of a normal man. No one knew why. Perhaps it was one of the things that had led to Gaimos's eventual demise. Jealousy was a mighty weapon.

"How did your hunt go?" Chardis asked before Mun could remark. He walked straight to the fire where he could warm his frozen hands. His face was weathered and creased with a bright pink tinge.

Kavan rose respectfully. The pain in his ribs was still great and often unbearable. "It was bloody."

He brought out the werebeast's head and told them his macabre tale. Both Mun and Chardis listened with rapt attention. Their gazes fell as Kavan briefly detailed the murdered family. Chardis wasn't pleased by the trail of bodies ranging the fields surrounding his village.

The Constable rubbed his chin, lost in thought. "With all the snow we've been getting, those bodies will already be covered up. We won't be able to dig them out until spring. How many did you say you found?"

"Three along my track. The last was a squire in the middle of the field by the cottage," Kavan answered. "If I had stopped to bury them, the beast would still be loose."

"No fault in that," Mun muttered.

"Are you certain this was a werebeast?" asked Chardis.

Kavan nodded. "Aye, though something about it doesn't sit right with me. I've traveled this world for many years and have never heard of such a creature loose before. Legends say they used to be all over this part of Malweir, but none have been seen or reckoned on in generations."

Now it was Chardis' turn to think. "So why now? And why here? We're a simple people and have little to do with the modern world. There are no riches or prospects for such. It doesn't make sense."

"Who can say what makes the heart of evil beat? There's more, however. A question and a problem have been plaguing me since my battle. I think this was no ordinary werebeast."

Chardis raised an eyebrow. "What do you mean?"

"I cannot be certain, but I believe the creature I killed was once a man."

"Impossible!" Mun sputtered his mouthful of tea onto his lap.

Kavan wanted to agree, but circumstances were already different. His shoulder-length black hair swished softly against his neck as he shook his head. "Nay. For in those horrid eyes, I beheld emotions. It knew pain and fear and had cunning beyond measure. This beast wanted to die. It wanted me to kill it. Some foul purpose claimed that man and perverted him into a nightmare from legend."

"You speak ill tidings," Chardis cautioned. "Word of this can't get out to the people. There will be panic. A witch-hunt will ensue to find who did this. I suggest we leave that problem for another day." He paused, carefully choosing his next words. "I suspect you'll want your payment for the head in that bag?"

"And to be shown a tavern where I may get my fill of ale and wenches."

Chardis smiled. He motioned Mun to open the small safe and handed Kavan a pouch of coins. The knight expertly weighted his palm before tucking the leather pouch away.

"Twenty golds as agreed," Chardis told him. "A shame we had to do business in the first place, but I'm glad you finished it. Mun, mind the office. I think I could use a good ale as well."

Old Mun grumbled under his breath and went to stoke the fire again. He was just glad to be done with the Vengeance Knight. Times were troubling enough without one of them lurking about.

Kavan and Chardis stood beside each other just outside the building. The air was crisp and chill with winter's kiss. Their breath came out in thin plumes of steam. Spring was only a few weeks away, but this late storm refused to let go. The sky was clear and moonless. Kavan stared up at the purity of the night sky and marveled at the contrast of dark and bright. Thousands of stars winked at him. He was about to comment when the sky suddenly flared to life.

Hundreds of streaking lights slashed across the sky. There were so many, they veiled the stars. More and more thundered down. Kavan's mouth dropped open. He'd seen the occasional shooting star but never anything of this magnitude. Many cultures saw shooting stars as a foul event and shut the doors and shuttered the windows at the sight of just one. He was never one for superstitions, but his hunt of the werebeast left room for doubt.

Chardis made a quick warding gesture and started to move. "This is not good."

The meteor shower continued. Neither man spoke again until they were inside the village tavern. Many of those gathered clearly had also borne witness to the celestial event, for the mood was dark, sullen. The gentle crackling of the fire overpowered what sparse conversation there was. Chardis led them to an empty table on the far side of the room.

"What can I get you boys?" a serving maid asked as she walked up with a bright smile. Word of the storm had reached her and sent shivers of fear down her spine, but she was wily enough to capitalize on it.

Kavan smiled back. He stole a glance at her supple form and felt familiar stirrings. She wasn't the most beautiful woman he'd ever seen, but she was pretty and inspired a great many ideas. "What do you recommend, my dear? My friend and I are thirsty, and I'm paying."

Her eyes twinkled at the last. "The mulled wine is particularly good, I think. The ale is fine but not as strong as it should be. Don't tell Harding I said so, Constable. I don't think he'd appreciate me sabotaging his business, as it were."

Chardis waved off her concern. "No worries, Tarryl. I think the wine will do. Something to take the chill off is all we need."

"I'll be right back," she smiled and walked away.

"Nice girl," Kavan remarked.

Chardis shook his head with a rueful glance. "What will you do now?"

Kavan took his time to get his thoughts straight. "I really don't know. As I stalked the beast, I thought of heading off to another village on another hunt, but the questions in my mind demand answers. I would know where this beast came from."

"You can't solve all of Malweir's problems," Chardis advised. "The beast is dead, and our threat has passed. Let it rest and move on to better fortunes."

"If I could, but it's not that easy. If there is one of these creatures, there must be others. One man might not be able to solve all of the world's problems, but he might just make a difference with the right ones."

The young serving girl, Tarryl, returned carrying two pints of the strong red wine. Her gaze lingered just a while longer on Kavan after he paid her.

"The task you propose may last a lifetime. Are you prepared to spend the rest of your days on the hunt?" Chardis asked him.

Kavan drank deep from his mug before answering. "If I must. Tonight was a sign, Chardis. I feel it in my bones. I must go back on the hunt."

Both men sat and drank in silence until a shadow fell over them. Kavan looked up first. His eyes narrowed suspiciously at the seemingly drunken man teetering before them. Hand crept towards the hidden dagger at his belt. The drunk spied this and immediately held up his empty hands.

"Speak quick," Kavan warned, his voice a low, throaty growl.

The drunk did, leaving the Gaimosian in muted shock.

THREE

Propositions

"A hunt, you say?" the newcomer asked in wine-laden speech.

Kavan dropped his hand unseen to the hilt of his sword. The man staggered before clumsily finding refuge in an empty chair. No one else in the room bothered to look their way. He nodded once to the Constable before resuming his gaze on the Vengeance Knight. He reeked of manure, and his clothes were filthy. His graying hair was stringy and bore the look of not having been washed in months. Still, Kavan leaned forward.

"Not that it's any of your business, of course," he said with measured tone.

The drunk laughed. "Business is business, eh? Was a time I hunted myself."

Chardis had heard enough. "What are you up to, Therdin? We have enough to think on without your drunken stupor."

Therdin threw his hands up in defense, or at least tried to. "I'm meaning no harm, Constable. I jus' couldn't help but overhear yer conversation. If it's a hunt you want, I heard tell o' one down south. One more massive than any in recent years."

His eyes never left Kavan. For his part, Kavan didn't blink.

"You be interested?" Therdin asked.

Kavan leaned back and drank a mighty gulp. "I'm still listening, aren't I?"

Therdin slapped the table, laughing loudly. "I like you, Knight."

At the mention of his title, Kavan shifted his gaze over the crowd. The last thing he wanted was to draw attention. "Lower your voice if you wish to speak to me."

Therdin seemed taken aback, but the moment passed. Tense silence settled over the table. Therdin sat with a smug look, as if knowing what the answer was going to be. Chardis motioned for another round. He was tired and ready to return to his wife and warm bed but something in Therdin's behavior whispered caution.

"Your words are twisted," he said at last. "There's no hunt going on here."

Therdin shot him a drunken stare. "No, not here. Word's come up from Aradain of trouble brewing. Folk say King Eglios is asking for help. Say he's got a big hunt lined up."

"What kind of hunt?" Kavan asked.

Therdin smiled. "Ah, so you can do more than just threaten, eh? I heard tell o' strange creatures and dark magic roundabouts that way."

"Magic?" Chardis asked.

"Aye. Magic."

Kavan said, "Magic hasn't been used in years. Whence comes this magic, then?"

Even as he said it, Kavan didn't believe it. The werebeast was enough to convince him otherwise, though. His thoughts turned to leaving and finding the answers for himself.

"For myself, I cannot say. Though some say the ruins of Gessun Thune have been uncovered."

The Vengeance Knight suppressed a chill. Gessun Thune was a place of ancient evil from the time of the dawn of the world. Tales of murder on a grand scale still haunted children who misbehaved. No one had ever proven the existence of such a place or bothered speaking of it in public for a long time. Kavan remembered coming across vague references to it at the great library in Greeves.

"Gessun Thune is a legend, and even if it were real no one has seen or heard of it in this lifetime," he gently rebuked.

"Be that or not ain't for me to say, but I hear what folks say," Therdin shot back. "You didn't think that beastie you killed was one of a kind, did you?"

Both Kavan and Chardis tensed.

"What do you know of the beast?" Kavan asked.

Therdin shrugged off their concern. "Like I said, folks talk. There's been odd killings going on up and down the Kergland Spine all winter. Nothing natural about half-eaten bodies and busted up homes. Bears and wolves been scarce in these parts in my lifetime. What else coulda killed them folks?"

"I think you've had one too many drinks tonight, Therdin. How about I help you home? I'm sure Shella misses you," Chardis said after passing a nervous glance to Kavan.

"Nonsense, Constable. They ain't made enough for me to have drunk enough!" he boasted loudly.

Both men were instantly worried that his liberal speech would start a panic, or worse. That was the one thing neither needed. Chardis prided himself on maintaining a sense of peace, and Therdin's drunken behavior threatened to undo it. Kavan, on the other hand, had no desire for the entire village to know he was Gaimosian. The name inspired harsh repercussions.

He needn't have worried. Chardis kindly assisted Therdin to his feet and half-forced him outside. Once away from prying ears, the Constable slammed the drunk against the cold wall. "Now you listen to me. I don't want to hear another word about magic beasts or ancient ruins. People here don't need that kind of hassle in their lives. Kavan did what I paid him to do. You take yourself home and sleep this off. Tomorrow, we'll pretend this never happened."

He slapped Therdin firmly on the shoulder and sent him on his way. Only when he was gone did Chardis exhale his frustrations. He knew as much as the drunk that dark times were astir. The question was what could any of them do to stem the tide and maintain a measure of normalcy? Not wanting to stand in the cold any longer, Chardis collected his empty thoughts and went back inside. Sometimes, answers came rather than being found.

"That was interesting," Kavan said lightheartedly as Chardis sat.

He agreed, but for other reasons. "The cold makes a man want to keep warm. Ales work just as well in the right circumstance."

"And it is a cold night."

They continued making small talk for another hour and three rounds of mulled wine. Both carefully avoided talk of monsters or magic. Tarryl continued flirting with Kavan, and he enjoyed it. Chardis soon excused himself, leaving the Vengeance Knight half-drunk and alone again. Like most his kindred, he preferred it that way. Kavan had come to appreciate those moments of extended silence.

Tonight was one of those moments. Between his attraction to the young serving girl and the effects of some very good wine, he was more than ready to find a soft bed.

Tarryl sauntered up with an easy smile. "Another pint, sir?"

"No," he smiled back. "I've had more than enough drink tonight."

"Perhaps I could get you something else?" she asked with the slightest hesitation.

Kavan gave her his best impersonation of a gentleman. "Perhaps you could. Tell me, what time do you get off?"

Tarryl flushed.

Therdin hustled away from the cold-hearted Gaimosian, hoping to never run in to another one for the rest of his days. There was danger lurking just under Kavan's skin. Danger that turned blood cold. Therdin had seen it before, though not to such ravaging extent. Best stay away. He'd live much longer.

Stumbling through the village, at least so far as the far edge where he finally felt comfortable enough to abandon his drunken guise, Therdin hurried to his rendezvous point. Old trees lined the one lane road stretching south. Leafless branches twisted like gnarled bones, adding to the illusion of wickedness said to haunt the forest. Therdin knew better but wasn't one for quick speech. His was a thankless task, one from which there was but minimal reward. So long as the villagers believed ill resided in the forest he was decidedly safe.

He reached the small clearing, no more than a missing tree or two, and waited. Night continued to deepen and with it the bone numbing cold. Winter had no love for this part of Malweir. Fresh snow covered that from the previous storm. Therdin absently glanced around the semi-darkened area. A slight shiver took him and soon he couldn't stop. Only when his teeth began clattering together did his contact emerge from the night.

Dressed entirely in thick, black robes and knee high boots, the figure marched up to the villager. His head was hidden beneath a heavy cowl, only his breath coming in frosty plumes suggested he was human and even that was suspicious as far as Therdin was concerned.

"Well? Did he take the bait?" the figure asked with much impatience.

Therdin bobbed his head submissively. "I told him, Master. And he listened good. Not sure if he's bound for Aradain or not but he was real interested."

Hands gloved in the finest leather stretched from the ends of his sleeves to clasp and clench. "Pray that he does. I require the Gaimosian to reach Aradain in time or..."

Therdin continued to bob his head, praying his audience ended before a foul thought could take hold.

"Return to the village and follow the Gaimosian. I will contact you once it is determined that he is heading in the proper direction. Do not fail me, Therdin. The Gaimosians have been a plague on existence for too long. It is far past time to finish what our fathers began. I will see their entire bloodline eradicated. Now go, leave me."

"Yes, Master Corso," Therdin said before scurrying back to the sleeping village. He didn't slow until reaching the tavern's front door.

Alone again, Corso stood watching his servant fade into nothing. His thoughts swirled around impossible scenarios. So many of his kind had been killed his own bloodline was at the point of extinction. All because of the Gaimosians. His hatred towards that warrior breed stretched deep into the past, propelling him down roads few should ever willingly travel.

A time of blood was coming. A time when the very soul of the world would be pierced and his revenge finally obtained. Oh yes, blood would soon run free. Collecting his robes, Corso returned to the night. There was much planning to be done before his victims arrived in Aradain.

Kavan awoke with a groan followed by a long stretch. Days and weeks on the hunt had left his body bruised and beaten. The sun hadn't risen yet, but it was time to be moving. He looked fondly over his shoulder at the sleeping Tarryl. She'd easily been his most memorable and enjoyable experience since arriving in this backwoods village. The people were friendly enough, but he was born for a different, more violent life.

From the age of five, the boys of Gaimos were trained in the finer arts of warfare. Scholars and philosophers were brought in from the corners of the world to further the boys' training and education. Looking back, Kavan wondered why it had taken so long for the rest of Malweir to attack. Power was destructive, and the people of Gaimos had paid for it with their lives.

He left the past where it belonged and leaned down to kiss his companion's naked shoulder. Tarryl smiled in her sleep and rolled over. Kavan let out an amused chuckle before slipping out of bed. Naked, he stood in the chill air of the room. The fire had died out sometime in the middle of the night. Frost coated the windowpanes. He wasn't looking forward to leaving so soon but couldn't help but feel the pull of his training. Aradain was a long way away, and he had a nagging feeling that time was important. If his guess was correct, he was going to need help along the way.

Kavan went through a series of stretches, trying to alleviate some of the tension in his body. Scars littered his lean, muscular frame. A spear thrust to his right thigh. A pair of arrows to the right of his heart. Sword cuts crisscrossing his back and chest. Indeed, the life of a Vengeance Knight was not for the weak of heart. Temptation whispered for him to return to bed, but he refused. He had many leagues of travel if he was going to succeed in finding the right ally necessary to confront the rumored evil hiding in the ruins of Gessun Thune.

His thoughts wandered as he dressed, and he was surprised to find he was afraid. Aradain was a relatively small kingdom over a hundred leagues away. He'd been there once before. King Eglios had just ascended to the throne and was working towards his eventual reputation as a hard man. Three times he'd led his armies to war. They were defeated twice. Kavan knew the ineptitude of their military made Aradain a laughingstock among the neighboring kingdoms.

This was a common theme among the western kingdoms. Normally, he'd see no cause for concern, but the stunning victory of the third and final war gave him pause. The army of Aradain had virtually smashed the small kingdom of Barduk in a matter of days. Barduk no longer existed; it had become an annexation of Aradain. Eglios wasn't known for his strength. Rumors of an impending invasion from the south had surely forced the king's hand to desperate acts.

Kavan knew he had no choice but to go to Eglios and learn the truth. Deep foreboding troubled him. Fully clothed and armed, Kavan gave Tarryl a final kiss and slipped out the door. The smell of fresh bread and roasting meat stirred his appetite. He made his way to the kitchens to fill his pack. The owner's wife smiled and pinched him on the cheek before refusing his coin. After all he'd done for their village, a pack of rations seemed insignificant. He thanked her for her generosity and headed outside.

The predawn air was crisp and burrowed under the edge of his cloak. Kavan briefly considered going back inside until it warmed up. When it came down to it, he was Gaimosian and unused to a life of comfort. This was what he was. Hardship was a constant companion. It made him harder while weakening others. The journey to Aradain was long and trying, and he didn't know where else it would take him along the way. His conscience told him not to go alone, but he needed to go now. There would be time enough for rest when they laid him on a pyre.

Deciding there was nothing for it, Kavan shouldered his pack and set foot on the road. Halfway through the village he passed the Constabulary. He expected Mun to be peering out from behind curtains but was surprised to find Chardis himself sitting on the porch in wait.

"I figured you'd be sneaking out right about now," Chardis said as he packed his short-stem pipe.

Kavan placed a foot on the first step and eyed Chardis with respect. "It's easier this way. The folks that don't want me around can't complain, and I get where I need to faster. It doesn't do much for me to sit around and wait for things to happen."

"That's no way to live a life, but that's just my opinion," Chardis commented. "You'll be heading for Aradain then?"

Kavan nodded.

"Can't say as I agree with that. Therdin may have been drunk, but I think he knew what he was saying. Aradain is a troubled land. Some folks say the king has gone mad." He shrugged. "Doesn't matter. I hope you find what you're looking for. You've done enough to earn that peace already."

"It's never enough," Kavan solemnly replied. "There's a chance that werebeast was but one of many. If that's the case, there could be a lot more murders this side of the Spine. Someone needs to do something about it, and right now I figure that is me."

"You're an interesting sort, Kavan. I'm glad to have met you. May fortune smile upon you."

Kavan nodded his thanks. "And you."

Stepping back onto the road, he let it take him towards what would turn out to be his destiny. Chardis watched him go before heading back inside. He fixed Mun with a stern glare.

"I want you to take that head outside of the village and burn it. No one knows we had it. Am I clear?"

Mun nodded without saying a word.

FOUR
A Noble Thought

The pristine fields of snow stretched for as far as he could see. Sparse groves of pines and firs peppered the fields and rolling hills. Winter, Kavan decided, was his favorite time of year. Of course he could do without the cold, but a man in his profession wasn't prone to being choosy. Besides, he'd always figured it was easier to get warm than it was to cool off.

Endless leagues of lightly forested, rolling hills stretched off into the distance, reminding him of just how small one man's problems can be. Since the fall of Gaimos Kavan had roamed Malweir in search of purpose, meaning. Cold injustice ran like a plague through what were supposed to be the civilized kingdoms. Finding employ was no issue.

He'd been across the face of the world numerous times. A sad part of the life of what few Gaimosians remained. Thoughts of his homeland were forced deep, buried under the thick crust of a hard life few others bore. Kavan had been very young when Gaimos fell but that pain, that irrepressible sense of horror remained with him to this day.

Born hard and toughened continually to the point where Gaimosians became the premier fighting force in all Malweir, his peers had once been legion. Great companies were employed by neighboring kingdoms to quash petty rebellions or border disputes. Gaimos might have easily conquered the known world, but theirs was a force for good. Very seldom did their Knights ever stray from the path of righteousness. Which, in the end Kavan decided, had led to their downfall.

Was it any wonder why so many kingdoms banded together to rid the world of the power that was Gaimos? Naturally it hadn't made sense in the thrall of his youth. He was cast out from all he knew. Left to fend against the wolves of the world while the ashes of his people scattered on the cold winter winds. Humbled, and frightened to no small measure, Kavan walked away from what had once been a pristine kingdom, resplendent with statues of great warriors and thinkers alike.

What he found elsewhere left ill flavors swirling on his tongue. Malweir was a corrupt place. Many kingdoms were mired with cruel politicians and half-hearted monarchs. While never hiding his true identity, for the sin of vanity wouldn't permit such, Kavan took the odd job here and there until his reputation began to grow. It wasn't long before he was sought after, and with good reason. Gaimosians were the very best at armed combat. Warriors without peer. His blade solved the problems of a great many all while claiming only modest recompense in exchange.

Kavan learned, very early on, that money only went so far. There was no point in hording vast wealth while entire villages languished under the yoke of indentured servitude. He took what he needed to get by, always keeping a purse filled, for Gaimosians were without home or land. They roamed the world untethered. The rest he donated to those in greatest need. Selflessness had ever been among his best qualities, almost rival to that of a master swordsman.

His life took on no discernible pattern. As casual and free as the easterly wind just before dawn, he blew from kingdom to kingdom righting old wrongs and preventing new ones. As spiritually satisfying as his occupation was, Kavan often longed for that solitary life he so voraciously defended. Home and hearth were not in his future and truly only faded tatters of imagination from his past.

He often longed for the day when he could finally lay down his sword and take up a family, a home, a stable environment to call his life. Kavan smiled warmly at the thought despite knowing it was far off, if ever. Gaimosians the world over, no one had ever bothered figuring out how few remained, continued with their existence as if machines. If there was an endpoint, Kavan certainly wasn't privilege to it. All he knew was the inexorable pull of some faceless hand continued to drag him forward through one horrendous situation after the next.

When the time finally did arrive where he had earned the right to set down his sword, Kavan vowed to never look back. But first purpose must be filled.

He reined in his horse and pulled the round leather canteen from a saddlebag. The cool feeling pouring down his throat was refreshing, almost enough to help him forget the hardships of traveling alone across practically inhospitable terrain. Any simple pleasure taken from witnessing the vast expanse never fully translated to the reality of crossing it. And, even though he bore special fondness for winter, he didn't relish the idea of marching across an entire kingdom swathed in snow and ice.

Right now, he wished for a warm fire and a mug of ale. The rest would sort itself out quickly. Melted snow dampened his boots to the point where he found it difficult to feel his toes no matter how much he wiggled and flexed them. Frowning, he couldn't help but shiver as the chill crept up through his muscled frame. Kavan made up his mind then and there. It was time for a change.

As much as he relished the thought of sticking around this part of Malweir and continuing his hunt for the werebeasts, he knew that the only true way to defeat them was by going to the source. Kill the host and the plague died. Thoughts swirled like freshly blown snow. Centering on his problem, Kavan recalled his conversation with Therdin.

Aradain. King Eglios. Those two names overpowered his rationale. Was there some hidden connection between the werebeasts and the king of Aradain? Possibly. Anything was possible in this world. But what would Eglios stand to gain from such a... hostile relationship? Kavan failed to figure out any plausible answer aside from the collection of more power. Power, after all, was what made the world spin. He'd long figured that the sun would eat the moon if only it could catch up to it.

Saying, for the moment, that he believed King Eglios had some nefarious purpose in mind, Kavan tried to think of how anyone could come to control such monsters. Malweir had more than its fair share of bloodthirsty dragons, demons with a penchant for stealing children, and just plain bad people, but very few had ever been able to control a werebeast population. At least as far as Kavan recalled. That Eglios could do so now suggested he would be in league with a darkness far greater than any the Gaimosian had fought in a very long time.

Such conclusions led him down dark roads he was loath to travel. He was going to need help if there was any chance of succeeding. But who? Where to begin? Halting his horse again, the Vengeance Knight closed his eyes and drew his breath to bare minimums. Liquid fire sparked deep within his blood. Surging. Pulling. Leading him towards the southeast.

His eyes opened with the shock comparable to being struck by a crossbow bolt. Pain intensified through his entire body. He began to sweat. Suddenly exhausted, Kavan slumped in the saddle to the despondent snicker from his horse.

The bond. The blood tie that all Gaimosians shared. He had summoned it in the hopes of finding others to aid in his self-appointed quest. Normally anathema, working together with other Knights was his best and, most likely, only chance for success if the problem was as systemic as Therdin seemed to believe.

Not that Kavan took the drunk's words for granted. Men like that were always looking to improve their own station at the expense of others. Therdin wouldn't have divulged such knowledge without the whisper of promise, whether from Kavan or someone else. It wouldn't have surprised him if the drunk had been put up to it for some personal gain Kavan wasn't privileged too. It was a sad fact he'd witnessed too many times.

Regardless, Kavan abandoned the wasted thoughts occupying his mind. Therdin was in the past, an already fading dimension not worthy of remembrance. What little he had offered threatened to grow stagnant if Kavan failed to act quick enough.

Southeast.

Kavan glanced across the frozen hills towards the unseen horizons. He knew that imposing mountain ranges lay ahead, filled with rivers and danger. Beyond that was the great Jebel Desert, an endless sea of golden sands filling the middle of Malweir. He reached down to give his horse a reassuring pat on the neck. Having bore him through battle and travel, the steed was as much a part of the knight as his sword.

"Come friend. We must go in search of even older friends. The desert calls," he whispered.

His horse snickered and began to plod ahead. There was yet many weeks of travel before reaching the near western fringes.

FIVE

Poor Timing

Hours blended into days. Days into long stretches of seemingly indeterminable time that only a Gaimosian Knight could endure without fracture realities. Kavan and his ever-faithful horse continued ever east in search of the closest Gaimosians. Deep snow drifts gradually gave way to jagged cliffs and mountain peaks rising high into the clouds.

With only a silent horse for company, Kavan struggled with that ever present, if expertly hidden, desire to rethink old problems. Thoughts of what he might say, how he might react upon reuniting with old friends troubled him to no end. He hadn't seen another Gaimosian in years, much less the one he had sensed through the bond. While not the warm-hearted friends lesser men might otherwise be, Kavan felt a closeness that could only come from sharing intense moments in death laced combat. To even consider working with his old mentor again after so many years was a conflict of emotions he wasn't entirely prepared to deal with. Fortunately, the weather was able to sooth his aching mind.

Over the course of his travels he'd shed the heavy fur cloaks and now found genuine sweat making his skin clammy. Any grievance of the cold or penetrating winds of deep winter he might have bore were cast aside in favor of new disagreements over the humid nature of the lands bordering the desert.

He rode into the border town shortly before dusk. Already his nerves were on edge. Having been here before, and somewhat loath to repeat the experience, Kavan came in expecting a fight. Not that there was anything special about this out of the way, virtually forgotten part of the world, but he'd been in several just like it and they were all the same. Searching the past, he recalled having to kill two men on his last stay.

No doubt the past was doomed to repeat.

"Folks around here don't much care for your type," a grizzled voice snapped as Kavan tethered his horse outside the lone inn.

Winds howled down the road as if answering the challenge.

Kavan's head dipped slightly and his hand dropped to his sword. This took less time than he expected. "Folks need to mind their own business."

"Gaimosians seem to draw a crowd. Best you climb back in that saddle and head out, boy."

Turning, Kavan readied for the inevitable fight. Braggarts were good for little else than skewering with a blade, at least as far as his experience went. No doubt he'd make quick work of this one, provided he wasn't able to drive him off first. He pulled an inch of his blade free to loosen it.

Three men, all foul looking and ill tempered, were arrayed before him. One was missing an eye, the scars on that side of his face already faded. He was clearly the leader, for the others were almost skittish, as if they understood the truth of what they were attempting. Kavan pitied them. Almost.

"This is your only chance. Walk away now and there won't be trouble," he warned, though deep inside he knew they wouldn't comply.

It was a sad state of the human condition when pride interfered with common sense.

"Three on one is pretty good odds, even 'gainst one of you." He spat a wad of partially chewed iron leaf. The acidic flavor poured from his mouth in vapors.

Kavan's smile was grim, almost sad. "It's really not."

He moved, seizing advantage before the others had the chance to react. His sword hissed free, eager to kiss the open air again. The Gaimosian danced with the skill and grace of a venerable warrior. A hand was hacked free. Blood curdling screams followed. A second move and he skewered the man on the right. Blade punched through flesh and bone before twisting and jerking free.

A rope of hot blood splashed on the one eyed man's boots. He hadn't the chance to close his mouth from spitting before Kavan's blade gingerly touched him just below his one good eye. He began to tremble.

"Not wise, friend," Kavan admonished. "I told you to walk away."

Rage and fear conflicted in his eyes, but he was wise enough not to speak lest Kavan's sword drive into his flesh.

Kavan glanced at the man's partners. The one had died and the other had fallen mercifully silent. His screams reduced to mere whimpers as he clutched at the stump of his arm. Kavan frowned, for there was no more distressing sound than a grown man whimpering.

"See to your friend before he bleeds out."

He whipped his sword away and back into the scabbard. Disturbed with his actions, the Gaimosian paused before returning to his horse. "Do not let me catch you again. Fate will not be so kind twice."

Confident that no more would occur, Kavan went about his business. It was only when the growl of an empty stomach stole his attention that he realized he was famished. Room secure, he headed back out in search of a meal. He only made it a few meters before being confronted once more.

"Well, well, I hadn't expected to see you slumming in this part of the world," a burly old veteran said with genuine smile.

Kavan returned the smile and finally allowed his defenses to relax, slightly. "Dag! I was sure you'd be dead by now."

"Death doesn't want me I'm afraid. But you, from what I hear Lord Death has been stalking you for quite some time."

The two embraced. Kavan winced from the force of Dag's slap on the back. His friend may have been older, but he lacked nothing of power.

"What brings you around here?" Dag asked.

Kavan opened his mouth but paused, unsure of what he should say, for the details still weren't settled in his mind. The confusion laced his eyes, prompting Dag to nod thoughtfully. Ultimately Kavan decided that such a conversation wasn't for the open street. The pair headed off to the nearest kitchen where the food was overpriced and under flavored. Just the way a man used to always being on the move appreciated. Only after Kavan's stomach was full and his taste buds left in utter confusion was he ready to tell his tale.

Dag sat through it listening intently. His mouth dropped at the details of Kavan's battle with the werebeast. In so far as he knew there were no more of the dangerous, virtually mythical creatures, left in the world. For the Gaimosian to have stumbled upon them now whispered dark tidings. Much of the tale became more manageable to accept by the time they reached the bottom of their second pitcher of ale.

"You lead a charmed life," Dag announced with an exaggerated flourish. Foam peppered his upper lip.

Kavan grinned sheepishly. "Not by choice. It's hard when you know nothing else."

Yet another sad fact Dag was all too aware of.

"You think there's a connection with the king?"

Did he? "I...I don't know. There's been a few other caravans I've come across along my way here. Some didn't know anything, others pretended to know too much. One or two told it true. Whether the king of Aradain is directly involved with the werebeasts remains to be seen but all information points to his kingdom as the launching point."

"It's been a long time since I was last in Aradain," Dag said suggestively.

"No, Dag."

"No what?"

Kavan set his empty mug down. "Stay away. If this turns out to be half as bad as I think it will Aradain will best be avoided."

Brows furrowed, eyes drawn together, Dag replied, "I'm a grown man capable of making my own decisions, be they bad or good. Well, more bad than good of late but that's not the point! You see, I've got a good group of people working for me. They watch my back and take care of them. If we want to go to Aradain that's our business."

"You do want to go?"

"Who said that foolishness? We haven't made up our mind is what I'm telling you. Malweir's a big world. Plenty of places for a man of my quality to get into a little mischief."

Indignant, Dag crossed his arms and leaned back into the rickety chair. Rope stretched, threatening to break against his weight. He frowned, silently cursing everything in town for being, well, old.

"Mischief? I seem to recall a night a few years back when you and I were standing up to our ankles in blood and a stack of corpses," Kavan reminded.

Dag beamed. "Damn straight. That was a tough fight but they just wouldn't stop attacking." His face darkened slightly. "We made enough to pay the widows of the boys we lost."

Kavan caught the attention of a serving maid and signaled for another pitcher. Another drink to honor those who had fallen over the course of his career. The list was long but every name remembered.

"Look, Kavan, if this Aradain business is as tough as you think I don't understand why you need to get involved. There's got to be easier jobs throughout the kingdoms. No sense in risking your neck for a cause not your own, at least my mother used to say."

"I didn't think you had a mother," Kavan countered.

"Says the Gaimosian," Dag glowered. "Why are you really getting involved? This can't all be from some blind sense of nobility."

"It's not. Dag, thus far I've killed two of the werebeasts. The last one nearly got me. I've seen what just one can do against unprotected civilians. Can you imagine what several can achieve if unleashed on a village? I won't allow that to happen, so long as it is within my power to prevent it."

"Honor then," Dag grumbled. "Don't make any sense dying for nothing I suppose."

"No it doesn't. That's why I don't plan on dying."

"No sane man plans on it, Kavan."

"As you like to point out, we Gaimosians aren't known for our sanity."

Dag nodded sagely in agreement. "Best of luck to you, my friend. Know that if you need me, I'll be there. Maybe not as fast as I once was, but sooner or later."

"Thank you, Dag. Your offer means more than you know."

"I know!" he beamed. "S'what makes me special. Where are you heading to now? Aradain's the other way last I recalled."

"Out into the Jebel Desert. I'm going to need help and there are other Knights nearby. Strength in numbers and all that."

"Good plan. Well, Kavan, I do believe it's well past my bedtime. I'll make sure you don't run in to any other issues getting out of here," Dag told him. "Until the next time."

They clasped hands and Kavan watched his friend shuffle through the growing crowd. Once again the Gaimosian was alone with naught but a quest and the strong desire for companionship. Whatever may come, the desert awaited. After that, well, that was anyone's guess.

SIX

Pirneon

Night had grown eerily silent. The lack of a moon cast a menacing pall over the still sands. Even at midnight, the air languished from heat. Sweat poured down the soot-blackened faces of the hundred warriors lying in the waist-high patch of desert grass. Ever so slowly they inched forward. They'd been crawling towards the enemy camp since dusk and were almost in position to attack. Their leader gained the crest of a long dune and fixed his spyglass on the cluster of tents. He sighed as much from frustration as relief.

A quick scan told him everything he needed to know. The oversized tent in the center, ringed with partially attentive guards, meant only one thing. The Satrap was here. His death or capture would signal the end of the war. The task wasn't going to be easy. Camped below were close to seven hundred of the Satrap's elite. Seven to one wasn't good odds by any means, but Pirneon had been through much worse. One thing he'd learned from his time among the tribes of the Jebel Desert was that life may be hard, but warriors were often soft.

Having done his share of killing, Pirneon of Gaimos knew hard men. These desert dwellers were soft when it came to open conflict. He didn't know the reasons behind such behavior, nor did he care. What mattered was getting paid for his services. Even now, Barum, his squire and aspiring Knight, was preparing their departure. Desert life didn't agree with the aging knight.

Anything besides the task at hand was wasted time. Pirneon cleared his thoughts. First the Satrap, then a new job. He glanced left and then right. With no way of knowing if his forces were all on line, he was mired by constant delay. The desert tribes were not professional warriors as he had been for his long life. The once Knight Marshal of Gaimos frowned but could do little about it. He whispered orders to the sergeants on either side. They were supposed to be the pride of the Caliph's army, but he found them sloppy and woefully underprepared for what needed to be done.

Most were peasants in disguise. His opinion of the Caliph left him with vague doubts. The ruler of the desert was an unremarkable man. Copper skinned and swarthy, he lacked strong moral character despite his quest to unify the desert tribes under his banner. Pirneon had taken an instant dislike to the man. But work was work, and so long as the gems and gold kept coming, the knight planned on fulfilling his part of the contract.

Muttering a prayer under his breath, Pirneon decided it was time. Spring had come and, with it, the desert rains. He'd timed the attack in this camp according to the court magician's weather predictions. It was now or never as far as Pirneon was concerned. He rose slightly and signaled the handful of archers directly behind. Theirs was the most critical role in the assault. Satisfied they were preparing, he turned back to the camp. Only four sentries could be seen patrolling the outer perimeter, giving him a false sense of security. Once they were dead, the avenue of approach for his force would be wide open.

He thanked his good fortune for having led the scout the night prior. Having been a soldier for decades, Pirneon preferred to do his own reconnaissance before a major operation. It was paying off now. His own intelligence gave him detailed ingress and egress points along with the meager defensive strong points in the Satrap's perimeter. Getting in wasn't going to be much of an issue. Getting out….

His biggest ally in the camp was routine. By now, the sentries were already complacent in their daily activities. Soldiers often have a tendency to relax when duties became routine. Routine kills. That was one of the Gaimosian military academy's main tenants. Pirneon hoped to use it to his advantage.

He raised his arm enough for the archers to see. Arrows were knocked, bows drawn. The moment was now. He dropped his arm. Six arrows thrummed through the darkness. Pirneon's heart refused to beat. His entire plan hinged on the sentries being killed without noise. Only seconds went by, but it felt like an eternity. Five of the six shafts were true, and the sentries dropped dead.

Pirneon already had his raiders up and moving before the last body hit the sand. Sword in hand, he charged silently down the dune. The soft sounds of a hundred others accompanied him. Pirneon raced past the feathered corpses. There, half of his force split off to the tents filled with sleeping soldiers. He directed a handful to snatch torches and burn the camp. The confusion alone should prove enough for him to reach the Satrap and do what needed to be done.

Cries of alarm went up from around the camp. Flames sprang to life as the dry rotted fabric of the tents burned. Pirneon led the handful of men crowding him. This was the only chance he was going to get.

"Come on," he snapped. "Kill everyone in the way, and don't stop until we gain the command tent."

The soldiers around him slashed their way through the camp with vigor. Pirneon found the indiscriminant slaughter a useless act. It served to slow their advance and inspire thoughts of revenge when the smoke cleared, threatening to provoke a wider war. The Satrap's tribe was well connected and still had many allies. Any extended violence would keep Pirneon in the desert longer. He despised the desert. Snarling at his lazy thoughts, the Gaimosian hurried.

Slowing to a creep at the edge of the last row of tents, Pirneon got his first good look at the command tent. More than two dozen alert and decidedly dangerous guards were posted by the front. They were heavily armed and expecting trouble. The battle raging throughout the camp scarcely interested them. Their sole purpose was to protect the Satrap. Swords drawn and archers ready, the guards were vigilant. Pirneon scowled.

At least twenty meters of open area separated his raiders from the tent. The swordsmen weren't an issue. It was the archers who worried Pirneon. Those crossbows were more than a match for even the most heavily armored. Having insisted on stealth over protection, Pirneon's raiders would be woefully exposed. Their black tunics and pants wouldn't even slow the bolts. The potential for slaughter was high but worth the risk as far as Pirneon was concerned. He gritted his teeth and leaned back as the rest of his forces caught up.

Most were bloodstained, and all were panting heavily. Pirneon found their lack of skill and discipline disturbing. The Satrap should already be in chains. Instead, he was forced to delay because of the sloppy barbarism of his allies. That ignorance was going to cost them dearly. Pirneon had no qualms about sacrificing a few for the greater good. Intensified sounds of battle drifted to him. All elements of surprise were lost. They were going to have to scrape their way out of the camp whether they succeeded or not.

"Now! Rush the guards. Take down the crossbowmen first. I'll grab the Satrap," he ordered.

Pirneon saw the fear in their eyes and almost sensed a trap. For the briefest of moments, he felt his soldiers plotting against him. The moment passed, but doubts lingered. The motley group Caliph Adonmeia had given him wasn't fit to muck out stables, much less win a war. He smiled cruelly.

"Attack!"

The intensity in his voice gave them a start, and they paused for a split second in shock. One by one, they gathered their wits and charged. Howling and bellowing ancient war cries, they rushed towards the guards. Pirneon stood fast and watched the scene play out. The guards remained motionless. The raiders ran in an unorganized mob. He idly wondered how those fools would feel if they realized they were never meant to be more than a diversion. The thought almost made him smile.

At five meters, the guards fired. A dozen crossbow bolts slammed into the massed ranks of enemy warriors and nearly halted the attack. Seven raiders dropped dead or wounded in gargled cries and a spray of hot blood.

The front of the mob collided with the consolidated ranks of guards, and even more fell. Swords clashed with wild swings. The guards held. Without armor, Pirneon's raiders were waiting targets. The ground soon grew slick with blood. Another salvo of arrows sliced into the back of the mob before they recovered enough to counterattack the flanks. With the archers successfully engaged, Pirneon moved.

He was only going to get one chance. The Vengeance Knight danced past the battle, not stopping to fight unless absolutely necessary. Sped, strength, and conditioning brought him past the battle and into the tent. Common sense told him there'd be additional guards and servants inside, and he'd already drawn daggers. The tent flap brushed aside, and Pirneon immediately pitched forward into a somersault.

The move caught the pair of guards unawares, giving him the moment he needed to attack. Pirneon stabbed from his knees. The daggers sunk deep into exposed thighs. Both men cried out. Pirneon rose and slit the throat of the nearest guard. Confusion in his eyes, the guard futilely clutched at his throat as he fell. The second guard recovered better. Firelight reflected off the curve of his blade. Pirneon backstepped and let him come. The guard drew back to strike. Pirneon darted forward, getting inside the guard's reach. He slammed his dagger up through the lower jaw and into the brain. The immediate threat neutralized, Pirneon scanned his surroundings.

The Satrap sat on a modest throne in the center of the tent. Horror blanched his features. Beady eyes peered out from beneath a gold turban encrusted with emeralds and rubies. He'd clearly not been expecting the amount of raw violence brought against him. His mottled grey beard and moustache concealed his mouth and jaw, hiding his other emotions. Old eyes the color of forged steel settled on Pirneon. He then did something the Vengeance Knight didn't expect. He nodded his head in respect.

"You are one of them, are you not?" he asked after recovering his senses. "A fabled Vengeance Knight."

Pirneon sheathed one of his daggers and stepped forward. "Yes."

The Satrap stood. "It is said among my people that none are your equals in battle. That the very name strikes fear in the hearts of the young and old. That you have come to dispatch me is indeed a sad day for the desert tribes."

"No," Pirneon said. "I haven't come to kill you. Adonmeia needs you alive to end this war. I am to deliver you alive and unharmed."

A flash of a smile. "Adonmeia wants us all dead. You included. He wants the desert for his own and will not stop until all bend knee to him. Whether by your sword or another's, I am a dead man."

"The politics of the situation don't interest me. I've been commissioned on specific purpose. We can do this dignified."

Outside, the muffled sounds of combat were continuing at a greatly reduced pace.

"There is no dignity in being a hostage."

Pirneon paused. Something in the Satrap's words didn't sit well. That funny feeling of betrayal returned.

The Satrap noticed his hesitation and pressed. "You don't know, do you?"

"Know what?"

"As we speak Adonmeia sends his army across the desert to kill my people. Our villages are already under siege. He will slaughter every man, woman, and child. Adonmeia is a monster who employs monsters."

Pirneon stopped. A horn rang out, and the battle quickly faded.

"If that were true, I'd know," he replied. "I'm one of his generals and on the war council. There has been no talk of such actions."

The Satrap fixed him with a sorrowful look. "Adonmeia listens to only one man. All others are but expendable pawns. I am already dead, Vengeance Knight, but so are you."

Pirneon's thoughts got the better of him. Bradgen. Adonmeia's right hand and enforcer. Any move would have been filtered through Bradgen. Suddenly nothing made sense. A Gaimosian in name and deed, Pirneon had always held to a strict code of honor. He didn't kill for sport or pleasure and viewed this act of kidnapping for the purpose of cold-blooded murder beneath him. For Adonmeia to have fooled him so completely left him knotted with grave doubts.

The Satrap nodded. "At last you begin to understand. But it is too late."

A handful of soldiers burst into the tent. All were covered with blood and belonged to the Satrap. Pirneon knew he'd never be able to fight his way clear. Even so, he drew his sword and prepared. Glory would come.

The Satrap held a staying hand. "My soldiers have not come to kill you."

"Might as well. I don't see any alternative. There's only one way this can end. If what you say is true, my life holds little value," Pirneon snapped.

"Enough have died already. There is another way. What remains of your assault force is fleeing back into the dunes, but it is not enough. If my people are to live, I must surrender."

A collective gasp escaped the soldiers. Even Pirneon was at a loss. He slowly lowered his sword. There was no real threat here. The Satrap issued orders in his native tongue. Several soldiers left to relay them throughout the camp. What little remained intact was about to be broken down for movement. Camp was being struck.

"Take me back to Adonmeia. I will not let my people be slaughtered out of false pride. Others have fought, and all have died. Whole tribes no longer exist. That shall not be our fate."

He removed his turban and walked close enough to Pirneon to lay a fatherly hand on his shoulder. "This is the way of the desert. A hard life, to be sure."

Pirneon remained in shock and awe of the man before him. If other leaders held the same quality of character as the Satrap, the world might have been a better place.

SEVEN

Prisoner

It took them more than an hour to reach the pre-designated rendezvous position. The night had grown cold, but they were still covered in sweat. Pirneon was feeling the weight of his advanced age, though not from the battle. The Satrap, Habrim, walked at ease, as if freed from any tension. His words weighed heavily on Pirneon's conscience. The entire operation had gone sour the moment he'd entered the Satrap's tent. More than ever, he was thinking his decision to come into the desert was a mistake. He'd taken the job after a period of restlessness resulting from unemployment. Life was hard enough without being paid. When the Caliph's agents entered his chambers he virtually leapt at the opportunity, though he had little opinion about the desert.

Neither man spoke as they trekked across the dunes. Sand got everywhere, practically coating them, much to Pirneon's dislike. *Just another reason to never return. Whoever created sand sure didn't like people.* Pirneon let his guard down for the first time since entering the desert. Habrim's men posed no threat as far as he could tell. Adonmeia's men more than likely thought him killed. It was a recurring theme he'd gotten used over the years since he'd fled Gaimos. Not that he minded. Being thought dead was useful. Infinite possibilities opened up when the enemy figured you for dead.

He didn't bother binding Habrim. That would only slow them down, and the Satrap seemed almost as eager as Pirneon to see this affair through. A dread sense of foreboding pained him. Habrim knew that every delay was potentially fatal to his cause, a fact he went to length to impart that to Pirneon as they set out. Visions of massacred bodies now tormented the Gaimosian as he walked. They stopped only long enough to relive themselves and take a bit of water. Even at night, the desert was a formidable opponent. Dehydration was a constant threat.

Pirneon uncharacteristically halted Habrim. Pulling him close, he whispered, "I promise I will not let Adonmeia kill you."

Habrim said nothing. They continued again, climbing the last dune, and arrived at the edge of the rendezvous point. Pirneon helped him kneel and let out a shrill birdcall. The wind carried it softly. No answer. He frowned. Another call sang out, followed by another. He waited, his battle-hardened mind already racing through potential scenarios. Finally, the call was returned. Relief conspicuously absent, Pirneon took the small piece of rope from his pack and bound Habrim's wrists loosely.

Faces turned to look up at them as they stalked down the dune. Pirneon felt a growing sense of respect for the Satrap after he offered no resistance to being bound. That respect turned to disgust as he fixed his attention on the remnants of his raiders lounging sloppily at the bottom of the dune. They were not the same men who had set out with him earlier. What he saw was a bunch of frightened men thankful to be alive. Of the hundred raiders he'd been given command of, less than thirty remained. Seven of those would not see the dawn.

The mass carried themselves without poise. Shoulders were slumped. Heads hung low. No Gaimosian worth his salt would ever allow defeat to willow him so. Victory and defeat were mere facets of understanding. Whispers spread as, one by one, heads turned to watch Pirneon march towards them. A corporal, the highest-ranking raider left alive, finally climbed to his feet to confront the pair.

"We thought you were dead." It was more question than comment.

Pirneon hid his defensiveness. The malevolent gleam lurking just behind the corporal's eyes was troublesome, further signifying the extent of the danger Pirneon was in. "So did I, but with the guard distracted, I was able to enter the tent and kill the Satrap's defenders. I made it through the back with him before the enemy came in force."

The lie flowed smoothly off his tongue. He'd lost all respect for Adonmeia's forces. They'd shown their true worth, and it was cheap. Pirneon figured his best bet was to keep to his promise. Habrim might very well be the hope for the stable society the desert tribes were searching for. He decided to turn the conversation and force the warriors on the defensive.

"What about you? I thought for sure you had all been slaughtered."

The corporal dropped his head from the sting of the words. "We managed to burn half of their camp before the enemy grew organized. We fought hard but were outnumbered. A horn sounded, and we knew more were coming. Those of us still alive…left before they could kill us all."

Pirneon caught the pause, knowing the corporal struggled not to say they had turned and fled like cowardly dogs. He bit the inside of his cheek to keep from lashing out. Not only had they run without knowing if their mission was a success or not, they had left him to die. Not a one deserved to live, but it wasn't his decision to make. If they'd been sons of Gaimos, they would have been stripped naked and banished into the mountains for a year. They would be allowed to return if they survived. Before the Fall, not one banished warrior had returned. Pirneon reckoned this lot would fare no better.

He leveled his sternest gaze on the broken men. "Pray we deliver our bounty to Adonmeia alive else your heads will roll. The Caliph does not look kindly on failure."

"But I...."

Pirneon took a menacing step forward. "But nothing. You left me without securing the Satrap. You turned and fled the field of battle. As the highest ranking left alive, all responsibility now falls on your shoulders. You will answer to the Caliph upon our return. Do not anger me further, or I may just forget we are allies."

That last took all the wind from the corporal. No man in his right mind dared cross a Vengeance Knight. Pirneon's harsh reputation among the desert tribes was well deserved and, he hoped, enough to see him through to the dawn. He was a cruel man to work for and a soldier without remorse. That earned enough respect from Adonmeia, or so he assumed.

"Yes sir," was all the corporal could reply.

Pirneon didn't ease up. His life depended on it. "Get this rabble up and moving. We leave in an hour."

Strapping their gear to their backs, the bedraggled group set out for camp. Dawn was still some time in coming. Pirneon didn't particularly care. Marching at night was to their benefit. He knew that Habrim's forces weren't a threat, but his suspicions had been gnawing at his confidence ever since assaulting the command tent. The Satrap had been expecting him. It was the only way he could have been captured so easily. Pirneon couldn't keep the now almost permanent frown from marring his features. Questions plagued him. Why would Habrim willingly surrender, knowing that death was an inescapable conclusion?

That ill feeling continued to strengthen the longer they marched. He didn't know what to make of the current situation, but one thing became abundantly clear: there was more going on in the desert than he'd previously assumed. Pirneon dropped back to pull even with the corporal. It was time for answers.

"How many enemy soldiers did we kill last night?"

Confused, the corporal asked, "Sir?"

"How many do you think we killed?"

He wasn't sure. "Maybe seventy to one hundred. Most of the men ran through the tents before the heavy fighting began. Every tent I entered was empty."

Empty tents meant Habrim had been prepared for their arrival, waiting. What was he up to? Pirneon wasn't sure, but no answer would be one to look forward to. The first rays of sunlight broke across the far horizon. It was going to be hot soon, and they still had more than a league to march. That league was all the time Pirneon had to reassess his situation.

"Thank you. Pass the word along. We stop at dawn for five minutes," he ordered.

"Yes, sir."

Leaving the corporal about his duties, the knight fought the urge to go and question Habrim. There could be no signs of collusion, or his neck would pay the price. Treason was already a very real fear. That marked him an instant target. With no loyalties to either man, he was a loose end. His best and safest bet was to deliver Habrim alive as promised and slip away before Adonmeia was the wiser.

The reality was far different. His oath to Habrim overrode any monetary commitment to the Caliph, at least as far as Pirneon was concerned. Honor demanded to be upheld. Adonmeia was a brutal man with an almost savage ferocity lurking beneath the surface. He was not one to be crossed, and Pirneon recognized he was putting his life in jeopardy just by conversing with Habrim. Should Adonmeia find out....

Still, Habrim was the more honorable of the two. Personal feelings held little regard when it came down to it, even for a knight of Gaimos, but Pirneon couldn't help but figure he'd made a massive mistake by signing on with the Caliph. His thoughts were broken as the reduced company of raiders ground to a sudden halt.

Pirneon watched with disdain as the men slumped down on their packs to lick their wounds. Most of them were stained with blood or bore injuries themselves. They were worn down and near broken. He couldn't stand the sight of them. Memories of fleeing Gaimos as it finally fell returned to him. Not even the broken army, what little remained of it, showed such despair. Watching the raiders act as if their world had just ended disturbed him.

Having seen enough, Pirneon decided it was time to speak with his prisoner. He strode purposefully to where a handful of guards loosely observed Habrim, knowing that none would oppose his will in so long as they believed he still held authority under Adonmeia. Most raiders refused to make eye contact or walked away as he approached. Pirneon snorted his displeasure.

"I need to speak with the prisoner," he barked at the nearest of the guards.

The guard looked skeptically at his peers. Pirneon stepped quickly to his face. Sunlight began to glare behind him, adding to the unspoken menace he presented. "Don't forget your place," he warned through clenched teeth. "I act in the Caliph's name. Question me, and you question him."

The guard blanched and motioned his peers away, leaving Pirneon and Habrim alone.

"Impressive, but it won't last long," Habrim said without looking up.

Pirneon crouched down and offered his canteen.

"Thank you."

He nodded in reply. "You knew we were coming. Didn't you?"

The elder Satrap smiled thinly. "The desert holds many secrets."

"As in a line of scouts running the dunes unseen?" Pirneon asked with an arched eyebrow.

"We are at war, Vengeance Knight. Would you leave your camp undefended?"

The question was double edged. Pirneon now had no doubt that Habrim had meant to surrender long before the raiders arrived. But why? He'd seen his share of intrigue and politics getting involved in wars but often managed to avoid them. Generals needed to be on the battlefield, not mired in pointless plots. Here the desert ways were differed. Rulers and military leaders were expected to have their hands in every aspect of war.

"Why would you let us march into your camp and kill your men? You could have had us all before we crested the final dune."

"Deception is sometimes necessary in the grand scheme of war," Habrim replied before drinking deeply.

Pirneon felt he was closer to the answer that would unravel the mystery but was still missing the final few pieces. He'd come across others who had thought that, by surrendering, their people would be spared, and they'd all genuinely done so for the good of the people. Habrim was different; that much was obvious. He surely wanted to save his tribe, but some other agenda propelled him forward.

War had been going on for almost a year before Pirneon arrived. Adonmeia threatened to raze the desert with his ambition. The notion sent shock waves across the desert as war spread. War. The word suddenly felt wrong. Pirneon glanced to Habrim with unveiled eyes. The Satrap wasn't planning on surrendering. He wanted to become a martyr and raise his people.

"This is all part of your plan," he whispered cautiously.

Habrim remained silent for a moment. "Tell me, knight: what did you think when you first came into the desert? That the war was a simple feud between rival tribes? That Adonmeia wanted to end it and bring about lasting peace? We have been at war for more than ten years, not the one you mistakenly believe."

"But why? War isn't good for any culture," Pirneon argued, not knowing what else to say about the revelation. His words were hollow, for was he not from famed Gaimos? A military society that eventually caused their own downfall? Pirneon suddenly viewed the Jebel Desert as a very dangerous place.

"There comes a point when one no longer questions. Actions are all that remain if the future is to come. The tribes of the desert have been mocked and laughed at by those who dwell beyond our borders for a very long time. You know this, Knight. The stiff wind blows change."

"How many?" Pirneon asked, his mind racing. A slight breeze wafted through his almost silver hair.

Habrim smiled again. "More than you could guess. Adonmeia is in for quite the surprise."

He said nothing more. The conversation was finished. Leaving his canteen, Pirneon stormed off. He'd discovered just enough to make the immediate future terrifying. Habrim's words troubled him to no end. He ignored his raiders as he marched past. They were now more of an enemy than Habrim ever was. Visions of huge armies of men running parallel to his current position were almost enough to make him send out scouts. How much time did he truly have left?

If Habrim intended to sacrifice himself in order to unify the tribes, time was running short. Adonmeia would no doubt want to toy with his prisoner before killing him. That left Pirneon in a bad way. Compounding matters, he didn't know whom he could turn to for trust. A final battle was about to play out, and he was trapped as deep as possible. What he needed was time, and that was one commodity he didn't have.

"On your feet! Get moving!" he barked.

Better to get it over with now.

EIGHT

Trapped

The sun was already sweltering by the time Pirneon marched his men past the outer perimeter of Adonmeia's camp. Dark-skinned soldiers stared angrily at the survivors of the raid. Pirneon paid no attention and marched with the pride and authority befitting one of his station. It was a natural arrogance born from years of violence. At the moment, he felt anything but. Sweat coated his body in a thick sheen, and his water was almost gone. It was already midday, and temperatures were well over one hundred degrees. Pirneon hated the desert and regretted his decision to leave one of his canteens with Habrim.

A burly captain with golden torcs on his upper arms approached them. A large jewel-encrusted saber was tied in a red sash at his waist. Pirneon reluctantly halted his company.

"Where's the rest?" the captain growled. His displeasure at having to serve under one of the Vengeance Knights was obvious.

Pirneon had no love for the man, for they had clashed once before. "Dead."

The captain eyed him suspiciously but didn't push the confrontation. Pirneon brushed past with an air of authority and kept going. Sand had gotten into his boots and made for a very unpleasant walking experience. He was tired, filthy, and hungry. There'd be time to bandy words with common soldiers later. Right now, he still had a third of a league to go before reaching Adonmeia's tents.

More soldiers lined the avenue to watch them. None of the survivors had any fight left in them and walked by with hollow stares. There was no sense of victory. No pride in a job well done. Those watching could only guess at the horrors they'd seen the night before. All were secretly glad they hadn't been selected for the mission. The only thing that inspired confidence was seeing Habrim shackled and in chains. With him here, they knew their long war was almost over.

Pirneon ignored the stares and growing chorus of jeers. Prisoners such as Habrim deserved to be treated with more respect, he believed, but the man he worked for was a second-rate barbarian and inspired ignorance among his men. Howls of glee soon erupted from the throng of surrounding soldiers. Rocks and clumps of horse dung were flung at Habrim, striking several of their own people in the process. If Pirneon had his way those responsible would each lose a hand.

His thoughts continued to darken at the sight of the man pushing his way through the crowds to reach him. Standing at shoulder height, Bradgen was slight of build and far from imposing. His skin always appeared greasy, unkempt. His hair, jet black, ran down in a jagged line past his slender shoulders. The corners of his eyes were tucked and drawn back, giving him a sinister air. A thick moustache accompanied his long beard. His clothes were expensive and well tailored, suggestive of his standing. Pirneon despised the man and had no doubts that he would flee rather than be confronted in a fair fight. Pirneon knew Bradgen was one of the most vicious and sadistic men he'd ever encountered.

The sheer duplicity in his smile told Pirneon all he needed to know.

"Your mission was a success," he said in a nasal voice.

"At cost. We lost almost three quarters of our men," Pirneon replied.

"A minor consequence. You of all people should understand the need for sacrifice."

Pirneon remained silent, quietly comparing Bradgen and Habrim.

"The Caliph will be pleased with this. Come, let us take the prisoner away and see to your rewards. I have a feeling your services will no longer be necessary now that Habrim is safely in our custody. I'm sure you are anxious to be on your way."

"What about the remainder of the war?" Pirneon asked.

Bradgen paused just enough to arouse suspicion. "Events are underway to ensure the proper end is metered out. The Caliph will soon be crowned lord of the desert."

They stared at one another a moment longer.

"But come," Bradgen continued. "Enough talk of war and kings. You and your file are heroes now. I'm sure the Caliph will wish to reward you handsomely during the banquet this evening."

"Banquet?"

"Yes. The Caliph felt, as did I, that your victory was inevitable and all should know of your courage and dedication to our people. Think of the boost in morale this will inspire among the ranks."

Pirneon wasn't overly concerned about morale. He was more worried about the enemy forces he was certain were gathering nearby like a terrible storm in the restless dune. It was only a matter of time before that storm struck. He doubted he or Barum would live long enough to witness it. Something in the way Bradgen's narrow eyes stared at him as they wound through the camp unsettled him. Pirneon began searching for evidence of concealed archers strategically placed along their route of march. That

Bradgen was armed and more than willing to kill him if the opportunity arose went without saying.

Pirneon was caught in a dangerous game well beyond his ability to undertake. He cursed his ill fortune. This was the third consecutive job that had ended poorly. He'd narrowly escaped the last job with his hide intact.

He briefly recalled when Adonmeia's agents first approached him in a border town in western Averon. Capture Habrim and end the war. That was his charter. It sounded simple enough, but even then he'd held reservations. Rulers were deceptive by nature, and Adonmeia was a master. It was his way or no way. There was little room for the free will of a Gaimosian in the new desert empire.

"Adonmeia had no way of knowing I would succeed," he ventured.

"Name me one ruler you have come across who plans to fail," Bradgen countered. "Kingdoms aren't built on bodies. We need people to serve in our new empire. Habrim's capture gives us that resource."

"Slaves."

"What's in a name?" Bradgen smiled. "The important thing is that you were successful, and our plans can continue from here."

Pirneon took ill at the thought of Habrim's people being reduced to slavery. "What happens to Habrim?"

"That is for the Caliph to decide. Reinforcements are already pushing forward from the southern tribes. Perhaps you noticed the open areas in camp? The war will soon be over. Habrim is the catalyst."

He was bragging now and probably felt there was justification for it. Pirneon knew escaping became deadlier. He ran over a dozen different scenarios, and none had worthwhile outcomes. His best bet lay in killing Adonmeia and Bradgen at the banquet and escaping in the confusion. However unlikely, it was still possible. He needed to get to Barum at once.

Hundreds of large canvas tents were being erected on either side of the avenue. They were clearly expecting the arrival of a massive number of troops. A major offensive was about to begin, not the gentle subjugation Bradgen explained.

"What of my payment?" Pirneon asked after deciding he wasn't to glean any more useful information.

"All monies will be paid as soon as the prisoner has a collar around his neck and is on his knees in front of the Caliph."

Deciding there was no harm in risking it, Pirneon admitted, "I gave the Satrap my word he would not be killed."

Bradgen paused. "Ah…did you? The ever-famous sense of Gaimosian honor. His fate is no longer in your hands, but rest assured all will be properly taken care of. Don't trouble yourself over such a trivial matter. Habrim will be dealt with, and you will be on your way."

They stopped outside of Pirneon's tent.

"The Caliph will expect you at dusk. We have much to celebrate."

Pirneon stood a while longer to watch Bradgen and his retinue slink off with Habrim in tow. The Satrap glanced towards Pirneon before they were lost in the crowd. Pirneon understood that no one was going to be killed at least until the banquet—for good or bad, he wasn't sure. If his fears were realized, the enemy wasn't going to wait very long to attack.

Sighing with frustration, Pirneon went inside. He didn't like having his hands tied, but there seemed little he could do. This close to Adonmeia's quarters and already under suspicion, his every action would be watched and closely monitored. No doubt, spies and assassins were already assuming their positions around his tent.

Barum looked up at the sound of his arrival. Young and with almost mousey brown hair, the squire was pleased to see his master return unharmed.

"We've been watched more closely of late," Barum told him. "I think they are about to make their move."

"Tonight," Pirneon confirmed.

He was pleased with how quickly Barum had caught on to their situation. He was a good squire and well on the path to becoming a good knight.

Barum nodded. "I figured as much and already packed most of our equipment. The horses are prepared as well. There are enough rations to see us out of the desert."

"Leaving might be more difficult than I had anticipated."

Barum paused.

Pirneon continued, "Our beloved Adonmeia has arranged a victory celebration in my honor this evening."

"Weapons restricted, no doubt," Barum added. "I don't like it. That worm Bradgen has been collecting more power ever since we arrived. He's got the most loyal men and gold. This is a dangerous game."

Pirneon folded his arms across his chest. "Agreed. This certainly gives new thought to the desert tribes being little more than barbarians. I also wouldn't be surprised to find he has more troops loyal to him than to Adonmeia."

"This will get bloody."

"If we survive to see it through," Pirneon agreed. "There's more, though. My belief is that Habrim wanted to be captured. I have a feeling that, once he's killed tonight, a vast army will sweep into camp to claim revenge."

"But he was promised to be a political prisoner, not executed."

Pirneon grinned. "Indeed he was. I hate to admit it, but I think we are in over our heads…again."

"Worse than Antheneon?"

Pirneon laughed. "Much worse, and there's no innocent princess involved this time. Any suggestions on how we might escape?"

"Not really. Even if this banquet is going to distract the rest of the camp, I can't see him letting you just walk out. Adonmeia is a petty man."

"Best get out my dagger vest. I'm going to need it."

Barum grumbled under his breath but snatched up the vest already laid out on the simple folding wooden chair in the corner. The vest held a dozen three-inch blades, concealed and honed to razor sharpness. They'd saved Pirneon's life on more than one occasion, and he hoped they would again tonight.

"The sooner we leave this place, the better," Barum commented as he handed over the vest. "Can't we find an easy job in a cooler climate next time?"

Pirneon stripped off his torn and stained tunic. "You're forgetting one thing. First, we have to find a way out of this mess."

He finished stripping out of his fouled clothes and headed for the private bath chamber he'd insisted on upon accepting this job. As usual, Barum had anticipated his needs. The bath was filled with lukewarm water, the best they could manage given the almost murderous heat in the middle of the desert. Pirneon was tall for a Gaimosian at almost six and a half feet and was forced to scrunch up to fit into the metal tub.

One of the older knights still alive, he'd been there from the beginning of the war until the Fall. After the breaking, Pirneon and a handful of others had returned to their ruined lands to gather what they could of the codes and traditions before going into hiding. There, they had trained the youth and carried on the old ways. The following years had not been kind.

Pirneon slid deeper into the water and closed his eyes. His silver hair draped over the edge. As tired and filthy as he was, he wasn't about to let this simple luxury go to waste. His eyes closed. Barum entered what felt like mere moments later to wake him. Groaning his way out of the fouled water, Pirneon dressed in a clean tunic and pants while concealing his vest. He didn't want to go through the formality of the banquet but knew his absence would arouse suspicion. The only way to survive was to go through the motions and kill those responsible before they killed him. A sad song, to be sure, but one he'd grown accustomed to playing.

He halted at the tent entrance and laid a fatherly hand on Barum's shoulder. "Have the horses saddled. If I don't return, you know where to go. Speed and fortune, my friend."

Barum nodded. "I'll see you soon."

Pirneon smiled tightly and left.

The sun was beginning to set and, with it, their futures.

NINE

Betrayed

The main tent set up for the Caliph's banquet was hundreds of meters long and half that wide. Thousands of soldiers and acolytes filled the tables and chairs. Adonmeia and his closest advisors and generals sat at a long table filled with different meats and vegetables. Pirneon considered asking where they managed to find so much fresh fruit this deep in the desert but found the notion mildly inconvenient. He didn't care. Well-honed instincts had him already searching for the easiest exit point. Killing Adonmeia meant nothing if he couldn't escape.

At the same time, Adonmeia's narrow eyes were focused directly on Pirneon. The Vengeance Knight knew he was a target, despite Habrim's chained figure on display. Assassins and second-rate cutthroats lined the crowds waiting for the word. They were poorly disguised and stuck out to a trained eye. Adonmeia watched but didn't move. Pirneon sighed and marched with all the poise of a veteran warrior to the head table. He stopped short and bowed.

"Rise, my friend," Adonmeia said in a light voice. "It is we who should all bow to you. You've brought me my most hated enemy and given us the opportunity to successfully end this war. You have no idea how much this means to me."

The Caliph was dressed in ornate robes that sparkled and flowed in a hideous array of bright colors and cheap jewels. Adonmeia was the type of man who wanted to be more than what he truly was. Overweight and balding, he portrayed himself as the gracious savior of the kingdom. The reality was anything but. He'd grown up poor and an orphan. As a youth, he had been forced to steal and murder to get by. Now was no different. Some said when he smiled all you could see was daggers.

Pirneon graciously waved off the false accolades. "I merely did what you commissioned me for. Losses were more than expected. They should be recognized as the true heroes."

Adonmeia dismissed his comments with a wave. "Losses that have already been replaced. Come, sit and enjoy this feast in your honor. It is a glorious victory we celebrate."

He clapped his hands twice, and a serving girl brought Pirneon a porcelain mug of wine. Bradgen sat Adonmeia's opposite side and casually watched as the Pirneon claimed his seat. For the slightest moment, Pirneon feared the wine was poisoned. Outright murder wasn't in Adonmeia's bag of tricks, however, for the Caliph was of a subtle nature. Killing Pirneon at the beginning of the banquet would plunge his army's morale. Pirneon figured his death would be rigged to look like a jealous soldier who, in turn, would be killed to remain quiet.

The charade continued for another hour. Jugglers and acrobats performed, and bards sang tales of the greatness of Adonmeia and his glorious crusade. Pirneon thought it was more a circus than anything important. Anticipation was building despite his years of training and self-control. He almost couldn't wait for Bradgen to set his plan in motion. He ate sparingly, and his eyes never stopped scanning the crowd. He'd already picked out three of his potential assassins. They seemed nervous and skittish, enough that Pirneon knew they were false attackers. A fourth assassin sat not far from the head table. Pirneon was almost impressed. The man had the eyes of a professional killer and was as composed. That made him the primary target.

Adonmeia abruptly stood. The tent gradually fell silent as all heads turned towards the Caliph. Pirneon caught the malevolent gleam in his eyes, wild and lusty.

"This is the dawn of a new era for our kingdom. No longer will the tribes waste their futures trying to kill each other."

A cheer erupted. Men hammered their mugs on the table. Adonmeia held his hands out for silence.

"After so long, our most hated enemy has at last been humbled. The enemy alliance has lost its head thanks to the services of our esteemed Vengeance Knight. Satrap Habrim is now in custody!"

A pair of guards hauled Habrim to his feet and dragged him before the assembly. Bradgen shifted his gaze to his placed killer and nodded so slight Pirneon almost missed it. How Habrim managed to maintain his dignity was beyond him. A great cheer arose through the crowd.

"This usurper thought to keep us from our destiny," Adonmeia roared over the noise. "His ragtag filth of tribes wanted us to rot and suffer in poverty and famine while they grew steadily stronger. Is this fair?"

"No!" came the rousing shout in reply.

"And when we were at our weakest, they meant to attack! To crush us under their wicked heel and make slaves of us all!"

Pirneon listened intently, not for the message but for what wasn't said. There was a sense of magic in the words, and the lie was presented flawlessly. He'd seen no indications of an invasion of any fashion. His suspicions were that Habrim's people were the ones in suffering and Adonmeia wanted to crush them a little harder. Politics of the desert were often cruel without discrimination.

"Destiny is with us. With the usurper on his knees and in our grasp, the enemy will lose heart and flee before the might of our scimitars!"

Another great cheer arose.

"Bring me the prisoner!"

Adonmeia wore a smug look as Habrim was pushed and prodded before him. The air of intensity rose sharply. All within the tent felt electricity charging the atmosphere. This was a moment they'd long been waiting for. Habrim was taken to a small raised platform behind the head table. A guard lashed out when Habrim moved too slow, catching him behind the knee. A sickening crunch was heard as Habrim fell. With a nod from Adonmeia, the executioner stepped from behind a section of paneling.

Pirneon felt helpless. His promise to the Satrap was in vain, and there was nothing he could do to stay the moment. He was forced to turn to his own plans. Habrim had made his choice and—if this was, indeed, part of a conspiratorial plan—was prepared for the consequences. Now it was time for Pirneon. He folded his arms inconspicuously across his chest, hands stealthily slipping into his tunic and grasping the hilts of a pair of daggers.

The head table was curved, with the horns facing row after endless row of diagonally placed tables all filled with now-frenzied savages. Oil lanterns hung high above their heads, giving him enough to see by. Bradgen had no doubt placed him at the end of the table nearest the others on purpose. With no one between the killer and Pirneon, he had a clear avenue of approach. Pirneon knew that he'd strike first as soon as Bradgen gave the signal.

Adonmeia slowly walked behind Habrim and leaned down.

"This is your end, my brother," he said in a voice only they could hear. "Once you're dead, the desert is mine."

Habrim shifted his gaze up to the hate-filled eyes leering down on him. "You were never a brother. Our mother gave birth to us, but any relation ends there. Once I'm dead, you'll soon follow. You have no idea the wave of violence you're about to unleash."

Adonmeia hissed at the insult. He rose and nodded to the executioner. Sword in hand, the black clad man kicked Habrim in the back and forced him down until he was laying prostrate on the platform. The crowd tensed.

"Have you any last words, brother?" Adonmeia snarled.

Habrim placed his forehead on the platform and quietly began to pray. The executioner had a clean blow to the neck. Adonmeia raised his arm high. No one breathed. Pirneon's fingers twined inside his tunic. The cool leather on the dagger hilts tingled on his fingertips. It felt good to be touching a weapon again. He looked right. Bradgen's eyes widened with unfettered joy. Time slowed. The moment was now. Adonmeia dropped his arm. The sword came down. Silvered steel gleamed in the lantern light. Blood splashed on golden robes. Bone and flesh were torn. Habrim's head rolled away. Soldiers howled in delight. A lone man slipped out unnoticed through the back. The executioner reached down and snatched Habrim's head by the beard and handed it to Adonmeia. Triumph etching his face, Adonmeia presented the head to his warriors.

The world exploded.

Bradgen spun on the Caliph and plunged a table knife deep into his belly. Adonmeia gasped in shock and pain as Bradgen stabbed repeatedly. The killer behind Pirneon rose swiftly and closed on him. In one fluid motion, Pirneon whirled out of his chair and attacked. His dagger pierced the killer's throat before twisting sharply and ripping a wide vertical gap. Hot blood sprayed across the floor. Pirneon was already moving as a pair of killers shifted to block his path. Bodies struck the ground. Adonmeia's head nearly clipped Pirneon's heel as the Vengeance Knight lunged at the killers. Both fell with daggers in their hearts.

Soldiers were moving. Many were frozen in shock, but a core group had secretly secured the exits and was striking down those known to be completely loyal to the Caliph. Pirneon tried to use the confusion and make his escape when a bone-jarring blow struck across the back of his head. Darkness took him.

Pirneon awoke to the sharp sting of being slapped in the face. His head pounded unlike anything he'd experienced before, and it took a concentrated effort just to open his eyes. His vision was blurred, and he saw three of everything. Another slap jarred his senses.

"Wake up, dog."

Much as he tried, Pirneon drifted back into unconsciousness.

He finally awoke some time later and discovered he was in a dark tent. A single low-burning torch illuminated the far corner by the tent flap. He sensed more than saw the pair of guards watching from the shadows. Every small movement sent shivers of pain through his body. Pirneon tried to place a hand over his eyes, but they were bound by heavy chains. Without any hope of breaking his bonds, he could only wait for one of the guards to make a mistake.

He felt more than heard the tent flap brush back. There was little doubt as to who had entered.

"At long last, our mighty Gaimosian Knight is in his proper place," Bradgen crooned. "You should never have come here, old fool."

Pirneon struggled to laugh. "I agree. Be a good whelp and send me on my way, then. We can both forget this episode ever happened."

"You're about to be sent somewhere, just not where you wish. Perhaps in the next world you can meet some old friends. The desert no longer has need of your services. You and your kind are nothing more than cheap mercenaries acting on a bankrupt honor code. There is no place for you in the new world."

Bradgen paced. Dark blood stained his tunic.

"Much like the departed Adonmeia," Pirneon said.

"Adonmeia was simplistic at best. A farmer's son who thought to rise to power and glory. He was weak and trusted too freely."

"So you murdered him."

Bradgen fumed. "I did what was necessary for my people! I don't expect an outlander like you to understand our ways. Life here is pain. I've secretly built a federation of tribes with the capability of uniting the entire desert. We will take our place atop Malweir's power struggle."

Pirneon decided to continue fishing for time. "And then what? There's no way the rest of the world will allow you to succeed."

"Then we make our war on the world," Bradgen snarled.

"You're mad."

"Too long have our tribes been laughed at and looked down on. No more. All of that ended an hour ago. Adonmeia and Habrim were the last of the old guard. They needed to be removed for the good of the future. I would expect one in your position to understand."

Pirneon did, though without agreement. "You want it all, don't you? What shall your title be in this new world order? Sultan? Overlord? God-king?"

Eyes twinkling with the lust for power, Bradgen leaned a few inches closer. "A small price to pay for so noble a quest. What else could the man who conquers the world be known as? Nations will tremble at the very thought of my name. Despair will sweep across all Malweir, and I shall ascend to a place never before imagined."

Pirneon laughed again. "You honestly believe these half-assed soldiers can contend with the great armies of the world? Neither you nor your ilk are fit to lick the shit-stained heel of a Gaimosian's boot."

Bradgen lashed out with a heavy backhand, splitting Pirneon's upper lip. "Just where is mighty Gaimos now? Ashes in the wind. A whispered name heard only in shadows. Don't compare your failure to what is coming."

A loud explosion rocked the ground, closely followed by several more. Shouts of surprise arose through the camp and were quickly mingled with the cries of the wounded and dying. Bradgen and the guards were thrown violently to the ground.

An armored figure burst into the tent. "Sir, we are under attack!"

"By whom?" Bradgen snapped.

The soldier trembled. "We don't know."

Bradgen snarled and picked himself up. He grabbed one of the guards by the shoulder in passing. "Kill the Gaimosian. Whatever else happens ensure he dies."

TEN

Escape

Aphere watched the explosions rage across the enemy encampment with grim satisfaction. She'd orchestrated numerous campaigns throughout the years, but this was proving to be the most satisfying. Thousands of warriors lay waiting in the night for the signal to attack. At forty years old, Aphere was no stranger to war, and she fully intended to prove her experience tonight. A nearby horse snickered in anticipation. She smiled, grim yet serene in the wild chaos erupting around her. Even the animals could feel it.

The crimson glow of so many fires gave her an almost legendary silhouette. To friend and foe alike, Aphere appeared a lovely goddess of war come into the world to wreak untold vengeance. Slight of build and standing a whisper shorter than the desert warriors, Aphere was in peak physical condition. The crimson band on her head held back her auburn hair, giving her a hard look that frightened many.

It was almost time. She drew her sword and called for the commander of troops. Weeks in the desert had left her an angry woman.

"Ma'am?" he asked with a thick accent after stalking across the dune to reach her side.

"Commander, sound the horns to advance. Catapults continue firing until we breach the perimeter," she ordered.

He nodded and rode off. "Sound the horns…."

Baleful calls went up in the night and were answered by a dozen more from all sides of the besieged camp. Aphere began the slow ride into the carnage. Smoke rose in dark columns from the score of fires already raging. She could make out bodies lying at twisted angles, broken from the ferocity of her assault. The surrounding night came alive with the jangle of hundreds upon hundreds of cavalry lurching forward. Infantry followed in tightly packed ranks ten across and twenty deep. Archers came next. Wearing no armor, they were able to dart through the ranks to get within bowshot and reform in loose ranks.

Aphere watched as flight after flight of arrows sped towards the enemy. She didn't enjoy killing, but it was a major aspect of her trade. The Gaimosian Knight spent many nights wrestling with that demon. Some of her kind admonished her weakness while others approved and took the same methodical approach. She didn't know if she'd ever be able to beat the demon, but so long as her tactics proved successful and the field was hers at the end of the day, nothing else mattered.

The last flight of arrows hissed past, and she kicked her horse into a gallop. War cries erupted from her ranks as the cavalry charged. The thunder of so many hooves on the hard sand trembled the core of the night. Adonmeia's forces, confused and unsure, struggled to form a ragged defense as the mass of steel and flesh neared. Thunder boomed as the cavalry struck. Horsemen plunged past the defenses in a grim wave of death. Soldiers were pierced and hacked. Others were trampled underfoot. The sheer weight of the attack pushed Aphere and others deep into the heart of the camp as catapult rounds continued to explode at random.

The guard grinned cruelly as he slowly drew a rusted dagger. Pirneon recognized him as the spineless corporal from the raid. He wasn't surprised.

"I'm going to enjoy this," the corporal sneered.

Pirneon said nothing. He could do no more than watch as death came for him. He didn't flinch as the blade inched closer. The last thing he wanted was to give the coward the satisfaction of hearing him scream. Both guards leered. He judged them for what they were: weak men who took advantage of the helpless. Pirneon gave himself a last curse for taking this job in the first place.

"We're going to make you scream, old man," the second guard told him. "You got a lot of my friends killed last night."

They shared a laugh as the corporal nicked a shallow gash below Pirneon's right eye. He barely blinked. Hate-filled eyes stared back at the guards with contempt. He dared them on. Dared them to do their worst. He was the only one who noticed the slender figure slip into the tent.

"Brought another of your friends to help?" Pirneon mocked and motioned towards the flap.

The corporal turned and caught a sword across his throat. He hit the ground hard, rolling with both hands clutched to his neck in a futile attempt to survive. Blood spurted between his fingers. The second guard made a call and attacked Pirneon, knowing he wouldn't be able to kill both. There was a slight *whoosh*, and the guard's head sailed from his body. Pirneon tried to blink the blood out of his eyes.

"I would have come sooner, but the tent was well guarded, and they've been searching for me since the banquet," Barum explained as he set his sword down and began unfastening the chains.

Pirneon eyed his squire appraisingly. Barum was dressed as a normal desert man. He was ready to become a knight. "I lost sight of Bradgen in the chaos. Whoever is attacking is doing so in force. We must escape now, while there is still time."

"Have you any idea who is attacking?" Pirneon asked, secretly suspecting Habrim's plan was unfolding.

"No one seems to know. Their numbers are great. I think we are surrounded. Adonmeia will not win this fight. Half of the camp is already in flames."

Pirneon grimaced. "Adonmeia was murdered at the banquet. Bradgen now commands. Where are the horses?"

"Confiscated, along with everything else we had. Soldiers came the moment you left. Getting out of here won't be easy."

Pirneon nodded. "I feared as much. We'll have to take what we need and pray the attacking forces let us go unhindered."

Barum produced a set of traditional desert robes. "I brought these. They might not fit so well, but no one is going to be paying us much attention in all this."

"Well done, my friend," Pirneon said as he threw the robes on over his clothes.

They stripped the dead guards of their weapons, such as they had, and entered the chaos of the night. Sights and sounds of carnage were on a grand scale. For the slightest of moments, Pirneon remembered the final night of the Fall. He gripped the rusted dagger tighter and shook the waking nightmares away. He didn't know in which part of camp he was imprisoned and decided to let Barum lead their way.

The squire moved with an enhanced sense of assuredness, stopping only once to rearm off a pair of arrow-slain warriors. The flat blade of a scimitar felt good in Pirneon's hands. He tossed aside the rusted dagger and kept moving. The body count rose the closer they got to the outer perimeter. Arrows jut up from the sand and bodies alike. Screaming grew louder.

"This way," Barum hissed, and he led them into an empty tent moments before a host of retreating soldiers rushed by.

"Flame the tents. I don't want anyone attacking us from behind."

Barum's head snapped up.

Pirneon shook his head. "We only kill if it's necessary. This isn't our war anymore. Let them waste each other. Our only goal is to escape."

Barum took a dagger and sliced a jagged tear in the back of the tent. After scanning the immediate area, they made their way down an abandoned avenue between tents. The false security wouldn't last long. Flames already turned the night sky a haunting red. Soon, the enemy army would sweep through the tents. Pirneon knew there was only way out of the camp.

"Barum, we need to kill a pair of riders and take their mounts," he whispered.

Barum barely nodded, understanding fully what was expected. Nothing stirred. This part of the camp had been turned into a graveyard. Hundreds of bodies littered the sand in awkward angles. Blood ran so thick the sand was hard pressed to absorb it. Pirneon stepped over several moaning figures. A quick glance showed their wounds to be mortal. He let them die.

The sound of hooves beating suddenly came from everywhere. Pirneon threw Barum to the ground and dropped down after. They lay amongst the dead, unmoving and silent as riders stalked through the sea of bodies. More than one spear was jabbed into a back to ensure the dead were dead. The horses came closer. Pirneon clutched his sword but, with his eyes closed, couldn't be sure where the enemy was. A nearby body cried out as the spear sank through his heart.

"Come on. These are all dead."

Pirneon held his breath until the riders went off in search of new sport. Only then did he open his eyes and look around. Alone, the pair picked up and hurried off before another patrol arrived. Thick clouds of black smoke obscured their sight. Their eyes burned, and it became difficult to breathe without choking.

Barum finally got his chance to act a short time later when he stumbled upon a pair of dismounted riders burning tents. He and Pirneon attacked while the riders were distracted. They closed the gap in seconds and cut the riders down from behind. Pirneon's sword ripped a deep gash diagonally down the first's spine, severing the spinal cord and killing him painfully. Barum stabbed with all his strength and was rewarded with his sword plunging through the rider front and back.

"Quickly, before others come," Pirneon said, taking the time to wipe the blood on the dead man's jerkin.

Barum ripped his sword free and snatched the reins before the horses could bolt. The desert-bred stallions were smaller than the northern breeds, but they were bred for battle. Barum whispered softly to calm them. They snorted and stepped back. Gradually, both horses calmed to the point where it was safe to mount them. Pirneon had just placed a foot in the stirrup when a soft yet uncompromisingly stern voice halted him.

"My, my, what have we here?"

Pirneon stepped back down and prepared to do battle. He turned, weapon raised. Fires raged behind the lone rider confronting them, preventing either from making out more than the vague outline.

"You kill two of my men and think to flee into the night?" The rider laughed. It was a raw sound, throaty and harsh.

A woman! Pirneon peered harder. There was something familiar about the voice.… Extending his arms, he lowered his sword until the point rested in the sand.

"Go no further — not until I discern your true intentions. Two more bodies amidst all this won't matter come the dawn," she warned.

He wasn't sure, but the voice almost sounded…playful.

"You can see we're not from the desert. We seek only to go our own way and leave this behind," he said, hoping to appeal to any humane side she might possess.

She laughed in response. "Two innocent travelers in the vast Jebel Desert who just happen to stumble across a massive civil war. How convenient. More like mercenary spies, I expect."

Pirneon tensed, anticipating the attack. Instead, the woman eased from the saddle and, hand on the hilt of her sheathed sword, advanced close enough for him to clearly make out her face. Shock registered, and he could merely stare back with an open mouth.

She laughed even harder. "Ah, Pirneon. Don't you ever get tired of choosing the wrong side to work for?"

"Aphere?"

She curtsied.

"What are you doing here? I wasn't aware of another knight so close."

Folding her arms across her chest, Aphere said, "Right now, it looks like I am keeping you two alive. Mount up and stay with me. The battle is just about finished, and I could use your help getting all of this settled. The Caliph's forces seem to lack the taste of battle tonight."

Relieved beyond belief, both he and Barum did as instructed and rode off in search of the head of the whirlwind. The battle continued to rage. Come the dawn, there would be no prisoners, and a sea of bodies would stretch for nearly a league.

ELEVEN

Aphere

"You knew this was going to happen, didn't you?" Pirneon asked as they rode.

Aphere nodded. "I was also one of those who slipped into the back of Habrim's tent when he let you take him. I didn't agree with letting my employer commit suicide, but he was nice enough to pay me up front."

"You let Habrim die for all of this?"

She kept her sorrow hidden. Habrim had treated her like a daughter. "I argued, but they refused to listen. He insisted this was the only way to end the war. At any rate, Salac is in charge now. His retinue is at the command area and searching for Adonmeia. This war is over."

"More than you know," he told her. "Both Adonmeia and Habrim are dead. Bradgen usurped the power and almost executed me as well, but Barum arrive just in time to get me out of a bind, as it were."

Her eyebrow raised quizzically. "That makes sense. Breaking their lines was much too easy. Our scouts were hesitant when one of the spies sent the signal just after nightfall."

"What signal?"

"We had spies in position to watch for Habrim's murder. Once he was dead, they were to come outside and light off one red flare. That's how we knew of his passing and began our attack. His death galvanized the eastern tribes," she explained emotionlessly. "I conferred with my generals as soon as you escaped with Habrim. After much deliberation, it was agreed that we wait for one glass before sending all our military might at this camp. Catapults and cavalry were already en route from different camps scattered in the desert. The campaign proved more problematic in planning than execution."

Barum listened closely. Experienced as he was, he was still a squire and willing to learn from every situation. He noted the nonchalance of their tones and how they stalked across the killing grounds. They had no fear. Forgetting his place, momentarily, Barum gazed upon the smoke and sweat stained Aphere. Even through the grime he could see her beauty. His cheeks flushed, slight enough not to go noticed, or so he hoped.

"Thank you, Lady Aphere," he blurted uncharacteristically. "Your timing was impeccable."

She flashed a quick grin, briefly displaying her ivory teeth. "No thanks are necessary, Barum. I did what any Gaimosian would have."

Unsure how to accept his sudden attention, she turned hers back to Pirneon. "Adonmeia being murdered by his own men is ill news, Pirneon. If Bradgen escapes, he can rally parts of the army that haven't arrived yet. This war could continue."

"You sound as if you have vested interest in this," Pirneon added.

She stiffened. "My business is my own."

"Fair enough."

They rode in silence for a while, letting the fading sounds of battle pull them ever forward. Aphere began feeling uncomfortable the closer they got to the command tents. Finally, she looked at the now-haggard Pirneon.

"Habrim was a good man. Those are few in the desert."

Pirneon said nothing. Life as a Gaimosian knight was hard and often lonely. The normal family life simply didn't exist for them. Chances were good that Aphere never knew her father. Pirneon had been taken away from home at the age of ten and tested to see if he had the mettle to become a knight. Once he passed the tests, he had been led away to the ancient training grounds on Skaag Mountain. Fifteen long summers had passed before he was allowed to come down from the mountain. Pirneon imagined it had been much the same for Aphere's father. True warriors seldom made good parents. Aphere had been born well after the Fall, so at least her father had survived. Pirneon was almost jealous of that. He'd never known what a family was. At least she'd been given the opportunity.

"One thing bothers me," he said at last.

She bit back a laugh. "Just one? This whole damned desert is a bother."

He cracked an almost imperceptible smile. "Only one pressing at the moment."

"That being?"

"When I was in Habrim's camp I couldn't sense your presence. Here tonight, I couldn't either. How is this possible?"

"I was forced to put up shields to remain closed to you," she answered.

"Shields!" he exclaimed. He'd heard of this being done before but had never seen the application. The Gaimosian ability to sense one another was one of the things that made them so lethal on the battlefield. Her concealment was troubling. "How is this possible? The bond should not be severed so easily."

Aphere sighed, already dreading the conversation. "I learned this about a decade ago when I was in Harlegor. Kistan taught me how to twist the bond just enough to hide from unwanted eyes. It took me a long time to master the talent, but it has come in handy several times."

Pirneon was confused. The thought of hiding from a fellow Gaimosian incensed him. "Why would you do such a thing? The bond is what makes us special. It is one of the remaining ties we have to the fatherland."

"Pirneon, Gaimos is gone, and we must find new ways to survive and remember home. Many of us never knew Gaimos. I agree that the bond is important, but it has changed in some of us in ways I can't explain. I daresay it is almost…magical. Did you know Kistan could actually throw bolts of raw energy at people?"

He hadn't, and the prospect frightened him. Surrounding kingdoms had banded together out of fear of Gaimosian power. These mutations threatened to spark a witch-hunt of such proportions that it could only result in the utter extinction of his race. However, this was not the night for such deliberations. He shifted the conversation.

"Why did you use them against me? If I had known you were working here…."

"I am sorry for that, but we believed total surprise was best. I knew you'd be able to sense me and couldn't take the risk. If we'd have spoken, you would have known our plans and put the entire offensive at risk. We had to keep you blinded in order to succeed. The more you knew, the more dangerous it became for you and us. It was the only way."

He understood the need for total surprise but found his mind greatly disturbed by the revelation. *How many others share this power? Have you any idea what it means for our kind? We will all be damned. He decided to be wary of her, at least until she proved herself or they parted ways.*

"It would have been nice knowing I was up against you," he said after a long pause to sort out his feelings.

"To what end?" she asked. "Gaimosians don't fight one another."

"You could have quit."

"As could you," she countered.

He genuinely laughed for the first time in days. "It appears neither of us had much of a choice. What's our next step?"

"Sort this mess out and find a cooler place to work," she suggested.

The battle was over, for all intents. Dead and dying littered the field. The smell of so much fresh blood permeated the air. Dawn would see a host of vultures flocking in. Barum found a spear along their route and now held it at the ready. Many of the tents remained untouched despite the commander's standing orders and provided perfect ambush points for any of Adonmeia's men still with fight left.

"Who is this Salac?" Pirneon asked.

Aphere said, "He is the new Satrap. You'll meet him soon. I suspect the moment will be bittersweet since it was your actions that helped him unify the east and kill his father. He is Habrim's oldest son."

Pirneon sighed. This new bit of information changed nothing, but it did extend a degree of complication on his part. He felt no remorse for his deeds, nor should he have. He'd been paid to do a job. Habrim was another casualty in an unjust situation. If Salac had qualms with him, they could settle later.

"We should leave the horses. With a little luck, Salac and his generals will have Bradgen in custody by now, or dead," Aphere told them.

Young for a full-blooded knight, she displayed maturity well beyond her years. He'd heard of her, but they'd only met once in passing long ago. Still, he was honestly impressed with what he saw. Capable military commanders were a commodity these days. One with a sense of compassion was practically unheard of. Pirneon felt she had a long and prosperous career ahead of her, despite her mutation.

Barum took the reins of their horses and waited outside the command tent. His station as squire didn't afford him a place at the command staff. The pair of knights walked to the cordon of guards.

"Carry on, gentlemen," Aphere ordered once they snapped to attention.

"Impressive. They could almost pass for real soldiers," Pirneon said quietly once they were out of earshot.

"I should hope so. I spent the better part of the past two seasons training them," she replied.

They entered the enormous tent to find a large crowd gathered. One spotted her and made his way over.

"Lady Aphere, we were beginning to grow worried. You have not been seen for some time," he said with an inviting smile.

"Calm your fears, Minister. I was merely seeing to a colleague. May I present Sir Pirneon, knight and former Knight Marshal of Gaimos," she announced just loud enough for those assembled to hear.

Suspicion flared briefly in the Minister's eyes as he bowed crisply. "It is an honor, Knight Marshal. But enough of formalities; Salac is anxious to share the good tidings with his favorite general. Come."

"It has been a long time since I was the Knight Marshal," Pirneon said to Aphere.

She shrugged. "These desert types stand on titles and formality. If I had just introduced you as Pirneon the Gaimosian, Salac might have had your head for your part in his father's death. I did you a favor."

"Memories of Gaimos continue to raise caution and old fears across the lands. It is not wise to throw them about so casually," he scolded.

Aphere shot him a disparaging glare and pushed through the crowd. He had no choice but to follow. Many in the crowd were old and spattered in drying blood. Their armor was tired and abused from constant exposure to the harsh desert elements. Each man was proud and strong in his own way. Shields were cracked, helms dented. Several bled but remained in good spirits. These were the crème of the eastern tribes.

Following her lead, Pirneon stopped and watched.

She leaned in to whisper, "That's Salac in the dark blue turban. Remember, he is now the sovereign ruler over all the Jebel Desert. Do not dismiss him lightly."

He supposed he understood her sudden hesitancy. However, Salac was hardly the first king or lord he'd stood before. Pirneon was about to tell her so but wisely decided to hold his tongue. Their situation was still much too perilous for his liking. He folded his hands in front of his waist and waited.

Salac stood with his hands on his hips. His skin was dark, making his almost black eyes appear hollow. His nose was long and hooked at the tip, further strengthening his angled face. Pirneon's eyes glanced to the scimitar tied to his waist. It was a weapon made for killing, not the ornamental toy of a boy ruler.

"Welcome back, general," Salac said after noticing Aphere. "I believe this day belongs more to you than to any other. It is only fitting you have come to celebrate with us."

Pirneon was instantly wary, knowing how well the last celebration had fared in this camp. He had no desire for a repeat.

Aphere curtsied. "I just came up with the plan, Sultan. Your men executed it very well."

"Indeed," Salac agreed. His sharp eyes fell on Pirneon, and he stiffened. "I have seen you before."

"Indeed you have, Sultan."

"Last night in my father's tent. You came to kill him." Venom dripped from the words.

"He is the one I mentioned," Aphere stepped in, hoping to avoid bloodshed.

"What is your name?"

"I am Pirneon, son of Gaimos."

"Gaimos is dead, much as my father," he snorted. "A regrettable act of war, but one both my father and I deemed necessary. But I am being rude. I am Salac-ib-Habrim. Let us save titles and stature for another time. Tonight,

I wish to celebrate the end of the war and a new dawn of peace for the tribes of the desert."

"Tell me, Salac, is there one among your prisoners named Bradgen?" Pirneon asked.

"Should there be?"

He shook his head. "It would be in your best interest. He killed Adonmeia and took control of the army last night. Without him in custody, the war won't end."

Salac's eyes narrowed dangerously. He barked for his minister, sending the man scurrying off shouting orders in a high pitched shrill. "We shall soon know if he is still here. Checking the dead will take a very long time, however. Will you identify him once we have him?"

"My pleasure," Pirneon replied with a wicked gleam in his eyes.

Salac clapped his hands twice, and music started from the far corner of the tent. "Then come, let us break bread together and form ties of fellowship. Tonight is a special night, and, though you have been my enemy, I name you friend. We would not be standing here tonight were it not for you."

Pirneon wasn't sure how to respond. That familiar nervous feeling rippled through him again. The last time he had been here with talk of feasting and celebration, he'd nearly been killed. Escape hadn't been possible then, and he knew it wouldn't happen this time either if things went sideways. His only security came from having another Gaimosian with him. Blood didn't fight blood. He was forced to rely on that alone.

The feast lasted hours, much to Pirneon's dislike. They were all exhausted, him perhaps most of all. A series of unending speeches spanned the event, and the men roared and cheered throughout. Pirneon found himself nodding off somewhere in the middle before a sharp elbow snapped him awake. Aphere ensured Barum was fed and taken care of as small groups began to gradually excuse themselves. Not even the generosity of the newly pronounced Sultan was enough to keep them on their feet after a long, hard-fought battle.

"What next for these two knights of renown?" Salac abruptly asked as dawn broke the night sky.

"Other kingdoms have need of our services," Pirneon replied between stifled yawns. "One cannot know which way the wind shall blow."

"It's a vacation for me," Aphere hesitantly smiled. "I heard of a nice place to the east of Averon. Quiet and out of the way."

"The perfect chance to collect your thoughts. You have surely deserved it, both of you," Salac agreed.

The minister suddenly burst back into the tent. He immediately dropped to his knees and bowed his head. His cheeks were red, and he was breathing hard.

Salac raised a benevolent hand. "Rise, my friend. What is it? What has you so excited?"

The Minister grinned. "Sultan, we have him. We have found the traitor Bradgen."

Pirneon was instantly on his feet. His dagger was already in hand. More than anyone else, he desired revenge.

TWELVE

Just Dues

Soldiers pushed and dragged Bradgen across the same raised platform on which Habrim had been killed. He was bruised and bloody. His once fine robes were torn, soiled. Nothing about him suggested his former standing, yet, despite his fall from grace, his eyes still bore a timid defiance. He grunted as he was shoved to Salac's feet. The iron chain attached to the collar around his neck kept him from enacting any thoughts of treachery.

"This is the man who so casually murdered my father and sought to rule the world?" Salac spit. "Tell me why I should not bleed you here and now."

Bradgen placed his forehead on the ground. "I did what needed to be done for the good of the desert. All I wanted was to make our kingdom strong again. Adonmeia and his Vengeance Knight went mad and made sport of killing honored Habrim! They were reckless and cruel. I did what I could to ensure our people remained strong. Both men paid for their crimes before you arrived."

"I'm curious as to what crimes I was punished for," Pirneon said after a stern look from Salac.

Shock rippled across Bradgen's face as he lifted his head enough to see Pirneon glaring at him. "You! You should be dead. Great Sultan, this man is a poison to our kind. He cannot be trusted."

Salac slapped him hard enough to bring tears. He looked to Pirneon, his gaze softening slightly. "I believe you now. He is an evil this kingdom can ill afford. Many thanks for bringing him to my attention."

"I'd prefer to take him to the netherworld." His hand, after sheathing his dagger, rested comfortably on the pommel of his sword.

Salac laughed, crisp and unusually wicked. "There will be no need for that, dread knight. Guards, cut out his tongue and eyes and turn him loose in the deep desert. Never again shall this filth taint our lands."

They dragged the screaming Bradgen away. Aphere winced at the sound. She'd never advocated torture, and there was no honor in Bradgen's punishment. None could survive the desert crippled so.

"You do not approve?" Salac questioned. "He received no more than he deserved. A message needed to be delivered. Usurpers shall suffer the worst of fates."

Aphere held her tongue, though inside she believed she'd misjudged the quality of Salac's character.

"Think no more on this. The night is nearly done, and we are all tired. Go now and rest. I shall have my men supply you and see to your mounts. You may depart at your own discretion."

Both knights offered short bows and turned to leave.

"Pirneon."

He slowed and turned back. Pirneon's eyes were already steeled in anticipation of what was to come.

"I shall never call you friend, no matter what I announced before the others. You may not have killed my father, but you willingly came to do so. My gratitude is given for your part in ending this war but should ever return to the desert and I catch wind of it, I will hunt you down with every asset available. Your fate will be worse than Bradgen's. Good day, sir."

Pirneon nodded again and stalked off.

Aphere had been waiting for him just outside the tent. "What was that all about?"

"Just a friendly reminder that my time here is ended. What are your plans from here?" he asked.

"West is the fastest route out of the desert. I was thinking about heading for the Kergland Spine and then south to one of the seaports. It shouldn't be too hard to secure passage aboard a merchant vessel."

"You still mean to go to Averon?"

"Yes. I cannot say why, but I feel pulled there. What of your plans?"

He paused; until now, he hadn't given it much thought. The simple act of getting away was all that had mattered. "I'd like to return to Skaag Mountain. I need meditation to heal my mind. Too many wrong decisions have plagued my inner thoughts of late. I must attend to those demons before returning to the campaign."

"Perhaps we could travel together for a while?" she offered.

"Perhaps."

The solitary lifestyle was hard on every Vengeance Knight and he'd been at it for much longer than either she or Barum. Her youthful company might inspire him again and ease some of his loneliness.

They walked back to where Barum waited. In their absence, he'd laid out their gear and readied the mounts. All three were tethered to a nearby tent stake. Aphere was impressed, not having a squire of her own.

"All is prepared. Your tent is on the left, Lady Aphere," he said.

"Thank you, Barum," she told him with a genuine smile.

Pirneon squared off on her. "Shall we leave at dusk? I don't relish the idea of traveling in the hot of the day."

"Until then."

They entered their respective tents and collapsed.

The sun was setting by the time the Gaimosians mounted and headed out. An honor guard had been assembled to see them off. Aphere had been named a hero of the realm for her actions in the war, and, so long as she traveled with Pirneon, he had nothing to fear. It was a title neither sought nor accepted. Of Salac, they saw naught.

The stench of burning bodies choked the air. Disease spread quickly, and fire was the best way to prevent it. The pyres burned for many days, and, when it was all finished, this site would forever be known as the Hall of Death.

Pirneon and Aphere rode away without looking back. He was glad to finally be rid of the desert people. Their ways were primitive, violent and crude. It was a land where strength of arms was the only respected power. Salac might have won a great battle, but it might be years before the desert unified. When that day arrived, woe to Malweir, for their savagery would threaten the very pillars of society.

They rode through the night and didn't pause until the pale glow of the massive pyres was lost to the night. The air was pure and crisp. A slight chill settled over them. The desert was cold at night. Temperatures dropped more than fifty degrees once the sun set. Pirneon enjoyed the solitude of the darkness. It was nearly perfect with no moon, and thousands of stars dazzled the skies.

Halfway through the night, they began alternating riding and walking to rest the horses. The pace was gentle, undemanding. Pirneon stopped them every so often to rest, knowing the sun would be murder on man and beast alike.

"The sky is so beautiful," Aphere said, her gazed fixed longingly on the stars.

"It is, indeed, and shall be more so once we leave this cursed kingdom."

She scowled at his derision. "The desert isn't so bad. One can learn to make peace here."

Pirneon grunted. "Peace, perhaps, but look around. Everything is the same for as far as the eye can see. I need mountains and trees. Green grass and gently babbling streams. The doldrums of this place would ruin me."

Her laugh was light and vivid. "You manage to find the worst in things. Not everything has a dagger waiting in the shadows."

His scowl went unseen in the night. Barum knew better and was forced to stifle his laugh.

"Tell me more about this…special talent you have," Pirneon said after a time.

"What can I say? One day, I woke up and felt different inside. It really is almost unexplainable. The feeling came and went at first. I'd get flashes when I least expected them."

His eyes turned cold at the thought. "Could it have to do with the manner in which you were raised?"

"No. At least, I don't think so. I was raised to follow in the code of the knights. My father did his best to train me in the old ways."

He wasn't satisfied. "You were not trained on Skaag Mountain. Knights connected with an ancient power in the depths of the mountain. The order of scholars believed that's where we learned and developed. Some argued the power stemmed from the very heart of Malweir. Growing up so far away from Gaimos could have distanced you from the source enough to mutate your bond."

"I have made the pilgrimage to the ancient training grounds and felt the stirrings of the old power, Pirneon. Yet it has not changed me. Kistan goes to great lengths to ensure we each attain our full potential, without becoming a threat."

Pirneon said, "He was considered a recluse even among us. Spent most of his time in the deep forests. Some say he often spoke to Elves and other Fey creatures. For myself, I have seen neither. One day, he rode off into the east towards the forest of Relin Werd. When he returned three years later, he was dressed in simple blue robes. Gone were his weapons and horse. He claimed he no longer followed the code, for it led only to death. He was laughed at and shunned.

"I was one who did not believe him. Right before the end, he gave away all his possessions and whispered a harsh prophecy on our lands. In one score and a day, the pride of this people shall shatter, he said. Kistan was driven from Gaimos and proclaimed a heretic."

Pirneon's voice faded to a whisper. "Twenty years and a day later, his prophecy was fulfilled."

One of the spare mounts snickered and dropped its ears flat.

"At any rate, I'd believed him dead."

"He's anything but. Far to the east lies a great lake, named Thuil by the Elves. Do you know of it?" she asked.

He did.

"Kistan has made it his home. For the last fifty plus years, he's built a private community on the shores of the lake. There are folk of all races there: Dwarves, Elves, Trolls, even a Sprygg or two."

"An odd assortment. To what end?" he asked.

"He's teaching them."

Pirneon straightened and reined to a halt. "Teaching them what?"

Dark visions of a more twisted, abstract Gaimos sprang to life.

"To find an inner power and develop it to maximum potential. None can say where the power comes from, for only he and a handful of others are from Gaimos. To my knowledge, they use their talents for good, though I did not stay long. The calling brought me back west."

"These are dangerous tidings you speak of," he admitted. "Our kind was given the bond as a gift from the gods. Now you tell me it has mutated? Changed? We have squandered our gift and will pay for our sins. Untrained power such as this has the potential to tear all Malweir apart. Kistan could well be marching us towards a final doom."

Aphere regarded him sharply. "Pirneon, his students are forbidden to carry any sort of weapon. They had but a handful of retainer guards to ward off brigands and such, but no more. He preaches peace."

"How many do you think have answered his calling?"

"Maybe a hundred," she quietly answered.

He clicked his horse forward. Strong premonitions burned, leaving a frightened feeling in the core of his being. Arguing with Aphere wasn't going to solve anything. He felt the taint in her bond and was disgusted. The bond was sacred and holy to their blood. Any transformation should be considered abhorrent, but he withheld his judgment. As former Knight Marshall, he was trusted to be fair and impartial. He knew what needed to be done, though he remained hesitant.

"I think one day I will go see Kistan and learn the truth behind his teachings. Whether it bodes ill or not I will discover soon enough," he said.

"Fair enough," Aphere said.

Dawn streaked through the sky by the time they stopped. They helped Barum erect a large canvas lean-to large enough for the three of them and their horses. By dusk, they were heading west again. Pirneon figured they were still at least a day away from the edge of the desert and even further from the Kergland Spine. Cresting a large series of dunes, they looked down upon a sprawling complex of tents. At last, they'd arrived at the way station. Drenched in sweat and bordering dehydration, they were more than ready to resupply and rest before heading out. He figured they'd need at least a full day in order to recover from their trek across the desert. Less than an hour later found them bathed and eating roast lamb in a large common area tent.

THIRTEEN

Old Friends

Aphere splashed the cool water on her face before dunking her entire head. Several onlookers watched her waste of water suspiciously. They whispered and murmured of the insolent woman who dared show her face among the tribes. Talk turned towards punishing her until they spied the amount of weapons strapped to her body. One by one, the onlookers drifted back to their business.

Caravans geared up and hired additional guards for the long trek across the warring desert. Many of those at the way station were permanent fixtures. Some rotated in and out of passing caravans while others remained to tend the shops and various businesses. Dark tanned women concealed behind diaphanous veils waited in perfumed tents for weary travelers to spend their coin and forget their troubles. Old grey beards sat around ornate water pipes gilded in gold. They drank from tiny glass cups of hot, heavily sugared tea. Trays of dates and other desert fruits filled the huge tables of the dining tents.

Pirneon took it all in with casual interest. His time among the desert tribes had left him with a sour taste, and he cared nothing for them. The way station was perhaps the calmest place he'd visited since coming to the Jebel Desert. He drank his tea and watched. No matter how long he remained here, he'd never understand how they could stomach such a drink in this heat.

Aphere slipped onto the bench opposite him and popped a lemon wedge into her mouth. Her lips puckered, and she scrunched her face tightly before spitting out the rind.

"Have you felt it?" she asked of a sudden.

Pirneon nodded almost imperceptibly. "We have. There is another Gaimosian here."

"Should we go find him?"

He shook his head. "No. I've a feeling he will come to us. Besides, he is an old…friend if my senses are accurate."

Aphere wanted to say more but decided against it. Being the junior knight, she was still trying to learn her role in their group.

"Did you sleep well?" he asked in unexpected amusement.

She shrugged. "Well enough, I suppose. It felt good to be on an actual mattress. Almost like being back in civilization again."

"I found it rather discomforting," he admitted. "It's been a long time since I was afforded the simple luxury. The desert has changed me."

"How so?"

"How else can you explain me drinking this damned hot tea in the heat of the day?"

Aphere burst into laughter. Pirneon followed, as did Barum.

"What else shall we do to occupy our time while here?" she asked after recovering. "I haven't had a good sparring partner in over a year."

"None in Salac's army could match you?"

She snorted. "It took at least ten just to tire me."

His eyes shone brightly beneath his bushy eyebrows. "No need for so many today. I accept your offer. You and I shall dance swords tonight."

"I look forward to it," she smiled back.

They finished their meal in relative silence.

Aphere ran her hand down the flat of her sword. Like herself, the blade was well tempered and slender, more of a rapier than the huge broadsword Pirneon preferred. Only one side of the blade was sharpened. The sword had a slight curve to aid in slashing without losing stabbing power. His sword was made for brute force. Double-edged and heavy, it was a weapon perfected for cleaving and hacking limbs. Since the dawn of Gaimosian culture, blade masters had taught that the sword was an extension of the knight who wielded it.

Both knights went through a series of stretches. Combat didn't afford such luxury, but injuries happened more often than not when one was ill prepared. Barum marked the training area and stepped back. He was given his own set of drills to practice while they danced. In the end, each knight would offer him a chance to come and test his skills. It was a ritual as old and tried as their very order. Finished stretching, the knights faced off and bowed.

"Begin," Pirneon commanded.

Aphere drew her sword back, angled sideways and shoulder high. Pirneon took a half step back and raised his broadsword overhead in a high guard. Neither betrayed a hint of emotion. Nor did they notice the growing crowd around them. The Knight Marshall struck first, bringing his sword down towards the exposed side of her neck. Aphere sidestepped and blocked the blow by crossing her body.

Weight and size were to his advantage, and he pressed hard. Clang. Clang. Steel sparked as it struck steel. Both gave everything, losing themselves to the dance. After twenty minutes and several near-deadly blows neither had scored a point. They halted long enough to catch their breath and drink a little water.

"It seems we are quite popular tonight," Aphere said after wiping the sweat from her face. "I'm not used to being watched by so many non-participants."

"Perhaps you'd care to challenge some of them instead?" he asked.

"I haven't beaten you yet, or perhaps I would."

She walked back to the center of the pit and raised her sword in challenge. Pirneon followed.

"Begin," she said and aimed a slashing blow across his stomach.

"Thank you for that," Pirneon told her over a breakfast of brown fruit with bright green flesh and honeyed water. "I always welcome the challenge of youth."

Aphere smiled. Her shoulders were sore. "You didn't do so bad yourself. I was hard pressed just to defend."

Pirneon returned the smile and thought of his own aches. He was nearly three times as old as Aphere and suffered from too many pains to note. They served as constant reminders of the passing time.

"It felt good to spar with one of my own blood again. I'd almost forgotten what it was like to face a talented opponent," he admitted. "Barum, you did exceptionally well. You are about to become a fine knight. There is nothing more I can teach you. When we arrive at Skaag Mountain, I shall confer upon you the title of Gaimosian knight. It will be yours to seek out and train others of the blood."

Barum was instantly humbled. "Thank you."

A server presented them with cups of hot tea, which Pirneon subconsciously took and paid for. He shook his head as the hot liquid burned down his throat.

"I simply don't understand these people," he muttered and set the empty glass down.

Aphere snickered. "That doesn't prevent you from enjoying their drink. He barely left the table, and your glass is empty. Barum and I haven't even touched ours yet."

"Bah…" Pirneon scowled and looked away.

A shadow fell across the table, causing them to look up. Pirneon's eyes went wide with recognition.

"I've been searching for you for a long time, Pirneon."

"Kavan?"

The knight smiled and clasped forearms with his former teacher. "There is a matter I must discuss with you — one I believe to be of grave importance."

They made a place for him and bade him sit. Pirneon caught the server's attention and ordered more tea. Aphere concealed her amusement. They ate and drank with minimal conversation, for Kavan was both tired and hungry. Once sated, Kavan lit his oak stem pipe and began his tale.

"I believe there is some dark power at work in the world. In the past year alone I have come across several werebeasts," he told them in serious tones.

Aphere's eyes narrowed, for these creatures were known to her. The prospect of facing one sent shivers coursing through her. Pirneon leaned back. A worried look creased his brow.

"Werebeasts? There's been no sighting of one in over a millennium. Are you certain?" he pressed, not willing to give in to hysteria without vetting thoroughly.

Kavan nodded. "Aye. The first damn near killed me. It left a terrible trail of bodies until I ran it down and finished it."

"Think it possible you killed the host?" It was rumored that if the werebeast who'd initially born the disease was killed, then all of those it had turned would wither and die.

"No, for another came across my path a few months later. There's more to this tale, though," he said.

Pirneon frowned. "More?" he asked.

"These were not the beasts of legend. I saw too many human features in them. They looked crossed between man and beast. As if a vile power transformed them into abominations."

Pirneon shifted his gaze to Aphere and struggled to rationalize his private fears before they led him to false accusations. She met his gaze, daring him to speak.

"There is no power in Malweir capable of such a thing," Pirneon said finally. "Not even dragons are rumored to be so strong."

In truth, dragons were rare, mysterious beasts. Few alive claimed to ever having seen one, for the great wyrms stayed in their lofty mountain haunts deep in the most isolated parts of the world.

"What could have done such?" Aphere asked. Despite Pirneon's obvious prejudices, she knew this matter had no connection to Kistan and his enclave.

"It is rumored that Gessun Thune has been rediscovered," Kavan told her. A dark glow haunted his gaze.

She shook her head. "I'm not familiar."

"It is an ancient place of evil," Pirneon cut in. "Back when the world was young, there was a war among the gods. They came down onto Malweir and wrecked the planet in their rage. Mountains shattered. Rivers dried up.

The planet was left barren. When the rebellion ended, the gods of light abandoned what was left and banished the dark gods to another realm. They say Gessun Thune was the spot of the final battle. Some fell powers are said to infest the very ground."

"Surely that is just an old wives' tale," Aphere said.

"Most myths are rooted in truth," Pirneon answered. "Legends say that, after the war ended, new races crept into the world. None knew from where. They gathered at Gessun Thune and cast a great spell upon the world. If any ever discovered the ruins, evil would be loosed again. Aphere, I believe this place to be very real."

Kavan agreed. "As do I. How else can we explain such nightmares walking the lands?"

"There must be something else, especially if this foul place has been discovered."

Pirneon rubbed his temples. "Tell us, Kavan, where is Gessun Thune rumored to have been discovered?"

"West of the Kergland Spine. There's a small kingdom called Aradain. King Eglios has ruled there for some years now. Villagers south and east of the capital are frightened to their bones at the portents. For it, Aradain suffers. Folk speak of plagues and random disappearances. The shades of their ancestors have stopped coming."

"But it's been how many thousands of years since the war? This could be just a rogue sorcerer tinkering," she pressed, unwilling to blindly accept what he was saying.

"Perhaps," Pirneon seconded.

"Pirneon, there's more. Even now, Eglios is organizing a large-scale hunt to track down this evil. If they unwittingly stumble on whatever the source is, there could be doom for us all."

"Ominous events unfold in the west, it appears," Pirneon finally agreed.

"I have traveled many leagues to seek your counsel. Will you ride with me, old friend?" Kavan asked. He set his pipe on the table.

Pirneon clasped his hand firmly. "I shall. I think this is a test we were born to take."

"I'm coming as well," Aphere told them.

Kavan grinned at her eagerness, wondering if it would remain after they squared off against more of the werebeasts.

Pirneon added, "Naturally, your company is welcome. I think the more help we get, the better this affair will end. Four Gaimosians! This will long be a moment remembered!"

They toasted to their success with a fresh round of hot tea.

Kavan joined them in the dance of blades that night. The crowds doubled. Men continued to grumble over Aphere's disregard of their customs while exchanging bets. Soon, the sounds of steel striking steel filled the skies over the way station. Some feared these strange warriors were gathering for some unholy tournament, for surely their size alone marked them as demons. No mortal could dance so gracefully with swords and not be wounded.

Kavan strapped down the last of his saddlebags. He looked up to watch Aphere do the same. He found her exceptionally attractive, though younger than he. She carried herself with poise and a grace ingrained through rigid discipline. She turned and caught him staring. Her cheeks flushed.

"I've not seen you before," he told her in the hopes of dissuading her from thinking he had been ogling her. The attempt was lame. "Where did you grow up?"

"North, past the Thed Mountains in a kingdom called Delranan," she told him.

"My travels have yet to take me there."

"It is a hard land. Winter is long and especially fierce. My parents' parents thought it was the perfect environment to raise and train future knights," she said. "We grow hard, like the grey stone of the mountains. I recall many winter nights in the mountains training and drilling with the sword in naught but a tunic and breeks while my father sat watching beside a small fire. I was not allowed warmth until he was satisfied with my performance."

"A hard life," Kavan nodded. "I think all of us were raised similarly. Not as oppressive as the north, the jungles near the Bay of Cuerlon bear a killing humidity." He paused to grin in fond memory. "Pirneon pushed me hard and is responsible for the man you see standing before you."

She shared his easy smile. "This is the first time I've been around so many of our kind in years. I wonder if it was like this after the Fall."

"Perhaps."

They left the conversation at that and went to find Pirneon. It was no surprise to find him sipping his tea quietly.

The next day found them far from the way station. Each was lost in various thoughts. Pirneon dwelt on the possible connection between the taint of the bond and the sudden reemergence of Gessun Thune. He knew there had to be more than just what was on the surface. The lore of the gods was a fascinating subject. If evil ever did return, it would be through the remains of the dark gods. How would Aphere hold up to such twisted mutations? He decided that it would be his sword ending her if it came down that.

Kavan tried to push aside thoughts of the werebeasts for now. Aradain was still several days away, and he made more pressing issues to deal with. Aphere dominated his thoughts. There was a subtle lust deep inside. She intrigued him.

Aphere, oblivious to his rising desire, thought back to Kistan's teachings. His training had been instrumental in controlling her newfound powers. If she concentrated hard enough, she could make small objects move with her mind.

Barum the squire looked to the coming day when he would finally be named a knight of Gaimos, one of the new generation of Vengeance Knights. His excitement was curtailed only by the scorching heat of the sun and thoughts of how lovely Aphere looked each time he opened his eyes.

Sand eventually gave way to sparse clumps of dried grass. Soon, the ground was littered with grass and rough stone. The landscape changed from tan to blanched green. The sun burned less hotly. They had finally come to the edge of the Jebel Desert. Pirneon's spirits improved almost immediately, though he was left with the desire for a glass of tea.

FOURTEEN

Groskus

Groskus was a typical border town. Filled with petty villains and thieves hiding from authority, the town thrived on lawlessness. Nestled in a narrow canyon three leagues west of the Jebel Desert, Groskus went largely unnoticed. Massive boulders much larger than many homes dotted the open plain leading up to the hidden town. The stores and shops were obsidian to match their surroundings. People in this part of the world were a superstitious lot, tending to believe there were tormented souls trapped in the rocks. Most of Groskus was built underground and deep into the canyon walls. Those few roofs that were exposed were covered in dried thatch.

Some called Groskus the mouth of the underworld. At night, smoke poured up from the ground to mix with the eerie glow of fires. The town took on an air of nightmares unseen anywhere else in Malweir. Travelers warned each other to stay clear, for surely nothing but doom awaited any foolish enough to stop. This worked well for the residents, for they had established their town with specific purpose. It was the first and last stop for the rich merchant caravans moving across the desert.

Twenty leagues west of Groskus ran the Fench River, a tributary of the greater Thorn River flowing south from the Northern Seas. More than a kilometer across at its widest, the river cut diagonally down after following the lower part of the Kergland Spine. A handful of enterprising men constructed a ferry to make crossing easier and charged an exorbitant price. It helped that the ferry was the only manmade construction for almost one hundred leagues.

The western shore of the river led up to the slopes of the Spine. Rolling hills almost immediately gave way to jagged mountains. The Kergland Spine was one of the greatest ranges in Malweir and more intimidating than most believed. Hundreds of lives had been lost in the dark canyons. Folks said a tribe of Trolls lived among the peaks and Goblins in the caves below. Hunters reported having seen massive pits filled with bones.

The one-eyed guard to the southern entrance of Groskus gripped his spear haft and watched as the Gaimosians rode into town. He recognized the dark haired one and snarled. Reaching up, he touched his empty eye socket and remembered the day the dark haired man had taken it.

"That one is watching us too closely," Aphere said. Her hand was already moving towards the small handheld crossbow concealed under her riding cloak.

Kavan looked up and scoffed. "I shouldn't worry about him. He learned his lesson the last time I rode through. Thieves are generally cowards."

They kept riding down into the narrow crevasse. The further they went, the more the walls above them curled in, giving a claustrophobic atmosphere. Hundreds of arrow slits and murder holes lined the jagged walls. Pirneon casually wondered how many men they had to defend the town in the event of an attack. The lay of the land left but one vulnerable point. Any assaulting force would have no choice but to funnel down the main avenue, through the gauntlet. It would be a slaughter.

A network of tunnels honeycombed the ground. The people of Groskus could flee long before the first catapult round was in the air. Enough weapons and supplies to last months were stored away in underground caches. The town was as much a fortress as it was a den of thieves — the perfect sort of place for renegade Gaimosians to conduct business.

"Keep your guard up," Kavan offered halfway down the path. "Groskus is one of the most dangerous towns in this region. There's not much good being done around here."

"What are those huge tents on the surface for?" Pirneon asked. He deferred to Kavan's experience, knowing the younger knight was the only one of the four to have been here before.

"Stables and such for merchant caravans. They're not allowed down in the town, nor would any sane merchant bring one down of his own accord."

Pirneon frowned. "How do they make money, then?"

"They let the exchange down here take control. There's no room for wagons, so the caravan masters don't put up much of an argument about it."

"That's convenient," Aphere remarked. "While most of the guards are topside, the merchants below are easy pickings."

Kavan agreed. "True enough, but we shouldn't be in any trouble. Only a fool would think to take on a handful of Gaimosians."

She hoped he was right.

The proprietor of the Hanging Man was fat by any standard. His flesh held a sallow look, and it had been too long since he'd last walked under the sun. Greasy, unkempt hair was slickened to his skull while pudgy fingers constantly worked and reworked the knots on the string he carried with him. Despite all his faults, Elic was one of the few honest folk in Groskus. He was also one of the few not afraid to stare back at a Vengeance Knight.

"Your journey was…ah, shorter than I expected," Elic told Kavan in a nasal voice. "I trust you found what you were looking for?"

Kavan set his sheathed sword on the bar top. "I did. I trust you've got room enough for me and my companions?"

"I'll have to check, but it shouldn't be an issue."

"Do that. We're tired from the road." Kavan eyed him hard, probing for lies or hidden truths.

Elic waddled away to check the ledgers. He already knew exactly how many vacant rooms he had and where most of his customers were at this very moment. Kavan's presence filled him with a deep sense of dread that left him doubting whether it was in his best interests to house the knight or not. Calmed, he returned and faked a smile.

"Yes. Yes. I have a few rooms still available," he told them. "How long will you be staying?"

"Long enough," was all Kavan said. He had no intention of telling their plans. That kind of information was dangerous in the wrong hands.

Elic blanched. "How many rooms?"

"Two."

"Right this way."

Aphere took a room to herself despite arguing that she needed no special treatment. That left the three men in one of the larger rooms across the hall. Barum took a spot on the floor, arguing that he wasn't a knight yet. Pirneon bickered and cursed but finally relented. His old body needed the straw-filled mattress more than he wanted to admit. Sleeping arrangements hashed out, they washed and redressed. It was nigh time for supper when they met in the hallway. Kavan caught the way Aphere's hazel eyes almost glared at them.

Pushing his empty tray away, Pirneon wiped the corners of his mouth and looked at Kavan. "Where to from here?"

"Cross the river at the ferry. It's another five leagues up into the Spine. We shouldn't have any problems with the passes this time of year. Once we're through, we can ride across Barduk and into Aradain. I figure it's about a two month journey."

"That will put us there around harvest time," Aphere said. "Wouldn't the king have had his hunt by then?"

"Several of them from what I hear. There are tales that Eglios has organized a hunt on the full moon of each month since their troubles began. Either he's a fool or he wants to be sure to rid his kingdom of those terrors for good," Kavan said.

Pirneon added, "It is possible that Eglios may be responsible for the werebeasts or at least have a hand in their uses."

"True, but that wouldn't explain why he's organized a series of hunts to eliminate the problem," Kavan absently tapped a finger against his temple. "I think there is something more sinister at play in Aradain."

"Such is the way of the world," Pirneon said. "We need to be cautious in our approach. If Eglios is the cause, he must not know our true purpose."

"Agreed."

"Has anyone been to Aradain before?" he asked.

Aphere had. "Once, when I was younger. The capital is surrounded on three sides by a great bog. Rantis, I believe the city is called."

"Good," Pirneon said and waved off a drifting cloud of smoke as it lazily went across the mostly empty common room. "We resupply here for the long journey and make our way to Aradain via Kavan's route."

"It's a four day ride to the mountains, and the ferrymen will expect a high toll for using their crossing," Kavan added.

"I can take care of that," Aphere offered. She'd made enough in the desert to last a dozen lifetimes.

She ignored Pirneon's wince. Even Kavan struggled to remain straight-faced. The former Knight Marshal's last job had netted only one gold and five silver pieces. Not exactly the king's ransom Aphere had earned working on the opposite side. They spent the next hour debating plans and tactics. Kavan warned them not to speak too loudly, else they'd draw unwanted attention beyond that from simply being Gaimosian. Too many greedy eyes and ears were fixed upon them already. Talk began to circulate in whispers. Kavan thought he spied the one-eyed man lurking just behind a corner but couldn't be certain without creating a scene.

"We're about to have company," he said quietly and finished his mug of weak ale.

Each scanned the room without moving their heads. The atmosphere of the common room had changed over the course of their conversation. Most patrons had their hands perilously close to their swords. Pirneon, ever one to take control of a situation, rose swiftly, startling most.

Caught, the patrons attempted to play it off, but it was too late. The other Gaimosians joined Pirneon and were careful to display the full force of their weaponry. Without a word, the knights filed out of the common room. Kavan, the last in line, snatched Aphere's mug and drained the last of her ale. He threw the empty mug down, shot a daring grin at any foolish enough to follow, and was out the door.

Barum stood hidden in the shadows just outside the tavern. The tip of his sword rested lightly in the muddied red clay of Groskus. He didn't have to wait long before Kavan's hunch paid off. Ten armsmen strode through the center lane of Groskus with swords barred and ready for use. They leered and gawked at the three knights waiting for them. Not one thought of the fourth they couldn't see. A burly man with large muscles and a shaved head stepped forward, assuming responsibility of what was to come.

"You've got brass balls coming in here like this," he bellowed in a deep voice. "'Specially you, dark hair. Think ye could take me brother's eye and not have ta pay it back?"

Kavan smiled. "I took it easy on him. You won't get the same luxury."

Anger flashed across the big man's face. "I see three o' you and ten o' us. We'll be enjoying this. But you, you we'll bleed last. Feed ya to the wild dogs in bitty pieces."

The armsmen laughed. Aphere yawned at their bravado. She'd heard more than she needed and decided Kavan had let it go on long enough. She raised her crossbow and fired in one fluid motion. The quarrel struck the big man in the forehead, pitching his corpse backwards. He was dead before he hit the ground. The others milled in shock, debating what to do. It was already too late. Even if they wanted to flee, the Gaimosians weren't going to let that happen.

Swords clashed, and a dark river of red blood soon flowed across the clay. A severed hand dropped. A head rolled away. Men screamed. Bodies collided and hit the ground. The survivors turned to flee only to run into Barum's blade. Three quick slashes, and the last two dropped dead.

"They had to have known what we are," Aphere said as she wiped the sweat from her brow.

"They knew," Kavan said. His hands were stained red. He looked sharply to Pirneon. "This won't be the last time. You can bet they had others watching in the shadows. More will come later tonight."

Pirneon cursed. "Damnation. Is there another place closer to the ferry where we can purchase supplies?"

"One or two small hamlets, though I doubt they have the capacity to sustain us for the long trip to Aradain," Kavan said after a little thought.

"It doesn't seem like we have much choice."

"What about the bodies?" Aphere asked.

"Leave them," Pirneon ordered. "It will serve as warning to the others. Perhaps seeing so many of their friends slain will give them pause."

They went back to their rooms in the leisurely manner that suggested confidence and packed. Once done, Kavan excused himself under the pretense of having business to conduct. Pirneon watched him go but said nothing. He was his own man and free to make his own choices. Besides, he knew where Kavan was headed.

Once downstairs, Kavan headed straight for the check-in counter. He reached across with lightning quickness and snatched Elic by the fat on his neck.

"Where is he?" he growled.

Elic sputtered. "Please...please, I ain't had nothing to do with it. Don't kill me."

"Kill you?" Kavan laughed. "That would be a waste of my time. Now, where is he? I won't ask again."

Elic broke and told him everything. Crying, the innkeeper sat huddled in the corner long after Kavan left. When dawn finally arrived, people found the body of the one-eyed man with his own sword run through his heart.

FIFTEEN

Hunted

Pirneon ignored the fresh blood staining Kavan's tunic when he rejoined them. They'd made it out of Groskus without further incident, but their luck failed there. Aphere and Barum managed to scavenge a sack of oats for the horses along with a few other items, though not enough to see them across the mountains. Kavan offered a half-hearted collection of various food items raided from the Hanging Man.

"There might be another problem," Kavan told them a half-day's ride out from Groskus. "The ferry is operated by men loyal to the crime lords in Groskus. Word may have already gone out about us. I don't need to remind you that the borderlands are lawless and dangerous. Even for a knight."

"How many normally garrison the ferry?" Aphere asked.

Kavan shrugged. "There were about twenty the last time I crossed. If the alarm's been raised, a whole company could be heading to cut us off."

"Lovely."

Pirneon sucked in his right cheek and checked the horizon. "We can't burn the ferry once across?"

"We'd be cutting off too many villages from the trade routes, not to mention the amount of lost revenue the caravan merchants would face. We burn the ferry and there'll be a hefty price on our heads," Kavan cautioned. "These crime lords don't forgive, and they never forget. I'd say we're already worth about a hundred gold pieces. Our heads are, at any rate."

"You're full of good news today," Aphere said and kicked her heels into her horse. "I'm going to go scout."

"Can't you use your newfound powers to halt them?" Pirneon harshly demanded.

Aphere winced. "It doesn't work like that, Pirneon."

She clicked her heels into her mare's flank and stormed off.

They watched her ride off to relieve Barum. Soon even her dust trail was lost.

"Determined woman," Pirneon said in a fatherly tone.

Kavan grinned. "She is one of us. How did you two come to be traveling together and what was that about powers?"

Pirneon offered a sly smile. "Opposite sides of the same war."

He paused to enjoy the puzzled look on Kavan's face before telling the rest of the tale.

"These are strange times indeed," was all Kavan managed when he had finished.

Pirneon kept riding.

They rode for nearly two days at a slightly quickened pace. Pirneon knew that an undetermined force was keeping apace of them, riding hard to beat them to the ferry. If that happened, the Gaimosians were left with two options. They could try to fight through the blockade or spend weeks riding up and down the river to the nearest ford. Both paths were equally dangerous, for even if they escaped the ferry ambush, they'd be harried until the brigands' vengeance wore out.

Kavan cursed his lack of foresight for not bringing a bow. He'd be able to strike out and whittle the enemy numbers down then. As it stood, that task fell to Barum. The squire was the only one with a long bow and would not suffer any of them to use his weaponry. Pirneon gave him a paternal look of approval and watched his squire ride off into the gathering dusk. The others stopped and make quick camp in a stand of sparse shrubs. It was late at night during Aphere's watch when Barum returned.

"I almost didn't find you," he told her after slipping from his saddle.

Aphere never stopped scanning the night. "Were you followed?"

"Not that I know of." He shook his head.

She let him bed down, deciding that he need only tell his story once before the entire group come the dawn. He thanked her and stumbled off, exhausted. Aphere continued her watch in silence. Her thoughts soon drifted towards Pirneon and his building disdain towards what her bond had become. It wasn't her fault, but he couldn't see it. She lacked the ability to choose how it worked or why. What little she did know was that she'd been suffering from constant and severe headaches until Kistan helped her cope. All his techniques worked splendidly, and she found herself with a much greater power than possibly imagined. Lost in thought, Aphere continued to watch for signs of their foe.

"I killed seven, but there are at least another twenty out there," Barum told them between yawns and a bite of a hard travel biscuit. "Their horses were tired and slowing. These men are pushing hard for the ferry."

"How did you come upon them?" Pirneon's gaze was hard, flint-like.

Barum swallowed. "I picked up their trail about a league away. Once I got within range, I used the rock formations for cover and picked them off when I could. They were on to me by the time I killed the seventh, so I ran back in the opposite direction to throw them off."

Aphere idly remarked, "It must have worked."

Satisfied, Pirneon stood and stretched his back. "Very good. I continue to be impressed, Barum. Would that we had more bows and more time; then we could whittle them down enough to make the remnants give up."

"There's no point in wishing," Kavan said. "The ferry is still a league away, and they've no doubt sent a runner ahead to warn of our approach."

Pirneon nodded grimly. "It seems we must make our choice now. Do we continue on to the ferry or head north to the nearest natural ford?"

"Four going up against forty isn't good odds, even for us," Aphere said. Her face darkened at the prospect.

"Agreed. Doing so invites death. Which ford is nearer, north or south?"

Kavan rubbed the stubble on his chin. "South, I believe. But there are rumors of some fell power in the mountains down there. Many travelers have gone through Lendren Pass and never been seen again."

Pirneon laughed. "I'd much rather face a monster than forty plus men intent on murder. How far away is the ford?"

"Maybe twenty leagues," Kavan replied. "There are a few villages and independent steads along the route. Remember, the borderlands are mostly untamed. All manner of creatures roam there. Most men will not come unless their need is dire."

"All this just to find out if a king has actually found where the dark gods were beaten," Aphere said in disgust.

Pirneon eyed her sharply. "Gessun Thune is perhaps the most evil spot in all of Malweir. If Eglios did indeed find this dread place, it would do well for us to take action. We may be the only ones capable of stopping the evil from spreading. Others have tried throughout the years, but only Gaimosians came close to succeeding. The werebeasts Kavan slew are but the beginning if the way is open again."

"Open?" she asked.

"Gessun Thune is said to be a gateway, a nexus, to another realm. The dark gods placed their power in the very ground where they were defeated, thus leaving a way for them to return when the time was right."

Kavan winced. "You believe that time to be now?"

"So it would appear."

"Then it would seem time is of the essence. We must be away before the brigands discover our change of plans," Aphere said.

The tiny band struck out for the southern ford. By nightfall, they'd ridden nearly twelve leagues, and there was no sign of pursuit.

The land gradually opened into grassy plains, brown and wind dried from lack of rain. The boulders were gone. The Vengeance Knights were able to gain speed and time. Pirneon stopped them twice at small villages to resupply and water the mounts. Villagers shunned them and only dealt with them when there was no other option. They'd been raided far too many times to trust heavily armed strangers.

It was late in the second day of riding when talk returned to the ancient ruins.

"How can we know for certain that all of these issues are caused by Gessun Thune? None of us are trained to deal with such power," Aphere said. Genuine concern twisted her face.

Pirneon empathized. He'd wondered the same since Kavan first found them in the desert. Gessun Thune was treated as a myth during the high time of Gaimos, often used by mothers to frighten their children into behaving. Not even the military training academy on Skaag Mountain bothered wasting time on nearly improbable events.

"Evil is evil," he tried to argue.

Kavan wasn't convinced. "That may be, but the power of the dark gods is well beyond anything we've encountered."

The conversation ended, for none had anything substantial to contribute. Speculation only went so far. Pirneon finally decided to allow a small campfire for cooking on their second night. He believed that the brigand threat was already gone and the knights would finally be allowed to relax, if slightly. Barum took his bow and returned with a brace of prairie rabbits for a thin stew. The meat was good, but rabbits have almost no fat, and eating too much would eventually weaken the knights.

Kavan thoughtfully gnawed on a leg bone and suddenly slapped his knee. The others gave bewildered looks.

"I just remembered," he explained after seeing their faces. "When I was a little boy, my father would speak of an oracle somewhere out west. If it exists, we should be able to find the answers we need."

"The Oracle of Wenx in Hresh Werd. Tis no myth," Pirneon confirmed.

They nodded in thought, silently deciding their next course of action. A day later, they crossed the southern ford and continued the trek west.

SIXTEEN

Attacked

Aphere tried, unsuccessfully, to shield her face from the lashing rain. Thunder and lightning rumbled through the foothills. Strong winds drove the rain down in sheets, each drop a stinging flechette from an angry god. She couldn't see more than a handful of paces ahead, and the rain-slickened ground had turned dangerous. Pirneon didn't want to turn back, for there was no telling how much longer the storm would rage. So she struggled on into the teeth of the storm.

The storm had struck as they crossed the river and hadn't let up in nearly a day. Pirneon pushed them as hard as he dared, but the going was slow. It took much longer than anticipated, but they finally crossed the five-league span to reach the foothills of the Kergland Spine where they now desperately sought shelter. Aphere's hope rose slightly as she spied a growing darkness in the gathering dusk. She pushed ahead and felt instant relief as the darkness opened into a cave mouth.

Dismounting, she drew her sword and stalked to the entrance. Mountain caves were notorious for harboring bears and other large predators. The air was musky but clean of any animal scent. The cave wasn't very large but should prove adequate to contain all of them. A fire was out of the question, however; with no dried wood, the knights would spend the night shivering. This was the worst part for her. They'd be forced to suffer through the night soaked to the bone and cold. Late winter storms had killed more unsuspecting travelers in this part of the world than anything else. Far from satisfied with her discovery, Aphere led her horse to the back of the cave and returned to fetch the others.

She didn't know how long she waited, only that the last of the light was nearly gone before she heard the clack of hooves on stone. The pale glow of Pirneon's lantern soon followed. Aphere let out a breath of relief. Born and raised in a kingdom like this, she knew the dangers of their situation more than any of them. Lord Death was out this night. Pirneon finally came into sight looking haggard and beyond exhausted. Steam trailed from his mouth with each breath.

She greeted them wordlessly and led them into shelter. They saw to their horses before settling down to a meager meal of dried meat and hard cheese. It did little to sate the growling sensation in their stomachs but successfully took their minds off the bone-numbing chill sinking deeper. Outside, the storm raged on.

"A cup of tea would do nicely about now," Pirneon commented as they watched the heavy rain pound down.

Aphere and Barum shared a smile while Kavan only looked at him with a wild eye.

"Tea?" he asked. "A fine ale would better ease my troubles. Winter doesn't want to let go here. If this storm worsens, we may find the way barred."

He left the last part of his thoughts private. Going around the mountains would add months to their travel time.

Aphere shivered. "Barred how?"

"Lightning and thunder can cause rockslides, or worse. The Lendren Pass is thirteen miles deep and treacherous in fair weather. The ground will be slick for days. There are some reaches here the sun does not kiss. Too, remember the tales of the monster in the mountains," he explained.

"At least we'll die dry and warm if the monster turns out to be a dragon," Barum mumbled.

They laughed and huddled a little closer as warmth slipped away.

The storm left them trapped for another day. A distant bellow, the screams from their deepest nightmares, echoed over the cold grey walls. Hands dropped for swords, but the bellow wasn't repeated. Pirneon organized a watch, for he would not have them come upon danger unprepared. The day passed uneventfully. Steady rain concealed most of the mountains, which suited them well. None wanted to be reminded of the gloom awaiting them. Halfway through the night, the storm picked back up. Lighting savaged the land, and Aphere trembled under the most terrible sound. She swore the mountains were crashing down on top of them. Uncharacteristically, she struggled with the urge to break and run for her life. Kavan snatched her back right before she stepped out of the cave.

"No!" he shouted above the storm. "You go out there and you're dead! Stay put until the storm ends. We will be safe here."

She reluctantly stayed, but that frightened look never left her soft eyes.

Dawn broke and, with it, the first bit of sunlight they'd seen in three days. They were eager to leave the confinement the cave had become, but storm damage was everywhere. Debris littered the trail, and the entire slope of a nearby mountain was gone. It had the appearance of being sheared off. Even Kavan balked at the sight, for no force on Malweir was that powerful.

He and Aphere agreed that it must have been when she had heard the awful sound the night prior. After witnessing it, he could scarcely blame her fear.

They had more pressing problems besides a distant mountain. Their clothes were nearly dry yet still damp enough to invite sickness and mold. The storm had rendered all their tinder useless. The mountains were unkind to unprepared travelers, even ones as hard as the Gaimosians. With no way to make a fire, they wouldn't be able to dry out or heat their dwindling rations.

"We'll catch a sickness if we don't change out of these clothes soon. With naught to strike a fire, I deem we might be in trouble," Pirneon warned.

Aphere clenched her jaw. It was a reflexive act she often failed to notice. "We need to get moving, then. The sooner we're across these gods-awful mountains, the better our lives will be."

"What if the way is blocked? Whatever caused that mountain to collapse could easily have done the same to block this pass," Kavan asked.

"There's nothing for it. We ride on and hope for the best," Pirneon said.

The bitter tone of his voice left no room for further conversation.

Each took a turn relieving him or herself in the back of the cave and wearily climbed into the saddle. They were all red-eyed and sore, the kind of sore only experienced soldiers could begin to understand. A constant burning sensation lingered in their eyes, and their muscles were cramped, aching from being trapped within damp confines for so long. Even the horses seemed almost giddy to be away.

"What of that bellowing we heard? It was no natural sound," Aphere said.

"The monster of the mountains," Kavan replied dryly.

As much as he enjoyed having others for companionship, Kavan quickly found himself wishing for the natural solitude of a Gaimosian knight. He'd had enough of working as a unit. Owing to the actions of others didn't sit well with him — or any of them, for that matter — but it for the greater good, he carried on. The moment when he could break away without guilt and strike out on his own again would be welcome indeed.

Reluctantly, Kavan was forced to admit that he needed the others. This expedition had been his idea from the beginning — all because he deemed it necessary to help in fighting back a plague of demons. Be that as it may, at least the demons didn't babble each waking moment. Kavan snickered.

"The world is still young, untamed," Pirneon said. "It could be a great many things. I don't think man has even begun to discover all the old races lurking in the dark places of the world. Be thankful there are no wild tribes of

Goblins this far west. Our troubles might never end otherwise. Goblins hold grudges until fulfillment or death."

"Goblins don't bother me so much," Aphere told them. "I rode with a Dwarven war band from the Bairn Hills to avenge a fallen kinsman once. We chased the Goblins down into their hole and burned them out. It was a good fight. We were outnumbered five to one. Damned creatures nearly hacked off my right foot."

Kavan shook his head. His thoughts turned inward, back towards his fell encounters with the werebeasts. Up to that point, he'd never come close to being bested in combat. The blow tempered his sense of superiority. Since then, he'd been forced to rethink matters. He realized his own mortality. Gaimosians were naturally long lived but not immortal. Lord Death stalked them like every other soul.

This cold truth forced him to reevaluate his position. Finding and stopping the source of the werebeasts was his focal point. Pirneon and Aphere were invaluable assets required to find success. He just didn't know where to begin. Getting to Aradain was a priority, but where to go from there? Fortunately, time was on his side. Lost in thought, he spurred his mount forward to take lead scout.

His dark eyes scanned the pass. There were hundreds of natural hiding places cut into the foreboding rock. Hundreds of places for ambushes. Outcroppings and shadowed draws lined the passage. Lendren Pass ran nearly twenty meters across at its widest and scarcely five in the deep mountain straits. It was nearly a mile up at its highest point and inhospitable nearly year round. Wiser people sought ways around the mountains rather than risk their lives going up and over.

He reached the first choke point and slowed. Dark shadows fell across the trail. A short ledge jutted out from the right a few meters above ground. Sickly strings of gangly moss draped down. Kavan wasn't sure, but he felt like he was being watched. He drew his sword.

"Come taste my steel, beastie," he challenged in a low snarl.

The horse, born and bred for battle, sensed danger as well. Its ears pinned back against the flat of its great head, and it let out a harsh snort. Together, they advanced on whatever lurked in the shadows. The rest of the world disappeared. Pirneon and the others were still a goodly distance behind, leaving Kavan to face the challenge alone. Just the way he preferred.

A damp coolness washed over him the moment he stepped into the shadows. Tiny hairs stood on end on the back of his neck. Kavan sensed the beast was near. He gripped his sword tighter. The horse carried on. Halfway through the shadows, the beast struck. Kavan ducked right just in time, narrowly avoiding a crushing blow from a war bar. He reflexively lashed out in reply, and steel met hardened iron armor. Burning pain lanced down his arm. The war bar came crushing again, smashing huge chunks of rock off the wall where Kavan's head had just been.

Kavan managed a good look at his foe and blanched. It was an Ogre. Nine feet tall and close to five hundred pounds of muscle and belligerence, the Ogre had a sickly green-grey pallor concealed beneath golden armor. His arms and legs were thickly corded muscle. A great horned helm sat wedged atop his massive head, a thick mane of jet-black hair running down his neck. The Ogre stank of death.

Roaring in frustration, the Ogre readied to attack again. Kavan spied bits of bone and rotting flesh stuck between razor sharp teeth. Cold black eyes glared back at him. The Ogre shifted his gaze to the horse with hungry eyes. Kavan struck. His sword cut a shallow blow on the top of the Ogre's exposed forearm, causing it to roar again. Kavan brought his sword up sharply to slice off one of the Ogre's fingers.

Dark blood spit from the wound. Using the same hand, the Ogre grabbed hold of Kavan's sword and punched the horse in the side of the head. Bones cracked, and the horse reared back. Kavan fell. Unhorsed and now weaponless, he slowly eased back to put distance between them. It wasn't much, but he was left with little options. His horse bolted away, back towards the others, in pain and fear.

Pain racked the Ogre's damaged arm. He looked down at the blade cut into his flesh and cast it aside with a snarl. Fixing Kavan with a lethal stare, the Ogre barked the laugh of a victor. It was a sound so deep and booming, it trembled the very rock face. Kavan readied for his death. He crouched low in a grappling pose and drew his dagger, the only weapon on his person.

The blade was slender, hardly more than six inches. He had no illusions about winning. The Ogre was too big, too strong. He'd swung with all his might and barely managed to cut through the iron-like hide. The Ogre sensed his despair, taking the time to set his war bar down and taunt Kavan. Hot spittle drooled down from the corner of his mouth. Kavan caught the hesitancy and understood immediately. The monster wanted the challenge. Forcing a shallow breath, Kavan braced himself. This was going to hurt.

Roaring in challenge, the Ogre charged. It was all Kavan could do to stay on his feet as the ground quaked from each footstep. Rock and dust drifted down from the mountains, and the Ogre struck. His massive fist caught Kavan in his side and drove the knight into the rock wall. Kavan fell in a heap of bruised flesh. Fire burned his lungs. He struggled just to breathe. The Ogre stepped back and waited, like a cat toying with his prey. Stay down or get up, Kavan knew he was a dead man.

His vision swam as he struggled to rise to hands and knees. He clutched the tiny dagger tighter. Blood and phlegm spilled when he coughed. His entire body felt bruised, battered. Nothing in his warrior training had prepared him for the savage beating he was taking. No man had ever killed an Ogre in single combat. Trickery was his only option but one he thought of far too late. Kavan managed to rise on unsteady feet. The Ogre bellowed laughter. Kavan grinned fiercely in reply. Sensing the end was at hand, the mighty Ogre took slow, measured steps towards his wounded prey.

Kavan, for his part, was forced to place a steadying hand on the nearest rock face. The Ogre kept coming. Kavan let him, having little choice. The ground threatened to tear. Bruised arm hanging limp at his side, Kavan waited until the Ogre's huge body blocked out the sun peeking over the ridge. He waited until all he saw was the bright golden armor charging to kill him. When he deemed the end was nigh, Kavan cast his dagger with all the strength he had left.

The blade shrilled through the air and struck true before the Ogre could react. Ichor and blood erupted from the ruptured eye as the blade drove deep into the socket. Unbelievable pain shot through the Ogre's head, and he screamed. The very sound threatened to bring down the heavens. The Ogre raged, arms flailing and thrashing wildly. Kavan was knocked to the ground again and tried to crawl away before being trampled. A large chunk of rock landed squarely on his back between the shoulder blades, pinning him to the ground and knocking him unconscious.

Howling in pain, the Ogre turned to see his meal stricken down. He roared at the body in an ancient tongue. The gods had stolen his chance for revenge. Reaching down to snatch Kavan up, the Ogre jerked upright suddenly. New pain, deeper than any he had ever felt, burrowed into his body. Turning, he spied another three humans racing towards him with weapons barred.

A second arrow glanced off his armor just under where the first was lodged. A wild looking maiden rode at the front of the group. In her hands was a spear meant to skewer creatures his size. The Ogre saw death and turned to flee. He dropped Kavan's body and sprinted up into the crevasse leading to his caves. Behind him, the maiden let out a victorious whoop and halted her horse. That was her mistake, the Ogre thought. For he'd return to strike again as soon as the sun began to set. He retreated with murder on his mind.

SEVENTEEN

The Ogre's Lair

Kavan awoke to intense pain. Every inch of his body was sore. He didn't want to move but knew he must if he wanted to live. The Ogre was toying with him or already had him trapped. Either way presented grave danger. All Kavan knew was that he had to get away and warn the others before it was too late. He tried to rise, but the pain was overwhelming. Darkness took him again.

"I think he's coming around."

Kavan's head felt horrible. The fierce pounding threatened to burst through his temples. Stars dazzled his vision each time he tried to open his eyes.

"That thing did a number on him. He's lucky to be alive."

He wasn't sure who said what. Vague recognition entertained his thoughts. He opened his mouth, but no words came out. Kavan swooned and passed out. When he awoke again, it was to the sounds of fire crackling gently. He felt warm, dry. Surely, his mind was playing tricks.

"Well, come on then," he managed to croak. "Finish me off already."

He caught the soft chuckle of a feminine voice.

"There'll be no finishing off today, Kavan. Relax and regain your strength. You were very nearly killed."

"Aphere? Where am I?"

His surroundings slowly came into focus. The fire brightened the area enough to show him the walls of another cave.

She smiled, cupping his cheek. "Yes, it's me. You're fortunate to be alive. I haven't seen one of them in years."

"Mountain Ogre," he struggled to say.

She snorted. "That was damned foolish to do alone."

"Where?" he asked again.

"Gone. It ran off after Barum put an arrow in its throat. He and Pirneon are out hunting it now."

Pirneon stalked up the bloodstained path. His eyes remained constant, searching, scanning. Barum was a few paces behind, arrow loosely nocked. They knew the Ogre was wounded, though how badly remained to be seen. The older knight smiled grimly when he came upon Kavan's dagger lying beside a ruined eyeball. Kavan had given a good accounting of himself despite being impetuous. Pirneon pointed at the eye so Barum could see and gestured up a small crevasse.

"He's gone back to his hole, most likely," Pirneon whispered. "That will make him harder to hunt. We must be cautious."

He knew from past studies that Ogres of any type were vicious and often vengeful. There was no doubt it would soon be coming back to finish Kavan off. Too, he couldn't just walk away from such a severe threat. There was no telling how many innocent travelers the Ogre had already killed or how many more it would if Pirneon let it go. He tightened the grip on his spear and followed the blood trail deeper into the Ogre's hole. The stench was overpowering. Untold years of rot and decay spoiled the air. Almost noxious fumes seeped from the ground. The Gaimosians backed away before it was too late.

"Place your kerchief over your mouth and nose," Pirneon advised.

Barum finished tying his off and asked, "Do you think my arrow was successful?"

Pirneon shook his head. "No. Ogre's have tough skin. It was a lucky shot you made to hit him in the throat, but I doubt your arrow did much more than anger him."

Again, they entered the hole. The blood trail thinned before eventually fading away to a lifetime of grime and stains etched upon the stone. The light was dim, turning the tunnel entrance into a haunting scene. Pirneon listened for sounds of his prey but heard naught. They advanced. The ground grew slick. A small stream trickled down from the ceiling. The sheer stench of waste and filth turned Pirneon's stomach. There was no doubt that this den belonged to the Ogre.

He pushed forward, hoping the rest of the hole wasn't so bad. Pirneon didn't slow until they came upon a small bend. He paused, again listening intently. Again, he was disappointed. The Gaimosian eased slowly ahead and was rewarded with a view of a large cavern. Small fires burned low across the floor. There was no immediate sign of the Ogre. Frustrated, he signaled Barum to follow. Once the squire had a clear line of fire, Pirneon took stock of the chamber.

There was a crudely made stone cot in the far corner. A bed, most likely. Large boulders clearly used for sitting circled one of the fires. A pile of old clothes and bones lay heaped along the near wall. Pirneon spied numerous glimmering objects. The Ogre's horde. All the treasure taken from countless victims through the years lay forgotten and unprotected. He edged closer, growing bolder. It was just beyond the fire that Pirneon felt his stomach lurch.

Thousands of bones littered the ground. Most were human, though several different animals were mixed in. A natural ledge running the length of the back wall made for a shelf that contained a row of polished skulls. The Ogre kept trophies. Pirneon was disgusted. He'd seen the worst men had to offer, but this was unlike anything he'd ever witnessed.

"Help," he heard a small voice groan.

Barum shifted aim effortlessly. Pirneon spun around and leveled his spear. Partially concealed behind a rounded boulder sat a small figure in a cage. He was naked and no more than two feet tall. Filth covered his body, and he had the look of having suffered great abuse. Rage consumed Pirneon, for at first glance the figure appeared no more than a child. Then he noticed the narrow eyes and pointed ears poking out from beneath mousey brown hair. The small face looked back at the knight with abject excitement. He reached out to grab the bars and began babbling.

"Oh, please. Please help me!"

"Who are you?" Pirneon asked, wary of a trap. Here, of all places, he wasn't about to take unnecessary chances.

The small figure rose and said, "Geblin. I am a prisoner."

"Why should we believe you? You could be a pet set here to lure us to our deaths," Pirneon's voice was hard.

Geblin appeared frantic. "You must believe me! He is coming back, and when he does, he will kill us all! Please! Free me, and I'll show you the secret way out."

Pirneon didn't move. Part of him wanted to believe the story, but an equally large part wasn't trusting. Still, he couldn't abide any living creature being locked in a cage. He was about to order Barum to free Geblin when the little creature's eyes went wide with fright.

"Behind you!" Geblin cried and curled up in a tight little ball.

Barum spun and fired. His arrow bounced off the iron armor and skirted the rock face. Pirneon used the distraction to charge. The Ogre's mass was so great Pirneon was hard pressed to strike any of the vital areas. Instead, he stabbed the spear for the Ogre's unprotected groin. Barum fired twice more. The first shaft brushed past the tip of the Ogre's nose while the second splintered against his skull.

"Waaugh!" Geblin cried above the din.

The Ogre kicked at Pirneon with a tree trunk of a leg longer than Pirneon's spear. Pirneon's reflexes saved him from being crushed under the monster's heel. He used his momentum to dive forward, throwing down his spear and drawing his broadsword as he rolled and came up behind the Ogre. Pirneon slashed across the back of an exposed knee. Tissue and tendons ripped apart. The jagged lined shred the back of the Ogre's leg even as Pirneon swiped across the other. The Ogre managed one step before crashing down.

Pirneon leapt onto his chest before the dust rose. He stabbed down hard, driving his blade into the Ogre's leg and didn't stop until he felt bone. The Ogre thrashed and rolled, trying desperately to get his hands on his murderer. Fast as the Ogre was, Pirneon was faster. He had his spear back in hand before while the Ogre remained disorientated. Barum rushed forward but was forced to leap back or risk being crushed beneath a calloused hand. The Ogre bellowed again. Geblin's weak cries joined the chorus.

"Stay back!" Pirneon warned Barum.

The squire exhaled a deep breath and took aim with his long bow. The black feathered shaft thrummed free and sped the short distance to its target. Tempered steel drove into the Ogre's exposed face, piercing his septum before bursting into the brain cavity. The Ogre let out a final roar of defiance before his tongue lolled out of the corner of his mouth as he died. Remorseless, Pirneon stabbed his spear through the Ogre's throat to ensure it was dead.

"Ware!" Kavan shouted and struggled to find a weapon he no longer had.

Aphere, startled by the outburst, laid a reassuring hand on his chest. "Be calm. You were having a dream."

He tried to get up again and winced as extreme pain lanced through his body.

"Stay still as much as possible. I think you've got a few broken ribs and possibly internal bleeding. You are fortunate to be alive."

"I don't feel fortunate. How long have I been out?" he asked.

"A few hours."

"You didn't need to stand watch," he said, his tone suddenly turning…affectionate.

Aphere stiffened, turning back to the mountain pass. "I did what any good Knight would have. Think nothing more of it, Kavan. Let us hope Pirneon and Barum return soon. I am eager to be away from this dreadful place."

Kavan frowned. "They should be back by now."

She shared his apprehension and struggled just as much as he to resist the temptation to seek Pirneon out. Honor demanded she stay by Kavan's side until he was able to fend for himself. Pirneon, being the former Knight Marshal of Gaimos, would have to take care of the Ogre with only Barum. She turned her attention back to the tiny fire they were fortunate to have.

Aphere managed to drag together enough small bushes and broken twigs to get the fire started, but it wouldn't last long. There wasn't enough natural fuel in the mountains. Seizing advantage of the moment, Aphere had put together a small pot of stew with what ingredients they had in their saddlebags. It was thin and bland.

"Do you believe this oracle is capable of helping us?" she asked as she handed him a bowl some time later.

Kavan accepted graciously and swallowed a mouthful of the piping liquid. "It can't hurt. We'd be riding into Aradain blind otherwise. This is one time I want as much advantage as I can get."

"Ominous words for a Gaimosian."

He scoffed, letting her anger rise slightly. "If you'd fought those werebeasts, you'd be feeling exactly the same. They weren't natural."

She rose suddenly with the grace of a cat and drew her sword.

"What is it?" he asked.

"I thought I heard something."

Aphere blocked the cave entrance. She couldn't hope to fight off the Ogre, but there were no easily accessible escape routes in the darkness. The scraping noise gradually got louder. Closer. Her heart slowed as she dropped into a deep sense of calm. It was an old trick Gaimosians had been using for centuries. Despite this, she felt small, almost insignificant in the smothering darkness.

"It is us," Pirneon called out in a gravelly voice before they edged into view.

She breathed a small sigh of relief and sheathed her sword. Aphere spied tiny movement between Pirneon and Barum. *Where had they found a child?* She eyed the small figure cautiously. Some mysteries were potentially too dangerous to know. She opened her mouth to ask but decided against it. Much to her surprise, Geblin sped past her guard and the prone Kavan to revel before the warmth of the fire.

"What is that?" she leaned close to ask Pirneon.

He handed her Kavan's spear and shook his head. "That is Geblin. He's a Gnome."

"A Gnome?"

"Aye. I'd keep a watch on your purse. He's already tried to lift mine," Barum added. "He doesn't seem too thankful for being rescued."

"What of the Ogre?" Aphere riffled through the pack at her feet and handed the Gnome a bowl. Geblin greedily snatched it and waited impatiently for her to fill it.

Pirneon said, "Dead. Barum is quite the marksman."

The squire bowed his head, cheeks reddening slightly. Aphere smiled in delight. The group then settled down to eat their meager meal before the fire. It had been an exhausting day, and there was much still left to be done.

EIGHTEEN

Corso

Howling winds buffeted against the black stone tower. Dark clouds snarled past. A mist shrouded the lower levels as if concealing some foul purpose. The very night was alive with repression. It was only fitting for the work being done. The lone tower was the only structure for leagues. It reached high into the sky, a relic from the old times when the First Races came into Malweir. Made entirely out of black granite and marble, the tower hummed with latent power. None living knew who had created such a thing or why. There were no legends, no dust-covered tomes explaining its purpose. It was forgotten by all but a few.

Cruel intentions surrounded the area for leagues. A wicked forest of vines and thorns, tangled limbs and gnarled trees had grown around the tower, lending a special brand of malevolence. The ground was littered with poisonous plants and lurking predators. A single path led from the forest edge to the base of the tower, a path that was only known by one. The secret had been handed down through the ages to those deemed worthy of beholding the dark power contained within.

So it was the current keeper of the knowledge entered the foul wood at dusk, for not even deepest night was safe for the chosen. Ancient wards protected the tower from prying eyes. He didn't mind the wards; after all, he'd been responsible for reestablishing them once he assumed the role. Dressed in dark robes with a hood covering his head, his stride was powerful, confident. The woods stirred around him. Malicious creatures hungrily waited to see if he would make that fatal misstep.

At last, he arrived at the tower. His bony hand slid from the confines of his robe to point at the lock. Green light glowed from the tip of his almost skeletal finger and pulsed into the lock. A series of clicks echoed through the dusk, and the door groaned open. Pausing to give the forest a final look of warning, he entered the tower and began the long climb to the top.

This was the first night of Spring, a special time for the followers of the power. The robbed man, Corso, tirelessly climbed the thousand steps to the upper floor. Fitting, he mused, for he was also one thousand years old. Ten centuries had he wandered across Malweir, tending the ways left behind by the dark gods. Tonight was the culmination of his long existence, a moment he'd striven for his entire life.

The moment was bittersweet. In order for his plan to work, he needed to die. His one solace came from knowing that his actions would send more of the pitiful remnants of the Gaimosian race to their dooms beforehand and then after. He gained the landing, lost in conflicting thoughts, and used the green light to open the final door. Corso entered, drawing a shuddering breath as he passed through the electric tingle of the invisible warding. Tiny sparks reached down into his soul. The power was raw, unpredictable and strong enough that should any attempt to break in the tower would explode.

A waist high pedestal rested in the center of the room. There were no windows or other furnishings. Only the pedestal. Atop the flat surface sat a dust covered ball of solid onyx. Corso halted before it and bowed reverently. He began to chant in an ancient tongue that hadn't been heard on the wind since the war of the gods. His eyes rolled back into his head, leaving in the small orbs vast emptiness. His arms stretched wide. Fingers pointed at the marble.

The marble ball began to spin, rising gradually up from the stone. Corso directed all his thoughts and power at the ball. It spun faster, becoming a blur. The same green glow emanated from the marble, bathing Corso and the chamber. Corso's head snapped back with an audible crunch. He screamed at the top of his lungs as green flames belched from his mouth. The magic lasted but a second before darkness claimed the chamber and Corso collapsed. The ritual had begun. His fate was now entwined with the rest of the world's. Soon both he and Malweir would die.

NINETEEN

Geblin

"What do we do with him?" Kavan asked, gesturing to the Gnome.

One day had passed since Pirneon had returned with the little creature, and Kavan was beyond fed up. They'd been forced to drag him to a small runoff pool Barum had discovered and scrub Geblin clean. He'd fumed and protested the entire time, but it was well deserved. The Gnome stank of Ogre. Aphere held his head underwater to get his cooperation, and he hadn't stopped glaring at her since. He'd already tried picking each of their pockets, crying that it was in his nature and not to beat him. He complained about everything and was never satisfied. When Pirneon scolded him for acting like a crotchety old man, he fumed and folded his thin arms across his chest, claiming he was hardly out of his tweens.

Aphere looked sharply at the pouting Gnome. "Put him back in the cage and be done with him. He is a most infuriating creature."

"That would only lead to his certain death," Pirneon cautioned. "He is harmless, for all of his faults. A bit of a nuisance, yes, but harmless nonetheless."

"Then we go in the opposite direction if you don't want me to kill him now," Aphere warned.

Pirneon sighed. He admitted his own ire was raised at Geblin but not enough to wish him harm. Abandoning the Gnome now was just as good as putting him back in the Ogre hole. But they didn't need another traveling companion, another mouth to feed. Geblin was a liability and, if Gessun Thune had indeed been discovered as Kavan feared, he'd only stand a greater chance of getting killed.

"Calm yourself, Aphere," Pirneon said. "As he said, it's in his nature."

"Being obnoxious? If he tries to lift my purse again, I'll break his little fingers," she vowed.

Barum chuckled.

"Be that as it may, we simply can't leave him in these mountains. He'd starve and die in a matter of days."

Geblin's head swung sharply at the mention of death.

"What I want to know is what he was doing in the Ogre cage to begin with. I didn't think Gnomes lived in these mountains," Kavan pointed out.

Feeling better, he was finally able to move on his own — a little, anyway. They'd bound his ribs to reduce the pain that had become a constant.

He'd survive but required many more days of recovery. He scowled and frowned upon Aphere's ministrations much the same as Geblin had.

"Geblin, come over here please," Pirneon called.

Hesitantly, the Gnome obeyed. He remained just out of arms reach, for his experience left no faith in his new companions. "What do you want now? Think I'm some kind of pet for your amusement, do you? Ha!"

"Ingrate," Kavan muttered.

Aphere added, "Just throw him off the cliff already."

Geblin cringed under the constant onslaught of threats. Pirneon held up his hands to quiet his friends. "I'd like to know what you are doing up here. How did you arrive in your situation?"

Geblin snorted and stamped his foot. "I was about to be eaten is what I was doing. Or didn't you notice the pile of bones?"

They heard Barum chuckle again from his guard post at the cave mouth. He found the Gnome's sarcasm quite amusing, knowing his master's famous patience was being pushed to the limits.

"We know that already," Aphere snapped. She had a mind to say more but held her tongue out of respect for the former Knight Marshal.

Geblin clenched his jaw, clearly debating the merits of telling them more. Finally, he sat down and began his tale. "Two weeks ago my brother and four cousins were returning from a trading venture in Groskus. We were drunk and happy. We never saw the Ogre until it was too late. One by one he captured us and killed us. He...ate my bro... That's my story, and I'll be telling you no more," Geblin said in an angry tone. He didn't expect them to understand or care. They were Big Folk, after all.

"Ill fortune indeed has been visited upon you," Pirneon said. Sadness clung to his voice.

Kavan added, "As it would have on us."

He was still sore about giving their position away so easily, despite the Gnome's story. Then again, if he hadn't been in such a hurry to be done with the group, they would have walked into a similar ambush. Kavan shook his head slightly. He felt he was the victim in a lose-lose situation.

Geblin fumed. "Ill fortune! My kin were slaughtered and eaten! That's not fortune; it's cruelty."

Pirneon said, "Yet you are still alive."

"Only because the Ogre wanted to fatten me up first," he admonished with a wagging finger.

"Nevertheless, you ought to consider yourself fortunate. The Fates spared you for a reason, Geblin," Pirneon soothed.

"For what? To show me the error in my ways or just to mock me until I die?" He grew livid. "Big Folk are all the same, Ogre or men. Your kind can be just as cruel as them! I won't stand for it."

"Then stand alone, and let us be done with you," Kavan fired back. "We saved your miserable life, and all you do is complain about it. Go back to where you came from and trouble us no more."

"Kavan," Pirneon warned.

"I owe this one no debt," Kavan snapped.

Pirneon struggled to regain control of the situation. "No. You don't. But I will not let him sit in these mountains to die. He comes with us until we're down and on the plains again."

Aphere walked away. She relieved Barum and stewed over the argument. There was no sentiment in her mind, for she cared little for the other races. Yet she couldn't deny Pirneon spoke true. What was the point in rescuing him only to leave him for dead? She may have understood but would never admit it aloud.

Kavan finally gave in, though with threatening undertones. "Very well, Knight Marshal, yet heed this. Should I find him stealing again, I'll run him through and leave the corpse for the crows."

Geblin felt the color drain from his face.

They stayed at the cave for another day. Barum went hunting and returned with a mountain goat. The knights ate heartily for the first time in days, especially after Pirneon returned to the Ogre's cave to get a supply of firewood. A single wagon rolled through the pass during their time of healing. They stopped and exchanged tales and what current events were engaging. Pirneon bade the driver to spread the word of the Ogre in Lendren Pass so that folk could travel freely again. The driver waved and continued east towards the ferry. Geblin should have joined them, but something stayed his legs.

They awoke the following morning refreshed and ready to be done with the Kergland Spine. Geblin stumbled about in a drunken stupor; he'd snuck off in the night to find the wreckage of his wagon and came upon an unbroken cask of wine. Kavan watched in disgust as the Gnome urinated on his own boot.

"Where do I ride?" he asked before sneezing into the palm of one hand and wiped it off on his trouser leg.

"Not with me," Aphere said and walked away.

"I'll take him," Pirneon said. "He'll not be much of a burden."

"Burden!" Geblin spat. "Who says I'll have you?"

Having heard enough, Pirneon snatched Geblin by the shoulder and hauled him to the baggage mount. He ordered Barum to ensure the Gnome was tied down. It wouldn't do for Geblin to fall off along their route of march. Barum chuckled again and produced a rope.

Kavan didn't feel like wasting any more time and rode into the lead. Within moments, he was far enough ahead to be out of sight. The Gnome's curses echoed off the pass walls. Kavan hoped there was only one Ogre, or they'd all be done for. Sighing heavily, he rode on.

TWENTY

Decisions

The rest of the journey through the mountains proved uneventful. Pirneon halted them a few leagues away from the base of the mountains where they made camp for the night. They could have gone much further, but the long days in the pass had taken their toll, and Kavan still wasn't back to full health. They found a small stand of silver oaks and started a fire. Aphere and Barum went hunting, coming back with a small stag that would feed them for at least a week. Kavan managed to find some edible roots and berries to round out their meal.

Geblin awoke sober and in misery. He snatched at the stew pot and was met with the back of the ladle across his wrist and a stern warning that, if he wanted to eat, he was going to wash in the nearby stream first. Glowering, he reluctantly agreed that his stomach was more in charge than his brain.

Talk of their next move was made over dinner. Geblin, as part of his penance for earning his keep, was elected to scrub the pots before rejoining them in a refreshing cup of tea after dinner. He tried to protest but was quickly coming to understand the terms and quality of his rescue.

"How far to Hresh Werd?" Aphere asked once things had quieted down.

Pirneon thought about it. "I'd guess close to five hundred leagues."

"That's a long ride," Kavan said.

"Six weeks at best."

Aphere yawned and stretched. "Do you think we have six weeks to spare?"

"We don't know the importance of events in Aradain. This might not even be Gessun Thune, but some other evil. We must also consider the way and reasons of an oracle. They rarely speak plainly. More like riddles and half-answers intended to get us to find part of our inner selves."

Kavan barked a savage laugh. "Get one in reach of my falchion and see how fast we get answers."

Pirneon shook his head. "No, Kavan. That is an impossibility. Oracles are well protected by elder magic. Some say they come from another world altogether."

The first twinkle of stars began to shine in the twilight.

"Pah!" Geblin grunted. His tunic was soaked, and he wore his usual dour look. "Oracles are nothing but drug addicted knaves. They serve no purpose but the trickery of the Fates."

All heads turned to the Gnome.

"What?" he demanded. "Your ears need cleaning?"

"What makes you think that?" Aphere asked. The tone of the conversation made her uneasy for reasons she couldn't explain. "Oracles have power."

It was Geblin's turn to shake his head, exasperated at their ignorance. "They help decide the future, don't they?"

"They influence our actions and deeds," Pirneon admitted.

"Which is the future. What do the Fates do?"

"Of course! They do the same thing but on a grander scale," Pirneon realized. "Impressive, my small friend."

Geblin offered a *hmph* and went back to the stream, grumbling.

Aphere stared up to the sparkling night sky. Her mind was filled with the wonder of too many things. Fates and oracles. Gessun Thune and dark gods. Then, there was Kistan and his growing movement. She felt overwhelmed, confused. She didn't know which direction her life was moving in. She was an honor-bound knight of vanquished Gaimos but felt like something else at times. The bond she shared with the others was changed enough to make her feel like an outcast. She felt uncomfortable at her deepest levels.

Then there were her companions. Kavan stared at her when he thought she wasn't looking, a passing longing in the back of his eyes. That he was attracted to her was beyond question, but why? She'd made no motions to attract such attention. As far as she was concerned they were peers and nothing more. Barum, on the other hand, proved subtly more fascinating. Quiet confidence defined him, almost making her wish he was more vocal, especially when assuming the role of Pirneon's conscience.

So. Two admirers and a long list of bad reasons to get involved. Aphere seldom found life played on an even field, but this experience might prove more maddening than it was worth. Still, she couldn't help but smile, always secretly, whenever she spied Barum blush at being caught looking at her. She sighed her frustrations.

Perhaps the oracle would be able to help. It was said that oracles know all and can give the answers to worthy seekers. Surely, she fell into that category. Wasn't this quest one of honor and value to all peoples of Malweir? She thought so, else she wouldn't have come. Aphere sighed longingly. There were too many uncertainties. The one thing she was sure of was that she was destined for more. Aphere quieted her mind as Kistan had taught her. She practiced using her thoughts to move objects until her guard shift was over.

"Today, we must decide our course of action," Pirneon said after a quick meal of cooked oats sprinkled with sugar.

Kavan rolled his eyes, tired of being part of a team, and went to empty his bladder. They'd been having the same conversation repeatedly since leaving the cave in the Kergland Spine, and he was sick of it. He was the type of man who made a quick decision and adjusted afterwards. All else was senseless banter. Pirneon was cautious by nature, perhaps too much so but at least understandable after his experiences during the Fall. Caution had the propensity to be both boon and bane. Kavan pulled his trousers up and looked upon the dew-laden plains of Ergos. The kingdom ran forever, all the way to the western coast. Most of it was grass covered with clots of trees and light forests. He turned back to the camp. At least the ride seemed easy enough.

"What say you, Kavan?" asked Pirneon. "Rantis or Hresh Werd?"

"I say the same thing I've been saying from the beginning. The Werd."

Pirneon watched the younger knight as he walked past. A very angry man, he concluded, but what he couldn't figure out was why. Clearly much had changed in the years since he had apprenticed a young Kavan. Surely, his life had been hard and long fought. It was no different for any of them. Pirneon decided to try and find out why. After all, they had more than enough time before arriving in battle. Mired in thought, Pirneon watched Geblin amble by as well. The Gnome presented another situation entirely. His kind was much hated in the western kingdoms. A single Gnome presented an easy target for drunks and thieves. Then again, he knew he couldn't take Geblin against his will, especially into a potentially dangerous situation.

"Geblin," he called.

The Gnome suspiciously turned.

"How far is it to the nearest of your kin?"

His eyes lowered. "Why? They won't take me back after this. I'd be a disgrace."

"I'm sorry," Pirneon gently said. "But we must decide what to do with you. It is a long ride to Hresh Werd. After that, we head into certain danger in Aradain. The chances of survival decrease with each passing day, even for one of us."

"You're just going to leave me here and bid farewell as you ride off like the gallant knight you claim to be? I don't think so. You found me, saved me, now it's your responsibility to get me to safety."

"This is about as safe as you can get," Aphere snapped, tightening the belly strap of her saddle. "With a little bit of work, you can make a nice living here."

He shot her a baleful look before realizing it.

"You may ride with us until you find a suitable place of your liking. Yet heed this: this is not a free ride. You will earn your place among us. No one eats unless they work. Such is our way. Can you abide by this?" Pirneon leveled his gaze and looked sternly down upon the Gnome.

Geblin shuffled his feet. "I can, so long as none of you threatens to hurt me again. And I can leave at any time I want."

"Leave now, for all I care," Aphere said. She, like Kavan, had had enough of his posturing. She'd never seen a Gnome before and never wanted to meet another if he was any indication of their race.

"Agreed," Pirneon answered for all. "I suggest you check your attitude around here, and don't try to steal from us again. Else I might not be able to save you."

Geblin paled and hesitantly agreed. A death wish was the one thing he lacked, and he decided that running afoul of these knights wasn't in his best interests. Gently this time, Pirneon helped him aboard the packhorse, and the small band was back underway.

The next three days went by without event. In fact, nothing changed. The grass remained the same. The stands of trees. Even the far horizons appeared constant due to the lack of mountains. The tedious nature of their journey caused them to let their guard down and grow lax, if but slightly. They rode. They ate. They slept. The next day, they did it all again. And the next day. Conversation had stalled. There was some speculation on what the oracle might offer on finding the truth of Gessun Thune. Occasionally, thoughts of the dark gods entered their sleep to induce nightmares. These were never shared or talked about, for the knights were too proud to admit to petty fear.

On the third night, they enjoyed a wild pheasant. Nightfall crept upon them. Barum took his turn on guard duty, given the early shift so that he could sleep through the night. Geblin, tired of the knights and their seemingly pointless wondering, stumbled off to a small crook in the nearest tree and grumbled himself to sleep.

"We should be coming upon a village soon," Kavan speculated. His time in the low country was minimal, leaving much to guesswork. "Our supplies are running low, and the horses need grain. About the only thing we have plenty of is the Gnome's wine."

"Only because I haven't let him have any yet," Aphere chided.

Kavan glanced at her, admiring the way her auburn locks fell over her shoulders. She stretched slowly in a display of deadly grace. She caught Kavan's look, and they shared a smile. He was beginning to feel better. The ride across the rolling plains of Ergos did much to not only improve his spirits but give his body time to heal. Even his animosity towards Geblin faded, if only just. Stripped down to undershirt and trousers, Kavan did his own stretching. Tonight was the first night he felt well enough to practice with his sword.

"The map says we should be coming upon the village of Bronf," Pirneon said. "We'll arrive sometime around midday, provided nothing happens along the way."

Aphere snorted a quiet laugh. "What could possibly happen? We've been in trouble since the final night in the desert. I wouldn't know how to behave if it all came to an end now."

Pirneon held his tongue.

"Are you ready?" she turned to ask Kavan.

"Give me a few minutes," he replied.

Her eyes bore a mischievous gleam. "I suppose you expect me to take it easy on you? Poor thing. Should I go get a stick to use rather than my sword?"

"Only if you want to get cut," he growled back. "I'm ready."

Steel met steel, and the glade erupted in the sounds of combat. Pirneon never once looked up.

"Damned fool humans," Geblin swore under his breath after being awoken. "Quiet that racket! Some of us are trying to sleep!"

Bronf was a one-road village with about twenty homes and a handful of necessary businesses. Location was the only thing of value Bronf had to offer. It was situated along one of the major trade routes running across Ergos. The chandlery was the only two-story building in the village and that but barely. Smoke drifted lazily up from the chimneys. Even though spring had graced the land, a chill remained.

Most of the thatch-roofed homes had modest sized pens behind them. Pigs and chickens were the mainstay. One of the larger farmsteads they had passed on the road into town held a hundred head of cattle. Farmers and villagers were spotted dotting the fields, preparing for the coming planting season. All in all, Bronf was like every other village across the face of Malweir. Cozy, quaint, and out of the way. The kind of village where everyone knew everyone, and there was never any trouble.

The Vengeance Knights rode into the village under the wary gaze of the villagers. Many suspected a raid. Pirneon saw it in their faces. A few mothers ran to get their children. Men reached for what meager weapons they had. The oldsters looked a little closer and frowned. It was worse than they'd initially thought. The newcomers were no ordinary raiders. They were Gaimosians.

None living had ever fought the Gaimosians, though some of their great fathers had. The next generations grew up with tales of horror. Some claimed the knights bore supernatural powers. Others said they were in league with the dark gods. Whichever tale be true, the people of Bronf weren't welcoming.

"Not exactly a friendly village," Kavan said. Try as he might, he couldn't get any of the villagers to look him in the eye.

Pirneon continued scanning for signs of trouble, even while giving the illusion of calm. He realized that many of the plains villages suffered from seasonal raids, and for four heavily armed riders to come unannounced could very possibly spell their doom.

"Yet not openly hostile, either," he replied. He nodded to one of the oldsters eying them carefully from a rickety rocking chair on his porch.

Aphere didn't feel calm, but neither did she have a sense of impending danger. "Do you think they know we're not raiders?"

"I'd say that was a good bet," Pirneon said and reined in his horse.

A lone man emerged to block the road.

"We don't be wanting no troubles from no G'mosian Knights," he told them in a thickly accented voice.

Kavan thought the man's tongue was too big for his mouth.

Pirneon held out empty hands. "We don't come bringing any trouble. My name is Pirneon, this is…."

The man spit. "Don't rightly care what you call yerselfs. Folks here have enough troubles to worry about, what with crops and children. You come a riding in here with all them weapons, and that be asking for trouble."

Kavan chewed on his rising ire. Finally, he couldn't take it anymore. "That's great. And you are who exactly?"

"Name's Hars, and I be the constable," he said with an inflated sense of self-importance.

"Constable Hars, we merely need to resupply and get a night's comfort on a real bed before carrying on," Pirneon told him. "We'll be gone by dawn and will pay fair wages for any goods."

Hars looked each of them up and down, as if deciding which was the most dangerous. "Chandlery be on your right. Ferrier is the next building down. We got a small inn on the outskirts a town. Food be good and at good price."

With that, he turned and walked away. By the end of the night, everyone in Bronf would know how he put these Gaimosians in their proper place in no uncertain terms. Of course, he left out the part about them being so well armed the four could easily have run through the entire village if they wanted. Some facts were best left unsaid. He didn't want the wrath of the dark gods to come down on him, after all.

TWENTY-ONE

King Eglios

The kingdom of Aradain was abuzz with rumors and gossip over the latest hunt. Twelve men went down into the recently discovered underground ruins, champions and master hunters all. Not a one had been seen since. As was the custom, Eglios declared a state of mourning to last no shorter than five days and nights. Names were added to the already growing monument in the town square of Rantis. Most of the kingdom's residents knew little of the goings on in the capital, though, so the losses from the hunt seemed unimportant, impersonal. Only when one of the dire beasts managed to escape into the countryside did the peasants react.

Rantis was a tightly packed city of nearly ten thousand people living on top of each other. Considered young; only a few hundred years had passed since men first settled on the bluffs. Aradain was neither prosperous nor desirable. The land itself was farmable, but there were no riches in the soil. No veins of minerals ran beneath the dark earth. Instead of mines, there were farmsteads stretching for as far as the eye could see. The line of Eglios had been born on the backs of peasants.

That latent anger manifested itself down through the generations until part of it consumed the mind of the current liege. Many nights Eglios sat alone on his gilded throne, stewing over his legacy. Other kings were made of vast wealth, their names carried down from ancient times through heroes' blood and temperance. Eglios was not so fortunate. A great bear of a man, he languished under the peasant rule. Near six feet tall and two hundred-fifty pounds, he was well into his forties. He'd lost his right eye in a border skirmish some years back when he'd stormed neighboring Barduk and almost doubled his kingdom.

Yet not even conquering another kingdom was enough to raise his stature amongst the other nobles across Malweir. So he sat and fumed, seeking new ways to earn a proper name for himself and for Aradain. It had been winter two years ago when the old stranger had ridden in under the blanket of a blizzard and promising to change Aradain's fortunes. Corso claimed to be a priest in search of the right king to serve.

Corso wove a web of lies and subtle hints in the king's ear. He whispered of greatness and the destiny of one of the greatest and most remembered lords in all of history. Eglios lit up at the thought and slept with dreams of glory. But Corso had other plans. He often disappeared for many days at a time, and where he went, none could say. Disappearances in Rantis and surrounding villages also rose. Most of the victims were homeless, drunken riffraff no one missed.

Peddlers and travelers often reported hearing high-pitched screams coming from a tangled wood in the dead of night. Worse, any who tried to investigate were never seen again. Folk soon learned to stay well clear of the black wood. All the while, Eglios turned to Corso for advice. He secretly began building an army geared for invasion. Bases were fortified and enlarged at various points across the fold. Arms and armor were being produced at incredible rates.

Corso came into the throne room one year to the day after first arriving in Rantis with a wicked a smile. He claimed to have found a place of ancient power that would make Aradain invincible. Eglios asked to see this power and was met with a staying hand. All in due time, Corso promised. And he proceeded to detail his plans. So it was that the ruins of Gessun Thune were uncovered and the door to the coming darkness found.

Key players mysteriously disappeared. Others, once opposing the king, suddenly changed their opinions and became loyal, if somewhat skittish supporters. A year later, Eglios sat upon his throne dressed in crimson armor emblazoned with a lightning bolt crossing a sword. He recognized, but would never admit, that none of it would have been possible without the staunch advice from Corso, who now stood before him, hands folded in his robes. The king eyed his advisor sternly.

"You're certain of this?" Eglios asked. His voice was deep and booming.

Corso nodded. "Yes, sire. They are coming to put an end to your reign."

Eglios rubbed his chin. "How many?"

"Four."

"Ha! Four have no chance of breaking through. My army is nearly four thousand strong. A pathetic four, even Gaimosian, cannot hope to lay siege and kill me."

Corso flashed a quick smile from within the shadows of his cowl. "But sire, these are no ordinary assassins. They are knights of Gaimos. They have certain powers."

"Powers or not, they are of little concern. Gaimos is a forgotten kingdom. Their kind has been all but driven to extinction. Our fathers did the world a favor by ending that threat long ago."

"Be that as it may, these knights are more dangerous than you imagine. Three others have already come to the hunts. They have to know about Aradain's plans," Corso teased, just skirting around the truth. "The Gaimosians must be stopped."

"Where are they now?" Eglios asked.

At last, Corso thought. "South of here. Traveling across Ergos, as my spies tell me."

"Ergos? I cannot send troops rampaging across two different kingdoms without risking open war," he sputtered.

"There is always the Fist."

"The Fist," Eglios whispered.

The Fist was a highly disciplined unit of five hundred men. They were hardened veterans from across Malweir who reveled in the gore of battle. Not even a handful of the legendary Gaimosians could match five hundred murderers.

"Very well," Eglios relented. "Send the Fist. I would have this threat ended before they bring us all to ruination."

"As you wish."

Corso spun on his heels and left the throne room. His mind was alive with the possibilities suddenly presented. If all went according to his carefully laid plans, the dark gods would soon be free of their prison and the Gaimosian threat removed forever. Free to bring darkness and ruin to Malweir and all who had prospered from their banishment.

TWENTY-TWO

Dreams

Early springs soaked the grasslands of Ergos. Kavan, once again riding ahead as a scout, pulled the collar of his jacket tighter to keep the rain from running down his back. Being wet was bad enough, but there was no sense in being uncomfortable as well. He patted his horse on the neck for good measure and continued to ride. It was just past midday, and the skies continued to darken. Kavan had been through too many storms and knew when not to take the weather lightly. He looked up into the clouds, confirming his suspicions.

A major storm was building, and they were caught in the open. A distant rumble got his attention. Thunder. The rain came down harder. He almost wished for the cave back in the Kergland Spine, but that was nearly two hundred leagues behind them. The best he could hope for was to find a stand of trees thick enough to buffer the brunt of the storm.

He started to question exactly how he'd begun this quest. The initial idea had been all his, but Pirneon seemed to have eased into the leadership role and decided the direction they would proceed. For a man used to working alone, that smarted. Kavan wasn't a soldier and didn't appreciate being given orders. More than once, he found himself biting his tongue rather than risk the cohesion of the group. Finding Geblin had almost been the breaking point. His previous encounters with Gnomes left him with little doubts as to why people were so prejudiced against them.

The only saving aspect of their adventure, at least as far as he was concerned, was Aphere. Attractive and intelligent, she more than aroused him. But that was also her downfall. He was very attracted to her and might have been interested in pursuing a relationship if only she wasn't a knight. The title alone meant solitude. He'd known love once before, but it hadn't lasted. She wasn't ready to commit to a man who was always in danger, and he wasn't prepared to abandon his oath. It was his life and purpose for being.

"Some life," he muttered as the rain fell harder.

The rain hit with force. Fat, heavy drops suggesting ill portent. The winds were picking up as well. Kavan settled himself in for a long, miserable day. Having a village nearby would have been nice, but Ergos was sparsely populated. They'd gone over the maps last night, as they had each night since leaving Bronf, and weren't expecting to come across civilization for a few more days. The only choice they had was to ride the storm out.

Once more, his thoughts drifted to Aphere. Of how her body seemed to flow when they sparred. The way her clothes downplayed the curves of her body. How her eyes seemed to catch the sun. Kavan sighed. He knew it was futile. They were both knights and had no business falling in love. The best he could hope for was a long, passionate affair before they parted ways. He brightened at the thought. That wasn't such a bad idea either.

It continued to rain harder. Kavan had resigned himself to the misery of the day when he spied a familiar and much needed sight in the distant gloom. A house. He'd stumbled upon a farmstead.

Kavan stretched out on a row of hay bales and let out a long groan that could only come from many hours in the saddle. He was sore and waterlogged. The ride to the farmstead had proved longer than he'd initially thought, so they'd gone for a few more hours before finally stepping out of the rain.

"It may only be a barn, but it has all the comforts of home," he told them with his hands behind his head.

Aphere shook her head. "Maybe if you're a cow."

He shot her back a playful look. "It's warm and dry, and the old man was kind enough to give us some hot food."

He'd also agreed to let the knights spend the remainder of the day and night in his barn free of charge. Such acts of kindness, while not altogether rare, were most welcome.

"Smells as bad as the Ogre den," Geblin said. His face scrunched in disgust.

"Oh, I don't know. I could get to like the place," Barum said.

Geblin snorted. "Bah! How can you live like this?"

"I suppose a Gnome hole is better?" Aphere asked.

Geblin grew furious. "We don't live in holes. We're a civilized people. Gnomes live in the forest, in the trees, and I'll be damned if I sit here and take your insults much longer."

She laughed again, mainly at the sight of the two-foot-tall gnome trembling with rage. "Trees it is, then."

He sat back down and continued to glower at her.

The rain fell harder.

Aphere awoke in the middle of the night covered in sweat. She instinctively reached for her sword. The only sounds in the barn were the slow drip of water from the roof and the breathing of the others. She pulled the steel from its scabbard anyway and climbed to the upper loft where she could see outside. Pirneon was there on his watch.

"You should be sleeping," he told her without turning. "It's not yet your turn for duty."

She eased closer. "I was…disturbed."

He craned his head. "By?"

"I don't know. A dread overcame my dreams. I have the feeling we are being hunted."

"Nonsense. No one has cause to bother with us," he assured.

She wasn't comforted. "I've felt this before, Pirneon, only not so powerful."

"When?"

Her brow furrowed. "A few days back, after we left that village."

"Perhaps it is just the dream. Our profession often spawns nightmares in the cold hours before dawn," he replied.

She countered, "This is more than a dream. Too many times, I've found myself looking over my shoulders. Evil stalks us."

"There is much evil in this world," he sighed. "All we can do is combat it when it surfaces and leave the world a better place in our passing. Do not trouble your thoughts unnecessarily over this. The trek to Hresh Werd will be long, and there may well be dangers along the way. These we shall face when they arise. Go back to sleep. Rest your mind as well as your body."

"You don't trust me."

Pirneon visibly stiffened at the accusation. While truthful, he wasn't prepared to deal with it directly, not yet. "I don't trust what I don't understand. You come with boasts and claims of this new power, an aberration of what the bond was supposed to be. I haven't seen any evidence of this power nor are you inclined to explain it fully. Perhaps if you were more forthcoming…"

"I can't explain what I don't know, Pirneon. This isn't something I asked for. It just happened. Who can explain why the sun rises? I am a child of my environment, nothing more."

"Perhaps. Perhaps not. Time will tell, but so long as I have reservations towards you I will remain uneasy."

Aphere knew from the finality of his tone that the conversation ended. She stewed over his words and silently fumed at the casual dismissal. *How could he be so blind? Surely the bond told him much the same?* At one point, her people had been considered among the best and brightest in all Malweir. Then ego had set in, and Gaimos had fallen. That deluded sense of superiority had led to their downfall, a fall Pirneon survived. Now he was the one showing the error of hubris.

She tried to shrug off the terrible feeling gnawing away and fall back to sleep. Thunder rumbled in the distance, low and menacing. As she lay her head down, heavy winds shook the bark. Sleep was a long time in coming. Aphere lay with open eyes and watched the storm renew.

The storm continued unabated through the next day, and they agreed to wait it out in the shelter of the barn. All, that is, but Geblin. The Gnome grumbled and cursed for the remainder of the day. The longer he remained with the knights, the more he couldn't wait to finally be free. Folding his wiry arms across his chest, he paced back and forth. No one paid his efforts attention.

Aphere had her own problems. She knew in her heart that something wicked was coming for them. Pirneon's nonchalance about her confession infuriated her to no end, but what else could she do? All she had was a feeling. A crawling sensation buried deep within; all she'd known threatened to change.

The urge grew stronger as the hours passed. She felt powerless. Aphere glanced around the barn, desperate for someone to confide in, but saw none. Pirneon had all but blown her off. Geblin was out of the question. Barum was becoming a good friend but still had much to learn about the world. That left Kavan. She wasn't sure, but she had a hunch he was leaning towards romantic inclinations towards her. Flattering as it was, his love was the last thing she needed — the last any of them needed.

Her thoughts drifted back to those cold winter days in Ipn Shal under the teachings of Kistan. There, Aphere had learned to control her mind and body. The Gaimosian bond in her had transformed into a wondrous thing, giving her gifts and advantages few others enjoyed. Her insights served to heighten her senses. That newfound awareness left her certain they were being hunted. By whom was the problem.

Aphere and Kavan broke contact and eased back from each other. They were covered in sweat and breathing hard. Their swords gleamed brightly in the emerging daylight. It had finally stopped raining in the small hours before dawn. Pirneon wanted to leave as soon as possible, but two days of being cooped up in the barn left them all restless and troubled. They danced swords and released any pent-up frustrations in the process. Aphere still couldn't shake the ill feelings, however, for they had only grown stronger. More than once, she found her mind distracted when it should have been focused on Kavan.

"You have good form," he said, admiring the sheen of sweat on the bared flesh of her arms. "But you're not paying attention."

Aphere lowered her sword. "I am troubled." Her voice was the barest whisper.

"Do you have doubts about the mission?" he asked, the concern showing deep in the wells of his eyes. He went to sit on a moss-covered boulder to begin cleaning his sword.

Aphere shook her head. "We're being hunted."

Kavan's head rose slightly. "By whom?"

"I don't know. The feeling strengthens every so often but never goes away."

"When did you last feel so?"

"Last night, just before dawn."

An ill feeling crept into Kavan. "Have you told Pirneon?"

"He dismissed me without any thought."

Kavan grunted. He wasn't surprised. Pirneon was an old man set in his ways and didn't take well to counsel. Convincing him of her revelations would prove difficult, especially given his attitude towards the inexplicable change of her bond. He didn't say it, but the once Knight Marshal was weary and mistrusting of them. Kavan knew better than to intervene in the matter.

Geblin sat chewing on a piece of straw, listening carefully to their conversation. He couldn't say why, but he also bore an ill feeling. He knew they were being tracked, and once they were discovered, the blood would flow. He thoughtfully searched for a way to save himself before it was too late.

High above the land, so high there wasn't a shadow, a terrible winged beast soared between the clouds. The cross between a dragon and a nightmare, the great beast had skin of leathered flesh and dull, grey scales. Mottled shades of red and black spotted its belly. Twin horns ran back from the forehead, accenting green eyes with a malevolent twist. Clawed hands made for rending flesh apart reflexively clutched at the empty sky as it scanned the ground.

The beast hissed as its rider jerked the reins to guide right. Air whistled off the almost bone-like membrane of its vast wings. Pharanx Gorg patted the beast on the neck and smiled. His prey was below. He was the leader of the Fist. Pharanx was a tall and bitter man. Tattoos covered much of his flesh, barely discernible from the deep bronze coloring of the sun. Ragged black hair blew wildly in the wind. Naked from the waist up, Pharanx peered down.

Once locked on, his coal black eyes never left the tiny band of Vengeance Knights far below. Vengeance Knights. He scoffed their arrogance. Soon enough, their name would be put to the test. The Fist had never run across one of the legendary Gaimosians before, and he relished the opportunity. But as much as he would have liked to attack now, he had other matters to attend to. Corso needed to be updated, and Pharanx still needed to move the main body of troops into position to engage. The assault would come fast and violent. He had little doubt of the outcome. The Fist was about to strike.

TWENTY-THREE

Hresh Werd

It took seventeen days to finish crossing the expanse of Ergos. The vast grasslands stretched forever. When Pirneon finally spied the fringes of Hresh Werd, his heart settled. It had been a long, largely boring ride. The weather had been mostly favorable, and the knights were able to make good time. One part of their quest was complete. The harder part about to begin. Somewhere, lost forever in the deep tangle of woods was the Oracle of Wenx.

Many had come in search of the oracle and his powers through the course of history, though few succeeded. Some disappeared in the heart of the Werd, devoured by the guardians. Others never made it further than the border before losing heart. Those rare few who went the distance came home changed. None ever spoke of what they saw or were told. Many went on to change the world while the rest stumbled into the doldrums of insanity.

Such was the power of the oracle. And here, on the far eastern borders of ancient Hresh Werd, stood the handful of Gaimosians seeking to right old wrongs and prevent the spread of evil.

"At last," Pirneon whispered.

Geblin felt cold as he stared into the impenetrable darkness concealing the forest. Fear crept into his bones. He whispered, "This is not good. Many fell deeds have been done here."

"Hush," Aphere cautioned. "You'll be safe with us."

"Or perhaps you'd like to go back to your Ogre hole?" Kavan laughed as he eased forward a few steps.

Aphere shot him a stern glare. "Geblin is right. I can feel the spirits trapped in the forest. We should be cautious."

Kavan drew his sword. "Let them come. I'll dispatch them to the netherworld once and for all."

"Listen to Aphere," Pirneon called back to them. "In this instance, her insight might prove useful. We should not dismiss her warnings lightly."

Anger flared at his words, but she held her tongue. She wasn't an oddity to be used only when it suited him. Whatever evil was hidden in the Werd was already at work on them. They needed to act wisely or join the spirits of the damned. Barum drew his sword with a heavy sigh and headed towards the trees. Geblin recognized his intent and buried his face in his hands.

"Where are you going?" Pirneon asked, his voice sharp. "We don't know what lies within. Let us wait for full light before entering."

Barum held up. He knew his actions had sparked the reaction he was hoping for. The miasma enshrouding Hresh Werd was beyond dangerous. How many seekers had made it this far only to succumb to the unique brand of madness engulfing the Werd?

"The forest is dangerous as it is; provoking wrath by entering in the dark would all but damn us," Pirneon continued once Barum halted. "We back away and set up camp by the stream we crossed earlier. We enter the forest at dawn."

Barum concealed his satisfaction as he sheathed his sword and wheeled about. He noticed Aphere's smile and nodded to her in respect. Without knowing it, Barum had saved them all from a terrible mistake. Three sets of dull yellow eyes blinked rapidly in disappointment and watched the group depart. The guardians of Hresh Werd sat and waited.

Kavan finished swallowing his last chunk of stale bread. "How can such a place have that dark a stain upon it? I thought the oracle helped people."

"Oracles are rumored to be neutral. Theirs ways are neither good nor evil. It is the nature of the oracle to speak what is and what will be."

"Then where did this evil come from?" Aphere asked.

Pirneon shrugged. "Who can say? We often need only look within our hearts to find evil."

Geblin snorted. His earlier fears had begun to diminish.

"Think what you will, but it is in all of us to commit some act of violence or evil. Would you have been trapped away for food if there weren't some dark intentions, Geblin?" Pirneon pressed. "Answer me not. For myself, I've killed more men than I care to recall. There was no pleasure in doing so, yet they are all naught but bones in the ground now. Perhaps their ghosts are in that forest waiting for me. Who can say?"

"Ghosts and oracles." Geblin frowned. "Have you ever seen either?"

"The world is filled with ghosts," Kavan interjected. "You need only look behind you to feel one."

Geblin clutched his knees to his chest and lowered his head. The longer he stayed with the knights, the more he hated them. He didn't know why he was still with them. There was no reason to be, and he'd had more than enough opportunities to slip away. The Gnome finally laid down and curled up under his blanket. He'd had his fill of talk of good and evil.

"Are there any other oracles in Malweir?" Barum asked as he watched Geblin go to sleep.

Pirneon said, "Not in this part of the world."

Aphere added, "I heard rumors of one in the far eastern kingdom of Gren, though I have never traveled so far."

"They say Gren is a beautiful land filled with wonder," Kavan said. "I would like to go there someday, when these nightmares are over and the werebeasts destroyed."

Werebeasts. No one had mentioned such in the better part of a month, yet that latent fear propelled them forward. For a moment, Kavan thought about old Mun and Constable Chardis. What had become of them? He and Mun weren't friendly, but Kavan didn't wish the wizened old man harm. The werebeast had come close to shattering that sleepy village. He cringed to think what might happen if another fell to prey while they were undefended.

"Do you think all of this could be because of the latent evil of Gessun Thune?" he asked of a sudden.

"Why would you ask that?" Pirneon asked.

Kavan tossed the bare bone away. "Aphere has been feeling haunted for weeks. I've already killed more than one of the werebeasts, and there are rumors of more causing havoc in the north. All of this began months ago. That is more than enough time for any evil to spread and grow."

"Hresh Werd is haunted, make no mistake, but I doubt the influence of the dark gods has extended to a self-exiled oracle. We are all tired and not thinking clearly. Let us sleep on it. I have a feeling the trek through the forest will be long and arduous. I shall take the first watch."

Pirneon rose, snatched his sword, and went off into the night.

The others looked briefly to one another. Aphere took his display personal. The skillset she had developed under Kistan's watchful eye, while fledgling and unpredictable at best, had given her newfound insight. Kavan once mentioned that perhaps the Knight Marshal wasn't changing at all and that he'd always been like this. Barum immediately disagreed and confirmed that his master was different since leaving the desert. Aphere kept her opinion private.

Kavan was the first to ride into the almost suffocating confines of Hresh Werd. He rode without fear or his weapon drawn. Two torches hung from his saddlebags in the event darkness overcame them. His eyes were narrow. They never settled on one spot longer than needed. He was a solid professional entering a potentially hostile environment. Caution and vigilance were his tools. Unthinkable creatures were said to lurk under the canopy of the Werd, creatures born of magic.

His mount snorted at the sound of distant footsteps crunching lightly on the deadwood and old leaves. Kavan flexed his shoulders as memories of his last encounter in a forest returned. He'd barely survived the werebeast's ambush then and vowed not to make the same mistake again. Reaching down, he pulled his sword loose and let it rest partially out of the scabbard. The time was approaching when he'd have need of it.

They stopped after a few hours to stretch and ease the burden of their horses. The forest seemed to creep in around them, lending a claustrophobic feel. The underbrush was thick, constricting. Kavan found it difficult to breathe. The heavy canopy blocked out the sun almost completely. Scarce patches of golden light streamed down inconsistently throughout the Werd, adding to the haunting effect. The trees were old, grown to massive proportions.

Hresh Werd was thought to be one of, if not the, oldest forests in Malweir. Only the Elves could say for sure, and they were a most reclusive people. Few had ever seen an Elf, and those who did spoke of them only in passing. Glimmers of shadow in the dark parts of the world. Some named them the wardens of the world. If such tales were true, Hresh Werd was long forgotten.

Tangled vines lay strewn across paths unwalked by man in years. The older trees were gnarled and twisted from passing centuries. Younger, newer trees shot straight like ash grey spears. Streams intermittently broke up the landscape. The strength of the forest was overwhelming. An ancient thing rested in the heart and, through time, and manipulations had manifested itself into every inch of soil.

Kavan, still trying to shrug off the feeling that they were about to get into a fight, turned to the others. "How do we know this is the right way?"

His voice was hushed, deliberate.

"The paths are overrun, but the deer trails should take us close," Pirneon guessed.

Kavan wasn't convinced. "What if this oracle has guardians keeping everything from intruding on him? Hresh Werd is a large forest. We could wander for weeks and never find what we seek."

Aphere suddenly bolted upright. Her eyes glazed over as she stared ahead. The others closed in around her, fearful and wary at once. She was frozen like a statue for a time, leaving them with naught to do but protect her. Whatever spell she was under was powerful, even for the Gaimosians to handle. At last, she drew a deep breath and collapsed. Kavan rushed to her side. He gently cradled her head on one of his thighs and checked her breathing. Satisfied she was in no immediate danger, he glanced at Pirneon.

"She appears unharmed," he said.

Pirneon knelt, genuine concern etched on his face. He was more worried over the power of the forest than her safety. Understandably so. The oracle could be set against them. This could well have been a warning. Part of him was sorely tempted to abandon the quest and ride north to Aradain immediately. He scanned the surrounding forests with one eye for telltale signs of ambush. He was only partially relieved to find nothing. If the oracle wanted them dead, this was the perfect time.

Aphere awoke with a ragged breath. Her body trembled. Sweat beaded across her brow and upper lip. She had a wild look, as if she'd glimpsed a revelation too stark to comprehend. Kavan held her tight. Whatever torments she'd been exposed to didn't prevent her from returning to her normal self.

"We are expected," she whispered with a shaky voice.

Pirneon jerked. "What?"

She stared back. "The oracle. He knows we are coming."

"How can you be certain?"

"He...he touched my mind," she stammered. "At the center of the Werd lie the ruins of an ancient temple. That's where we'll find the oracle. He's waiting for us. He shared his mind with me. Pirneon, this creature is as old as the dawn of the world. I felt such raw power, such knowledge. He knows of our quest and about the nexus."

"Then the oracle can indeed help us," Pirneon replied.

"There's more. He knows, and he's afraid."

They rode the rest of the day in silence. Kavan was both relieved and apprehensive. The uneasy feeling from earlier was gone. Whatever creatures the oracle used to protect the forest had been told to stand down. The mood of the group lightened, if only just. The forest seemed to open up, creating a clear path to the Oracle of Wenx. Only Pirneon continued to brood. His concern over Aphere grew, compounded now by the contact made with the oracle. Why her? That central thought dominated his mind. He couldn't make sense of it. Thousands of Gaimosians were born and died, and hers was the gift that somehow mutated? He found the notion to be abomination. This Kistan might be more trouble than he was worth. Again, Pirneon resolved to visit his fellow knight at the complex he was developing on the shores of Thuil Lake.

Pirneon found his gaze narrowing and constantly shifting back to Aphere throughout the course of the day. She was an enigma that tested the limits of his faith. Why her? He was the eldest, the most experienced of the surviving knights. By rights, the oracle should have contacted him. It was his right. *It should have been me!* So involved in his own thoughts, Pirneon failed to notice the forest thin.

Sunlight broke through to banish the gloom. Birdsong filled the treetops. Wildflowers replaced the vines and scrub brush. Dead leaves and broken branches turned into soft, lush grass of the deepest green. Broken marble columns dotted the clearing. What remained of a massive building dominated the center. Sunlight reflected off the stained alabaster walls. Kavan halted the group as they beheld a sight unseen by mortal eyes in a very long time. This had once been the epicenter of the lost kingdom of Wenx.

Before them stood a wizened old Elf in a faded brown robe, leaning on a walking staff. They had arrived.

TWENTY-FOUR

The Oracle

"My name is Anthemos," said the ancient Elven sage.

Age had not been kind. Once tall, lean, and proud, Anthemos was barely five feet tall and hunched over. His muscles had wasted away. All that remained of his youth was a sharpened mind through the unbending will of the oracle. His life was dedicated to the power of Wenx. Deep lines etched his weathered face. His eyes, once bright and full of promise, had a dull shine and were partially concealed beneath bushy eyebrows.

"Your coming is an ill tide for all Malweir," he continued in a gravelly voice. "Long has it been foretold that three sons of Gaimos would come in search of us to combat the sudden resurgence of ancient evil."

Pirneon dismounted and stood before the Elf. "You know us?"

Anthemos cackled in delight. "It has been foretold. The enemy of life is rising once again. Some are chosen to rise against it. You have been chosen. Such is the way of the world. All life is cyclical. Good banished evil once, long before Man came upon these shores. Now that same evil is trying to return. Darkness creeps across the lands. Are you strong enough to stand before it?"

Geblin yelped and hid behind Barum. Anthemos looked up with a forgotten twinkle in his eye.

"Do not fear, Geblin. Your part in this tale is long. Without you, these bold few stand little chance of success."

Geblin took heart despite the doubts manifesting in his mind. He was no hero, never wanted to be one. Time and again, he only wanted to be left alone and forget these reckless knights and their ceaseless battles. If what the oracle predicted was true, he might never have the chance.

"Come," Anthemos told them all. "The oracle awaits, and time is not in your favor."

Kavan alone kept his hand on his sword.

"There is no need for that, knight of Gaimos," Anthemos said. "This place is well protected by forces more powerful than any of you possess. Even yours, lady."

Aphere startled. She knew the oracle was aware of her power. The link between them had descended into the core of her soul. She was laid bare for them to see and now, standing before the Elf, felt naked. She was also emboldened. She might finally get the answers that had long eluded her.

"You're not the oracle?" Pirneon asked, too stern for his liking.

Anthemos continued walking. "No. I am but a humble servant. What strengths I have are nothing in comparison to the Oracle. Just as you, Knight Marshal of forgotten Gaimos. We are but singular drops in the vast ocean of time."

Pirneon took the insult in stride. It had been a long time since any had the audacity to talk down to him. "Let us see this wonder of the ancient world and be about our journey. As you say, time is not our ally."

The Elf barely sighed. He alone knew what future awaited these knights. Some would go on to fame and glory. Others would fall into ruin and darkness. It was the same from every group of adventurers come to seek the wisdom of the oracle. This band of heroes would fare no different. Sadness swelled in his heart. He'd been expressly forbidden to expose any sign of what fate belonged to whom. A wrong word had the potential to irrevocably damage the fabric of the future. The aging Elf held his tongue, content with his role as a mere observer.

They followed him into the temple ruins. Once past the outer façade, they bore witness to the most spectacular scene. Anthemos explained the ruins were designed to deter would-be treasure seekers and looters. A ring of marble columns surrounded circling stairs winding deep into the ground. Torches lined the finished flagstone way, reflecting hotly off the polished silver finish. Blossoming cherry trees were sprinkled at random among the columns, producing a serene effect. The sun was directly overhead.

All of this was impossible, yet the Elf didn't argue. He merely smiled and gestured towards the stairwell. The knights huddled together, silently conferring. Aphere didn't hesitate. She felt inexplicably drawn to the power of the waiting oracle. Since her initial contact, she felt more than what she was. She couldn't say for certain, but it felt as if her mental abilities and the change in her blood gift had developed beyond even the imagination of Kistan. If that were the case....

"Who built this place?" asked Barum. Both he and Anthemos walked at the rear of the group.

The Elf shrugged. "Who can say? The world is filled with many wonders and nightmares. This is a place of power. Much the same as the nexus you seek. What gods responsible for such have long since moved on to other worlds. All we can do is care for and treasure that has been given to us."

Barum eyed him quizzically. Anthemos held up his hands.

"Who knows the will of the gods? I myself have never spoken with one."

Fair enough, Barum thought. He decided to change the subject. "How long have you been alive? I've never met an Elf before."

"A good question. I can recall the war for power, now so very long ago. I saw the mountains grow from the earth. Generations have come and gone. My own kin are but dust in the ground. To answer the question, I am old, very, very old."

"I don't understand. What power can keep you alive for so long?"

Anthemos placed a fragile hand on his shoulder. "Some questions should not be asked. There are answers we don't want to know."

Down they went, until at last they stood at the entrance of a vast hall. A small path no more than a meter wide carved through the crystalline waters filling the hall. Light reflected from gems made the hall appear much larger than it was. They stared in awe, never having dreamed of such a sight. Here, hundreds of feet beneath the surface, was the most wondrous sight they'd ever beheld. As the awe slowly faded, the knights began to notice the rest of the hall.

The Oracle of Wenx sat at the center of a small isle in the middle of the hall. It was neither man nor any of the other races, but an ancient creature of forgotten magic. The oracle was a Wisp. Half as large as a grown man, the Wisp was a near translucent orb of pure energy. The center was violent red and orange. Sparks of electricity emanated from the surface, transforming the opaque body to shades of grey and purple. Raw power pulsed across the waters.

"What is it?" Pirneon asked.

Anthemos slipped to the front. "This is the Oracle of Wenx. It is the last of its kind, a creature born of pure magic at the dawn of the world. It is a Wisp."

"How can such a creature communicate with us? I see no eyes or mouth."

"The chosen has been selected," Anthemos announced. He faced Aphere. "Only one of you shall hear the oracle's predictions. Only one."

"It should be me," Pirneon pressed.

Aphere blushed. She felt his resentment pulsing towards her in dark waves. It made her sick, causing her to cringe inwardly. At the same time, his attitude enraged her. She was every bit the knight he was and the only reason he was still alive. His behavior was childish, unbecoming of a man in his position. Now was not the time to confront his foolishness, however.

"Should means nothing to the oracle. I would be cautious if I were you, Knight Marshal. You still have far to go on your journey. You have great need of the oracle's counsel if you are going to find success along your way."

Anthemos closed his thin lips and said no more. He idly fretted over having said too much already. He knew this wasn't his concern, nor could he have any part in it. Let them do as they will, he told himself. It was the only way.

Pirneon folded his arms across his chest and fumed. He was not accustomed to being treated so, despite the long years of exile and loneliness. The pain of hiding his true identity for a lifetime was unbearable at times. He had hoped it was all changing after Kavan sought him out. This quest could lead to the reestablishment of Gaimos and freedom for all their blood kin. It was a task he'd been born to accomplish. And it was being delegated to a woman barely half his age. He was disgusted, and it showed.

"Go, child," Anthemos urged her. "The oracle has been waiting for your arrival for so long. Go to him and learn what role you play in the fate of Malweir."

Aphere hesitated. She wasn't certain of anything. Kistan's teachings did little to ease her doubts or self-consciousness. Anthemos sensed this and went to her side. His stolid features loosened enough to show the depths of his sincerity.

"It's all right. He won't harm you. You know this to be true," he whispered for her ears only. "This is your destiny, Aphere. Follow your heart."

She did. Step by step, Aphere eased down the path to the waiting oracle. Her heart quickened the way it did before a battle. Her knees felt weak. Questions rumbled through her mind, threatening to break her resolve. *What am I doing? How can any of this be possible? I can't do this. I'm not worthy.* Sudden calm washed over her. Any doubts were crushed. She found focus and renewed purpose.

Her steps became strong, confident. Aphere marched down the path with utter surety. There was a sense of giddiness the closer she got to the Wisp. Giddiness she hadn't felt since childhood. The oracle whispered to her in a gilded warble. The voice had a touch of song that delighted her heart. The world lost all bitterness as futures and past were revealed for truth. At last, she understood what being a Gaimosian Knight was all about. She was Malweir. Aphere reached a loving hand out towards the Wisp.

"No! Do not touch him!" Anthemos shouted.

The scene exploded. Waves of pure energy rippled out from the two. Aphere collapsed in a heap of useless flesh. The Wisp disappeared into the vast nothingness from whence it had come. Kavan and Barum recovered first and ran towards her for the second time today. Only Pirneon stood fast and watched with narrowed eyes.

"We were afraid we lost you," Anthemos told her after she regain consciousness.

"Where am I?" she asked.

The Elf sage smiled down on her with fatherly love. "You are safe. We moved you into my cottage after your contact with the oracle." His eyes grew stern. "That was a very foolish thing you did. The oracle is a thing of pure power. You might well have disintegrated. As it stands, the oracle is gone."

"Where did it go?" Kavan asked from the high backed chair in the corner of the room. His eyes were filled with genuine concern.

"Go? The Wisp was pure energy, and her touch set it in motion. It has gone off to be with the rest of its kin. There is a place, rumored of course, where the source of all power lies. Good and evil reside within in a collection of listless souls. Its task was accomplished, so the oracle returned home."

Horror registered across her face. "I killed the oracle?"

Anthemos shook his head. "Don't be absurd. Nothing on this plane can harm a Wisp. You did release it. There will be a time when the Wisp will return to await another band of seekers, but that is a story for the future. Do you remember what the oracle told you?"

She thought for a moment. Visions and images swarmed back. She saw things she never dreamed possible and nightmares so foul they ruined the very soul. Monsters and unmentionable creatures crawled out of the darkness to assault the free peoples of Malweir. Only a select handful barred the way. Most of what she saw made no sense. They were a jumble of separate thoughts without reason. Aphere relayed all she remembered. Finished, she lay back down.

"Unfortunately, I am forbidden from explaining what you were privileged to witness. But this I will say, you are all now part of a vicious cycle. Evil is coming, and unless you heed the visions, Malweir shall be plunged into one thousand years of darkness. Let me tell you a tale, one as old as time itself."

He paused to ensure all were listening, especially the suddenly taciturn Pirneon. "Ten thousand years ago, our nightmares took shape and savagely tried to take over by enslaving the world. A great and terrible war ensued. Tens of thousands died without knowing why. Finally, after many long years, the evil was beaten back and banished from our world. The night was once again safe. To ensure this evil could not easily return, a group of sorcerers channeled their power and created three nexuses.

"It was there and only there this evil might manifest itself again. For as strong as the combined will of the sorcerers was, they failed in defeating evil once and for all. The dark gods were allowed to linger in their alternate dimension. Exiled, they continued to rebuild their power until one thousand years passed. On the day when the moon swallowed the sun, they broke free from their prison and resumed their war on the world."

Anthemos paused to drink from a clay mug. "The dark gods were eventually defeated but not destroyed. After all, how can one simply slay a god? So was born the vicious cycle that has plagued us ever since. Most of the peoples of Malweir are totally ignorant of the fact. Some are unwitting pawns in this cosmic struggle. Others choose to make their stand, be it for good or evil. That time is once again upon us."

"When?" Aphere asked. Her voice was but a whisper.

"The moon will eat the sun thirty days from today, and the nexus will reopen. The cycle will be renewed unless you follow the wisdom of the oracle," he said with sad authority. "Time is almost nigh."

Dread bordering on panic settled in. His words carried ill portent laced with dire consequences. Surely, the chances of surviving such a cataclysmic event were close to none.

"I will say no more on this." He paused to look each of them in the eye, as if testing the strength of their inner resolve. "Should you fail, should you decide not to undertake this quest, Malweir will be plunged into irreversible decay. The world as we know it will wither and die."

"Not to place any added pressure on us," Kavan muttered.

Anthemos smiled sadly. "None of us are so fortunate as to pick our destiny."

The knight stood and drew his sword. "Men, I can fight. Beasts and monsters will bleed just like you and I. But a god? How can I fight something infinitely powerful? There are limitations to strength."

Placing his hand on Kavan's chest, Anthemos said, "It is not through strength of arms but the depth of your heart that you shall succeed."

Even Pirneon straightened. Old Gaimosian pride resurfaced. His sense of honor replaced the burrowing resentment all but consuming him. He took courage from the Elf.

"You may spend the rest of the night here and depart on the morrow. This quest will take you beyond the edge of dawn. Rest now. You will have need of great strength in the coming days. Good night."

Anthemos said no more. His frail body seemed to shrink within his robes as he stepped out of the room. Rest as they would, the Elf sage still had much to do. The guardians of the forest would be restless by now. With the Wisp gone for the time being, it was up to Anthemos to use his magic to control them — a daunting task, to be sure, for Anthemos felt his lifeline slowly creeping away. He paused to glance back at his home. The fate of the world rested within. Not the worst he'd ever seen, but far from the best. He smiled, praying faith would be enough, and wandered off into the forest whistling an old song his mother had taught him.

TWENTY-FIVE

The Journey North

They emerged from the northern edge of Hresh Werd at midday. Kavan, as usual, pushed forward to scout ahead. He was glad to be rid of the confinement of the forest. Aradain was still far away, and there were a thousand places along their route of march to meet trouble or delay. Pirneon had kept them awake the night before with a dire warning. If the Wisp had known of their role in the defense of Malweir, it stood to reason those aligned with the forces of darkness were as well.

Ergos stretched for as far as the eye could see. The fertile grasslands comprised the majority of the largest western kingdom, stretching from the Kergland Spine in the east to the shore of the western ocean and north to the edge of a foul swamp so ancient most had forgotten its true name.

"The journey will be long and potentially dangerous the closer we get to Aradain," Pirneon told them before leaving the temple of Wenx. "Once across the plains we must decide to go through or around the swamp. After that lies the kingdom of your people, Geblin. Outsiders have seldom been admitted within their borders. Thankfully, we have our small companion here to help."

Geblin blanched. Going home had never been an option.

"Past that are the broken mountains of the Crags. They are sharp and cruel. Our goal lies just beyond. Rantis is but a day's ride north from there."

"Is there no better route?" Aphere asked.

"Surely, but the time it would take puts us well beyond the eclipse Anthemos warned of," he said.

They rode north. The trip out of the forest was uneventful. It was evident that the Elf had gone ahead to clear their path. Anthemos waited at the edge of the forest, watching until they were well out of sight. The fate of the world was no longer in his hands.

By dusk, the knights were tired of riding. Pirneon relented only after Kavan returned to the main group with his scouting report.

"There is a stream not far ahead. Few animal tracks. We should be able to rest in the stand of birch trees close by," he said. Sweat plastered his windblown hair to the sides of his face.

Pirneon nodded his agreement. "Lead us there. We'll rest for six hours and continue until dawn."

"Are you crazy?" Geblin barked from his baggage saddle. "There's no reason to go at night. You don't ever stop to consider anyone else."

Pirneon wheeled about and scowled down on the Gnome. "My considerations have to do with the good of us all. Your fate is in my hands as much as the other way around. It would be wise of you to cooperate. To answer your question, I am far from crazy. What I am is cautious. You heard the Elf. Evil is hunting us, and who knows when it will strike? Time is now our foe."

Aphere glared hotly at him.

"Master Pirneon, I think I see something through the trees," Barum announced with false excitement.

Already on edge, Pirneon stalked to his squire's side, where Barum pointed with his sword. "Where?"

"Just past that large boulder. I'm not sure what it was but it moved quickly."

Interested, the Knight Marshal clapped Barum on the shoulder. "I knew it. Come, let us see what we can. Hopefully we will strike first."

Barum cast a final glance at his companions and was relieved to see Aphere whisper thank you. Knight and squire headed off into the forest.

They didn't wait long to find the answer to Pirneon's question. The attack came shortly after sunset. The knights sat around their small campfire enjoying a meal of rabbit and wild carrots. Conversation again turned to what they might expect in Aradain. Aphere slipped out of the darkness with her sword drawn.

"Put out the fire," she warned.

Barum immediately began scooping dirt on the flames as the other knights readied for battle.

"How many?" Pirneon asked.

"Maybe too many to fight. They're dressed in black and wear no armor. I wouldn't have spied them if I hadn't heard their boots striking the rocks. The ones I saw all carried bows. I think they are trying to surround us."

Pirneon frowned. Too many to fight was a big number against so many Gaimosians. He instantly made his decision. "Barum, you and Geblin get the horses ready to move. Cross the stream and wait for us in the tall brush. Keep a watchful eye. The rest of you come with me."

Split into groups, they worked as quickly and quietly as possible. Pirneon's only hope lay in the enemy following the main threat, his three knights, long enough for Barum to make ready the escape. It was an old tactic he'd used repeatedly during the war of the Fall. Hopefully, it would work again. They'd barely made it away from the campsite when a shrill whistle blew across the fields. The arrow struck Pirneon in the high shoulder with enough force to knock him down. A trickle of blood spit out in a lazy arc as he dropped.

Dozens of dark figures swarmed. They attacked in two waves. The first crashed against the blades of the Gaimosians while the second, larger group established an outer cordon of the battlefield. Kavan parried a wild blow and flicked both swords right. His blade managed to cut deep across his opponent's throat. The next man was on him before the first fell away. Fortunately for Kavan, the man mistimed his attack and closed too much to escape. Kavan drove his sword deep into the soft flesh of the belly.

With Pirneon down, Aphere found herself besieged on two sides. Mercenaries pressed in on her. She was resigned to fighting strictly defensively. Aphere shifted her eyes from man to man, deciding which was going to strike first. Blade vertical, she beat back the fever pitch of their combined assault. One of them let out a startled gasp before he dropped. She didn't bother looking and blocked high, then lunged forward into the second. The man died before he had the chance to adjust.

The first attacker tried to rise but had been run through the ribs. Pirneon kicked the mortally wounded man from his sword and struggled to his feet. Pain lanced through his upper right body. The arrowhead missed his tendons and struck squarely in the muscle. The rush of battle drove the pain away, and he went after his next target.

Kavan slashed hard, catching a man in the neck. Ropes of hot blood streamed away. He followed the movement through, spinning around to drop into a low crouch. Instincts took over. Decades of training and battle-tested skills overpowered his enemy. He stabbed backwards blindly and was rewarded by the feel of steel sinking into flesh. Two more fighters leapt over their dying comrade and tackled the off-balance Kavan. His sword skittered away as the three grappled to the death. They traded blows, each one trying to cripple the other enough to deliver the killing blow. Kavan was hard pressed. The fighter kept him pinned to the ground, hammering his ribs and kidneys.

Pirneon's sword cleaved a horrible gash down the chest of one man and took an arm at the elbow of another. His breathing was heavy, ragged. A lifetime of battle did little when pressed by the quality and quantity of the mercenaries trying to kill him. Like wolves, six more slinked from the night to encircle him. Their exposed skin was darkened with mud and charcoal, making them nearly indistinguishable from the night. Pirneon took a defensive stance. He was suddenly unsure of his chances.

Aphere let out a sharp cry as steel sliced across her upper thigh. She hacked at her attacker and limped back. Sweat stung the open wound as blood spilled down her leg. The pain was sharp enough to remind her of her mistake but distracting at the same time. Even without seeing the other knights, she knew the situation was beyond desperate. Whoever the assassins were, they were well trained, coordinated, and knew exactly who they'd come to kill.

The enemy sensed victory and drew closer. They could feel the kill. The thrill of freshly spilled blood drove them on. In the darkness, their numbers seemed endless. Aphere felt the world slipping away. Control ebbed. Her senses blurred, threatening darkness. She tried to fight back, tried to overcome the power welling up as it threatened to consume her. She failed.

In a single moment, all the pain and horror, the frustrations she'd kept pent up, exploded outward. Violence flared to life. Her body became a terrible weapon of singular purpose. Aphere gasped and opened her eyes. Once soft and pure, they held wildness burning deep within. Red flames devoured her irises as the power snapped her body taut. Flames shot from her in destructive sheets, growing in intensity.

Crimson turned to wicked azure. Everywhere the flame spread brought ruin. Grass, bushes, trees, and people exploded in muted screams. Dozens of fighters were exposed to the brightening light. They froze for one fatal instant before the azure fire swept through them. Flesh and bone disintegrated. Naught but loose piles of ash remained.

Kavan watched in mute horror. He'd never seen a power so vile. The two men atop him broke contact and fled in the opposite direction. Struggling through his pain, Kavan rose and reclaimed his sword. His eyes were locked on Aphere, instinctively knowing he needed to stay clear. He wanted to vomit. Great wisdom had never been one of his stronger attributes. He staggered towards Aphere as she started convulsing.

Her body trembled from exertion. Sharp pain numbed her sense. Darkness swirled around, soothingly beckoning her to join it. Her mind shut down, and she let it claim her. Aphere collapsed in a ragged heap of abused flesh. Kavan was instantly at her side. He shook her gently, but she didn't stir. Quiet desperation flooded into him. Was she dead? The fear of the unknown reached out to him. Lost in his own thoughts, he failed to hear Pirneon arrive.

"Is she dead?" The front of his shirt was covered in blood, most of it his. It was through force of will he remained standing.

Kavan placed his ear on her chest. Her body was strangely cool. After several long moments, he finally caught the gentle beat of her heart. "No. She lives."

Pirneon looked around the battlefield. "We must leave. There is no promise our enemy will not return. Can you get her to her horse?"

"I think so. Pirneon, who attacked us?"

His face darkened. "Mercenary scum from across the world. They are known as the Fist. Once hired, they won't stop until we are dead or their masters call them off. Quickly, now, we must leave."

The heavy sound of hoof beats rode upon them. Barum and Geblin had arrived. The looks on their faces showed Pirneon everything. The squire slid down to help Kavan strap Aphere into her saddle. Sitting atop his packhorse, Geblin shut his eyes and whimpered softly. Now more than ever he wanted to slink away and be forgotten. The tiny band of wounded Gaimosians mounted and struck north. Pirneon constantly looked back. The conflict with the Fist severely compacted their quest. He only hoped they could make it to the swamp unhindered.

TWENTY-SIX

Evil Moves Forward

Corso sat in the dark sanctum rubbing his aching temples. He was using too much power to control King Eglios. Fortunately, Eglios was seduced by his desire to be accepted amongst the other nobles and rulers in Malweir. He was blinded by the promise of power Corso sold him. But Eglios wasn't the problem. Corso's thoughts turned back to the approaching Gaimosians with uncomfortable frequency. Their involvement was the crucible upon which his entire plan hinged.

He'd studied the histories, both public and the ones thought lost forever. It was in these special tomes that Corso first learned of the dark gods and the awesome power they commanded. He'd fallen sway to that lure of power and devoted his life to their silent teachings. Locked in their eternal prison, the dark gods whispered to his dreams. They taunted him with images of invincibility and his rise as regent of Malweir upon their return.

Corso had never been a strong-willed man. He'd spent most of his life sneaking out back doors and spending money on alcohol and petty women. It wasn't until he'd stumbled upon this ancient tower that his life took focus. And focus it did. He spent his waking hours devouring the lost knowledge and was quickly subverted. He grew stronger, smarter. Corso embraced the darkness as much as it held him.

For a time, he wondered what it all meant. What end was this building towards? The answer came in a dream. Voices whispered for him to go to Aradain and gain the confidence of the king. Corso laughed. That proved easy enough. Aradain was a peasant kingdom wishing to be more. Corso orchestrated the invasion and takeover of Barduk. Eglios drank the victory in and craved more. Just like that, Corso gained his kingdom.

His troubles came from the remnants of Gaimos. Considering the knights knew virtually nothing of their latent magical abilities, Corso hadn't figured on them being a major factor. It was their power, not his, that held the keys to opening the nexus. It was also their power threatening to stop him.

Curious to the limits of their strength, Corso ingeniously implemented a series of hunts under the guise of ridding the lands of strange monsters suddenly harassing the countryside. Several Gaimosians had arrived in response. All were ignorant of their true role in the world. All were swallowed by darkness. Sadly, none was strong enough to open the nexus. He needed more.

They would come. Only this time, he knew, they were coming to kill him and put an end to his mad quest. It was an unknown game they'd entered. The Gaimosians pushed hard to gain Gessun Thune, so hard they'd already sought out the Oracle of Wenx. He hadn't expected that development and was forced to bring in the Fist.

Corso had no liking for the mercenary scum. They didn't take sides or become involved in petty political affairs. Mercenary swine, they were a step above barbaric. Brooding, he heard the telltale call of one of their flying beasts. Corso gathered his robes and left the sanctum.

The beast had already landed and Pharanx Gorg dismounted by the time Corso arrived. Pharanx's long hair blew lightly in the wind, ever tied in a top knot. Corso stared at him from beneath his cowl. Pharanx bore a wild look, one neither was accustomed to having.

"You said nothing of magic!" Pharanx accused.

Corso stood his ground. "You told me your men could handle this. Is this not the case?"

Pharanx drew his short sword and pointed it threateningly at his employer. "Thirty-six of my men are dead because of your secrets. I am not prepared to stand before such power. Thirty-six of the finest men, Corso. All dead in the blink of an eye."

Interesting. Could it be one of the Gaimosians actually learned how to use his gift? He didn't see how. All the ones who'd come to Rantis proclaiming to champion the people never had a clue as to what they truly were. Hearing Pharanx's claims might compound the future.

Corso held his hands up in a soothing gesture. "Stay your anger, Pharanx. I am not your enemy. Surely you know that."

"After this last battle, I am no longer sure," Pharanx countered. "They never had a chance. We ambushed the Gaimosians perfectly. I put fifty of my best in wait. Good as the knights are, I wasn't taking chances."

"What happened next? Tell me everything."

His inner desire needed to know. He had to know if these were the knights with enough strength to open the nexus. Pharanx went into great detail, leaving nothing out. He faltered only when he came to describing the murdering fire of the Gaimosian witch. Corso pressed on points, and Pharanx told him more. The give and take prolonged their conversation until it began to drizzle.

At last, the Fist leader finished his tale. He wanted to leave here and never look back, take the Fist east to greater glories where the outcome wouldn't be in doubt. But the professional in him made him stand. If he left now, their reputation was ruined. Chances were good that the Fist would never be hired again, and he'd be murdered by his own men. Long and hard, he deliberated the course of the future. *Most likely I'll be dead before this ends anyway*.

The mercenary let his face slip back into a mask before looking at Corso again. "What do you wish of us now?"

Corso's smile remained hidden. There'd been a moment of doubt about whether the Fist would abandon him. Not that it particularly mattered. Events were beginning to unfold as the tomes predicted. "Where did the Gaimosians flee to?"

"North. My scouts track them, but at distance. They will eventually arrive in Aradain."

"What lies between?" Corso asked.

"The great swamp and then the land of Gnomes."

The great swamp. The Uelg, an ugly name for an ugly place. Few alive were dumb enough to venture within. Rumors of a foul presence kept most away, but there were always those few who sought to challenge common belief. Their bones now rotted at the bottom of muck and mire. Corso knew what lay within. It was a terror the Gaimosians could never prepare for.

"Funnel them into the swamp, but do not engage them again. Not until you hear from me. This will be their ultimate test, Pharanx. If, indeed, they possess magic, it shall be sorely tested."

"If they escape into Creidlewein? Do we pursue?"

"The Gnome kingdom is of no concern to me," Corso dismissed with a wave. "We'll deal with that should the need arise. Push the knights into the swamp. All else will be taken care of."

"We shall do as you wish but know that I expect full payment once they are fodder for the swamp demons. There are less dangerous jobs in the far east we could be doing," Pharanx pushed.

Corso nodded. "So be it."

The commander of the Fist climbed aboard his beast and left Corso to his musings. Awakening the creature in the Uelg would be proactive enough to put an end to the false hopes of the Gaimosians. Those who survived, if any, would prove capable to end his quest. The nexus would soon be opened, and shades of nightmares would return. Malweir would once again know the true meaning of pain and suffering.

TWENTY-SEVEN

Truths Revealed

Aphere remained unconscious for the remainder of the night and well into the next day. Her indulgent use of power had left her near death as the others sat helpless. She lay strapped to her saddle, one step away from being a corpse and even further from the land of the living.

Still, the day passed swiftly. Pirneon pushed them as hard as he dared, and the leagues rolled by. Dusk was fast approaching when he finally called a halt. Kavan went back into scouting mode, for the countryside was unknown to them. The others established a small camp without fire. Pirneon debated the wisdom in this but decided not to take the chance of being carelessly discovered. He asked Barum to clean and dress his wound while Geblin saw to Aphere.

The Knight Marshal eyed her suspiciously. So much had happened so quickly, he felt his world breaking apart. The foundations of all he knew were being challenged by unseen forces far beyond his comprehension. He didn't know what to do any longer, and it frightened him. His was a life of trial and hardship. Pirneon hadn't had to work with so many others since the Fall.

He winced when Barum tightened the fresh bandage. The arrow had gone deep. Fortunately, it had missed all his major organs. The pain, however, was intense, enough that Barum continued watching over him throughout their ride north. Poison was a prominent concern with arrows. Pirneon wouldn't say, but the Fist were huge proponents of dirty warfare. *What have we done to invoke the ire of these mercenaries? Our enemies must be more powerful than we thought.*

Kavan eventually slipped back into camp and was met by an inquisitive Pirneon.

"Well?"

The younger knight nodded. "They still hunt us but from a distance."

Neither wanted to discuss Aphere's warnings or how they'd proven true. Pirneon wasn't mentally prepared for it.

"Last night frightened them," he said. "And with good reason. Aphere has shown us something destructive and vile. The Fist will not be quick to resume the attack."

Kavan sat down and rubbed his right thigh. "Pirneon, who are the Fist exactly? Why do they hunt us?"

Pirneon remained silent in his thoughts a moment longer. "The Fist are mercenaries. Men without beliefs or honor. Homeless vagabonds who abandoned their peoples. Malweir has no need of their kind."

"Are they evil?"

"Doubtful. I don't think they worry about good or evil. They're assassins for the highest bidder. Believe it or not, some of our own kind took off to join their ranks after the Fall. It is odd, because seldom have they crossed the desert in search of the hunt. The Fist normally work in the east, the lands of Gren and Antheneon. They must be getting paid a king's ransom to take us on here."

"Not if there are men of our blood among them," Kavan countered, the sudden fear of fighting his own people awakened.

Pirneon offered a sad smile. "No. There are no more."

He left Kavan to guess the meaning. Too many old friends had died on his blade. It was a burden only he bore.

"None of that explains why they hunt us. And now of all times," Kavan ventured. He ran a hand through his dirty hair. He was tired. Exhausted was more appropriate. Sleep beckoned. One question haunted him more than the others. "What is their strength? In the night, they appeared endless. We would not have survived if not for Aphere."

Pirneon's features darkened at her mention. "Five hundred has always been their size. No more, no less."

"Five hundred?" Kavan said in disbelief. "Pirneon, we cannot fight five hundred men. Not with the four of us."

"What do you mean four?" Geblin snapped.

They all turned to look at him in surprise. The Gnome stood before them with a scowl, seemingly permanently etched into his flesh, and tapping one foot impatiently.

"Be quiet, Gnome," Pirneon fired back. "None of us is in a mood to hear your antics."

"Antics, is it? You think you know so much about the rest of the world. Let me enlighten you for a change," Geblin was furious, his rage barely contained. "You want to know the truth of why I was in the Ogre cave? Do you? We'd gone there to kill it."

Eyes widened at the sudden, unexpected admission.

"That's right. Kill it. The Ogre was responsible for murdering dozens of my kin. We put together a raiding party and went to put an end to him for good." Geblin fell silent. Memories of his friends' last moments plagued him.

Kavan bore a wry grin. Even Barum was impressed.

"This certainly puts matters into a different light. Why the deception?"

Geblin snorted. "What makes you think I could trust any of you? Our races don't exactly get along. Even in the Spine, we have heard of the murdering Gaimosians. I took no chances and hoped for the right moment to slip away."

"You've had dozens of opportunities to leave," Kavan said.

Geblin hesitated. "I…I have a debt to repay."

"To whom?"

"To you, damn it! You saved my life, all of you did. I may not be of the same stature as you famous knights, but my honor is no less. You saved my life, and I'll not leave until that debt is repaid."

Pirneon's gaze softened. "Very admirable, especially considering our current situation. I accept your aid in this quest. Your debt shall be repaid."

The conversation ended in uneasy silence. Geblin's secret was a surprise none of them had been expecting. Kavan still wanted to bash his head in for the past but also discovered budding respect. Gnomes were renowned for being thieves, leading Kavan to wonder if more wasn't being said.

"Geblin, what is your specialty?"

Geblin's eyes narrowed. He lied, "I was a scout."

He'd just built the foundations of trust, but there was no reason to tell everything. Not yet, at any rate. There were some secrets too dark and uninviting that needed to be kept.

"Perhaps you can help me. We can split the duties. Two sets of eyes are always better than one," Kavan choked out. It was a stretch for him. There was no love lost between man and Gnome, but at least he was making the attempt. It was all he could do in the situation.

"I'll think about it," Geblin replied and turned Aphere. "What's wrong with her?"

"We don't know," Barum said. He'd been quiet throughout the exchange and for good reasons. His mind was preoccupied with thoughts of Aphere. The longer they shared company the more he found feelings intensifying. She was everything he had ever desired in a partner. But only if… He'd also been suspecting Geblin of hiding important facts and took personal interest in him. The last thing he wanted was to kill the Gnome.

"So much power," Geblin said and sat beside her prone form. He'd never admit it, but he was fond of her.

Barum hid a smile and went to finish taking care of the horses. Maybe their tiny company had a chance for success after all.

Kavan and Pirneon sat across from each other with guarded poise. Unspoken hostility lay between them. Kavan's concern for Aphere was equally matched by the growing anxiety over the divide between them.

Pirneon was a proud man, unbending. That exaggerated pride threatened to tear the group apart.

Kavan couldn't stand it any longer. "This must stop, Pirneon."

Pirneon eyed him dismissively. "I agree. She is becoming a mortal danger to us."

"Damn it, you! Not her. You know this," he growled back.

Pirneon shot to his feet. "She's the problem, Kavan! What she's becoming is an abomination. Everything she is has the potential to destroy us. No Gaimosian has ever had this taint. None!"

"Why should it be a taint? Why not a gift? After all, she was the one chosen to speak with the oracle. Not you or I. Without Aphere, this quest would already be lost."

"Lost! How can that be so? Our people have gone through generations in exile, all towards one goal. I've spent my life without wavering, always on a clear path. But her, what dark sorcery will she unleash upon us when she finally loses control?"

"She is not a threat. She never has been. We should all be dead. Whatever power she has can save our lives."

"As well as destroy us," Pirneon wagged an accusing finger.

Kavan folded his arms across his chest in frustration. "What, then, do you propose? Kill her now, and be done with it? Or should we just abandon her for the wolves? Tell me, oh wise Knight Marshal. What should we do?"

"Of course we don't kill her! That's not what I am saying. Aphere is a hazard. To you and to me, Kavan," Pirneon countered.

"Then leave. This is my quest. It always has been. I was the one who came to you for help and guidance. You've given it. Take Barum and go off in search of new, less dangerous adventures."

Kavan's words bit deep, but Pirneon stood his ground. Shock registered for the briefest moment. When he spoke, his words were deliberate, precise. "I cannot leave. The oracle said as much. If this quest is to succeed, I must be there at the end." He turned and began walking away. "Regardless of my personal feelings, I will fulfill my part. No one living or dead can say I quit before the task was complete. Mark my words, though, Kavan: no good will come of this."

"Like it or not, there is little we can do. It is the way of things to change." Kavan felt his anger release.

"When this task is complete, she and I will resolve our differences."

Kavan shook his head. "She's not the problem."

"Then I head east."

"To what end?"

Pirneon smiled darkly. "To find Kistan and see what atrocities he has been teaching his disciples."

They fell silent. Night came on, and they ate a meager traveler's meal. Kavan took first watch. That old itch was coming back. He wanted to be alone again. Working with so many others presented unwanted challenges. He'd forgotten all the insurmountable arrogance associated with teamwork. His feelings for Aphere were strong, though he doubted they signified love. Maybe, deep down where his most private feelings hid, he was worried about her developing powers. Maybe.

There was the slightest chance Pirneon was right. Aphere could be the end of their world. She wasn't alone. Kistan had recruited several of their kind and was instructing them in similar fashion. If just one of the others was as strong as Aphere, the balance of power in Malweir was threatened. The thought made him cringe. Too many had died for less over the course of history.

Their own history loomed much more prominently. Gaimos had been destroyed because of the same fear Pirneon now possessed. The fear turned to fervor and then riots. Citizens of the surrounding kingdoms begged for salvation against the witch-men of Gaimos. One by one the rulers fell in line with popular support, and a vast army was raised. The war was long, bloody. Tens of thousands died, but the outcome was never in doubt.

Gaimosian borders were steadily pushed back. Outlying villages and farms were burned to the ground. The Gaimosian army made one final, desperate stand on the slopes of Skaag Mountain. The battle raged long and furious. After six days, the remnants of Gaimos broke and fled. The ones who escaped went into exile until a time when it was safe to be seen again. Of Gaimos, nothing remained. Every city, every monument was razed. Pirneon feared a repeat if Aphere managed to lose control.

Kavan gave Aphere another glance and shuddered. Any earlier feelings he might have harbored for her were slowly fading. Love, he now understood, was fickler than his imagination. He played it off on having been away from quality company for too long. Regardless, he now knew that nothing would come from a relationship with Aphere. Her powers frightened him on deeper levels than love could stretch. She was an admirable woman and he prayed those times inspiring Pirneon's fear weren't returning. Only the Knight Marshal was old enough to remember the purging, though it was ingrained in every Gaimosian. The past must not be repeated. A touch of sadness reached Kavan's heart. A man without home or people shouldn't be subjected to even more torment.

They resumed their trek at dawn, and still there was no sign of the Fist. Kavan wanted to hope they'd given up and gone back to their masters in defeat. Common sense knew better. If the Fist were as persistent as Pirneon claimed, they would never stop. It was an uncomfortable feeling. Death was a constant companion for the children of Gaimos, lurking ever beyond reach. They never knew when the end would strike. Kavan could only hope it wasn't this day.

His eyes never stopped roving. Ambush spots peppered the surrounding area. He felt ill prepared. Should darkness creep upon them again, he wanted to meet it like the knight he'd been born to become. At midday, he halted and drank deeply from a canteen. The water was tepid and almost brackish tasting. Sweat trickled down his face. The weather was changing. It grew hotter, more humid.

He'd noticed the gradual change in terrain as well. Open grasslands gave way to thicker underbrush. The ground sloped up. Hills now dotted the countryside. Murky haze clung to the ground a short distance away. So near, yet unreachable. Kavan found himself almost wishing for the cold grip of winter. Still, he rode on. At last, he entered the mist and that border between light and dark. Kavan decided to wait for the others to catch up. A foul stench drowned the land. None of them said it, but they knew they had come to the edge of the great swamp.

TWENTY-EIGHT

Uelg

If ever a part of Malweir personified decay, it was the Uelg. A place so old man had no remembered name for it, the great swamp was all but forgotten by time. The very ground was a festering bog. It was a place where creatures came to die. The air was humid and ripe with foul stench. Nothing good lived within. Fumes and gases turned the sky sickly shades of decay.

"This is a dread place, Pirneon," Kavan said through the cloth covering his nose and mouth.

Mold covered the nearby vegetation. The ground sank as they walked. Kavan instantly grew concerned over stumbling across a patch of quicksand. Better men had come and died here.

"What choice do we have? It is still far to Aradain, and our enemy will not have abandoned their hunt."

"We could double back and swing east up into the Crags."

Pirneon frowned. "No. That's too dangerous, even for us. We are in no condition to fight, and the Fist is still out there."

Mist clung to the horses' ankles. Kavan glanced worriedly. "I feel something unclean about this place. The swamp is dangerous."

"Hopefully enough to deter the Fist."

"It will also give them time to circle around and cut us off," Kavan said. "It's impossible to move quickly through here. The swamp is old. Many creatures from the days before time wait within."

"This talk is going nowhere," Pirneon said with finality. "Push on and get it over with."

Geblin rolled his eyes at their banter. His people knew more about the Uelg than any other race, and these knights were too foolish to ask. The Gnome kingdom bordered the great swamp. Hundreds of hunters and wanderers had been lost to the perpetual murk. Gnomes were highly superstitious, and their eccentric losses soon spread. The Uelg became a house of evil, and the folk of Malweir stayed clear lest they, too, were swallowed.

Now he was headed directly into it. Geblin had begged for a weapon after revealing parts of his true nature and was rewarded with one of Barum's daggers. The Gaimosian blade was a sword in his small hands.

Leaning close to Kavan, he whispered, "We shouldn't be here. This place is evil."

Kavan offered a wry grin. Danger flashed behind his eyes. Then, he headed off to follow Pirneon. Geblin felt his already failing hopes of survival dash apart. He knew without a doubt that he was going to die here. He cursed the day the knights had rescued him from the Mountain Ogre. He cursed every decision he'd made to stay after.

"Take heart, Geblin. There are no finer warriors in the world," Barum told him in passing.

The Gnome snorted. "Words. Just words."

His was the last horse to enter the swamp, escorting Aphere along the way. He prayed to come out the other side.

The day crawled agonizingly along. Temperatures became unbearable fast. All five were soaked through with sweat and reek. It dripped down their backs, into their eyes. They found it hard to breathe as the swamp choked in around them. It was far worse than the closeness of Hresh Werd.

Vision was limited to a handful of meters. They caught heavy footsteps crashing through the unseen distance. Creatures of the old world, Kavan had said. The sounds made him want to break into a run but doing so would spell their doom. Mud sucked them ever downward. Boulders sprang up from the mist to block the already slender paths. Every footstep became a struggle just to move forward.

Fallen trees lined the paths. Mold drooled off slime-encrusted bark. Hot splashes sizzled over pools of acidic water. Other pools were coal black and bubbling over. The knights agreed that this was a world gone mad. Halfway through the afternoon they stumbled upon the remains of a gigantic beast long dead. Bleached white bones littered the area, most easily larger than a man. The rib cage blocked the path like an eerie tunnel. The knights stared in wonder, each wondering what sort of creature could have once walked the world.

Pirneon finally called a halt once they cleared the skeleton. His silver-grey hair was plastered to his skull. His eyes bore an almost hollowed out gaze. "Not even the sun."

Kavan drank deep from his canteen. "We could be going in circles, though it doesn't feel right."

"The Fist would be mad to follow us."

Kavan forced a laugh. "Just as mad as we are. Do you have any idea how big this swamp is?"

Pirneon didn't.

"We'll have to start looking for a defensible place to spend the night. This weather is taking a toll on the animals as well," Kavan said.

"Are you mad?" Geblin exclaimed.

A great and terrible roar shattered the still of the swamp.

"We cannot stay the night in this!"

Pirneon agreed but didn't see another solution. "Do you have a better idea?"

"This swamp is evil. You're damning us all."

"We've been damned for many long years, Gnome. Unless you have something pertinent to contribute, I suggest you keep your mouth shut."

"Then we sleep on the bones of my people," Geblin fumed.

Aphere awoke a short time later, dazed. Much of color had returned, though her body ached from such exertion. Borderline dehydrated and starving, she clumsily accepted food and drink while attempting to recall the events of the battle.

"I don't know what happened," Aphere told them.

Only Pirneon remained separate. His condemnation of her abilities wasn't about to shift simply because she woke up. Aphere was an abomination, and he intended to remind her so.

She finished the last bite of dried venison and washed it down with lukewarm water. "I thought it was the end. We were surrounded and about to be overwhelmed. I felt a rush through my veins. It was like fire spreading through me. I blacked out after feeling like I'd burned from the inside out."

"You've been unconscious for nearly two days," Barum said.

He finished repacking the rations and canteens. Nerves threatened to get the best of him. He felt like the swamp wanted them to stay. Barum felt restricted in unimaginable ways.

Kavan laid a hand on her shoulder. "Aphere, are you well enough to travel? We need to leave this place."

"I think so. I'm just tired," she replied, blinking thoughtfully. "Where are we?"

Kavan offered a sheepish grin and told her what had happened since she blacked out. An enormous shadow soared overhead, giving him pause.

"We must go," Pirneon said harshly.

Kavan nodded and helped Aphere ease into her saddle. Everything was against them, and it didn't matter if she was well enough to ride. The shadow passed again as the Gaimosians moved out.

They spent the night in silence, tucked away in a rotted copse of firs. Great branches bowed down; the browned needles swept outward in a protective fan. It was inadequate for cover, but the knights failed to find anything else. A brief dinner was eaten to the accompanying sounds of the night. Wordlessly, they bedded down and pulled their guard shifts, all the while praying nothing wicked came from the dark.

Dawn arrived without fanfare. The murk remained oppressive, nearly impenetrable. After a while, it began to dampen spirits and affect morale. Ever the swamp pressed in on them. Suffocating. Stifling. It was late afternoon when they stumbled upon a great lake in the middle of the swamp.

Aphere eyed the haze-covered waters uneasily. A warning went off in the back of her mind, a silent alarm alerting her to the pain of the future. She held her tongue, though, concerned with Pirneon's mistrust and growing intolerance. Still, she teased her blade from the scabbard just in case.

"What do you feel?" Geblin asked, startling her.

She looked down softly on the Gnome. Most of her earlier anger had dissipated. She smiled. It looked like Geblin wasn't going to be killed by them after all.

"A thing of great evil," she whispered so as not to arouse the others. "We are being stalked."

Geblin had suspected as much. "There's nothing for it. Only death haunts this land. I tried to warn him."

Aphere's eyes narrowed with the uncanny sharpness of a hunter. A dreadful scream wailed across the moors. Then their world erupted in violence. Leaves, muck, and branched exploded from the heart of the Uelg. The force of the blast knocked Kavan from his saddle. He hit hard, sinking into the rotting ground. Swords drawn, the others circled and prepared for battle.

Mist sped by them, drawn into a funnel of power at the center of a pool of black water. The air chilled. An overwhelming sense of dread spread from the gathering mists. Darkness took shape in the center.

"What evil is this?" Pirneon growled.

Kavan groaned and struggled to his knees. A thin sliver of blood trickled from the corner of his right eyebrow.

Geblin cried out, "Waugh! I told you! We're trapped!"

The Gnome drew his dagger and readied for death. A blast of power rippled from the dark. Frenzied winds lashed the swamp. Trees swayed, threatening to break. Barum's horse reared up and let out a frightened cry. They were forced to shield their faces from debris slamming into them. Their breath came in icy plumes.

Slowly, the figure in the center of the anomaly began to take form. Rank and fetid, the creature stood seven feet tall. Hidden beneath a molded black cloak, it raised an arm and gestured accusingly to the knights. Smoldering darkness pulsed from beneath his hood. Bone shone through the decomposing flesh of his fingers. What flesh remained was black, gangrenous. When it spoke, the voice came out in a tainted rasp.

"Blood must be paid," he groaned.

Barum's bow sang. The arrow hissed true, speeding towards the creature's hooded face only to disintegrate mere inches away. Ashes blew listlessly in the dying wind.

"You cannot harm me."

Again, he raised his arm, and waves of filth spread forth. Aphere began retching uncontrollably.

"Blood must be paid," he repeated.

Pirneon backed his horse away. He knew there was no winning this situation. Sword in hand, he struggled to find a way for them all to escape. He had trouble comprehending the monster attacking them. Never in his long, storied career had he seen such malevolence unleashed in a single being. It was as if the very soul of the underworld had spit forth this creation.

Geblin was instantly at Pirneon's side. Grim determination defined his face. "This evil is more than us."

The creature waited in the sanctuary of mists.

"Quickly, Gnome, tell me what you know of this foul creature," Pirneon whispered.

Black mist hid the lower body of the creature, adding a terrorizing feel. Geblin chewed his lip in thought. He heard death's soft whispers of temptation in the back of his mind. It called to him, to them all. Geblin shivered. He knew exactly what evil confronted them, and that scared him even more. Too many of his kin had been claimed in this manner.

"It is a lich," he said, "A devourer of souls."

Pirneon gripped his sword tighter, as if that would provide the resolve he required. A lich was a being from the old world, where men held power over life and death. This one should have died out with the rest of its kind. Once a man of incomparable power whose soul refused to die, the lich was neither living nor dead. Legend spoke of ancient sorcerers who did not accept death as the end. They performed spells and rituals to the dark gods in order to live forever. Immortality was exchanged for their souls.

"How can men defeat such as this?" Kavan whispered. His resolve was shaken. Doubt crept in.

Geblin searched the mists until he spied what he was looking for. "There! The gem atop his staff. We must destroy it. It's the only way. Can the lady use her magic?"

The lich had but one weakness. The source of his power was both boon and bane. Trapped within an amethyst gem was the soul of the undead.

That gem gave the lich unlimited power, both over the living and the dead. Destroy it, and the lich would die.

Pirneon shifted his gaze back to Aphere. His hatred and mistrust were temporarily gone. Sadly, Aphere was in no condition to fight. Her last efforts had drained her completely, so much he was certain she would die if she tried to use it again.

"No. We must do this," he said in a measured voice.

"Then we will die," Geblin replied.

Barum fired again, and again. Both arrows burned to ash. The lich howled in fury. His gem flashed brightly. A quake rippled across the ground. Spouts of flame slashed up from the bog. Wails of unimaginable pain rode the winds as hundreds of partially decomposed figures began crawling from the earth. The dead rising from the grave. Kavan returned to his normal self and grinned savagely at the prospect of a fight. One by one, the dead drew rusted weapons and attacked. Kavan rushed forward to meet them.

His sword sliced deep, ripping strips of desiccated flesh and ichor away with each swing. Hands and heads were cleaved off. Torsos were brutally slashed through, but for every one Kavan slew, more would arrive. The rest of the Gaimosians entered the fight at his sides under the watchful gaze of the lich. Only Geblin held back.

Most of the dead were Gnomes. His heart ached for his fallen kin. Anger and horror collided in his heart. So many of his people had been killed here. So many. Geblin felt the blood rage steal upon him, and he leapt into battle. His sword slashed and cut in reckless abandon. More than anything, he wished to send their trapped souls on to their final resting place. A liberation of the spirit. Tears streamed down his face as he slew Gnome after Gnome.

The lich watched the battle, waiting until the Gaimosians had expended their strength to lash out with the full majesty of his power. They, like everyone else, would soon belong to him. Then an unexpected panic suddenly gripped him. The lich froze, trying to scry the source of his unrest. His yellow eyes fell on the near prone female knight. Sparks of power, unseen by the mortal eye, crackled off her flesh. His gem flared warning. The lich howled, and his minions redirected their attack against Aphere. Organs and limbs littered the battlefield in gory mess. The smell of death was sickening, overpowering. Sword arms grew tired as the Gaimosians collapsed their defense to shift around Aphere.

Bodies began to pile up. The dead were desperate, knowing she posed the greatest threat. Driven by the lich's rage, they clawed and scraped closer to Aphere.

"Blood must be paid!"

The lich aimed his staff and spoke words of power. Purple flames shot at her from the end of his staff. Aphere barely managed to glance up in time. She scrunched her eyes shut and flung an outstretched hand back at the lich. Pure energy exploded from her fingers, sending a wall of power to the reaching flames. Magic collided in a wicked explosion. The Gnomes closest exploded in a shatter of gore. The lich stumbled backwards. Pain hammered into him, and he knew fear. His staff was cracked down the length.

Pirneon caught the hesitation. "Now, Kavan! Attack. Destroy the staff, and we destroy him!"

Kavan leapt over several clawing Gnomes, sword arced high above his head. He raced through the throngs of the dead and the sucking mud of the Uelg. His eyes narrowed. He saw only the decrepit robed figure ahead. Kavan lost himself in the battle. It was a fight only one would walk away from.

The distance closed. Twenty meters. Ten. Kavan was upon him before the lich recovered. Steel flashed in the purple light. The lich threw forth his staff, seeking to rip Kavan apart, but the knight was faster. His sword ate through the mists until it bit deeply into the staff's rod. The lich had time to scream once before his carefully hoarded power was released back into the world.

The force of the explosion flattened everything for a hundred meters. Kavan was flung face first into the muck as the lich disintegrated above him. Both halves of the staff landed at his head. One by one, the Gnome undead lost animation and sank back into their swampy tomb. Geblin cried from his knees. At last, his people were free. The mists dissolved, leaving the swamp and returning to the same unfriendly miasma it had always been. The Gaimosians recovered gradually. Eager to be free from this place of death, Pirneon lead them on. By nightfall, they had reached the northern edge of the Uelg. The night had never been so inviting.

TWENTY-NINE

Ambushed

The Fist struck at dawn. Black clad warriors leapt from their ambush positions along the open lane north and closed in on the Gaimosians with alarming ferocity. On foot, they were no match for the speed and strength of trained warhorses. Darts and arrows hummed through the air only to fall short. The Fist surged forward. They were eager to close with the enemy and collect their bounty, all the while avenging the deaths of so many of their own.

They moved with deliberate caution. The danger of losing their prey was slim with the flying beasts scouring the skies. Pharanx Gorge jumped upon the back of his faithful pet and raced back to the skies. He enjoyed the hunt almost as much as the art of killing. Consumed by disappointment, he vowed to kill them all, even that wretched Gnome. Only the unexpected use of sorcery troubled him. Her, he'd kill personally.

"How many this time?" Pirneon asked.

They slowed to a quick trot, fearful of exhausting the horses so far from their destination.

Kavan wiped his face. "More than a hundred is my guess."

The Knight Marshal frowned. Odds were growing increasingly in the enemy's favor. He was surprised to realize just how exhausted he was. They'd been on the run for almost a week now since leaving the Uelg. All were borderline ineffective, pushed to the limits of even their great endurance. The Fist, on the other hand, were rested and eager. They held numbers; they had the advantage. Only death could be the outcome. Only pain.

"We have to find a way to even the odds or this will be a waste of trip."

"Agreed," Kavan replied. "But we are in no position of strength to do so. The land between here and the mountains offers little protection but will not swallow us from view of their damned flying beasts."

"There is a forest not far from here. It runs the length of the plain all the way to the foothills of the Crags," Geblin offered.

Pirneon swung towards the Gnome. "How far?'

He rubbed his chin thoughtfully. "A day, perhaps less. We need to find the nearby stream and follow it to the small lake in the middle of the forest. Trees are thick there. They should provide us with good cover, at least until my people discover us."

Kavan tried to hide his grimace. More Gnomes was not exactly the position he hoped to find himself in. "Are you sure they won't attack us? I couldn't handle you, and now we march willingly towards an entire tribe."

Barum started to laugh, and it quickly spread to the others. Even dour Pirneon flashed a grin. Geblin folded his arms over his chest and stared daggers, less harsh than before, at Kavan before he succumbed to a chuckle.

"I was merely getting you accustomed to my kind," Geblin snorted.

"We're wasting time. Can you lead us to this stream, Geblin?" Pirneon asked, the mirth gone from his eyes.

"Well enough," he replied in a hostile tone. His mistrust of Pirneon continued to grow the more he became attached to Aphere.

Pirneon gave a crisp nod. "Let us go. Even now I can feel our enemy's breath upon our backs."

The beleaguered group hurried on.

"How do you feel?" Barum asked as he drew alongside Aphere.

She offered a tired look. "Exhausted. This is turning out to be more than I signed on for."

He agreed. "I'm not even a knight yet."

"Nonsense," she protested. "Titles are superficial, Barum. You've performed above the expectations of even our greatest. You are a true knight of Gaimos in every sense of the word. Would that there were more of you perhaps our fates might be different." She smiled before changing the subject. "What will you do after your ceremony on the Skaag?"

"I haven't thought past tomorrow, to be honest. Malweir is a grand world. There is much I wish to see. Pirneon and I have gone through many trials, but the idea of being on my own, with the power to choose for myself, staggers my imagination."

She reached out with a tender hand. "Keep a hold of those dreams. In the end, they are all we have."

"I will, Lady."

His head swooned with the relief only a troubled heart could deliver.

Geblin led them successfully to the stream, and their pace quickened. Now that they had clear direction, Pirneon decided it was time to surge ahead. The Fist were close, but he didn't know where. He cautiously stole glances at the flanks as they rode. The terrain gradually changed. The ground sloped more, becoming rocky and less forgiving. He worried that, if the mounds got too high, the Fist would have them trapped. A simple ambush to split them up would finish the knights.

"Faster. The forest edge is not far," Kavan said as he doubled back. His face was etched with concern.

"What did you spy?" Pirneon asked.

"It's what I didn't see that bothers me. There was no sign of the Fist at all. It's almost as if they've given up."

"Not likely." Pirneon grimaced. A light breeze danced across his face. "We're being hunted methodically. It's only a matter of time before they strike again."

Kavan agreed. "This is good ground for attack."

A wicked screech shattered the air, cutting him off. The horses jerked in fright, threatening to spill the riders. Swords drawn, the knights looked about for the source of the danger. Another screech echoed the first, this one louder, closer. Their eardrums burned from the pitch.

"There! In the sky!" Geblin pointed up and cried.

The winged beast sliced through the low-level wisp of clouds. It was black as the darkest hell and bred for killing. Barum nocked an arrow and took aim. Even as he did, he knew it wouldn't matter. The beast was too fast and agile. Worse, it was being ridden by a Fist.

Pirneon let out a harsh gasp. "Will we ever be free of these cursed people?"

Kavan wheeled around, sword uselessly pointed skyward.

"Flee! Get to the forest edge!" Pirneon barked.

All advantage lost; the knights fled at speed. Pirneon was concerned, knowing that the rider could drop any sort of munitions down upon them. Speed of horse was their only escape. Hooves kicked loose dirt and scree. Fear lanced their eyes. The sky rider screeched again and swooped down.

Kavan led them at full gallop. The forest edge was only a few hundred meters away, but the sky rider was closing. Wild cries suddenly sprang up from the mounds on either side of the trail. He knew what they were without bothering to look. The Fist was upon them. Kavan pushed his horse harder. The forest was so close.

Trees loomed ahead now. They were almost to safety. Sweat coated the horses in glistening sheens. Mud kicked up as the band raced on. Days of early spring rains left the ground waterlogged, dismal. Dark green moss clung to rock and tree. All around the landscape painfully reminded him of the swamp. The sky rider screeched again and circled higher. He was powerless to do anything but watch as the Gaimosians entered the forest.

Kavan heard a voice echo on the wind. "Faster dogs! Lose them, and it's your head!"

The Fist closed on the forest.

Howls of rage, taunts, and roars echoed across the terrain behind them, forcing the beleaguered group ever on.

"Kavan, shift north," Pirneon advised between ragged gasps. "We need to reach the mountains before the Fist catch us."

The knights kept pushing, though the density of the forest forced them to walk. Much of the ground was slick, slightly treacherous. Thick vines hung down like nature's executioners.

"We're going to have to stop at some point. The horses can't take much more," Aphere cautioned.

Pirneon bit back on his pride. She was right, regardless of his personal dislike of her. It was time to accept facts. The reality that they might not survive long enough to reach Rantis and fulfill the oracle's prophecy whispered in the back of his mind. He had to use all his assets if he hoped to escape.

"Geblin, how far until we reach Gnome territory?"

"We're already in it," came the solemn answer.

Geblin reined his horse in and laid both hands on the pommel of his saddle.

"What are you...."

Geblin pointed ahead. Dozens of armed Gnomes emerged from behind bushes and trees. All were dressed in various animal pelts and armed to the teeth. All had iron tipped arrows aimed at the Gaimosians.

"Keep your hands in the open, and make no sudden move," Geblin cautioned. "They will kill you without thought."

The Gnomes converged. Angry looks soured their faces.

"Down, off your horses," their leader snapped. "You are now our prisoners."

Geblin was first to obey. Once down, he placed his hands behind his head and said, "There are others following us. We are not your foe."

"We shall decide that for ourselves, Geblin."

The knights exchanged confused looks. More was going on between the Gnomes than they understood. Geblin hung his head.

"Don't worry about your friends. We've been watching them for some time," the older Gnome said.

From the edge of the forest, screams and cries could be heard as battle commenced.

THIRTY

Creidlewein

"Why are you with these outlanders, Geblin?" the Gnome pressed.

They were alone. All the knights were being guarded around a small cook fire. Confused, they hadn't put up a fight and were secretly grateful for the Gnomes' interference.

Geblin sighed. "That is a long tale. It all began in the Kergland Spine."

"Where are the others you left with? How is it you alone managed to survive?" the older Gnome said with barely contained anger.

Geblin jabbed a finger at the other. "Don't you dare accuse me, Flade! I did what needed to be done, as any of us would."

Flade rose, hand dropping dangerously close to his weapon. "You are wrong! My father never would have left his friends to die! You abandoned him, Geblin. You abandoned him and left him to die."

"Flade, listen to me," his voice dropped low. "I did not leave your father to die. Let me tell my tale, and you'll see."

Geblin returned to them as the sun started to set. He had a defeated air. Aphere moved over to him, offering a canteen of fresh stream water. He took it wordlessly and drank deeply.

"I'm sorry," he told them all.

She gave a short smile. "For what?"

He looked into her soft eyes and felt pangs of regret. "I tried talking to him. I tried, but Flade wouldn't listen."

Pirneon, from atop a large boulder, looked at the Gnome and asked, "What are you talking about? Who is Flade?"

"He and I grew up together. We were never really friends, more like childhood rivals. Both of our fathers were on the council at Creidlewein. Flade never had the temperament to get along with others. When his father chose me to be his apprentice, it devastated Flade. Our friendship, what little there was, ended that day and we've been rivals ever since."

Kavan fought off a yawn. "Why should he be so accusatory towards you now? Didn't he realize you were trying to save us?"

Pirneon shot him an angry glare.

"It goes far beyond that. Flade's father was the head of our expedition into the east. I watched the Ogre spear him to a tree and rip him in half. Flade blames me."

A great uproar disturbed the hasty encampment. Scores of Gnomes returned from the deepening gloom of the forest. Fists pumped in the air. Gnomes howled and shouted war cries. Logs were heaped into the fires as the last of the warriors slipped through. A celebration was in order.

The Gaimosians watched the Gnomes with inspired interest. All of those returning bore weapons too large for them to use. Swords and spears fit for human cavalry were carried in numbers. Kavan was the first to spy the strange flag carried to the camp center. Pirneon followed the flag until he felt his mouth drop open. It belonged to the Fist.

"Geblin, can you find out what happened? That banner is the Fist. I've seen it once before, and if my guess is right, these Gnomes just scored a great victory," Pirneon said. His voice contained a twinge of excitement.

If the Gnomes did, indeed beat back the mercenaries, the knights' chances of reaching Rantis improved dramatically. Geblin rose and approached the nearest guard. They spoke in hushed tones in their native tongue.

"What are you thinking?" Kavan asked.

Pirneon explained his plan. He'd developed several courses of action, all driven towards their same goal. Unfortunately, all of them put Geblin in integral roles all the way to Aradain. The oracle had told them how important all of them were to stopping the foul power rising. If Pirneon used the Gnome like he wanted, it would turn Geblin into an outcast and leave him hated for the rest of his days. That was provided any of them survived the coming struggle.

"We can't ask him to kill his own people," Aphere said, aghast.

Pirneon's gaze narrowed. "We may have no choice. Time is running out. How long can we truly be expected to remain their prisoners?"

"But his own people? That's like one of us being asked to kill another," she persisted.

"We all have difficult choices to make," he snapped, louder than he wanted. "You spoke with the oracle. Remember his words, Aphere. We are all necessary and have but days left to us."

Seventeen days remained until the next eclipse. Aphere dropped her argument and sat back down. An eerie premonition bothered her for reasons she couldn't explain. Geblin returned moments later. His eyes were livid with rage.

"They caught the Fist just inside the forest. They claim they killed all twenty of our pursuers," he told them.

Barum said, "That's a good thing, right?"

"Not really. Now we're being taken to Creidlewein and the council. They'll decide what to do with us."

Creidlewein was a quaint city nestled in a wide gorge in the northern part of the forest. The iron-grey mountains of the Crags could be seen in the distance. City streets were paved in cobblestone, adding homeliness to the stone and thatch houses. Men and women went about their business, pausing to stare at the humans being escorted down the main boulevard. Children played in a nearby park. None of the knights expected to find a city so tranquil and organized this deep in the forest.

"This is amazing," Aphere told Geblin.

He snorted. "You humans are all alike. How does it feel to find your prejudices empty? You thought we'd be grubby and cave-like, didn't you? Ha! We're just as civilized as any other race in the east. Don't be foolish enough to think differently."

"Where are they taking us?" Pirneon asked. He was tired of bickering.

"To the council chambers. Pray they are reasonable."

Kavan asked, "Will they be difficult to persuade?"

Geblin shrugged. "Depends on how much Flade tells them before we are seen. I'd say our chances are slim."

"We can't afford to be prisoners."

There was no mistaking Pirneon's tone. He'd kill as many Gnomes as necessary in order to escape. They walked on in silence until a burly Gnome in forest greens stopped them at the foot of the red stone steps leading up to the council hall.

"They'll wait in the guard room until Flade is done speaking," told the Gnome in charge. Then he spied Geblin and frowned.

Locked in the tiny room, the knights were fed and given the chance to sit, such as they could. Pirneon longed for a carafe of hot tea — without the desert, of course. Kavan folded his legs and sat on the floor in the corner. This was a familiar situation, and there was nothing to do but remain calm and conserve his strength. He rested his head in his hands and drifted to sleep.

The warden returned and brusquely ushered them down the hallway a short time later. More Gnomes dressed in the same livery lined the way. All were armed with daggers and ceremonial swords that Pirneon doubted were capable of cutting much. They appeared professional and impressive. None of them bothered looking the prisoners in the eye, giving the Gaimosians the feeling of already being condemned. Heads held high and marching with pride, they followed the Gnomes into the foyer.

The warden faced them just beyond a double set of doors carved from white oak. "Do not speak unless you are asked to. Make no threatening gestures, or you will be cut down. These are the elders of the Gnome people. Treat them as such."

He jerked his head at the pair of guards flanking the doors. They pushed the massive doors open and waited for the knights to pass. The floor was marble tiled, sunlight reflecting from tall stained glass windows depicting scenes of ancient Gnome heroes and battles.

Gnomes were consummate craftsmen. This was evident in every aspect of the council chambers. They were naught but fairy creatures from book and legend to most of the world, but the knights were learning differently. The wood paneling was clearly done by masters, as were the chairs and half moon-shaped table dominating the room. Made from dark cherry trees, the table had served as the symbol of Gnome leadership for hundreds of years. Tonight, it would be used again. Twin fire pits added warmth on the chill spring evening. The tender flames licked up from the smoothly polished stone.

A chamberlain tapped an oak staff on the marble floor twice and stepped to the center of the chamber. On cue, the warden stopped his prisoners and arrayed them in a line facing the elders. Six wizened faces stared back at them. Each had a long, white beard. Deep lines creased their sun-darkened skin. Arthritic hands curled around scepters of office. One by one, the elders turned their attention to Geblin.

"Who speaks for you?" asked the oldest.

Pirneon eased forward half a step. The act was natural, so much so he didn't put thought in it. "I do."

"You are accused of invading our lands with the intent of beginning a war."

The Knight Marshal clenched his jaw. "We have done no such thing. Yes, we entered the forest, but it was in fear for our lives. All we wish is to be sent on our way north."

"Lies," accused another. Streaks of red ran through his beard. "You've even brought a spy."

All heads turned to Geblin. The Gnome stood firm, refusing to give in to their brand of humiliation.

"Who is that one?" Aphere whispered from the corner of her mouth.

Geblin glared at the elder. "A relative of Flade."

The elder continued, "We all know of Geblin's treachery. Flade has spoken of this traitor's deeds."

The chamberlain tapped his staff on the floor.

"We," emphasized the eldest, "know nothing of the kind. Geblin's innocence or guilt remains to be determined, Tordin."

Tordin fumed from his chair.

"How shall I address you?" the eldest asked Pirneon.

"I am Pirneon of Gaimos. Once Knight Marshal of the army."

"Vengeance Knights!" wailed a female elder on the end. She was small, even for her kind. "No good will come of this!"

The eldest raised his hand, clearly irritated at the constant interruptions. "Be silent, Slon. There's never been trouble between our two peoples. This is no cause to start."

"You remember the troubles Gaimos caused the world," Tordin hissed.

"Those days are long past." He returned his attention to Pirneon. "What were those men doing hunting you?"

Pirneon smiled inwardly. He'd been hoping for a sign of division; now all he had to do was exploit it. "We've been hunted by the Fist since leaving Hresh Werd and the Oracle of Wenx."

Pirneon went on to detail their adventures, omitting key elements that wouldn't work in his favor. The Gnomes devoured his tale while casting suspicious glares not only at the knights but at each other as well. He deliberately avoided any discussion of Aphere's magic, loathing the subject and its portents. By the time he finished, only Tordin continued to glower in hatred.

"More trouble from Gaimos," Tordin spat once Pirneon fell silent. "Their country has been vanquished for a normal lifetime, yet even now they bring the world to the edge of ruin. Notice how they said next to nothing of Geblin and how he came to be in their service?"

"Step forward Geblin," the eldest commanded.

Geblin did. The firm defiance he'd shown since being rescued in the Kergland Spine was all but gone.

The eldest looked down sternly. "Geblin, son of Thil, you are accused of betraying your people. What do you say to this?"

"There is no betrayal. Flade's father led a small band east to find new trade relations with the other kingdoms. We fell into darkness crossing the mountains en route to the great desert. A Mountain Ogre ambushed us and killed all but me. I was kept in his lair while he feasted on the dead. I was to be eaten next, but these knights rescued me first. I can't say why I chose to remain with them, but something compelled me.

"Either way, the journey led west and brought me closer to home. Only then did we learn of the dark gods and their demons. Think and do with me what you will, but do not hold them accountable," he ended with a shrug.

Tordin asked, "And why not? You've brought war within our borders. Why should we trust you?"

Geblin had had enough. "I don't care what you think of me. Your affiliation with Flade is well known by all. Keep these knights from completing their task, and none of your accusations will matter. We will all die."

The chamberlain slammed his staff with power.

"Order!"

The eldest rose. His impassive features successfully concealed his thoughts. "You shall remain here until we decide what is to become of you."

The Gnome elders filed from the chamber, leaving Pirneon and the others standing humbly. The warden was the last to leave. He paused at Geblin's side and clasped his shoulder with a sympathetic look.

"Don't you worry too hard, lad. The Eldest won't be fooled by Tordin's bias."

Then he too was gone. The Vengeance Knights stood and waited, knowing all too well the fate of Malweir rested on of a handful of Gnomes.

THIRTY-ONE

Breaking Point

Corso howled in rage and heaved his crystal goblet at the wall. Glass shattered. A guard flinched to avoid being sliced. Corso began to pace. The vein on his forehead pulsed with anger. The sudden incompetence of the Fist perplexed him. Once again, the mercenary regiment had failed him. Once more, the most feared and expensive killers in the world had been thwarted by lesser foes.

He supposed he should take some small measure of satisfaction. The Gaimosians were resilient, proving themselves worthy of any accolades. This group was certainly stronger than the last few he'd experimented on. Even so, the hour was almost upon him. Corso now had two problems impeding his task. Fifteen days remained before the eclipse, giving him little time to get the Gaimosians funneled into Gessun Thune and activate the key. The second was the Fist.

They'd done their part, to be sure, but it was sloppy and ineffective. Pharanx Gorg already knew too much, making him a liability. They would need to be dealt with before Corso could continue much further. It seemed each time he felt he was getting a grasp on the situation, another issue arose. The death of the lich was a setback. Put there when the world was young, Corso had been counting on the creature to thin out the Gaimosians. Not even the Gnome had died. Corso cursed. The Gaimosians were proving more his damnation than aid.

"Leave me," he snapped.

The palace guards filed out silently. Alone, Corso stalked to the back of his expansive office. An ornate orb sat upon a shelf, nestling high above a seldom used fireplace. A small section of the floor opened to reveal a dark and winding staircase. The steps were wide, dust free. He used it more often of late. He had to get to the dark tower quickly and undiscovered. Underground passages crisscrossed the city, giving him fast egress to his safe house. Corso saw an opportunity while the Gaimosians were captive. Fuming, he might just be able to rid himself of one problem now.

They waited in the council chambers until late into the night. Twice, the warden came with fresh fruits and water. He didn't speak, lest he be denounced as a traitor as well. Pirneon didn't like it at all. His thoughts were focused on Rantis.

"This is a waste of time," he snarled.

Kavan yawned. Pirneon's ravings were growing tiresome. More and more he was losing control yet it was decided that by virtue of rank that Pirneon would retain the mantle of leadership. Kavan prayed he kept it together long enough to see the task through. They were so close.

"Patience, Pirneon," he said with a slow exhale. "We have time yet. The Gnomes will let us go."

"Will they?" he snorted. "Nothing has gone right since leaving Groskus. We have been hounded halfway across Malweir by men and monsters. For what? So we can wage war against a forgotten evil? This quest is getting out of hand. Our talents are better used elsewhere."

Kavan finally snapped. He rose to confront his one-time friend and mentor. "Are you listening to yourself? You rave!"

"I rave? I speak only what is on all our minds. Tell me this is what you envisioned when you came to find me in the desert. Between her unholy magic and our pursuit, I'm surprised we're not all dead. Come what will this night, I am leaving," he barked.

Incensed, Aphere fired back. "We'd all be dead if I didn't take action. Consider it a boon I am here."

"A travesty of our people, I call it. You mind your own affairs, and I'll be sure to do the same," Pirneon threatened.

Geblin hung his head in disbelief. They were on the very brink of imprisonment or worse and were attacking each other instead of finding a solution to their problem. More than anything, he wanted to be done with them. He was about to say so when the door creaked open and the chamberlain entered. The Gnome slammed his staff twice on the aged marble and a dozen guards filed into to herd the knights back to the center of the chamber. The elders soon followed.

The eldest looked down on his prisoners. "Step forward, Geblin. It is the decision of the council that…"

His decree was interrupted by a series of bone-chilling howls. Screams followed. Guards drew their swords and crowded around the elders. Geblin felt his knees give way. Only Kavan betrayed no reaction. He knew all too well what sounds disturbed the night. It was a sound he'd hoped never to hear again.

"We need our weapons, now," he stepped forward and demanded.

Tordin gave him a wild look. "Prisoners don't make demands. You'll do nothing of the sort."

A werebeast had broken into the building, rampaging through the meager Gnome defenses. Loud crashes echoed dully from behind the heavy doors. The werebeast was going to kill them all if Kavan didn't act.

"Listen to me," he said in a calm voice. "You are under attack by creatures you can't hope to defeat. Give us back our weapons, and we can at least give you a chance of surviving."

"Why should we trust you?" Tordin argued.

Kavan stared blankly. "Because you're dead if you don't."

A shrill scream followed by a fleshy thud on the other side of the doors pushed the council into action.

"Release them and return their weapons," the eldest told the warden. He leveled his gaze on Kavan. "What awaits beyond that door?"

"A werebeast. More than one it appears," he said with the faint glow of a smile. Several howls sprang up throughout the Gnome city.

"We cannot survive," Tordin whimpered.

"I've killed these beasts before. Give me my sword."

The warden's hands couldn't move fast enough. He dropped several of the weapons in a clumsy attempt at passing them out. Another Gnome hurried to unlock the chains on the Gaimosians. The pounding on the door intensified.

"I have a family," the warden told Kavan as he handed over the sword.

Kavan drew the weapon and cast the scabbard aside. "We'll do our best. Is there another way out of here?"

"Yes, in the back, behind the table," the warden said, his skin a waxy pallor.

"Take the elders. There's nothing more you can do here."

He sputtered, "But...."

Another thud. One of the doors cracked.

"There is not time. All you'll be is in our way. Now go!" Kavan barked.

The Gnomes retreated a split second before the doors burst apart in slivers. A pair of werebeasts tumbled in with the debris. Geblin let out a high-pitched scream. The four Gaimosians dropped into trembling battle stances. Any previous doubt bled away at the nightmare sights confronting them. Only Kavan had any experience. Only he made a move, attacking while the beasts were still disorientated.

The first was covered in pitch-black fur streaked through with red and eyes of darkest amber. It rolled through the charge and sprang to its feet. Kavan leapt up to come crashing down on top of it. Steel ripped flesh as gouts of fur and blood splashed away. The werebeast howled in fury and jumped back as Kavan followed through. He slammed a shoulder into the monster. Already falling, the werebeast lashed out to clip Kavan's boot. Both fell hard.

"Barum, fire!" Pirneon ordered.

Screams outside amplified. Barum strung, nocked, and fired three successive times. The second werebeast staggered back. Dark blood flowed from the wounds, but it wasn't enough to slow him. Born of dark magic and ancient hatred, the werebeasts were among the premier evil. Killing just one was a test of skill and luck. Pirneon and Aphere followed Kavan's lead and attacked. Barum drew again but was forced to wait for the right target of opportunity. He eased back to block the escape passage.

Coordinating their attack flawlessly, Pirneon and Aphere slashed and hacked the wounded beast. It bellowed in rage but could do little to prevent more pain. One beast in hand, Barum shifted focus towards Kavan. He and the werebeast grappled on the floor. Claws dug. Teeth snapped. Kavan wrapped a powerful hand around the beast's throat and fought off being club with the other. Murderous intent flared in both as Kavan and the beast fought for their lives. Barum took the shot. The arrow pierced through both sides of the beast's right calf.

"Kavan, get clear!" he shouted. "I can't get a shot!"

Kavan couldn't hear over the thunderous roar assaulting his ears. This beast was stronger than the ones he'd fought previously. More savage. Kavan threw everything he had at the beast and it took it with wrath. He squeezed the beast's throat tighter.

Across the chamber, Pirneon and Aphere systematically dismembered their foe. Body parts lay steaming, rivers of hot blood running away. The werebeast was critically wounded but continued to fight. Aphere lunged in, stabbing the beast through the heart. It let out a gurgled cry before Pirneon severed its head with a mighty blow. Hearts racing, they turned to Kavan.

A squad of Gnomes burst into the chamber, brandishing weapons and shouting war cries. All had blood stains on their skin and clothes. They attacked with reckless abandon. Kavan took an accidental blow from a hammer to the leg before he managed to roll clear. The Gnomes struck with ferocity to match the werebeast and soon stood triumphantly over the corpse.

Kavan looked up to see the warden, blood stained and exhausted, standing over him with a wry grin.

"I told you we can fight," he rasped.

Kavan flashed a salute with his sword. "Thank you. Where is the council?"

"Safe. Locked away in a chamber far below ground."

Limping, Kavan dropped to a knee to look the warden in the eye. A flicker of compassion crossed his hardened face. "What cost?"

"We killed two others," the warden said, white-faced. "I'd guess some fifty plus Gnomes. The blood is…"

He trailed off. His eyes were unfocused, staring far away. Though he professed to be a fighter, he'd never seen the horrors of war firsthand. Now that he had, it was all he could do to try and forget. Those weren't just bodies on the streets. They were friends. Family. Tears threatened to spill, but he was too proud to let them in front of such warriors.

"I am sorry for your losses, friend. We never wanted any of this to happen. They only came here because of us. A very powerful, ancient evil seeks to stop us from reaching our destination. We must leave Creidlewein before more of your folk are killed," Kavan explained.

The warden bowed his head submissively. "There is a trail north, into crags known only to us. It should lead you through the mountains and into Aradain."

"I know it," Geblin said, coming to stand beside his friend. "A small goat path our hunters use in winter."

"Is it big enough for horses?"

"Should be," Geblin answered.

"There's more," the warden continued. "I heard more of these…beasts in the surrounding hills. They continue to stalk you."

Kavan gave a sincere smile. "The story of our lives. See to your people while we escape. Thank you for your help. We shall not forget the bravery of your actions."

"Luck to you, lad," the warden replied.

The Gaimosians busied themselves with battle preparations. Blades were tested. Bowstrings were drawn for pull. Daggers were strapped to thighs. Mental preparation was made in the hope that their cunning and strength would see them through to the source of this evil. Geblin finished before the others and went to the warden. The two Gnomes stared at each other. The warden spoke first.

"Father would be proud."

"I am sorry for what happened, but I couldn't save him," Geblin admitted with sorrow. "I…."

"It's all right, little brother. He knew before the end," the warden said.

They embraced.

"Geblin, it's time to go," Kavan interrupted gently.

Another howl shattered the moment.

"Go, and may the gods protect you," the warden wished.

The brother separated. Kavan led his group towards the broken doors.

"Not that way," the warden cautioned. "Use the tunnels. They are large enough for a grown man and run the length of the city. I will have your horses waiting for you on the other side."

One by one, the band of would-be heroes darted into the dark tunnel. One brother stood watching until they disappeared and closed the door after the last entered. One brother led the group through the tunnel with tears in his eyes. He had the overpowering feeling that he was never going to see home or family again. It was the hardest thing Geblin had ever undertaken. He led them on with stifled sobs.

THIRTY-TWO

Escape

They fled. Down through dark tunnels and winding passages far beneath the Gnome city. Geblin's brother had planned well and was true to his word. Their horses and bags were already waiting in a safe house under a dozen guards. The Gaimosians were impressed and grunted appreciation as they climbed aboard. Dawn wasn't far off, the first grey fingers streaking through the far horizon. Kavan hoped they could make the mountains before the werebeasts caught up to them. It was the only chance they had. Lose them in the confusion of the Crags, and they just might reach Rantis.

Torn between destiny and his past, Geblin was helped aboard the packhorse. He closed his eyes in prayer. There was nothing more he could do. Come the dawn, he'd be just another dead Gnome. He prayed for his brother, somehow knowing that his people would be safe when he and the knights were gone. Whatever evil wanted them dead was willing to slaughter anyone in its path.

"Geblin, we must ride," Kavan said.

The Gnome nodded solemnly. "I know."

The Vengeance Knight nodded back. Gently tapping his heels to shank, Kavan began their desperate flight into the Crags. Barum waited until everyone passed and then followed. His bow and arrow remained permanent fixtures in his skilled hands. Covering the rear was just as important as the front in this instance. He may not be a knighted man, but he was every bit as deadly.

Pirneon slowed the pace once he felt confident they were far from Creidlewein. "Geblin, what is the fastest path into the mountains? The werebeasts will find our trail soon."

"If they haven't already," Kavan added.

"The path begins not far from here. I'll lead," he told them.

Kavan bit back his pride. Much as he wanted to argue the point, he wasn't going to insist on being in charge when a better-qualified person was available. "I'll be right behind you, just in case."

Geblin snorted his amusement while Kavan turned his attention back to Pirneon.

"This doesn't feel right. We're being pushed. The two I killed before were solitary monsters who killed to eat, often for the sheer pleasure of it. These were different. Someone wants us dead. I don't know if we can best this evil."

Pirneon eyed his former pupil sharply. He knew Kavan was right, but what choice did they have?

"Does it matter?" he asked frankly. "We've been hunted and pushed from the day you found us in Groskus. Our hand has been guided by this unseen force. It seems our lives are not our own. The oracle confirmed as much. What choice do we have but to keep pushing ahead?"

"We push on," Kavan agreed. He looked to each of the others for confirmation.

Golden rays of sunlight began to filter down through the clouds.

"To what end?" Aphere asked.

Geblin merely shrugged. He'd learned there was no point in arguing when one of them made up their minds. It didn't help any that the oracle had effectively locked them into continuing this course of self-destruction, whether they wanted to or not.

"We're wasting time," Geblin said.

Pirneon gestured, and they were off. It wasn't long before they began the climb up into the mountains.

Daylight made their task easier, but the Crags were not known for their kindness to travelers. The path grew increasingly narrow and winding. Often, when cresting the height of a mountain, heavy winds and snows would sweep down and threaten to carry them away. Rumors of haunting were spread through local communities. People whispered of a restless spirit stalking the broken heights. More often than not, it could be attributed to howling winds caroming off the rock face, but folks were superstitious, especially during these troubling times.

Spirits or no, the Crags were the definition of danger. The range took its name from the amount of broken and jagged peaks stabbing up into the sky. Shadows and rain turned the paths into slick spots ripe for potential disaster. Winds turned to screams when caught in the right canyons. People did their best to avoid this lonely part of the world.

Midway through the day, the knights made it into the upper reaches. Pirneon halted them for a quick meal and for Kavan to double back. The old knight chewed absent-mindedly as he waited. The stone around him was dismal grey, void of life.

"I wonder now if some of those stories are true," he said after a long pull on his canteen.

Aphere tested out the stiffness of her shoulder. "How can you have doubts after all we've been through?"

He pretended to ignore her. She possessed tremendous quality, but that didn't prevent him from continuing his growing dislike. As far as he was concerned, she wasn't the same woman.

"Damn it, Pirneon. Look at me when I speak to you!" she snapped. She was just as tired of the game as he was. She also knew that the only way they had any chance of survival was through complete cohesion.

He raised a hand. "Stay your arguments. I know what it is you have to say, and I've no desire to listen. I think your powers are an abomination of all our kingdom once stood for. Yes, you have saved our lives, and that places me in your debt. However, I cannot and will not accept you. When this task is finished, I shall go and have a talk with Kistan."

She threw her hands up in exasperation. "To do what? Eh? Pout and scold him for being himself? You are a fool, old man."

He spied Kavan riding back into the defile.

"There is no sign of any werebeasts," he reported. A haggard look burrowed deep into his face.

"What of the Fist?"

Kavan shook his head. "Nothing. The only tracks are ours."

"They will not have given up so easily. The added threat of the werebeasts means their masters have upped the price. It is more important than ever that we reach Rantis."

Kavan remained silent, glanced at Aphere. Her face was twisted, distracted. Clearly, something stressful had passed between them in his absence. He decided to avoid the subject for now.

"I wish these clouds would pass," he said. "It would make it easier to spot those damned flying beasts."

"True, but they also provide cover. We have need of every advantage. Geblin, how much further to the crest of the range?" Pirneon asked.

"Less than a league. It will take the rest of the day so long as the weather holds."

"More than enough time for our enemy to consolidate and attack."

Geblin added, "The pass reduces the number of ways for their advance. These walls are too steep to climb, even for monsters such as they. It's front, back, or nothing."

"Gain the crest, and we look for a place to hole up for the night," Pirneon ordered.

Kavan and Geblin started forward. Pirneon waited long enough to give them a substantial lead before taking the others. He nodded to Barum in passing. The squire was growing more troubled the longer the quest went on. His master wasn't himself, and there was no obvious reason why. Barum watched Aphere and felt sorrow. Mixed emotions flushed her face. More and more, she realized her place was back at Ipn Shal, not here in the wide world.

"He was wrong," Barum offered in encouragement.

Aphere glared sharply. "It doesn't matter. He said his piece and is on his own. Sometimes our words can be as cruel as the most tempered blade."

"There is much stress in him these days. This task is taking a heavy toll on us all, him most of all. He just needs time to gather his thoughts. That's all."

Barum knew the problem went much deeper. An unsettling rage was growing deep within his master. One he couldn't figure out for the life of him.

"Pray for him Barum, pray for us all."

She rode past and said no more.

Nightfall dropped on them sooner than they anticipated. Occasionally, they caught the faint echo of an ominous howl. Geblin reassured them that the beasts were following other trails through the Crags. After all, he reminded, these mountains held hundreds of twisting paths, but only a select few ran through to Aradain.

They found a sizeable cave to spend the night. Pirneon allowed a small fire in the very rear for warmth and to cook a simple stew with supplies thoughtfully stashed in their saddlebags by Geblin's brother when the horses were escorted around. The mountain heights were cold, sapping strength from their bones. They found scrub brush in one of the cuts and pulled it over the cave mouth for cover. Geblin volunteered for first watch, eager to be away from his bickering companions.

For a time the only sound to be heard was the gentle crackling of burning wood. The Gaimosians stewed over earlier events. Only Kavan was left in the dark, though he'd mostly guessed the source of their problems. Tension filled the cave. Something needed to be said, if for no other reason than to calm nerves.

"Another day, and we'll be down in the foothills," he said.

Pirneon barely acknowledged him, "We'll make good time back in the flats. Unfortunately, so will our enemies."

"Is there anything along the path that can hinder us between here and Rantis?"

"No," Pirneon said. "The city is surrounded by a vast marsh on three sides. Previous monarchs built bridges to span the mire. It makes for good defense."

Kavan wasn't so sure. "Who in their right mind would build a city in the middle of a swamp?"

"A man afraid of something very powerful."

"How far are the ruins from Rantis? Do we go straight there or wait to scout things out first? I don't like going into any situation blind, but time is just as much our enemy as these damned monsters and Fist."

Pirneon finally raised his gaze from the fire. "What did you say?"

"Huh? About the monsters?" He shrugged. "Who else could have an interest in stopping us? The only logical conclusion is they are being controlled by someone with clear vendetta."

Light dawned in Pirneon's eyes. The thought proved disturbing but made total sense. Magic was an ancient tool that had practically been bred out of the bloodlines. Most kingdoms outlawed the practice after the last war. That someone still practiced arts long thought dead spelled ill for the people of Aradain.

"That line of thought puts us in a dangerous place. There's more, though. None of this feels right. It almost seems as if we're being herded towards a destiny beyond our grasp. An unknown darkness threatens to consume us. I know the taste of fear for the first time in decades."

The Knight Marshal went quiet and returned his gaze to the fire. He felt changes coming. They taunted him, manifesting in his dreams with promises of unparalleled violence. More than once he found himself thinking about the taste of blood. Why? What significance did that hold for a proven knight of Gaimos? Certainly, his honor and pride were stronger than the animalistic pull of the subconscious. He shuddered softly and tried to sleep. The others followed suit. Tomorrow promised to be long.

Dawn saw them back on the goat path heading north. By dusk, the knights rode down into the plains of southern Aradain. Rantis was still many leagues ahead. Thirteen days remained before the eclipse.

THIRTY-THREE

Mabane

"Listen to me, and listen well, for these are surely days of blood and darkness unlike any in our kingdom's history. Strange creatures stalk the night. We all know someone who just disappeared, never to be seen again. I say an ill wind has blown upon our fair land, and it's our obligation — nay, our duty — to stand up to this darkness and cast it from our shoulders!"

The speaker paused. Beads of sweat danced upon his upper lip. His simple robes billowed softly in the spring breeze. They were pure white, marking him a priest of an unnamed deity. His hard eyes stared into each of his listeners, prompting them to look away in shame or stare back boldly in defiance.

"Friends, the question is not if this horror will be visited upon us, nor when. The question is what will you do to confront it? Will you go and hide in your homes, huddled around the fireplace waiting for the dark hands of death to come a-calling?"

Several enraged shouts rose from the crowd. He smiled inwardly. The crowd continued to grow. Bigger crowds meant more men to fill the ranks of the coming hunt. He'd cast his hook and now waited for them to bite. He held up the stump of his right arm. Those nearest reeled back with gasps.

"You see, I'm no different than you. I've gone on the hunt, and I stand before you humbled in my failures. I wasn't strong enough. The damned beasts took my hand and half my arm. They took my best friend as well. But while we and the others did battle in those cold caverns, you and your ilk were safe from harm.

"Now, friends, it is your time. Time to do your part in ridding the world of their filth, their sickness. My name is Mabane, and I beseech you to stand. Stand for your honor. Stand for your kingdom. Stand for all you hold holy and dear. For your loved ones. For your friends. Stand! That's all I ask. Will you stand?"

The crowd erupted in cheers and roars of approval. Whipped into semi-frenzy, they started lining up to make their marks in Mabane's ledger. The drive for the next hunt was well underway. This same deed was being performed across Rantis. King Eglios had once again raised the call. The summons had begun in earnest. Mabane knew that many of these righteous volunteers wouldn't return. That knowledge pained him, almost as much as when he'd lost so much during his own ill-fated adventure last year.

Mabane was no priest. If anything, the guise was a sham. A shameless con in order to end the threat impeding Aradain's future. It was all because of the ruins, those damned ruins that men had accidentally discovered after a quake one balmy summer night three years ago.

Mabane looked up at a grizzly looking man blocking the sun. Partial recognition inspired him to speak.

The newcomer held up a hand to keep him quiet. "My brother was the one you spoke of. He'd be proud to hear you speak. Will you be joining us?"

Mabane clasped the man's shoulder. Of course. Friends often spoke of family, and his best friend was no different. "Indeed I shall. I may not be much good in a fight anymore, but I'll be damned if I sit back and watch. This is my kingdom as much as it is yours. Your brother gave his life to save mine. That is a debt I can never repay."

Satisfied, the man grunted and slipped back into the crowd. Mabane sighed. Painful memories resurfaced. His face flashed. He needed to escape and find a drink. His nerves had been shattered since losing his hand. The sweats had returned, and he struggled to fend off the tears threatening to spill. He excused himself from his scribes and slipped away.

Once out of sight, he pulled off his robes and headed to the nearest tavern. Just a few drinks, and all would be right again.

The liquor burned his lungs. At least that way he knew it was working. Mabane grimaced and poured another drink from the half-empty bottle. He thanked the man responsible for inventing the foul concoction and pounded a healthy mouthful. His eyes were screwed shut. When they opened, he found a stranger sitting across from him. Mabane blinked rapidly, thinking it an illusion of the drink. He was rewarded with a knowing smile as the stranger refilled his glass.

"My thannnks, friend," Mabane slurred.

The stranger remained quiet.

Mabane eyed him more closely, wishing he would stop swaying so he could get a better look. "Do I know you?"

"No."

The sharpness in his eyes whispered danger.

"Wha…what can I help you wif? A…as you can thee I'm bithee."

He smiled. "I heard you speak in the plaza. Good words. It was very compelling. I felt myself…moved."

Mabane spilled tiny rivers of ale down his chin as he drained his glass. "So youf joined the hunt?"

"No."

"W…hy are you here?"

He leaned forward. "I want to know what you know."

Mabane righted himself, growing angry. "Look, friend, s'been a long day, an I'm trying to forget abouth it. Stay or go. Don't matter. I'm in n'mood fer gammmes."

"This is no game. Too many lives have been lost for that. My associates and I have come to put an end to this evil before the darkness grows."

"S'what you need me fer?"

"You've been down in the ruins. I need to know what you saw, the layout, where the tunnels lead."

Mabane snorted. "Plenty o' folks ha' been down there. Ole Eglios has been having great huntsss for two years now. Find sumon else. I'm not yer man."

"You're exactly what we're looking for."

"Who are you?"

The stranger leaned back in his chair and poured them both a drink. "My name is Kavan."

They stared at each other, neither willing to make the next move. Mabane generally had good sense for people and, even in a drunken stupor, recognized trouble. Bravery wasn't one of his strong suits. He'd tried that once and came away missing most of an arm. Not that he was a coward, by any measure. He was a stand-up man who'd once been a loving father and husband. All that had changed one winter night when the werebeast burst into his home. Their faces still haunted him.

Then he had joined the hunt. Revenge had spurred him on to the point of madness. His beliefs had faltered, for how could any god allow such evil to exist and run about freely? No. The gods were gone or just didn't care. It was up to men to end the horror. In that blind fervor, he'd strode boldly into the ruins of Gessun Thune and barely come out alive. A wreck of a man, Mabane had turned to the bottle. The kingdom paid a meager salary for his recruiting drives. It wasn't much, but he had enough to drown his anguish on any given night.

"Tha ruins are a day norf o' here. I wish you good fortune, friend. I caa help."

"There is strength in you. You have only to find it again."

"You some kina priest?" Mabane asked.

Kavan shook his head. "The furthest thing from it."

"Then why are you s' damned interested in a drunk wif one arm?"

"That's my business. Just know that I'm not looking for a sword; we have enough of those. What I need is a guide."

Mabane stared back blankly.

"Wrong man."

Kavan dropped his shoulders in defeat. "I guess so. Enjoy your drinks."

He rose and started to walk away. He made it a few steps before turning back, as if a sudden thought had struck. "My friends and I have a room at the Green Lotus if you happen to change your mind."

He flipped two silver coins on the table and left.

Mabane stared after him for a moment until Kavan was lost in the crowd. He snatched up the silver and finished his drink. Several other patrons turned to give him awkward stares. They'd caught snippets of the conversation. Mabane was just another drunk. Another casualty in a brutal campaign that had claimed more lives than the last bout of plague. They shook their heads and returned to their own drinks, leaving him slightly drunker and deep in thought.

THIRTY-FOUR

Arrival

Kavan closed the door and collapsed in the aged wooden chair.

"Were you successful?"

He looked up at Pirneon. "I think so. It might take a while for him to come around, though."

"We don't have much time for him to reach this conclusion, Kavan. There are but eleven days left."

Kavan pinched the bridge of his nose. His head ached, a sign of dehydration and the compounding stress they all felt. "I know, Pirneon. We all know."

Frankly, he was as tired of the older knight's insistent personality as the others were. Only now was he beginning to show it. Kavan was suddenly reminded of how much he liked working alone. The look on Pirneon's face confirmed similar thoughts.

"It might be time to start thinking of going our separate ways."

Pirneon felt right saying the words. Not even Geblin seemed surprised. The more he learned of the Gaimosians, the more he wanted to return to Creidlewein, but the oracle had spoken. Sitting in the windowsill, Geblin returned his stare outside and allowed his thoughts to return to his brother.

Kavan let out a quick laugh. "You're not the Knight Marshal anymore. There is no Gaimos. There is no more code. We must fight just to exist. The only way we can survive now is by getting into Gessun Thune and sealing the nexus before it's too late. After that, we never have to see each other again."

Pirneon jerked back as if slapped in the face. "Very well. The mission must come first. After that, we are on our own."

"Agreed," Kavan and Aphere replied.

"How certain are you this man you found will come to help us?" he asked, driving past his confusion.

"Fairly. He's been hurt and is partially consumed by the need for revenge. I'm confident he'll come around."

"So long as he can get us into the ruins and down to where we need to go."

Barum looked up from oiling his sword. "It occurs to me that we've had all these discussions on the dark gods and the nexus, but none of us knows what to look for or how to close it."

All heads swung to the squire with approving eyes. At least he was thinking ahead. The only problem with that was that they'd opened an entirely new chain of problems they barely had time to solve. Aphere smiled in appreciation.

"I'd like to say he'll calm down, but we both know it's not true," Aphere told Kavan.

They walked through one of the many business districts in Rantis. Light crowds scattered among the different vendors and peddlers. It was unimpressive as far as capital cities went. There was nothing special in Rantis save the ever-present odor of the surrounding bogs. People were people, no matter what part of the world they lived in. The biggest discerning uniqueness in Rantis was the pall of terror that choked the air. The population was genuinely scared for their lives.

Kavan didn't know how to take the comment. He'd known Pirneon for decades and the man had always been the same stalwart character. "He's a proud man."

"Pride often turns to arrogance," she reminded him.

"We all have our vices," he replied.

"Kavan, he is growing increasingly unstable. I'm concerned."

Kavan sidestepped a pair of stray dogs marching down the street. "You'd do well to be worried about us all. If the beasts that attacked us in Creidlewein are any indication of what we're up against, the world is in dire straits. Which brings me to another point."

"That being?"

"We need more weapons," he said.

She innocently asked, "More or better?"

"A little bit of both, I should think."

They continued casually down the street, browsing through many goods and the various conmen associated with them. At last, they smelled the telltale fumes of furnaces. Haze clung to the street just ahead. They'd found the smithy district. Both knights examined several shops with an expert eye. A messy shop meant low quality. Soot-covered men emerged from their shops to entice the knights to come and further inspect their wares. Kavan and Aphere kept walking. They knew what they were looking for.

At last, they stumbled upon a plain, unassuming building. It lacked the flashy signs of the other shops, no gaudy displays of illogical weapons in the windows. The knights exchanged a nod and entered. The floor was recently swept. A modest assortment of weapons hung from the walls. Some were for sale, others a quiet display of immaculate craftsmanship. Kavan eyed the black ash crossbow with particular interest. The heavy sounds of a hammer striking raw metal echoed from the back.

A young woman emerged from behind a counter carrying an armload of wood. Any surprise at finding two well-armed and fierce looking warriors in her shop quickly faded as she saw the potential for another sale.

"I'm sorry. I didn't know we had customers," she said sweetly.

Aphere offered a genuine smile. "We were just admiring some of your work."

"It's not mine. Well, not most of it, anyway. My father is the master smith. I'm but an apprentice."

She met their looks with defiance. Slightly over five feet tall, her jerkin and trousers displayed a natural litheness from birth. Kavan admired her figure and soft, inviting face.

"I'm Aphere. This is Kavan. Could we speak with your father, please?"

The woman brushed a lock of striking red hair from her face. "Wait here. I'll go fetch him. I'm Phirial, by the way."

"She's quite the beauty," Kavan commented after she'd gone.

Aphere's eyebrow rose. "Easy, big boy. We came here for weapons, not to find you a wife."

He ignored the barb. Phirial returned a moment later with her father in tow. He was the typical middle-aged man who'd had a hard life. A growing waistline and thinning hair marked him for what he was. Sweat streaked the charcoal dust covering his face and hands, but his smile was honest. He wiped a meaty hand on his apron and reached out to shake both of their hands.

"Name's Nik. Phirial says you have need of weapons?" he asked.

"We'd like to upgrade our current stock, yes," Aphere answered.

"So you'd be joining that fool hunt, eh? Well, I'm not one to tell folk their business, but you'd be doing yourself a favor in leaving this cursed city now and head east. Get as far away from our problems as you can."

Phirial caught the hint of amusement in their eyes as she studied them. Each wore more weapons than she'd ever seen on a single person before, and they bore the poise of professional warriors. She instantly concluded that they were dangerous. Despite this realization, she had no concern for either herself or her father. Besides, she couldn't deny Kavan had the type of rugged handsomeness that could melt a girl's heart.

"We appreciate your concern, but our path is already set," Aphere replied.

Nik nodded. He'd seen hundreds like them. If they wanted to go off on some damned fool crusade, let them. It didn't matter to him either way. There'd always be someone else coming along to keep coins in his pocket.

"What exactly do you have in mind?" he asked.

Kavan said, "That crossbow looks inviting. How many more do you have?"

"Just the one. Give me a few days, and we can have a few more. How many are you needing?"

"Three full size and a smaller one."

"How small?"

"Like for a child?" Kavan said.

Nik looked at him quizzically but said nothing. Their business was none of his. "What else?"

Aphere said, "A few hundred bolts, five daggers and three more swords."

"Plan on going to war?"

"Something like that," Kavan replied. "What about caltrops?"

"Those are easy enough to make. How many do you think you'll need?"

"Several hundred would be nice. At least two or three sacks full."

Nik exhaled sharply. "That's a tall order. When will you be needing this by?"

Aphere answered, "As soon as you can have them done. No more than a week at the most."

"A week! You're not asking for much are you?"

"Can you do it?" Kavan asked.

Nik rubbed his thumb and forefinger together as he thought. It wasn't impossible, but it would put a major strain on his smith. "I suppose so, but it'll take many long nights. How will you be paying for all this?"

"Gold coin," Aphere said.

Nik rubbed the scar under his jaw. "Deal. Come to the back, and we'll discuss cost."

The man standing in the shadows across the street had seen enough. The knights had been inside long enough to strike an accord. That meant they were getting close to launching an attack. The king needed to be told. It was a dangerous time, having three Vengeance Knights roaming freely about the city on the eve of the great hunt. Their presence only had the chance to make matters worse. He needed to follow this pair back to their inn before reporting to the king.

Aphere and Kavan emerged a short while later. The watcher melted into the shadows and waited for the knights to get a good distance down the street before following. He passed a quick look to catch the name of the smith and hurried off. His master could deal with that threat. His sole purpose was to find the knights. Only then could he get paid and return to a normal life.

THIRTY-FIVE

Secret Meetings

Two days passed before there came a subtle knock. It was Mabane, come to take them up on their offer. His motivations were private. None of the knights questioned them. The pain of losing his family rippled through his drunken stupor to the point where he realized this was his only offer of redemption. He'd be a fool not to accept.

"So, I'm here," he said with empty hands.

Kavan invited him in. The smell of vomit and alcohol drifted off his clothes as Mabane entered. Kavan spared a glance down the hall to ensure their guest wasn't being followed before closing the door. Since their trip down to the smith district, he couldn't shake the feeling that hidden eyes were on them. Pirneon had gone off on one of his random walks. He'd been gone for most of the last two days, making this meeting with Mabane easier.

Mabane watched Kavan suspiciously as he made introductions. "You don't waste any time getting to business, do you?"

"There is no reason to," Kavan countered. "You know why you're here, and we know what we need from you."

"What exactly are you supposed to be? Some sort of avenging angels come to set the world to rights?"

"Of a sort," Aphere said. "Does it really matter?"

He shrugged indifferently. "Not to me, it doesn't. Anyone here got a drink?"

"No," Kavan told him. "We need you sober for this. No more alcohol until our task is complete."

"Or we're dead," Geblin muttered from his perch in the window.

Mabane looked up at the sound. His eyes widened.

"And you need a bath," Aphere added. Her face pinched in disgust.

Mabane gave her an indignant look. "I can leave just as easily as I walked in. Rantis is a big city. Go and find another guide."

"We don't want another guide. I chose you for a reason," Kavan reminded.

"And I choose to have a drink!"

Kavan leaned menacingly close and snarled, "If you ever mention alcohol again, I'll slit you from ear to ear. Now sit back, shut up, and stop being a pain in my ass."

Looking hurt, Mabane did as instructed. It was going to be a long night.

"Good. Keep doing as I say, and there's more in it for you."

Tamblin smiled greedily, forgetting her anxiety, and went back to work. She left Corso plotting his next move in the shadows. The hour was getting late, and he still had to find the key. Black robes whirling, he stalked back into the tunnels and his chamber beyond. There was still much to be done.

"I'm not saying another word until I get a drink," Mabane threatened.

Kavan dropped a hand to his dagger. Aphere mildly suggested he let her deal with the problem. He was more than happy to let her.

"Mabane," she said softly. "You answer the questions we have right now, and we'll buy your drinks. Deal?"

He nodded. "But no funny business. A man is only as good as his word after all. Or a woman, for that matter."

She glanced at Kavan. "There, you see? He just needed the proper sort of persuasion."

Kavan frowned but remained quiet as he went to join Geblin by the window.

Aphere continued, "How many different avenues of access are in the ruins?"

"Only one so far as I know."

"Just one?"

"Yes. They're mostly underground, you know. There's a few collapsed columns up top and a ruined building or two, but the rest of the city is buried in a huge cavern."

"Why would anyone build in such a place?" Barum asked.

"Who said it was people that did it? Could have been Dwarves or Goblins. The place is so old no one really knows for sure," Mabane said. "All we do know is that folks go down and mostly don't return. It's like the darkness swallows any trace."

"That's awful."

"True, but the survivors suffer worse." He held up his stump. "I'm one of the lucky ones. Least I can still walk and see. A lot of people around here can't say that."

"Why haven't the ruins been sealed back up if it's so dangerous? You'd think the king would show more concern."

Mabane offered a cruel laugh. "King Eglios isn't a fighting man. We might have taken over Barduk, but he never left Rantis during the campaign. General Moncrieff was the force behind that, him and the royal advisor. They do most of the dirty work. I guess that helps Eglios sleep better at night."

Aphere said, "But we've heard rumors of his lust for power."

"That part is true," Mabane admitted. "But Eglios is nothing without those two. I wouldn't be surprised if the whole army revolted without them around. This is a dangerous kingdom you've come to."

Kavan got up, feeling irritated. "We're getting off track. Is there any type of garrison at the cavern mouth?"

"Slightly less than a company of lancers. It's more of a token force than anything substantial. Moncrieff's a crafty one. He makes it look good by having soldiers in the nearby village. They go and light watch fires along the road leading up to the ruins and make random patrols throughout the general area. It gives people hope. The lancers couldn't stop the monsters any more than the hunts, but folks feel safe so long as they see an armed presence."

Kavan shook his head. None of this made sense. "There has to be more going on than we know. Think about it. A king whose only task is the welfare and continuation of his people, and he's doing next to nothing to keep them from being slaughtered? Why?"

"Who can speak for the mind of a king? Not me. Eglios does what he does for whatever his reasons."

"How many villagers have been killed by the werebeasts?" Aphere asked.

Mabane trembled. "Werebeasts? The demons of the underworld? We're not going to survive this."

"Leave that to us," Kavan told him. "Answer the question."

The drunk took a moment to get past the sudden revelation. Until now, the beast that had stolen his arm had been nameless, an abomination bereft of personality. "I'd venture hundreds, though the real number must be close to a thousand. They come and they kill and kill and kill. So much blood."

"Have any of the monsters been killed?"

"Some, but it takes many men to do so. Once one gets the taste for blood, it becomes nigh impossible to stop."

Mabane was on the verge of tears. They were about to lose him but still had many unanswered questions. Aphere took control, placing a tender hand on his shoulder. "Mabane, we've all killed one or more of these werebeasts before. Some not longer than a handful of nights ago."

His eyes lit up in wonder. Hope sparked. "How is this possible? Are you gods?"

She smiled sadly. "No, not gods. Just ordinary people trying to make a difference. We come from the land of Gaimos."

Gaimos. The name clicked in his mind, conjuring images of his father's time and the tales of war and bloodshed. Most of Malweir thought them cruel, malicious. The harbingers of death. That's why so many kingdoms had banded together. He suddenly found himself wondering if the world had been wrong all along.

"Gaimosians," he said. "You shouldn't be here."

"We go where we please."

"No, you don't understand. If word gets out about you, there will be trouble."

Aphere asked, "What makes you say that?"

"It is the same every time one of you arrives," he answered.

She stared back in shock. "Others have been here?"

"Several."

This was unexpected news. None of the four sensed another Gaimosian anywhere close. If there were others in Aradain, they'd learned to mask their presence.

"Where are they now? Tell us what you know," Kavan pressed.

"Gone. They came here just like you. Fools all, to think they could end the problems in the ruins. The king held big banquets and ceremonies. There was a parade the day before the Gaimosians headed north. What happened once they went down into the caverns, no one knows. Not a one was seen again. Not a one."

Kavan and Aphere exchanged worried looks. More was going on in Aradain than they had previously guessed.

"Thank you for answering our questions, Mabane," Aphere said as she paid him. "Please come back later. There is still much more we'd like to ask."

Mabane shamelessly accepted his payment and scuffled towards the door. Almost as an afterthought, he asked, "Just what do you have in mind?"

Aphere's look was resolute. "We're going to end the threat in the ruins."

"Then I'll be using this to pay for your funerals," he held up the purse.

The door clicked shut. Geblin closed his eyes and wished for home.

THIRTY-SIX

Allies No Longer

The ebony tower twitched ever so slightly under the raging winds. The night had an electric touch, as if the world knew what was coming next. Corso climbed the stairs. His mind was racing faster than he had the ability to process. Events were finally drawing to a close. He felt it riding the storms as the days crept slowly towards their extinction. The power of the dark gods strengthened. He'd never been this strong in his long, degenerated lifetime.

He wanted to smile but couldn't. There was still too much in need of doing. Foremost in his thoughts was the Fist. Pharanx Gorg and his band of cutthroat mercenaries had done their part, though it would have been better if they'd managed to eliminate some of the Gaimosians. As it were, Corso had much to dwell on. The Fist had become a problem and more trouble than they were worth.

Corso gained the upper level and paused.

"We don't like being kept waiting," Pharanx snarled.

A pair of guards flanked him. One was an Elf of extremely dark, almost grey, complexion dressed in purple and black. He wore a bandolier of throwing knives and had crossed swords on his back. The black moustache gave him an unsavory look. His sneer told Corso his inner thoughts. Dark Elf or not, he was no match for Corso's raw power. The second guard was just a man, probably from one of the northern kingdoms. The morning star hanging from his belt suggested arrogance all too common amongst the mercenary corps.

Corso looked up from his cowl. "I don't like wasting my time or money."

"We did what we could. Too many of my men were killed in this gambit," Pharanx pressed. His right hand rested dangerously close to his rapier.

Corso silently wished he'd draw. It would make his next task much easier.

"The losses are not worth what you are paying us."

"Don't over-inflate your importance in this matter. You were paid to bring me results. Results I have yet to see," Corso replied.

Anger flared in Pharanx's face. "My men died for nothing! The Gaimosians are too powerful. Then there were those beasts."

"What beasts?" Corso asked innocently.

"We were attacked outside of the Gnome city by some kind of predator. They were fast and ruthless. My men stood no chance."

"So the rumors are true."

"What rumors?" Pharanx asked.

"Nothing."

"Tell us, or I'll bleed you out on your fancy marble tiles."

Corso clenched a fist. It took all his might to restrain himself. "Very well. There have been tales of strange creatures coming from a site of unearthed ruins to the north. I'd thought these stories to be mere foolishness, but you confirm otherwise."

Pharanx spat on the floor. "Ruins and monsters are not my concern. We were supposed to be paid for rogue Gaimosians seeking to kill the king. You endangered my command recklessly. We demand double payment, and this contract is terminated."

"Choose your next words carefully, mercenary," Corso warned. "You're making me angry."

Pharanx and his men broke out in laughter. None of them viewed the crippled, hobbled old man as a threat. "Save your words for weaker men. We want what's coming to us."

Corso half whispered, "As you wish."

He flung his arms out. The world slowed to a sliver of normal time. A wave of impenetrable darkness pulsed from his palms even as the mercenaries rocked back on their heels, fumbling for their weapons. Eyes wide in shock, they watched helplessly as the black miasma washed over them with crushing force.

A thunderclap shook the world, and the blackness receded. Pharanx stood between twin piles of mangled flesh, blood, and bone. Steam rose from what remained of the corpses, drifting away into the chill spring evening. Pharanx, however, didn't suffer a scratch. Corso flung a bag of gold coins at his feet.

"Take your payment and leave this kingdom. Your kind is no longer appreciated here," Corso commanded.

"Those…those were my best men," Pharanx stammered.

Corso cast a wicked glare on the man. "Then you need better men."

"Sire, Minister Corso is here to see you," the page announced from the doorway.

Eglios continued rubbing his chin for a moment. He toyed with the notion of sending the page away without response. Corse was spending too much time in his presence lately, and it disturbed the king to great ends. Even so, it was difficult to tell the man no.

"Send him in," Eglios said with a dismissive tone.

Corso entered with his usual flourish. His crimson robes enhanced his disarming smile. Eglios rarely trusted a man who smiled at another. They either wanted something or were scheming. He figured it was a bit of both in Corso's case.

"What news this day?" Eglios asked.

"Nothing good, I'm afraid, sire."

His pained expression aroused suspicion.

"What now?"

"The Fist has failed. The Gaimosians are inside the city."

His one good eye narrowed. "What? How can this be?"

"The knights of Gaimos are renowned for their expertise in battle and subversive actions. They were simply too much for the mercenaries to handle."

The king raged. "You expect me to believe that a five hundred-man company couldn't stop four knights?"

"Sire, I —"

"We've been betrayed! I want heads, Corso. Pile them before my throne and you'll be rewarded."

Smiling to himself, Corso bowed. This was almost too easy.

"We must see to the Gaimosians first. I feel they are the greater threat. They could very well be planning on attacking the castle tonight. Your life is in jeopardy."

"They wouldn't dare. Not even a Gaimosian is dumb enough to kill a king in his own bed," Eglios scowled.

"These are ruthless devils," Corso countered.

"That may be, but they are not assassins."

"Are you willing to risk your crown on it?" Corso asked. "Remember, you have no heirs. The throne will fall to a nameless house and lead Aradain to ruin. All you have fought and struggled for will vanish without so much as a monument in your name."

Eglios slumped back into his throne. Defeat glistened in his eyes. "What should I do? I've worked too hard to let it end now."

"I suggest we take a different approach. These knights obviously know we are seeking them. We can use that to our advantage. Invite them in. Make them feel welcome and encourage them to become honorary champions of the hunt."

"And the creatures in the ruins will destroy them," Eglios concluded. "It might work, but how can we be sure they'll fall for it?"

"Their sense of honor, sire. Use it against them. Surely, they have heard the stories of how many innocent lives have been lost. Their vanity and arrogance practically demand they go."

"What of the Fist?"

Corso replied, "Brand them traitors and put a price on their heads."

Eglios' grin was savage. "Make it so. I'm glad you work for me, Corso. You'd make a vicious enemy."

Corso bowed again and excused himself. *At last*. The wheels were finally in motion. The dawn of the dark gods was quickly approaching, and he was about to reap the rewards from a thousand years of faithful service.

THIRTY-SEVEN

A Hero Falls

Rantis was awash with excitement. The hazy sun was barely in the sky, and word had spread through the streets that a handful of Gaimosian Knights had come from half the world away to rescue them from the demons in the ruins. Adding to that, constables and praetors hung posters decreeing the penalty for being a member of the black company of the Fist. The eclipse was ten short days away, not that the general population knew this or cared. The remainder of the week promised to be filled with excitement.

Huddled in a corner table in the common room away from the scattering of patrons, Kavan could only shake his head in disbelief.

"How did they find out?"

Aphere clenched a fist. "They must have spies watching our every move. But why? None of this makes sense to me."

Finishing his mug of coffee, Barum said, "It could be the Fist. From what we know of them, it seems unlikely they'll give up their hunt just because they are outlawed."

"True. They could be trying to draw us out, make us expose ourselves," Kavan conceded. He liked that option even less. That path meant a monarchy-sanctioned public execution. Mercenaries were one thing, but an entire kingdom was another matter altogether. What little he knew of Eglios and Aradain offered no suggestion that they were involved with external affairs. That meant one of the Fist had either gotten to the king or that Eglios himself was their employer.

Try as he could, Kavan couldn't find a single reason why a minor king should involve himself with a handful of forgotten people. So why? He asked himself the same question a hundred times and came with no conclusion. What motives could Eglios have for removing yet more Gaimosians from the world? He grew angry at the emptiness of any answer. Confusion threatened before realization dawned. Eglios wasn't the one. There was another, hidden in the shadows, pulling the strings. He slammed an open palm down on the smoothed over wooden table.

Aphere glanced nervously around the room before asking, "What are you doing?"

"It's not the Fist," he said.

"I don't follow."

Kavan explained as best as he could. Not having time to develop his thoughts, he often tripped over theories and assumptions.

"Who in Aradain has enough motive to want us dead?" she asked after he fell silent.

"That's the part that doesn't make sense to me."

"He does have a point," Geblin chimed in between bites of toast and bacon. Crumbs littered his shirt.

Aphere's eyebrow rose questioningly.

"Oh, come on," Geblin continued. "You can't tell me that you haven't felt herded since we crossed the plains. You mentioned being hunted several times, but what if we were being pushed in this direction? Whoever hired the Fist wanted us here in Rantis."

They stared with the combination of shock and respect. Three seasoned professionals hadn't been able to decipher the riddle while a relatively inexperienced Gnome had. Kavan looked upon him in a new light.

Geblin continued, "If I were you, I wouldn't worry too much about it. We have a bigger problem."

"That being?"

He smiled, his teeth crooked and stained yellow. "Where's Pirneon?"

None of them had seen the Knight Marshal since the confrontation on the first night. There was no telling what might have happened to him. The bond remained, meaning he was still alive and in the city. His ego may have been damaged, but, truth be told, he needed it. He'd been isolated from the rest of the world for too long. Pirneon had become his own law and executioner.

The pride of fallen Gaimos haunted them all, but none so much as the former Knight Marshal. He never spoke of it to them, but Kavan had learned Pirneon led the armies of Gaimos during their final stand. Ever since, he wallowed with conflicting senses of guilt and arrogance. Pirneon, more than any other surviving Gaimosian, wanted to see his kingdom reborn.

Kavan recognized the danger of that power and turned his back on it. He didn't need Gaimos. It was a myth he'd never known and a heritage he couldn't escape. Like many of his blood, Kavan eked out a meager living hunting bad people and monsters. He had a feeling this event was the culminating point of his trials. Sadly, Pirneon failed to see it so.

"He can take care of himself," Kavan said defensively.

Geblin shook his head. "That's not the part that concerns me. It's our necks if he does something foolish."

The knights glanced at one another. Visions of their future crumbling away danced just out of reach.

Pirneon ran his hand over the smooth flesh of Tamblin's thigh. She smiled in her sleep, encouraging him to continue. He found himself happy, content for the first time in years. All thanks to a girl who hadn't even been born when he was passing his prime. If only she'd come into his life sooner.

Stretching as he rose, Pirneon padded naked to the washbasin and filled it from a pitcher of fresh water. Sunlight streaked through the transparent lace curtains. He plunged his face into the basin. The cold water invigorated him. He hadn't felt this alive in decades. It took great control to resist crawling back into bed and taking her again.

Pirneon dried his face and hands and stared at his reflection in the wall-mounted mirror. Creases filled his leathered skin. Crow's feet, those telltale signs of aging, crowded the corners of his eyes. His beard and moustache were so grey they bordered on silver. The dozens of scars crisscrossing his chest and arms stood out pale white against his bronzed skin.

He'd felt used up until now. A growing part of his subconscious wanted to see the long years of strife and toil draw to a close, wanted to move on to the next life in the hopes of finding a better place. The handful of days he'd spent with Tamblin quieted those doubts. He now wanted to live like never before.

It wasn't only him. The very air felt electrified. He'd already listened to what the townsfolk were saying. How excited they were that the sons and daughters of Gaimos had come to solve their problems. At long last, he felt vindicated by genuine need. It was all he could do to keep from grinning from ear to ear. He was proud to be Gaimosian, and that pride would surely sustain him to the end of the day.

"Are you going to come back to bed and wake me properly or just stand there admiring yourself all morning?" Tamblin cooed.

He turned to see her naked form lying in wait. She was propped up on an elbow, exposing her breasts and side for his approval. She was everything he wasn't. Supple and comforting. The very smell of her was as an elixir. He felt desire growing as he ambled back to bed.

"What sane man could possibly keep away from your touch?" he asked as he slid on top of her.

She let out an impassioned sigh and wrapped her legs around his waist before hungrily accepting him into her.

Life seemed as if a dream, despite the potential impending disaster. Pirneon was alive, invigorated. His steps were lighter, quicker as they wormed through the crowds in the central market. Normally, he'd be seeking out potential threats or hazards. Today, he didn't care. He briefly entertained the thought of rejoining his comrades. Somehow, that didn't feel right.

It was good to be on his own again. He'd wasted too much of his life tied to the fates of others. Even Barum had been getting on his nerves of late. Since the fall of Gaimos, they'd been meant to be alone, working silently in the dark corners of the world. Between the four of them and that annoying Gnome, he'd felt stifled, handicapped in more ways than he cared to admit. Once again, it was time for him to strike out and make a name on his own.

"Pirneon, look at this," Tamblin interrupted his thoughts. She held a dress of purple fabric across her face. It was thin enough to display her curves. Lust stirred in his loins.

"I think you'd look stunning in that," he said.

In comparison, his long coat was drab and uninspiring. What it lacked in aesthetic value was more than made up in how well it concealed his weapons. Smitten as he was with her, he was still a warrior in a hostile environment. Pirneon was armed and ready for a fight should the need arise. He was about to say more when he spied sudden movement from behind one of the venders on the opposite side of the street.

Pirneon unbuttoned the bottom of his jacket and gently slid his hand closer to his sword. The movement, slight as it was, didn't go unnoticed.

"What is it?" she asked.

His eyes never stopped tracking his target.

"Nothing," he told her. "Keep shopping."

He made out three distinct targets converging from two sides. Pirneon judged them to be no more than common thugs looking for an easy score. None had the air of being part of the Fist. His hand clenched reflexively. This wasn't good. The situation didn't concern him so much as a much bigger threat. Too many people seemed to want him dead of a sudden. The thugs stopped a meter away and glared.

Pirneon faced the one directly behind him. He hardly noticed as the crowd began to thin. They recognized the problem and wanted no part in another murder. He took his enemy in, measuring him against all that had come before. The man had a foul odor. His clothes were torn and soiled. Overweight and dirty, he had a nervous look in his eye. Pirneon gave him a tight smile.

"Can I help you?"

The thug jerked a rusted dagger from his belt. "Give me your purse, and you and your lady friend can go."

"Come and take it."

The thug twitched, marking a certain wildness that made him unpredictable. Pirneon let out a calm breath. The fat one on his right was going to move first. The man in front was a decoy.

"Last chance, fancy man. You can't win, not against the three of us."

Pirneon stepped forward. "You and I both know that's not going to happen. You and your friends will be dead before you can flee. Leave now, and I'll forget I ever saw you."

Even as he said it, Pirneon knew they wouldn't back down. These men were either desperate or extremely well paid.

"Don't do it," Pirneon warned. "No matter what happens here today, you will be the first to die. Choose wisely."

The thug attacked before Pirneon finished talking. Fast as he was with his dagger, the Vengeance Knight was faster. Steel whipped free, cleaving through the thug's arm at the wrist. He screamed once before Pirneon spun and ripped his stomach open. Blood and bowels spilled to the ground. The thug fell in agony, thrashing and crying as death claimed him.

The other two wasted no time in attacking. Pirneon was off balance. He kicked out, his foot catching one of the rushing men in the stomach. The thug woofed and dropped his weapon as he reeled back. The second man stabbed. His blade sank an inch before Pirneon jerked back and regained his footing. Hot blood trickled down the knight's shoulder.

Compared to most of his previous wounds, this wasn't worth worrying over. He brandished his sword in a high guard and stormed at the thug. The man shrieked and ran for his life. He was too slow. Pirneon's sword ripped his back open from neck to tail bone. The third man was gone by the time Pirneon whirled to face him.

He was almost disappointed. He hadn't even worked up a sweat. With the threat passed, he bent down to the dying thug. Blood frothed around his mouth as the thug desperately tried to move. Pirneon shook his head and proceeded to clean the blood from his sword. The thug shuddered a final breath.

"That was incredible," Tamblin gasped.

He'd half-expected her to be overcome with horror. But here she stood, in awe and wearing a look of sheer adoration.

"I've spent a lifetime butchering men. These two weren't very good."

The crowds started to reform. People were eager to see his handiwork and afraid he might do it again. Gently, they eased in around him. All of it made him uncomfortable. His hand clenched his sword.

The fabrics vendor was the first to approach. He extended the purple dress with a warm smile. "This is for your lady, brave knight. Consider it a gift for ridding us of these criminals."

He accepted the gift with sudden uncertainty.

"You're one of them, aren't you?" A rather plump lady in a yellow dress asked. "One of those Vengeance Knights."

"Are you really going to rid us of the demons?"

"Our thanks and blessings to you, friend."

Tamblin snatched the fabric and hugged Pirneon fiercely. His heart soared as if freed from decades of self-repression. Finally, the name of Gaimos was about to be restored. He was a hero again, no longer perceived a murderer or convict. His smile was wide and fierce as he graciously accepted the offered praise and answered questions.

As before, Corso watched with interest from the shadows. The matching smile on his face widened.

THIRTY-EIGHT

Mabane's Choice

"Here's the first bag of caltrops," Phirial said, handing the sack over to Kavan.

He set the bag down and pulled one out, pretending not to notice how attractive she looked despite the lines of sweat and soot streaking her face and crimson hair. More than once, he'd found her to be the most striking woman he'd ever laid eyes on. He'd never admit it, but it was nonetheless true. If Phirial was aware, she cunningly kept it to herself.

Kavan was impressed with the craftsmanship. The five-pronged caltrop was razor sharp. They'd do their job well enough, providing it didn't rain and turn the ground around the cavern mouth into a swamp. He hoped the information Mabane had given them was accurate. Otherwise, they'd be walking into a slaughter tonight.

"Careful with those," she cautioned. "They're sharper than you think."

"I've handled these before," he said with a wry grin.

She offered a mocking smile in return. "I'm sure you have, but these are honed to perfection. Guaranteed to rip a horse's hoof to shreds."

"Perfect, but it's not horse I'm hunting," he let slip.

She froze. "You're going up there, aren't you?"

"Up where?"

Phirial waggled a stern finger. "Don't you condescend to me, Kavan. You and your friends are headed up to the ruins to meddle with those beasts."

"I don't know what you're talking about," he lied.

She laughed, the sound a golden song to his hears. "You're a terrible liar. Besides, it's unbecoming. A man of your stature is used to telling the truth and being honorable. I know what you are and what you're up to. At least, I think I do."

Kavan didn't know how to react. He found himself impressed with the young apprentice smith. Normally, he'd have cut his ties and disappeared for a while until people stopped asking about him. The situation in Rantis was unlike any he'd experienced. Word of their arrival had spread down to the lowest citizen, pushing the city into a fevered state. Whether they truly believed the knights had come to save them or were simply clinging to another hope remained to be seen.

Kavan looked deep into her emerald eyes and decided to take a chance. "Yes. We are the Gaimosians that everyone is speaking of."

"I knew it. No normal man comes in here asking for such a large order of weapons." She jingled the second sack. "Not like this."

"We're going to try and end the threat in the ruins," he said without knowing why. That was as much as he cared to tell her. The best thing he could do was redirect the conversation and keep her blissfully unaware should the wrong people come calling. They still weren't any closer to finding out who their true enemy was yet.

"I don't suppose you can tell me anything about it?"

"Who can't?" she answered. "That place is sheer evil, and only a fool would bother snooping around."

"Why do you say that?" he asked.

"Do you have any idea how many men and women have died doing exactly what you're planning? Hundreds. Those ruins are a path to the end of the world. All of them were victims of the king's hunts."

She didn't tell him anything new but confirmed facts. He felt the answers to all the riddles were close. He just didn't know how to unravel that key strand that would expose the truth. There were secrets here someone was trying very hard to keep. But who, why?

"Are you listening to me?" Phirial asked.

He jerked, taken off guard. "Huh? Yes."

She flashed a devious grin. "No, you're not. Your mind is already focused on getting your fool self killed. Eglios is planning a feast in your honor, did you know that?"

"He's doing what?"

"Word has gone out about one of you killing some brigands in the marketplace today. Eglios wants to honor the brave Gaimosians come to help Aradain."

Kavan felt sour in the pit of his stomach. He hadn't heard this. If what she said was true, and he had no reason to doubt her, Eglios was likely at the center of this mystery. It seemed that enemies were closing from all directions.

"We came to help the kingdom, nothing more," he stated.

"That's not what people are saying. They think you've come to seek glory on your own behalf. Some even hint at you usurping the king — the ones that aren't fascinated by your presence, of course."

He frowned. "We had a kingdom once, and it didn't turn out so well. You can keep yours. I came to kill monsters."

"I believe you," she said.

Phirial reached out and gently touched the back of his hand. "The ruins aren't hard to find. Ride north two hours on the old king's road."

"You've been there?" he guessed.

She shook her head. Crimson hair splashed smoothly over her shoulders. "We are discouraged from doing what you intend to, but the way is well known. Just follow the trail of bones."

He didn't need to ask her meaning. The prospect of seeing mutilated corpses and sun-bleached bones lining the path to Gessun Thune was expected almost as much as it was feared.

"I thank you for your advice, Phirial. Perhaps when we return, I can find some way to repay you?"

Kavan wasn't sure what made him ask. She was nice enough, but they'd only met three times. He had no doubts about his physical attraction to her. As much as he wanted to find out whether it was reciprocal, he became hesitant. Their odds of survival were grim at best, and he was loath to hurt her in the process.

"You must come back alive first," she told him.

He nodded once. The warmth of her hand felt good, good enough that he didn't shy away. "I should leave now."

Her eyes, soft and deep, whispered otherwise. "Will you come back?"

He asked in reply, "Should I?"

"You should if you expect to pay me for the rest of these weapons."

"Until tomorrow."

Kavan excused himself and left Phirial smiling.

Mabane was waiting in the room with the others by the time Kavan returned. He was nervous and jittery, more so than his usual drunken self. Aphere and Barum were busy strapping on their weapons and long jackets. Geblin sat asleep in a chair, his short legs propped up on the edge of the table. Spying the remains of a roast fowl and dark bread, Kavan sat down to eat.

"What?" he snapped between bites when he noticed Mabane staring at him.

"Nothing. It's just that we're all going to die tonight, and you want to sit down for a feast."

Kavan barked a laugh. "If I'm to die then it will be with a full stomach and a smile on my face."

"Relax, Mabane," Aphere said when he grew exasperated.

"How?" he fired back.

"Because we're not planning on getting into a fight tonight. All we want to do is go and look around a bit."

Mabane looked down at his feet. "Doesn't make a difference. Once they come out of their caves, we are all dead."

"Oh, shut up, already," Geblin cursed without opening his eyes. "I can't sleep around here. I'm finished with big people. If he makes this much noise out there I'm leaving you to your fates."

"Sort of reminds me of someone. I'm glad to see you had time for a nap," Kavan snorted.

Geblin's glare softened, if only just.

"Everyone calm down. Geblin is correct. You need to keep your mouth shut or we'll have no chance of success. Now, if we can manage to relax, it's almost time to leave," Aphere intervened.

Barum slid the last arrow into his quiver and smiled. There was much to be said for the direct approach. Still, it didn't quite make up for Pirneon's unshakeable leadership. He was a hard man whose demand for results often brought out the best and worst in his students. It was no accident that he'd been made the last Knight Marshal. Pirneon hadn't been seen for days now and, as worried as Barum was, he knew they were going to miss the old knight's skill in battle should it come to that tonight.

No matter what spin they chose to put on it, once the sun went down, the werebeasts were going to be out hunting. Only this time, it was the Gaimosians' turn to hunt them. There would be blood this night.

THIRTY-NINE

To the Ruins

The moon hadn't risen yet, leaving this part of the countryside under a shroud of impenetrable darkness. Heavy clouds choked the skies. Even if the half moon did come up before they entered the ruins, Kavan doubted it would do much good. Visibility would still be restricted. He knew from experience that werebeasts had better night vision, making them almost supreme nighttime hunters.

Leaving Rantis didn't pose much of a problem. The people tended to mind their own business when the sun dropped, especially after the killings began. There was a decided pall over the capital of Aradain. Kavan had little doubt that whoever was behind this growing nightmare intended on subjugating the entire population. Before their task was ended, he knew he was going to have to find that person and eliminate him.

They passed the last pair of unobservant sentries and continued north. Kavan got the feeling they were being followed not long after taking the king's road. He halted periodically to see if he could hear anything or catch the glimmer of movement in the growing darkness. Each time yielded nothing. He wasn't going crazy, but between them all, one of them should have been able to confirm his suspicions.

Geblin eased his pony up alongside Kavan. The Gnome had a sour look. It was the same Kavan remembered seeing back in the swamp. Not good, his eyes said.

The knights rode on, Mabane whimpering from his spot behind Barum. They'd feared he'd turn and run if he had his own horse, leaving them in a tight spot. Kavan had all but tied him to the saddle. Sober and terrified, Mabane was in no condition to help himself. The faces of those who had died the day his arm was taken haunted him. Too many times, he was forced to squeeze his eyes shut and burrow into Barum's back as they inched closer to the ruins.

Barum suppressed his scowl and kept riding. He was angered by the decision but understood the necessity. A grown man scared witless could have easily overpowered Geblin and betrayed them all. Even so, his most valuable weapon was rendered useless as long as Mabane rode with him.

The road was relatively smooth and easily traversable. Built long before Eglios, the road was one of the most advanced in the west. Kavan was impressed and would have been more if he'd never visited the great cities in the east. The ground gradually sloped up, the terrain becoming rugged. Vegetation died away as if wiped clean by some dark plague. Fragile bits of moonlight at last escaped through the cloud cover to deliver glimpses of a violent landscape where all life had died. Bones were sprinkled among the rock and stone.

I hope the oracle was right, or this is all for naught.

The clip-clop of hooves drummed a lonely beat. It was the only sound in the still of the night. Not even the wind had the courage to blow here. Kavan halted them a half an hour later. He turned to see Barum pointing to the edge of the next rise. Kavan nodded and slipped from his saddle. He drew his sword as Aphere and Geblin followed him. Only Geblin had one of the ordered crossbows. Phirial and Nik hadn't been able to finish the others in time.

Kavan helped Mabane dismount and then pulled him close. "Are you certain?"

"Yes, just over this rise," he whispered.

"Keep him here, and keep him quiet," Kavan ordered Barum.

The squire nodded. "For how long?"

"Two hours, and then we head back."

He didn't say more. He didn't need to. If they weren't back in two hours they would be dead. The trio set off with grim looks. At last, after weeks and months on the road, they were finally about to lay eyes upon a place of nightmares. Kavan crawled up the slope, spying the glow of torchlight flickering below. They weren't alone. He stayed the others and moved a little closer to investigate.

The area below was beyond ruined. Broken pillars lay strewn everywhere. Time and the elements had not been kind. Any decorations had long since worn away from the handful of buildings above ground. His gaze was drawn to the far side and the gaping mouth of the cavern entrance. Torches lined the path, giving him concern.

At first, Kavan didn't see anything. He focused and looked harder. Two werebeasts lurked just inside the cavern mouth, as if they were pulling guard. They were killing machines, but he wouldn't have thought any power could make them tamable. Were the knights already too late? He didn't dare risk attacking and possibly disturbing an untold number of creatures within. Kavan turned back before he was caught

He'd barely taken a step when his boot slipped on a trickle of loose pebbles. Kavan slid nearly twenty feet down the slope before he managed to stop. By then, it was too late. A howl rang up from the ruins. He cursed his carelessness. It wouldn't take the werebeasts long to find him.

"Back to the horses," he growled through his teeth.

Geblin readied his crossbow.

"What is it?" Aphere asked. She was already on her feet.

"Werebeasts. Two of them."

Another howl rang out, haunting in the gentle glow of torchlight. A second followed quickly, but from a distance. They'd been discovered. Small clouds of dust marked the werebeasts' passing. The howls grew closer. Kavan knew there wasn't any more reason for stealth.

"Run!" he shouted.

There was still a hundred meters separating them from Barum and the horses. They weren't going to make it. Heavy footsteps shook the ground. Geblin let out a startled cry as the werebeast leapt over the rise, fingers and claws extended. Tripping over his own feet, Geblin fired as he fell. The shaft struck the werebeast in the shoulder with a sickening thud.

Kavan shouted again, "Barum! Your bow!"

The squire was already ahead of him. He loosed the first shaft and had a second nocked before Kavan opened his mouth. Mabane knelt, cowering at Barum's feet. He held his hand tightly to his face. Tears streamed from between fingers. Mabane was so engrossed in his own terror that he failed to see Barum's arrows strike the werebeast in the center of the chest.

The force of the impacts drove the beast from its feet, sending the massive body tumbling down the slope end over end. Kavan didn't hesitate. He charged down after it, bellowing ancient Gaimosian battle oaths. He heard the signature snapping of bones. The very sound boiled his blood into a rage. Kavan jumped down onto the fallen monster and attacked.

Sword stabbed and slashed. Claws raked the air in a desperate attempt to survive. Blood and fur flew upwards. Kavan's assault was furious with no signs of slowing. He stabbed down a final time with all the strength he possessed and was rewarded by piercing the werebeast's heart. It convulsed once and let out a hideous, almost human rattle before dying.

Kavan struggled to his feet, knowing the second beast was near. "Quickly. There is another."

He and Aphere broke into an open run before noticing Geblin limping.

"It's just a sprain. Don't worry about me," he said as Kavan returned for him.

The second werebeast exploded from the shadows just as they gained the horses. Fortunately, Geblin was short, and the beast sailed over him as he dropped. His pony gave a strangled scream as the werebeast bowled it to the ground, wasting valuable time ripping out the pony's throat. That mistake proved costly. Aphere and Kavan took turns hacking it to pieces. The werebeast died without a sound.

Knowing time was short, they cross-loaded the equipment from the dead pony and helped Geblin into place behind Aphere.

"We must flee before more come," Kavan told them. "Back to Rantis, now."

The Gaimosians took off into the night, leaving the dead rotting behind.

FORTY

Audience with the King

"We've caught and executed another three Fist mercenaries," General Moncrieff told the assembly.

Corso offered an obligatory smile. Three fewer souls capable of ruining his plans.

"Surely those damned Fist will have taken the hint and left Aradain by now," Eglios said.

"Yet they have not," Corso added.

The king slammed a fist on the table. "How many men do we have to kill before they give up?"

"Milord, the Fist are as relentless as they are ruthless. It could be necessary to slay them to the last," Moncrieff stated.

Moncrieff was a bear of a man. He had a massive barrel chest and thick arms and legs. His salt and pepper hair was closely cropped. He had a hard, unforgiving face. Moncrieff was every bit the soldier. He'd paid his dues, starting as a junior ranker and working up through the ranks. When, at last, he'd made general, Eglios had used him like an iron rod. The victory over neighboring Barduk was heaped upon his shoulders while doing little to serve Moncrieff's interests. He was the type of battlefield leader who found victory in how few men he lost, not treasure or glory.

"Drive them from my city. Push them back across the Spine. I want them to fear the kingdom of Aradain, and Eglios."

"Doing so may prove more difficult than we previously believed. Most have already gone underground, splintering into small cells."

Corso added, "Milord, the Fist no longer have valid reason for remaining in Aradain. I fear an assassination attempt is imminent."

"They wouldn't dare. I am the sitting monarch of a rising kingdom. My death would spark a purge on scales unimaginable," Eglios sneered.

Moncrieff grunted. "The Fist are ruthless. Regicide would not be below them. If they have already targeted the throne, there is but one way to stop them. Let me send hunter teams throughout the kingdom to wipe them out."

"I don't feel that is wise," Corso cautioned.

Eglios glared down on his minister with menace. "Interesting advice considering this is all your fault. You brought these mercenaries here and then lost control. Were I a lesser man, your head would be on a pike in the corner of my throneroom.”

Rage echoed from the walls. It was at that moment Eglios realized he'd been complacent for too long. The time had come to retake his kingdom and become the ruler his father had envisioned.

“General Moncrieff, I want these assassins out of my kingdom,” he ordered in a threatening tone that left little to the imagination.

Moncrieff bowed. “Is there any particular method you prefer?”

“Kill them. Arrest them. I don't care which. Just drive them from my borders so we can return to the task at hand.”

Eglios turned his back on them and gazed longingly out the window. Saluting sharply, Moncrieff spun and left.

“You're still here,” Eglios said after hearing the clang of shutting doors. “I figured you'd be in a rush to leave.”

“There is one more matter requiring your attention.” His voice was calm, measured.

“That being?”

Corso cleared his throat in a false display of submission. “The Gaimosian knight will be here shortly.”

Eglios turned. “Which Gaimosian? You've overrun my kingdom with murderers and fallen warriors. I'm beginning to think you're trying to depose me and steal the throne for yourself.”

Corso ignored the barb. “The knight who stopped the robbery in the marketplace. He should be here shortly.”

“To be proclaimed a hero of the realm,” he smirked. “I want him thoroughly checked for weapons. He does not enter the palace grounds with so much as a dagger.”

“Sire, we should consider using him to our advantage.”

Eglios paused. He was a practical man at heart as well as an aspiring politician. Times often dictated the path of his career. Wolves prowled the shadows of his kingdom, forcing him to act now. “This plan of yours leaves great doubt,” the king admitted.

“All plans have inherent fallacies. You are forgetting that no one has yet to return successful from the ruins. This is almost too perfect.”

“Your scheming will be the death of me yet,” Eglios said after a moment's thought. “Very well. Bring him before me. I'll have his audience and then a great feast to reassure the people. You can take him after that.”

Corso bowed shrewdly. “As you wish.”

“Oh, and Corso,” Eglios called as his advisor walked away. “After tonight, I don't ever want to see that man alive again.”

Corso finally let his thin smile crease his face. “Naturally.”

Pirneon spent the better part of the day preparing for his audience with the king. He felt good finally being recognized, though grave trepidations lingered with the banquet. His last invitation hadn't turned out very well. The prospect of being honored won over reason, however. He'd been forced to live in the shadows for too long. Once again, the glory of Gaimos was given the chance to flourish. Pirneon relished the thought of speaking to the monarch. As Knight Marshal, he'd met countless politicians and ruling kings. Most wound up turning on him before the end.

He hummed softly to himself as he meticulously polished his sword and armor. Tamblin had helped trim his lanky hair and beard. Being with her made him happy, an emotion he'd feared was lost to him. For the briefest amount of time, he felt alive. He'd forgotten about his comrades and their foolish quest based on an oracle's whim. He occasionally missed Barum, ever the faithful and diligent squire. Barum was going to make an excellent knight. Just not at his side.

Pirneon made one of the most important decisions he could have. It was time to cut loose the trappings of his old life and become the patriarch to a new dawn. Destiny commanded he rise to a man of greater importance than the pitiful shell he was now. Smiling broadly, he fondly recalled his last kiss with Tamblin and marched to the palace.

A quad of armed guards, the king's finest, met him at the grounds entrance to escort him through the stone halls of Castle Aradain. The captain of the guard, a thin, pale man with gaunt features, proceeded to have him strip away his weapons. Pirneon did so, albeit hesitantly. Any nerves were calmed with the knowledge that a Gaimosian Knight was a weapon in itself.

"Wait here while I announce you," the captain said. When he returned, Pirneon caught the sly look in his eyes. "Enter. The king of Aradain awaits."

Pirneon strode past with an air of arrogance. That was all he could do in the situation. Weaponless and braced for treachery, Pirneon fully expected a repeat of his time in the Jebel Desert. He walked confidently into the throne room. Back straight, shoulders arched and chin held high, he showed no trace of coming from a vanquished people.

Eglios, Corso, and Moncrieff watched as the Vengeance Knight marched into the throne room. General Moncrieff snorted his opinion. His decades of experience stretched only so far in making him comfortable, especially considering the squad of crossbowmen concealed throughout the room. He looked to the others. If they were impressed, neither showed it. They sat. They watched. They waited.

Finally, Corso eased forward. He was all but a snake in his coal black robes. "Pirneon of Gaimos, Knight Marshal and honored guest of the kingdom of Aradain, I present you to our lord and liege, King Eglios."

Pirneon halted at the foot of the alabaster throne and bowed crisply. "My lord, it is an honor to be in your presence."

Eglios gestured with his right hand. "Rise, Knight Marshal. It is you who honor us. My cabinet tells me you had a part to play in stopping less than desirable deeds in the marketplace. My thanks to you for protecting my citizens."

"Order is the basis upon which the principles of Gaimos were founded. There can be no peace without order," he replied matter-of-factly.

"Indeed. These are perilous times threatening to subsume us all. I'm sure you have heard by now that we are under siege by dark powers?"

"I have, and I also come to bring tidings of hope to the people of Aradain. I have traveled far to fight these fiends. While I shall not bore you with tales of my journey, know that it was perilous and filled with many of these monsters you face. Sire, I am no stranger to their brand of evil, and I have come to pledge my services in the defense of this kingdom, should you have me."

Eglios listened with half-hearted interest. The words were all lies as far as he was concerned. He struggled to keep from ordering Moncrieff to kill him now. But a king must show compassion when often there is none.

"We gratefully and humbly accept your service. Perhaps this quest shall go a long way in the healing process between the kingdoms of the west," Eglios said eloquently and rose. "Tonight shall be a grand banquet in your honor. There has been need for celebration of late. I believe our citizens will rejoice to have a true hero among us. In the meantime, I would ask that you meet with my minister, Corso, and General Moncrieff, commander of my armies. They can fill you in on all that has transpired to this point."

All parties exchanged obviously pained bows. Corso led them away from the king after being summarily dismissed. Eglios had much to consider before the banquet. He trusted no one, especially Corso. More and more, the minister gave the impression of harboring devious intent. That little fact gave him cause for concern over Moncrieff's loyalty as well.

A dark plan hatched on his way back to his chambers. He'd heard of such a thing being done before, mostly rumors of great men willing to sacrifice for the greater good of their lands. Peasants often referred to such men as tyrants. Eglios shook his head. They were all close-minded people too absorbed in their trivial lives to understand. Yes, he decided, perhaps the leadership of Aradain could stand for a purge.

FORTY-ONE

Plans Within Plans

"I should never have agreed to come along on this damned fool quest," Geblin growled between gulps of ale. "I've near been killed a dozen times over and haven't stopped looking over my shoulder yet! Now this!"

He pointed at his bandaged ankle. It was sprained worse than they had previously though. Kavan insisted on fixing it properly upon their return to Rantis. To his credit, the Gnome kept his pain silent. He'd never admit it, but the oracle's words meant more to him than anything he'd ever been told. They gave him renewed purpose, a sense of belonging in a world that had been intent on abandoning him.

Despite all that, he cursed and growled more. "Look at this! I can't even put a boot on. Just how am I supposed to fight like this?"

Smoldering embers of rage echoed behind his hazel eyes.

Kavan rolled his eyes, lost in thought over the events of the night prior.

"Relax, Geblin," Aphere chuckled.

Geblin stared her down. "Easy for you to say. I don't remember seeing so much as a scratch on you…from last night."

"I'm willing to bet I have more scars than you can imagine. Besides, who says you have to fight? The oracle said each of us was important. He never said how."

Geblin grimaced and returned to his drink.

Barum entered a short time later. His face was twisted with worry. Fortunately, the common room was empty. People's attentions were focused on the grand banquet hall, not a handful of misfits keeping to themselves.

"What?" Kavan asked.

"I've found Pirneon."

Aphere leaned in from across the table. "Where?"

"He's being hailed by the king. Word is he killed a few thieves and is now being considered a hero of the realm."

"For killing thieves?" Kavan questioned. "That doesn't sound right. They must be up to some scheme."

"It seems he's proclaimed himself the Knight Marshal of Gaimos and come with the intent of relieving Aradain of the werebeasts. I think he means to go to the ruins alone."

Fear edged Barum's voice.

"Pah!" Geblin snorted.

"He'll be killed," Aphere exclaimed before remembering where she was. "We have to stop him before it's too late."

Kavan rapped his knuckles on the table. He regretted getting them involved on this quest. He should have lived up to his title and done this alone. "How? Pirneon is a good man, but he's stopped listening to reason. He's changed somehow along the course of our journey. He's not the man who taught you, Barum. Not any longer."

Aphere protested. "We have an obligation to protect our own."

"He abandoned us. Destiny has a place for us all. Ours lies separately."

They mulled the concept in silence.

Aphere broke the mood and asked, "What's our next move?"

Kavan shrugged. "I don't know. The rest of the weapons should be finished tomorrow. That gives us six days until time runs out."

"The situation isn't quite as perilous as the desert was," she replied. She was tired, almost lost. A small part of her wanted to cave now and rejoin Kistan on the shores of Thuil Lake. The loss of the Knight Marshal and his denouncing of her abilities drained on her hope reserves.

Barum looked at her quizzically. "In what way?"

"We know who our enemy is."

Kavan disagreed. The werebeasts were a convenient scapegoat and surely responsible for multiple deaths, but they had to be controlled. Someone was holding their leash. The question failed to produce answers.

"The monsters have to come from somewhere."

"Could it be the nexus is already opening? Releasing them into our world?" Aphere asked.

"I don't see how. The dark gods are supposedly locked away for all eternity."

"That means they have agents here in Rantis," Barum said.

"Making our task more difficult," Kavan added. "We not only have to fight werebeasts but find this agent before it's too late."

"I knew it!" Geblin cursed. "You people are going to be the death of me. I need another drink."

"Speaking of drinks, where is our drunk friend?" Aphere asked. She was anxious to change the subject, lest those demons continued crawling up her spine.

Kavan gave a half-hearted smile. "Passed out in the room, I imagine. There's no way he can get out."

"Unless he breaks the door down."

"Or goes out the window," Geblin added.

Aphere laughed. "After the other night, I wouldn't put anything past him."

"Damned near had a heart attack," Kavan said.

They sat and drank for a while longer. Conversations never ranged back to Gessun Thune or the dead. They tried to think of mirth and old times, when all of this was unimaginable. Geblin remained true to form, griping the entire time. In his own way, the Gnome eased tensions. Eventually, all talk faded, and they decided to retire to their rooms. Kavan was about to push away from the table when a dangerous looking man entered.

His demeanor gave the Gaimosian pause. He was a killer. Two more entered behind and took flanking positions. Definitely killers, Kavan decided. He dropped his hand down to his sword and waited as they stalked toward him. The first man took a seat across from Kavan and stared hard.

"You the Vengeance Knights?"

Kavan stiffened. "I'm sorry, but you're mistaken."

The leader laughed. "You killed enough of my men for me to know otherwise."

"Fist," Aphere exclaimed from the stairwell and reached for her sword.

"Stay your hand, Gaimosian. We didn't come here for a fight."

"What do you want then? To taunt us before resuming your bounty?" Kavan asked.

"Nothing of the sort. My name is Pharanx Gorg, captain of the Fist. Yes, we were hired to kill you...."

"Didn't do a good job of it," Geblin mocked.

Pharanx bit back on his anger and continued, "Our motives were purely monetary. We're mercenaries, not assassins. You were just a job. That contract is now absolved."

Kavan didn't particularly care. "You've come to make nice? Is that it? I can recall killing at least five of your men myself."

"As I said, we are not assassins. Matters have changed here. My people are being hunted down, killed where they stand. Rantis has become an evil place," Pharanx explained.

"We know all of this," Kavan replied. "Do not come to us seeking forgiveness. There is none to be had."

Pharanx smirked back, finding a sudden liking for the character of the man he'd hunted for weeks. "Perhaps you should let me explain what has transpired since your arrival in Aradain."

He waited until he had their full attention before continuing.

"There's no reason for him to be telling us the truth," Aphere cautioned.

Kavan sat on the small cot, hands in his face, hoping to take away some of the compounding stress. A lifetime of hardship told him it was a futile gesture. "What choice do we have?"

They'd left the common room shortly after the Fist commander finished his tale. Naturally, their first instinct was to discount everything the mercenary said. They'd been mortal enemies until this point. Kavan had his own doubts towards the situation. The tone in Pharanx's voice and his demeanor whispered truths. Not for the first time during this ill-advised adventure he found himself mired in confusion.

"This is a dangerous game we're playing, Kavan," she continued. "There is too much intrigue, even for us."

"I thought you said this was less dangerous than the desert?" he brought up in a lame attempt at humor.

"What I said has little meaning anymore if this Fist is telling the truth. Do you really thing the king is involved?"

Kavan shrugged. "Possibly. Either way, our list of enemies has changed again. The whole of the kingdom may well be in league with this mystery advisor."

"I wish Pharanx had been able to give a name," she said.

He forced a laugh. "That would make it too easy."

She agreed. "What's our next move?"

"I go to check on the weapons in the morning. You and Barum see what you can learn on the streets. If this plays out right, we'll ride out to meet with Gorg at dusk. I have the feeling we're going to need as much help as we can get."

He bade her good night and retired to his room. Sleep was a long time in coming.

FORTY-TWO

Phirial

Phirial swept the floor in the main showroom with a smile on her face. Thoughts of the dashing Vengeance Knight entertaining her. Her father was in the back, stoking the furnace for the day's work. Every day was the same grueling process. They started not long after sunup and finished well after dark. She occasionally snuck dreams of a different life but was never able to figure out what it would look like. Working with her father was honest but trying. It made her stronger, a well-balanced woman.

That balance had shifted immeasurably when Kavan strode into their shop. She'd taken an instant liking to his handsomeness. While he was the best-looking man she'd seen, he also had a charming demeanor. She caught herself wondering what was beneath those worn clothes more than once. Every time Nik asked why her cheeks were flushed, she passed it off as heat from the furnace.

Phirial knew today was just another in an endless stream, except for Kavan coming back to check on his order. She'd gone to great lengths to wash her hair and find a dress both appealing and practical for working in the forge. Nik, for his part, knew exactly what she was up to. He remembered being smitten with a young lass on more than one instance before meeting her mother. Happiness was hard to come by in these dark times. His only concern stemmed from her being hurt. He'd lived almost a decade without his lovely wife, and the loss continued to pain him every day. Nik prayed to the gods that they kept her well.

"Come, now, father," she told him merrily, "Our customers should be here soon."

He hid his smile. "It's just another sale, Phirial. There's nothing special about these blades. Is the front clean?"

"Spotless," she confirmed.

He could say what he wanted, but she knew the truth. They'd spent more hours on these weapons than any other. It was as if the blades were being forged to serve higher purpose. Phirial was proud of her father's dedication to his craft. Though Kavan might never say it, she knew he was going to take those blades up to the monster pit and rid Rantis of them once and for all.

Nik nodded once. "Good. Now finish those inventories before they arrive. I expect these people to take their merchandise and leave soon enough,

214

but what I don't want is to be caught short. There's two extra sacks of caltrops and about a hundred crossbow bolts in the back."

"I'll go and put them by the counter," Phirial volunteered.

Her father grunted his approval before returning to the forge. Plunging the cast iron poker into the smoldering coal, he figured they would be hot enough to work with by late morning. Nik felt old today. He watched the embers with limited interest. Lethargy settled in. He wasn't sure why. On the contrary, his life had been going well recently. Demand for his products boomed with the announcement of each hunt. So what was the problem now?

He didn't have an answer. The question never changed, though. He'd been asking himself the same thing since his wife's death. None of his success bore meaning. If it hadn't been for Phirial, he was convinced he would have taken his own life. She was all that was important to him now. Nothing else mattered. If he didn't have her….

Nik let the thought pass. More important issues consumed him these days. His biggest concern came from the Gaimosians. Until a few days ago, his business had been filled with glory seekers and bounty men. He wasn't sure what to make of the Gaimosians yet. The old stigma applied. Having so many in Rantis would eventually lead to trouble. He exhaled slowly and went to work. Life was always simpler with a hammer in hand. The Gaimosians would come, take their weapons, and be gone. With any luck, that is.

She knew she was wrong for acting like a smitten teenager hoping for her first kiss. Phirial spent half the morning scolding herself and the other half-stealing peeks out the front window. Nik knew better than to interfere with the affairs of a woman, even one so young as his daughter. Glad her father chose to leave her alone, Phirial grew restless. Where was he? The question burned. She cleaned and cleaned again in frustration. At least her struggling desires produced positive results. She was almost about to give up when she spied Kavan's confident swagger marching down the street. Less than an hour had passed.

Kavan entered the smithy with his casual smile and bowed pleasantly. He tried not to let her see how his eyes drank in her beauty. That would have produced much embarrassment on both sides. No doubt, her father had a sword nearby in the event the knight grew a little too familiar. That scenario had played out too many times in the past, and he had no desire to live through it again. Phirial was in her mid-twenties and capable of making her own decisions, or so he hoped.

"Good morning," he said.

She returned his smile. "Good morning to you, Sir Kavan."

He winced. "Please, there is no sir. I'm just a man, much like your father."

The bitterness in her smile lessened. "My apologies. Were you able to test your new weapons?"

"We had a fair demonstration, yes."

"Are they adequate?"

He nodded. "More than adequate. We're looking forward to seeing the rest of them soon."

"You and the woman?"

There was no mistaking her meaning. Phirial was jealous of Aphere. Kavan tried to keep from rolling his eyes. This was the last thing he needed. Both were attractive. Where one was innocent and sweet, the other was a trained killer with a seldom-seen vulnerable side. He no longer held illusions about Aphere. His feelings had shifted to Phirial. What he didn't need was any jealous interference that might jeopardize the quest.

"Aphere, yes," he confirmed. "She is a Gaimosian Knight, as am I."

"I see."

Point of fact, she didn't see, and she was already hard at work on figuring out how to make him hers.

"Is your father in?" Kavan asked, suddenly uncomfortable with the conversation.

"He's in the back. I'll fetch him for you."

He watched her go with new interest. The way her simple dressed hugged her curves was enough to stir the fire in any man. Phirial was truly a lovely woman, one he might even see himself settling down with once this nasty affair was ended. Kavan let his gaze shift to the weapons lining the back wall. Each was exquisitely crafted, the sign of a true master. Nik and his daughter were thoroughly dedicated to their craft, speaking volumes for their work.

Nik emerged, wiping his hands free of the charcoal stain. "Phirial tells me you approve of my work."

Kavan shook his hand. "Indeed. We're anxious to get the rest. Your skills are perhaps among the best I've seen in all Malweir."

"Your words honor us."

"I merely speak the truth," Kavan replied.

Nik nodded. "The rest of your order is complete. I've thrown in a few extras for good measure. I'm guessing you'll be needing them."

Kavan produced a small purse and handed it to Phirial. "The money is all there, including a little extra for you having to rush."

"Thank you," Phirial chimed in.

They exchanged smiles.

"I don't suppose you'll change your mind," Nik probed.

"It's much too late for that."

Nik scrubbed his chin. "Never did have much use for destiny. I've always believed men make their own futures."

"I wish that were so. The gods have other ideas for some of us."

"You Gaimosians sure are an odd lot. I'll give you that."

Kavan stifled his laugh. "Can you blame us? We've been to the mouth of the black pit. The enemy rests deep inside in unknown numbers. There is more, however. I think you and Phirial should leave Rantis. It's no longer safe here."

"Where would we go?" Phirial asked. She was more startled than anything.

"Anywhere but Rantis. The streets will run with blood, and soon," he said with reluctance.

Eyes narrowed suspiciously, Nik asked, "What cause would you have in saying that? The hunt is almost upon us. This might be the last one."

Kavan picked up the hidden meaning immediately. "We didn't come here for your kingdom. What's left of my people are scattered across Malweir. There will be no rebirth for Gaimos. I assure you."

He wanted to say more, wanted to tell them how he believed Eglios might be involved in the plot to free the dark gods. It all sounded ridiculous, even to him. Two months ago, he'd been trying to make an honest living when he'd heard a drunk mention Aradain and monsters. Part of him felt like riding back south to confront that drunk. Kavan sighed. Doing so wouldn't produce any worthwhile results, though it might make him feel better.

The bigger problem stood before him. He genuinely liked the blacksmith and his daughter. Good people were hard to come by. Malweir was a dangerous world filled with all sort of wicked creatures and bad men. These two deserved a good end to a happy life. If Eglios was indeed involved, there would be terrible retribution in Aradain. Few would survive the coming slaughter. Those who did would spend the rest of their lives in slavery.

"How can we be sure? Everyone has heard tales of your kingdom, your bloodthirsty ways. You can't honestly expect us to believe you have our kingdom's best interests at heart."

Kavan was taken back. He hadn't come expecting to be attacked. Years of solitude helped calm his anger and prevented him from launching into tirade against Nik. After all, the man was a simple blacksmith trying to do what was right for his family. Men like this were usually ignorant of the ways of the big world.

"We came to end the werebeast threat. Nothing more. Besides, not even three Gaimosians can capture an entire kingdom," he told them. "Although we do have a very precocious Gnome in our midst."

Even stern Nik chuckled. "Very well. I don't suppose we have any choice, do we? Your weapons are ready and wrapped up. Take the extra quivers and sacks of caltrops. Werebeasts or soldiers, you're going to need them."

Sad as his words were, Kavan felt Nik's sorrow. Too many innocent people had already died for the crimes of a few. Now, it was all about to happen again.

"Don't make me regret my decisions," Nik told him and then returned to his forge.

"If we survive, you will be well compensated," Kavan assured him.

His words fell on deaf ears.

Phirial waited expectantly. For all her father's strong words, her mind was already set. "My father is a proud man. He's spent many years living with the grief of losing my mother. He just wants what is right for me."

"I respect that," Kavan said.

Phirial placed the purse in their moneybox.

"You're not going to count it?"

"Should I?"

He shook his head.

"Good," she smiled. "I knew you were an honest man. Would you like some help carrying all of this to your horse?"

"It would be a pleasure," he replied.

They loaded the packhorse, taking care to cover the weapons with a riding blanket lest the city patrol run across them. Kavan didn't know how deep the treachery stretched, and he wasn't about to take chances now — not so close to the end. Six more days were all that remained before the moon ate the sun. She gave the horse a soft pat on the neck.

"I don't suppose I'll ever see you again," she asked.

Would she? He didn't know. He wanted her to. Gods knew that he did. But a romance in the middle of the brewing storm wasn't the wisest course of action.

Holding the reins, Phirial stepped closer. "You didn't answer my question. Could it be nerves?"

Kavan swung up into the saddle and took the reins. "In the morning, perhaps I can come and call on you. I haven't been able to see much of the city I'm fighting for."

Phirial smiled and went back inside.

FORTY-THREE

Corso Rising

Dusk settled over Rantis. From the confines of his official offices, Corso watched the explosion of colors raging across the sky. Blues struggled to survive against the onslaught of red, yellow, and orange, all being driven by the gathering darkness. This was his favorite time of day. The death of each day offered the promise of the rise of his masters. With the night, so, too, came the gods. With the dark gods came the promise of unimaginable pain and cruelty.

Corso stood with his hands clasped behind his back and watched the day die. The illusion of perfection shattered with the heavy knock upon his door. Irritated, he squeezed his eyes shut. Hundreds of years imprisoned among these peasants, and he was still forced to suffer them. Corso whirled on the door.

"Enter!" he barked.

The massive oak door swung open, and a man in simple emerald robes hurried in. Bald, without brows or eyelashes, he bore the look of a man unused to being out in the open during the light of day. His boots clinked across the polished marble floor. He stopped a meter away and submissively dropped to one knee.

Corso's anger subsided, albeit slightly. "Report."

"Master, the Gaimosians are moving. I caught their new leader, a man named Kavan, visiting one of the local blacksmiths on several occasions. This morning, he left with a horse heavily laden with new weaponry."

"They could be preparing to join the hunt," Corso theorized. He almost felt foolish for suggesting such a thing.

The spy lowered his head. "We thought so, too, at first."

"But?"

"The Fist commander has made contact with them."

So, Pharanx Gorg has sought out the Gaimosians. This is an unexpected turn of events. "When?"

"Early last night. He and two others approached the knights in one of the local inns. They spoke for a time, and both groups parted."

The spy was clearly uncomfortable. He'd heard rumors of too many men in his profession disappearing after delivering an unfavorable report to Corso.

"What did they discuss?" Corso pressed. He was too absorbed in his thoughts to worry over the pathetic life of his spy.

Bowing lower, the spy said, "We caught whispers of an alliance and something about an abandoned fortress to the north of Rantis."

Kalad Tol? What significance lies there? The old fortress had been the original capital of Aradain when the first king broke away and declared his freedom. That was two hundred years ago, and no one had used it since. At least no one from the kingdom. Thieves and outlaws often holed up there to wait out the king's justice.

"This could work to our advantage," Corso muttered. He turned his back to finish watching the sunset. "Take your men and move on the smith. Burn it to the ground and kill any you find within. Make it look like an accident."

"Yes, master. The Gaimosians?"

Corso almost laughed. "Those few killed over fifty of the best mercenaries in the world without sustaining a single casualty. What makes you think you stand a chance? No. Leave them to me."

"Yes, master."

"Leave me," Corso snapped.

The door clicked shut.

Corso began to feel nervous. Gaimosians. The Fist. Moncrieff. The nexus. It felt like the world was tearing apart in several directions. He was almost paralyzed from making a move out of fear. What if he made the decisions and the dark gods weren't freed? An eternity of torment and misery awaited his soul. It took many long moments of deep thought before he made up his mind.

His first move would be against Pirneon. The Knight Marshal was by far the biggest threat. With that obstacle removed, Corso knew nothing could stand in his way. Hopefully, Moncrieff would keep the Fist and Gaimosians occupied in Kalad Tol long enough for the eclipse to pass.

Yes, Corso decided, it would begin with the former Knight Marshal of Gaimos. He changed back into his robes of state and went in search of the general. The time had come to make his move.

Tamblin collapsed on top of Pirneon. She was out of breath and covered in a sheen of sweat. Her hair was a mess while her eyes bore a distant look. Most importantly, she was thoroughly satisfied. Locks of blond hair dangled over his face.

"That was incredible," she managed between gasps.

He was in no position to argue. When she finally slid off him and onto the cool silk sheets of their king-sized bed, he made his way to the washbasin.

The room he'd been given in the palace was a bit hot but otherwise fit for a king. Certainly deserving for the Knight Marshal. He looked back at the beautiful woman lying in his bed and felt satisfied for the first time in seventy years.

"I can't believe I'm actually sleeping in the palace!" Tamblin exclaimed. "Me, a plain old serving maid."

Pirneon sat on the edge of the bed. "This was one of my conditions to the king."

She gave him a look of flat disbelief. "Are you serious?"

He lazily traced the line of her thigh muscle. "This is the first time that I've been truly happy. I owe it all to you, my sweet Tamblin. You've given me my life back. For that, I can never repay you."

Her arm snaked around his neck, and she pulled him close for a deep, passionate kiss. Soon, he was on top of her, and the sounds of their lovemaking echoed through the room.

Pirneon opened the door with the hostility of a man who didn't want to be disturbed. Naked, he stared down at the palace servant.

"My apologies, lord," he said, "but Minister Corso has requested your presence."

"For what?" Pirneon asked, secretly glowing at the honorific.

"Such is not my place to know. He and General Moncrieff await you, and I am to take you there."

Pirneon wasted no time in thought. "Very well. Wait here while I get dressed."

"As you wish."

"Ah, Knight Marshal, we've been awaiting you," Corso said with a fake smile.

He was one of three people seated around a massive wooden table littered with gouges and cuts from idle knives. Pirneon immediately felt that the size of the table made their gathering inadequate. It was a scenario he'd seen many times before. Little people trying to act important. Pirneon ignored the comment and took the remaining chair. He ignored Moncrieff and the other man.

"What is this about?"

Oddly, the third man kept his head down, refusing to make eye contact.

"We've decided that the time has come to strike," Corso explained. "Our enemies are gathering, though it's of no real concern to you. The threat in the ruins must be dealt with first."

Pirneon wondered what Corso meant by enemies. Every kingdom had foes, but Corso was right. It wasn't his concern. He'd come to end the werebeast threat. The rebuilding of Gaimos became a side quest, but one suddenly obtainable.

Corso continued, "What is important to you is the fact that the ruins will be unwatched. We can arm a small group and slip inside, forever stopping the monster threat to Aradain. With the monsters eliminated, our armies can move on the Fist and crush them at last."

"The Fist?" Pirneon asked, his interest suddenly piqued.

Moncrieff growled. "Those bastards have been plotting to kill the king and take over the kingdom. Our spies have just brought word that they're holed up in the ruins of Kalad Tol. I'm taking the army to put them down."

"I've had my experiences with them as well. I had not heard of their designs to conquer your kingdom, however," Pirneon said.

"Malweir is a dangerous place, as I'm sure you are well aware, Pirneon. Do not concern yourself with the Fist. Our army is enough. You and I, along with a small detachment of special guards will depart before dawn. Entering the pit is always safest at first light."

Pirneon leaned forward to study the faded map laid out on the table. Advancing on a position without proper reconnaissance sat ill, almost making him wish for Kavan and the others. Then his old arrogance returned, and Pirneon knew he would be better off alone.

"Do we have any idea how many werebeasts are within?" he asked.

"No. There have been few survivors from the hunts. It is murder on a grand scale. We estimate several dozen, though," Moncrieff added.

"A noble task. I will do what I can to end your nightmares or give my life trying."

Corso stood and clapped. "Very well. We meet at the stables one hour before dawn. Then we shall truly see what happens beyond the edge of dawn."

"Until the morning," Pirneon excused himself.

There was much to be done and little time in which to prepare. Moncrieff departed right after, for he, too, had much to plan. He felt the most alive out of them all. A professional soldier, Moncrieff reveled in the sudden chance to defend his kingdom and protect the crown.

FORTY-FOUR

Kalad Tol

The tiny band of Gaimosians rode into the crumbling ruins of Kalad Tol under the watchful eyes of the Fist. Dressed in their traditional black camouflage, the mercenaries were almost invisible to the unsuspecting eye. Kavan counted heads the closer he rode. He didn't like the circumstances or trust the Fist, but he felt like he was left with little real choice.

As agreed, the Fist scouts met them on the outskirts of Rantis and guided them back to the ruins. They'd been instructed not to speak, especially not to answer any questions. Gaimosians were dangerous allies and worse enemies. Should both parties survive the coming fight, they might easily turn on each other. Kavan welcomed the silence, patiently taking note of defenses, personnel, and access points.

"That's far enough," Pharanx Gorg said from atop the battlement.

"Tell me again why we're doing this?" Aphere said.

Kavan kept his eyes locked on the Fist commander. "To improve our odds of surviving. I don't think it will come to a fight but be ready just in case."

"You hope," Geblin added wryly.

His people had only been attacked because of the Fist. The enemy might never have found them otherwise.

Pharanx stepped down to greet them. "I have to admit, I didn't think you'd actually come here, all things considered."

"Trust has to begin somewhere. At this point, we should all be worried about our necks," Kavan said.

"Agreed. Shall we go inside? I fear prying eyes might be curious."

Men came up to take their horses to the stables. The smell of roast meat hung in the air. Fires burned in many parts of the main courtyard, giving warmth to those men not fortunate or high-ranking enough to get a spot in the barracks. Aphere spotted stacks of weapons placed along the walls and counted more than a hundred sleeping men alongside them. The Fist had claimed these ruins as their own, for the time being. This made them more than enough of a threat for any field army willing to break on their walls. She had little doubt that the stores were fully stocked and the coffers filled. A freshly dug well and numerous construction areas confirmed her suspicions. The Fist intended on making this a home.

Kavan said, "You're not planning on leaving, are you?"

"We have had to change certain plans," Pharanx admitted. "This is, in fact, the first time since I joined the Fist that we have founded a base. Surely you can see the need for a large, powerful mercenary force to not be bogged down in one place for too long."

"You won't be able to hold off Aradain's army for long," Aphere commented.

Pharanx gave a polite smile, the kind suggesting he knew more than he was willing to discuss. "We'll hold long enough against Moncrieff. It's the other one that worries me."

"What makes him so dangerous?"

They hadn't gotten to discussing the mysterious benefactor during their last meeting, leaving Kavan mired in confusion. He knew, without doubt, that the man responsible for hiring the Fist in the first place was behind most of the trouble plaguing this kingdom.

Pharanx faced the Gaimosians. "He is altogether evil. I can see it in his eyes. The very air around him suffocates with it. My men fear he practices foul magic."

As much as he'd been wanting confirmation, Kavan felt icy shivers ripple up his spine. "A sorcerer?"

"Worse," Pharanx said. "It'll be a day of celebration when he is finally struck down."

Aphere suddenly understood. "That's why you're still in Aradain. For him."

His expression took a sudden violent turn. "He betrayed us and sent my men into a slaughter. I want his head. Honor demands such and so much more. He'll find the true meaning of suffering when next we meet."

They entered the command center where a modest feast was laid out in welcome to the Gaimosians. Officers and senior sergeants busied themselves with maps and reports. A portly man with dark hair stood off in the corner arguing logistics with a man half his age and clearly his superior.

"Don't mind them," Pharanx said. "Sergeant Mapin often gets excited about his work. But come, I've had my adjutant prepare some food and drink. I always find it easier to conduct business on a full stomach."

Geblin hobbled to the table. "A mug of ale would warm me up, that's right. But this will work."

"Help yourself. Between you and me, Mapin is also an amateur brewmeister. It's one of the few indulgences we get."

The Gnome took his first sip and immediately felt like he'd been punched in the gut. He gagged, eyes watering. His throat burned in protest. He expected smoke to come out of his nose and mouth.

Pharanx laughed, deep and hearty. "My apologies, but I did say he was an amateur. It only burns for the first few mouthfuls. Two or three glasses, and you won't remember your name, little Gnome."

Talk quickly turned serious. The Fist leadership converged on the main table to listen and add intelligence to the battle briefing.

"It is a tower of the darkest obsidian less than an hour south of Rantis. That is the source of his power," Pharanx explained.

Kavan studied the map, gauging the distance from Kalad Tol to Gessun Thune and then back down to the obsidian tower. "No one has tried to sack it yet?"

"The forest is protected by unnatural creatures. Some say they are born from the very bosom of the old gods." Pharanx spoke closer to the truth than he knew. "The entire area breathes of evil. I will not risk my men to do so. No. Our best chance is to catch him alone and in the open. I've had men watching him and his associates since they turned on us."

"How many?" Aphere asked.

"Why?"

She exhaled mild frustration. "Because there have been public executions of some of your men over the past few days. Special army squads constantly patrol the city in search of anyone affiliated with the Fist."

All conversation stopped. Until now, it had only been a whisper they refused to believe. Aphere didn't like everyone staring at her, or being the bearer of bad news, but she was a Gaimosian Knight. Such was her solemn duty.

"I'm sorry," she added softly.

Pharanx frowned. Others began whispering frustrations.

"I suspect they've rounded up many more, innocent men, and charged them with being Fist as well," Kavan said.

"That would explain why so little word has reached us. I took a great risk by coming in search of you. He must be preparing to strike."

"It's much worse than that," Kavan added.

"What do you mean?"

"There will be an eclipse in six days. Your benefactor will attempt to open the nexus, a path between dimensions, and free the dark gods from their prison. All Malweir is in jeopardy."

Pharanx paled. "How would you know that?"

"The Oracle of Wenx told us," Aphere said.

Another bout of murmurs spread through the room. Pharanx idly traced one of his facial tattoos in thought. "The oracle."

"How can this be?"

Only Geblin remained smug. He almost enjoyed seeing so many humans rendered speechless. Forget that he had felt the very same way in Wenx. The decision to stand and fight had never been difficult. He'd feel better in the underworld knowing he gave his all for friends and family. It was a small comfort. He sat and watched the mercenaries to see how they would fare under the same condition.

"I've heard legends of the oracle," Pharanx said. Clearly, he had difficulty assimilating this new information. He'd never signed up to fight gods. "His words are to be revered. This changes everything."

"Not for us," Kavan replied.

"I don't follow."

"We came to Aradain to put an end to the threat in the ruins. We've been charged by the oracle to stop this evil and keep the dark gods in their prison. This is a task appointed solely to us. All we needed was to know who their agent on Malweir was. Thanks to you, we do." Kavan decided now was the time for a good, strong drink. Or even a bad one. He filled his mug.

Pharanx joined him. "What's your plan?"

Kavan struggled to swallow the bitter liquid. "We had thought of charging down into Gessun Thune and sealing it off. The oracle only confirmed our quest, not the method."

"Attacking the pit is suicide," Pharanx said. "Eglios has held more than a dozen of his hunts. Some of the bravest men in this part of the world died down there. You risk your lives foolishly."

Kavan already knew that. "That's not entirely true. We have a guide who participated in one of the hunts. He took us to the ruins two days ago."

"You Gaimosians are a dangerous breed. All your plans are based on not knowing who to direct your attack against. When will you change?"

Smiling, Kavan wished he had a better answer. "Our goals are the same. We both want this madman stopped. I propose an alliance, at least until this mess is done."

"An alliance?" Pharanx stared back wide-eyed. "The Fist normally works alone."

"I don't think either of us have a choice," Aphere said. She was more than willing to have the small army of mercenaries at her back — anything in order to survive.

"She speaks true. Very well, an alliance is formed, but on condition," Pharanx told them. "When we catch this man, I get to be the one who slits his miserable throat."

"Done."

The door burst open, and an Elf dressed in black, worn leathers entered, out of breath and disheveled. His eyes were wild. Fist members crowded in behind him, eager to hear what had him spooked.

"Calm down, Pelios. Take a breath first," Pharanx said.

The Elf obeyed, finally regaining his stoic composure. "Moncrieff is assembling an army. They're coming here."

"When?"

The word was measured, fatal.

"Two days, maybe less," Pelios replied.

Kavan ran a hand through his hair and sighed. "Are you certain this is not just part of the coming hunt?"

Pelios noticed the Gaimosians for the first time and stiffened. They had been the enemy the last he knew. Pharanx caught his eye and shook his head. The Elf relaxed, if barely. "No. The army doesn't gear up for the hunts. We overheard some of the soldiers mention an assault on Kalad Tol. They're coming here to annihilate us."

Kazme jerked his sword from Nik's corpse. The assassin looked around the forge while his men ransacked the place. Blood dripped down the blade, landing on his boot. Kazme snarled and stabbed the body again in frustration. He'd just bought these boots.

"Where's the girl?" he said menacingly.

"We can't find her. She may have left before we had eyes on this site."

Not likely. He'd timed his attack perfectly, waiting until the last lamp went out before breaking in. The old man had put up a mediocre struggle before dying with a blade through his belly. The redhead was nowhere to be seen. Corso was not going to be pleased. Kazme briefly gave thought to killing him companions and burning the bodies, but that would be a waste.

"Burn it," he commanded. "Burn it to the ground and turn this city upside down. I want her found and dead before dawn."

They began spreading the embers. Cries arose a short time later as flames spread to the neighboring structures. Nik's smith burned to the ground.

FORTY-FIVE

Grief

The trip back to Rantis was fast, uneventful. The only thing out of ordinary was the unusual amount of traffic on the roads. Bounty hunters, mercenaries, and adventurers began their pilgrimage to Rantis and the great hunt of King Eglios. All came seeking glory in one form or another. Most would find only death. The Gaimosians avoided them. Times were foul, and these additional people would only get in their way.

Little could they know that, at the same moment, Pirneon was finishing the last of his hot tea while preparing for his own hunt.

By the time they arrived back at the inn, all were exhausted. The sudden increase of long nights followed by troublesome days left them in need of a large bed and hot baths. Kavan trudged up the stairs with barely enough strength to unlock his door. What he saw then was beyond reckoning.

Phirial looked up from Mabane's embrace. Tears had stained her face. She saw Kavan and rushed into his arms. Mabane wiped his own tears.

"I didn't know what to do," he said weakly.

Kavan wrapped her in his embrace, whispering soft words of soothing.

"It was horrible," she sobbed.

The others filed in. Barum closed the door and worried.

"They killed him, Kavan," Phirial cried. "They murdered my father."

Aphere immediately crossed to the window and scanned the streets below. Barum drew his sword and waited in the event the enemy was about to ambush. Kavan felt a piece of him break. *Not her. Not her too.* Geblin climbed onto the low bed and struggled to hide his tears.

"Phirial, I know this is hard, but we need to know who did it," Kavan attempted to soothe.

"I don't know. Three men broke in. My father pushed me out the back and went to stop them. I wanted to stay. I wanted to...."

She broke down completely, all but collapsing in his arms. Kavan felt torn. His feelings for her threatened to overcome a lifetime of soldiering. He wanted to grab his sword and find those responsible. Duty came first. He stood, Phirial in his arms, helplessly trapped between duty and heart. All he could do was hug her tighter.

"I see one hiding in the alley across the street," Aphere confirmed. "They tracked her here."

"Unless we've been watched the whole time we've been in Rantis," Barum suggested. He kept an ear to the door, listening for boots.

Kavan put the facts together. "It has to be Eglios. With the army getting ready to move, the king needs to shut this city down."

"Once his enemies are removed, nothing can stop him," Aphere concluded. "The whole kingdom will be against us."

"We must leave immediately." Kavan's words bore finality.

Mabane glanced up. His reluctant help had become a death sentence. If indeed they were being followed, he knew he wouldn't last the night. "What about me? They'll kill me as soon as you leave."

Kavan fixed him with a hard stare. "You come with us."

"But...."

"Unless you care to fill a hole come dawn. We have allies in the countryside. It'll be safe enough for the time being." Even as he spoke, Kavan knew the words weren't entirely true. He had no idea how large a force Moncrieff was assembling or how hard they planned on hitting Kalad Tol. Still, a few hundred mercenaries offered better protection than a handful of knights. There was still a chance.

"We should go now before others come. Use the hunt for cover and head straight for the fortress," Aphere said.

Kavan nodded. "Pack. We leave at once."

Phirial stopped crying long enough to look up into his determined eyes. "What about me? I have nothing. They took it all."

"Our first stop will be the forge. Collect what we can and —"

She cut him off. "They burned it down. I have nothing left in my life, Kavan."

His eyes watered, genuine tears that hadn't been shed in many, many years. "You have me."

There is was. His decision made. He'd committed to her safety and whatever hardships that entailed. Kavan didn't bother looking around to catch the open-mouthed stares from the others. Even Mabane jerked back in shock. He knew what he'd done the moment he'd said it. He just prayed the complications didn't prove too much.

Barum cracked the door to check the hall. It was the middle of the day, an unlikely time for any attack. That didn't prevent the knights from using caution. The man who had hired the Fist very much wanted them dead, giving Kavan little reason to doubt that had changed recently.

"Clear," Barum said.

Kavan pointed. "Move."

Easing the door open, Barum slid into the hall and hugged the wall as he made for the stairs. The others filed behind with Kavan pulling the rear guard. He wondered how they'd come to this. A hobbled Gnome, a drunk, and the daughter of a dead blacksmith. Life had been so much simpler a few months ago. Lamenting old grievances wouldn't change anything, so he focused on the now. He'd been thrust into the leadership position, and it was now his responsibility to keep them alive through the coming storm.

He sighed. Once they reached the horses, their chances would improve considerably. Combined with the diversion he planned; the knights should be able to exfiltrate the city undetected. Kavan decided there was no point in concealing their true nature. They advanced with weapons drawn, enough to deter any fool looking to score a quick bounty.

Kavan tossed the room keys as well as a small purse filled with silver coins to the frightened innkeeper and watched as Aphere led the others through the kitchens to the modest stable in the rear. Satisfied, Kavan headed for the front door. There was never a doubt about what he intended. He decided to sheath his sword so as not to draw undo attention. He walked confidently into the crowds without being recognized. The crowds provided camouflage, allowing him to slink across the street. He caught sight of his target and grinned.

The risk was relatively small. Kavan was counting on the lookout not paying attention. The gap closed. He figured the lookout was searching for Phirial and would fail to notice him until it was too late. Kavan palmed a dagger as he neared. With a quick movement, the three-inch blade drove between ribs to puncture the heart. He let out a strangled groan before collapsing in Kavan's arms. Kavan wasn't satisfied until he watched the eyes roll back into his head and smelled the fresh urine spilled down his trousers. He dropped the body in the alley with the dagger still embedded.

"Any problems?" Aphere asked after he rejoined them.

Kavan mounted his horse. "No. It was fast."

Phirial caught the drying blood on Kavan's sleeve. Hate burned brightly in her eyes. "I hope you made him suffer."

Her words spit vehemence. No amount of bloodshed would be enough to erase the pain of losing her father. Kavan empathized with her but lacked the comforting words she needed. He'd never been particularly compassionate, seldom feeling anything remotely comparable to sympathy. He merely nodded and rode forward.

"Was there any sign of more?" he asked Aphere.

"None that we're aware of. Mabane knows a back way through the city. We should avoid contact, at least until we gain open ground."

Mabane looked serious for the first time since joining them. He wasn't sure where his life was headed anymore. Death loomed ever closer, a fact he had once accepted and, oddly, looked forward to. He knew he should have died long ago. Perhaps that would have been best, but time and foul memories conspired to reinstall his will to live.

"The way leads through some of the housing areas. Patrollers are about the only ones who ever look there. The army is forbidden, or at least they used to be."

"The army has no reason to know who we are yet," Kavan deduced.

That was not entirely true. Pirneon had somehow been subverted and could well have given the enemy a fully report on why they'd come to Aradain. Kavan struggled with this concept. Gaimosians were many things but not traitors to blood. More distressing, Kavan couldn't feel the Knight Marshal any longer, and he didn't know why.

"Where is everyone?" Barum asked.

Mabane answered, "More likely at the grand parade. Eglios has one in honor of the brave souls come to attend the hunt. It's a small concession, all things considered. There's food and drink, whores of all sorts, and a festive environment. None of it really matters."

They made their way through the virtually deserted housing area. Stray dogs and cats stared back from trash piles or empty alleys. Actual people were few. They heard the muted bustle of activity in the business district announcing the opening procession of the hunt. Kavan frowned with disgust. The entire charade was developed to keep the population from learning the truth of Gessun Thune. The enemy hid his work in plain view. With so many dying at the hands of werebeasts, the ruins had been turned into the center of a great many fears. No one in their right mind would dare go there, making it the perfect scenario.

It took almost no time before they reached the gates and were out onto the winding road through the bogs. Kalad Tol, and their fates, awaited.

FORTY-SIX

A Dream in Ruins

Pirneon stood atop the small rise gazing down into the mouth of the black pit of Gessun Thune. He felt no fear, no hesitation. All his life had been a series of trials pushing him to this moment, the culmination of every despicable deed and hardship suffered in the name of his vanquished kingdom. Chest filled with confidence, he mentally prepared for battle. Both his sword and senses were sharp. He'd never been more ready. The first cracks of sunlight were streaking into the night sky. He paused to watch and thought of happier times.

"It will be safer once the sun rises," Corso told him.

Pirneon nodded. He'd been told the same repeatedly during their trek to the ruins. He was a man unaccustomed to taking advice, tired of suffering lesser people. Arrogance demanded satisfaction. Only he had the ability to destroy the werebeast threat permanently.

"What sort of numbers are there?"

"None know for sure," Corso lied. "The monsters sleep during the day, almost in a state of hibernation. They won't impede you."

He stared deep into Corso's eyes in search of deceit. "Where will your men be positioned? This needs to be executed quickly and with precision."

Corso had brought six men, all acolytes of the dark gods.

"They'll be stationed on either side of the opening. I'll accompany you."

Pirneon scowled. "I didn't come here to fight alongside anyone. We tried that on the path to Aradain. It was a terrible mistake. Gaimosians are meant to work alone."

Corso smiled politely. "I'm afraid it's not that simple. The werebeasts are creatures of dark power. I alone have the knowledge to counter that. You will need me to extinguish the source and win your war."

"The source?"

"All of these creatures stem from a single source. Legends say that they rest at the heart Gessun Thune. It is that source we must find and destroy."

He failed to mention anything about the nexus, or dark gods, leading Pirneon to question Corso's integrity. Pirneon naturally assumed the source was the key to finding and destroying the nexus. It was a simple task.

"Very well, Minister. Do us both a favor," Pirneon suggested. Corso folded his hands in front of his waist. "Stay out of my way. I don't want your blood on my hands."

"Indeed. I shall keep that in mind."

Grunting his approval, Pirneon then asked, "May we begin? Daylight has broken."

"Take up your positions. Do not let anything out alive," Corso ordered his disciples. "If we don't return by nightfall, see to yourselves lest you join us in oblivion."

"There will be no such ending," Pirneon snapped. "Come."

He led the way into the valley with sword in hand. Corso followed at a reasonable distance, smiling wickedly the entire way. He'd come to hate Pirneon in their short time together. The man's arrogance was his undoing, a sad state that had led to the ruination of an entire kingdom. *No wonder Gaimos was destroyed.* He focused his thoughts on luring Pirneon into the alteration chambers where magic would run its course. Only then would Corso be able to complete his task.

Pirneon demanded silence once they left the slope. Corso's six men slinked into position, putting on a show of being afraid. They hid in the rocks and waited. Mildly satisfied with their amateur professionalism, Pirneon turned to the gaping maw just ahead. The very air reeked of evil, stifling, with murderous intent. He choked on sulfuric fumes sprinkled with brimstone. This was unlike any place he'd ever experienced.

Nothing lived. The ground was moist, almost disgustingly soggy. Mold covered the rocks and boulders. Pirneon tied a scarf over his lower face. Then he spied the greenish mist pulsating from deep with the cavern. He spared a glance at Corso, who feigned ignorance. Together, they crept into the cavern.

Pirneon caught the erratic drop of water from somewhere in the gloom. The sound echoed loud enough to cover their footsteps. He smiled savagely. Every little advantage brought him a step closer to the end and the glory he deserved. The oracle had been wrong to choose Aphere and her vile taint. Once he finished with the werebeasts, he decided he would seek out every twisted Gaimosian and cleanse the bloodlines.

His suspicions arose suddenly when he failed to spot any bones. Hundreds of men had come down here, yet there wasn't the slightest hint of remains. The werebeasts were carnivorous, but he had never met an animal who feasted upon bone. He tightened his grip on his sword, fully expecting an attack to come at any moment.

The path was midnight black and restricting. He could feel the walls slanting in on them. The only source of light was the strange green mist. Pirneon began to feel misgivings. Something was wrong here, but what? He disregarded the feeling as superstitious nonsense; after all, the gods had fallen here. He pushed deeper until the path began to widen.

The mists deepened. Claustrophobia subsided, just. Pirneon found he had room to swing his sword, the only truly important factor concerning him. Corso a step behind, he traveled deeper underground. Overwhelming dread awakened, building to the point it threatened to consume him. There was nothing natural here. He had a host of questions needing answering, but Corso was determined to remain recalcitrant.

Eventually, they came into a massive cavern, awash in the green glow. They stood at one end and gasped. Pirneon could make out the remains of dozens of buildings. It didn't seem possible, but Gessun Thune had once been a city. *What foul manner of creature once dwelt here?*

"This was once the home of the Edaas," Corso whispered, coming alongside him. Pirneon eyed him sharply. "Death cult of the dark gods."

Pirneon reeled. The oracle had been right all along. Pirneon was now the true hand of destiny. His mind swirled, lost in the cyclopean vision of the future. "What happened to them?"

Unseen in the mist, Corso's face hardened. "There was a crusade, similar to the one against Gaimos, to exterminate them. Kings and nobles banded together to destroy the Edaas. Only a few managed to escape, just over a thousand years ago."

"The ones who did have carried on that legacy," Pirneon guessed.

"And once again, Malweir stands on the brink of the abyss."

Pirneon wasn't satisfied. "What is the connection with the werebeasts?"

"No one knows. They only began appearing two years ago."

Pirneon didn't like the answer but knew there was little he could do about it. Corso was proving to be worthless.

"We're wasting time, Knight Marshal," Corso hushed. He knew Pirneon wasn't ready to accept the truth, wasn't ready to learn how evil had adapted through the centuries. It was time to prod.

"There!" he exclaimed.

Pirneon followed his finger. "What?"

"To your right. See where the glow is brightest? There rests the source."

"How can you be certain?"

"The ancient scrolls in the library mention it," Corso lied again. "It must be the source. Quickly, before it is too late."

Pirneon sat alone at a small corner table. The common room was mostly empty. An elderly couple sat in front of the gently cackling fireplace. A group of young men were opposite him, playing some sort of dice game. Empty chairs filled the rest of the tables. He ate a hearty meal of roast lamb and spring potatoes, finishing it with a mug of local ale. The taste was weak but didn't stop him from ordering another.

"You look sad," the serving girl said as she replaced his empty mug with a full one spilling foam over the sides.

"Most people are, in my experience," he replied.

She flashed a grin. "Nonsense. Life is what we make it. You can't live with regrets. They'll only eat you up inside."

"What's your name?"

"Tamblin."

He returned the smile. "I'm Pirneon."

"Pirneon? I've heard that name before."

His smile hardened. "It's common enough where I come from."

She shook her head. Blond curls whisked over her shoulders. "Not around here. There's some kind of myth wrapped around your name. I just can't remember. Some great warrior, or something. Oh well, I might remember before the end of the night."

Tamblin walked away with the empty mug, leaving him in a better mood than he'd been in for a long time. He watched her leave. She was certainly attractive enough, if a tad plump. Her long hair was of the purest gold, outstanding against her pale blue dress. Her smile could melt ice. Pirneon found himself suddenly at ease. It was an odd feeling, to be sure, but one he was interested in developing. He decided to take the rest of his meals here rather than with his quarrelsome companions. At least in this place he was welcome.

Tamblin glanced over her shoulder once more before slipping into the kitchen. She set the mug down by the washbasin and slipped out the back door without being seen. The alley was dark, inspiring an inkling of fear even though she'd walked it several times before. A hooded man emerged from the darkness, blocking her path.

"Well?" he asked.

She trembled slightly. "I got him interested, just like you said."

"Will he return?"

"I think so. His face lit up when I mentioned the great warrior bit. He'll be back," she said.

Tamblin caught the small purse tossed at her.

They slipped through the ruins. Pirneon scanned the cracks and shadows for signs of the enemy. Surprisingly, the way was clear, prompting new worry. Where were all the werebeasts? They should have at least been aware of the humans' presence by now. Pirneon began to sense a trap, but it was far too late. They had almost reached the glow.

A ring of shattered columns lay in ruins surrounding the glow. Bright green light shot straight up from the ground. The opening! Pirneon felt his blood go cold as he gazed upon the gateway to another dimension. Through here, the dark gods threatened to break free.

The air was suddenly hot. Sweat ran freely down their bodies. Pirneon felt miniscule. For the first time in his life, he felt inadequate. This place was death itself. He took a reluctant step forward, searching for something to strike. A lodestone. Anything that might signify the power of the source. The only threat came from the glow. His first instinct was to shy away.

Suddenly, the glow took on life. It pulsed the closer Pirneon got. The Gaimosian took that as a good sign, for the nexus knew he was here to kill it. He took another step, but it became sluggish. His footsteps were heavy, lethargic. Tentacles of mist circled around his legs. His thoughts became clouded. Pain spread from up his feet. He tried to turn but was rooted in place.

Corso watched with a wild look. Realizing he was betrayed, Pirneon struggled to reach him, to throttle him quickly, but he was caught. The first howl shattered the stillness, followed by dozens more. Pirneon's sword dropped. He was caught helpless in a trap. His eyes widened with genuine fright as werebeasts of various shapes and sizes started crawling into the ruins. The creatures ringed the area and watched. Pirneon had been tricked from the beginning. Corso was the enemy he'd rushed blindly to fight.

"Corso!" he raged.

Corso waited until his prey was surrounded, not that he needed additional security. By now, Pirneon was hopelessly trapped in the poisonous gas. Casually folding his arms across his chest, Corso joined his pets. Pirneon watched in horror as the monsters parted and bowed reverently to their master.

"Poor, poor fool. Only now you begin to understand," Corso began. "It was me all along. I pushed you where I needed you to go from the very beginning. That part was too easy. Your arrogance became my greatest strength."

The pain reached Pirneon's groin. "Why?"

"I've waited a thousand years to free my masters and take revenge against the sons of the usurpers. My agents helped cause the fall of your beloved Gaimos. Yes, it was your people who led the war against the Edaas, my kin. What better revenge to take than with the blood of Gaimos?"

Sharp pains lanced Pirneon's stomach. He gritted his teeth.

"You, Knight Marshal, are going to be the instrument of their final demise. But not like this, oh no, not in this form. The magic of the nexus requires the strongest soul to open or close it."

"I won't help you," Pirneon grunted through the pain.

His body suddenly felt…wrong. As if it was changing. His muscles spasmed violently. The very blood in his veins caused him intense pain. Realization crashed like breaking waves upon the rocky coast. This was impossible.

"You understand now, don't you? The mystery of the hunt is at last solved, but too late to save you. The Edaas learned how to turn men into beasts long ago. These werebeasts have done my bidding for a millennium. Eglios was fool enough to supply me with a steady stream of fresh specimens."

"How?" Pirneon struggled.

Corso shrugged. "There's no point in not telling you. You'll become my willing slave as soon as the transformation is complete. Then you shall serve my will and bring about the end of the world. You really were no different. Seducing you was just as easy as playing on Eglios' emotions. But for you I took a different approach. What better gift to give a man than what he didn't have?"

He paused, turning suddenly. "You may come out now."

A slight figure in black robes eased forward. Pirneon felt his soul shatter as Tamblin removed her hood, grinning malevolently.

"She's been my servant since I found her as a child. I knew you wouldn't be able to resist. Her charms are…quite remarkable, aren't they?" His finger gingerly traced the curve of her jaw.

Pirneon renewed his efforts to escape, but his body revolted. Sharp pain consumed him, hungrily devouring him from the inside. Corso's laugh echoed throughout the cavern.

"You won't remember this, but the pain will be extraordinary. When next we meet, you'll kneel before me and swear fealty.

Corso walked away, Tamblin in tow, leaving Pirneon to his demise. The werebeasts gathered closer and watched as their ranks grew yet again.

FORTY-SEVEN

The Hunt

Rantis was alive. Trumpets and drums boomed loudly over the roar of the gathered crowds. The smells of roasting meats filled the air, enticing hungry stomachs. Today was the commencement of the hunt, what the people hoped was the last. Knights, squires, bounty hunters, soldiers, and the average man seeking glory filled the palace parade grounds, close to three hundred, in all.

The people cheered as the parade lurched forward, winding through the city. Flags and pennants waved from the tallest buildings and most windows. The heroes drank it in. Never before had any experienced such a sendoff. Most had barely seen twenty summers. The few that had were old, long in the tooth. Weapons of every sort could be spotted under heavy coats or strapped across gambesons. Rusted armor of veterans mingled with the almost polished leather of the young. These weren't the best, or even the bravest, but they were all willing to end the tyrannical threat assaulting Aradain, for the right price.

Eglios sat upon the throne. His crown was heavy, much as it always was on this fatal day. His mind was cluttered with the hopes that this would be the last time he needed to send innocent men into harm's way so that his kingdom might be set free. Eglios closed his eyes and prayed.

"Sire," Corso interrupted from the doorway. "It is time to greet the hunters."

"Of course," he replied without conviction.

The king rose wearily. His hair was mostly silver now. The lightning bolt on his crimson breast had lost much luster. Eglios donned his black cloak. It was heavier. He suddenly felt very old, almost used up. "Perhaps we won't have need for this again."

Corso remained stoic. "I have a feeling we'll find success, sire. All the signs are right. We can't lose, not with the eclipse about to happen."

Eglios didn't bother with the explanation. He'd been told the same thing for months now, and nothing changed. No matter how many times Corso sought to reassure him, he still cringed under a nagging despair. He knew, deep in the corners of his mind, that Aradain was doomed. But why? His enemies had gone. The Fist was on the run, and the Gaimosians were all but disappeared. Even that pompous Pirneon had gone off to the black pit.

So why do I wake up with dread each morning? His sense of wrongness grew. Eglios slowly walked across the throne room. Sunlight streaked lines of light through the enormous windows but offered no warmth. He always felt so alone on this day. The world seemed to have abandoned him.

"Are you all right, sire?" Corso asked.

Concern steeled the king's face. "I'm tired, Corso. Tired of all this. Tired of sending people I don't know off to die in a struggle we are blind to."

"Sometimes the most difficult task for a ruler is to risk the lives of his people for the greater good of the kingdom."

"How many have to die before it's enough, or too much?" Eglios asked.

"I don't have that answer. This will soon pass. The future will turn this all into a distant memory."

Placing his hand on Corso's shoulder, Eglios said, "You are a good friend. I could not have asked for a better minister. Come, let us pay our respects to these brave few."

Corso closed the door behind them. *All too easy.*

Moncrieff met them at the end of the granite-tiled hall. He was in his finest dress uniform, complete with ornamental saber. Escorting the hunters to the pit was normally his function, this proving to be the one exception. Eglios knew of his true mission, had approved it himself, if but hesitantly.

"Sire," Moncrieff bowed. Rows of medals jingled softly as he moved. "The assembly awaits."

Eglios nodded. "Is all else ready?"

"Preparations will be finished by evening. Some of the scouting elements have already pushed out. The main body marches at dawn."

"The same as our hunters."

Moncrieff replied, "Yes, sire. I have one battalion of the House Guard dispatched to escort detail. They should arrive at the forward camp unimpeded."

He didn't say what they both thought. Once the guards finished escorting the hunters to the camp, their task was complete. The hunters were on their own.

"Very well. Let's go and bid our well wishes to this latest batch," Eglios said. Some of his old confidence was returning.

A pair of guards, Damos and Kern, dressed in the house colors of crimson and black, snapped to attention as the king marched by. He'd always made a point of knowing his people by name. They were charged with defending the throne, and he could think of no better gift to bestow upon them.

Eglios stepped onto the second floor balcony to the cacophony of cheers and whistles. Doves were released from the surrounding roofs. Horns blared out. The crowds cheered louder in one of the few times they had to feel good. The blanket of repression hung low over most. Though each of the previous hunts had ended with despair, the people felt that this was the time the enemy would be broken and evil defeated. They cheered and didn't stop until long after Eglios raised his hands for silence.

"Good people of Rantis," he began. "Friends of Aradain and brave souls from across the world, I welcome you to this once proud kingdom in the hopes you will soon liberate us from the dark stain. All of you know our plight. An ancient evil has come to claim us. Our people are hunted and killed. They disappear in the middle of the night. We've tried, the gods know we've tried, to put an end to this menace ourselves. We were found wanting.

"I organized the hunts as a way for the best and bravest in the world to take up arms and win both honor and glory. This is the most holy of crusades. All you need do is reach forth and claim your glory. Do you seek it?"

The youngest, most influenced, of the crowd cheered, brandishing swords and pikes. Again, the people of Rantis cheered. Eglios almost felt it.

"Do you seek riches?" he shouted.

The very foundations of the palace shook.

"Then go forth in the name of all that is just and right and stake your claim in the annals of history. Each of you who brings me the head of one werebeast shall receive enough gold and gems to become a king yourself! Go! Go now, and may your blades strike true!"

The hunters filed out of the parade grounds under the intense cheers of the people. Flowers and incense were thrown at them. The sun was bright, shining. The day was perfect. Hope filled the city. Today just might be the day. Eglios watched them go. He wanted to believe, but past experience forced him to think otherwise.

"You have doubts, sire?" Corso asked above the roar.

"When does a king not? There are days when I feel the world is against me. I often wonder why the gods chose us for this calamity. But the gods do not answer. This is a cursed time we live in."

"Your words were strong, inspiring."

Eglios snorted. "Pure drivel. This hunt will fail just like all the others. Of that, I am certain. I pray, General, that our armies are as up to the task of removing the threat in Kalad Tol as the hunters believe they are in the ruins."

"Have no fear, sire. The outcome is all but decided. We have but to march, and the deed is done," Moncrieff said confidently.

"Good. Once it is complete, I want you to swing north to the ruins and finish this once and for all. Kill any that get in your way and bring the mountain down on top of the cavern. This kingdom will be free again. Good day, gentlemen."

Eglios left them to their business. He had much to prepare for and so little time. Moncrieff took his leave as well, letting Corso stand and watch the last of the departing hunters. He gently punched his fist into the railing. Eglios was beginning to act impulsively. He threatened all Corso had worked so hard for without realizing it. Five more days until Corso was freed of the pathetic ministrations of Aradain. After that, they'd all kneel before him.

Corso wasted no time stealing away from Aradain. His own work took him back to the obsidian tower. *Let Eglios do as he wishes. None of it matters. Fire and darkness will soon dominate this kingdom. Pain and suffering will be delivered upon them all. This is my hour.* His anger lessened by the time he reached the tower.

A pair of werebeasts snarled dangerously as he exited the tunnel. Hidden expertly, they kept those unfortunates who'd stumbled into the forest from entering the tower. Corso ignored them. Once the best and bravest in the world, they were now his willing servants. Corso climbed to his private sanctum, pausing only when he spied the small river of blood trickling from beneath the door. He smiled and went in. The beast that had been Pirneon stood over the freshly murdered Tamblin. Blood covered his mouth and chin.

FORTY-EIGHT

Heroes Gather

Guards raised the alarm the instant Kavan and his group were within range of Kalad Tol. Men hastily dressed in full armor. Pharanx Gorg strode purposefully to the wall. His eyes blazed with focus. It was only a matter of time before either Kavan returned or Moncrieff found them. The mercenary captain glanced up to the endless blue sky. Today was a good day for battle.

"Riders approaching, sir," the sergeant of the guard announced.

"Give me the glass."

Wurz, a stout, violent Dwarf, offered, "Might be scouts. That or Moncrieff's sent a party to talk us into surrender."

Looking through the glass, Pharanx told his second in command, "Sorry to disappoint you, lieutenant, but it's just the Gaimosians, with a few extras. Open the gates. We've got company."

"Aradain is coming apart. Minister Corso seems to be running his own secret police, doing as he wants under the protection of the king. Assassinations, murder, arson. I think this is just the beginning," Kavan told those assembled.

Pharanx asked, "Has the army deployed?"

"We don't know."

Wurz scratched his dark brown beard. "It's a safe bet they have. We've already killed a good number of scouts. The bastards are coming."

"I agree. The attack will come soon. With the hunt beginning, they'll have the perfect cover to mobilize. No one will question the deployment."

"Convenient for Eglios," Aphere said. "No questions means no explanations."

Kavan added, "This kingdom suffers from rot. Perhaps we should turn our focus towards weeding it out once we're done with Gessun Thune."

"That leads us to a dangerous place," Aphere cautioned. "We fight wars for people, not to overthrow declining monarchs."

"We owe the people of Aradain a new freedom. I'd expect no less from any of you," Kavan retorted.

Pharanx disagreed. "She's right, Kavan. None of us came here to remove Eglios. For all we know, he has the support of the kingdom. Politics are not our business."

"You're all mad!" Mabane exclaimed.

Pharanx barked a quick laugh. "Indeed we are. You tell me. You're a citizen of Aradain. Are you satisfied with the way your kingdom is ruled? How much has that arm cost you in life?"

"I'm still loyal," Mabane said, some of the fire burning out.

"Are you?"

Pharanx wore a malicious grin. For all his bold words, Mabane knew he was outmatched. He felt like weeping inside. He wasn't half the man he used to be. Somewhere along the desolate path of his life he'd lost the very core of what made him a man. Mabane's alcohol abuse left him hollow. His friends deserved more. His kingdom deserved more. He deserved more.

Mabane stood slowly and leveled his gaze at the mercenary. "I am a man of Aradain. I know I'm not what I once was, but neither would you be if you saw half of what I have. I'm no great warrior or descended from an ancient land. I'm just a man. Do what you have to do and leave our kingdom in peace."

He left them in stunned silence, having spoken his piece. Satisfaction made him walk taller, each step proud. Let the killers speak and plot of usurpers or death. He wanted no part in it. He'd help them with their task and do his part in ending the werebeast threat, but after that, he intended on striking out to reclaim what was lost.

Pharanx Gorg waited for the door to close before saying, "I think I'm going to like that man."

Kavan found Mabane sitting alone in the mess. A plate of half-eaten roasted plains lizard sat before him, accompanied by a still full mug of ale. Mabane spied him coming and stiffened reflexively. This was a moment when he needed to be alone.

"Strong words," Kavan said as he sat.

Mabane shrugged. "I said what needed saying."

"There are too few men like that in the world."

"I don't care about your crusade, Kavan. The moment this is ended, you'll never see me again."

Kavan sighed. "It's not my crusade. Destiny handpicked us all. We are the agents of the gods, for good or bad. That's not why I'm here."

"What reason, then?"

"Something wrong with your ale?" Kavan asked.

Mabane cut off a laugh. "This is piss water."

They sat in silence for a moment. One struggled with what to say while the other tried to find a way to avoid the conversation entirely.

"I know what it means to lose everything," Kavan finally spoke. "A family. A home. My people had it all taken from us. Folk talk about how evil we were, how corrupt. In truth, we Gaimosians were just like the rest of you. We only wanted to be left alone."

"This qualifies as being left alone?" Mabane mocked.

"There will come a day when the hatred fades, when the vengeance in our souls doesn't burn so bright. You lost your arm and your best friend. Hundreds more lost their lives, for what? So a crazed king can sit there and feel good about himself because he believes he's doing the right thing?" He shook his head. "This is a world that cares nothing about people like us, Mabane. You know that, though you may have forgotten it. All we can do is try to make it a little better in the time we are allotted. That's it, nothing more. In the end, we all turn to dust."

Kavan rose to leave. He made it to the door before Mabane's weak voice stopped him. "Kavan?"

He turned.

"Thank you."

Kavan nodded. "Enjoy your piss water."

"They're moving at last," Pharanx confirmed.

It was already midmorning. Tension filled Kalad Tol. All were veterans but waiting for a siege to begin inspired thoughts of desertion. Even the Gaimosians began to feel the pinch of being trapped.

"The hunters are en route to the ruins. Moncrieff should be here by dusk."

Kavan stared out across the supple, rolling hills of northeastern Aradain. It was so unlike the bog-mired south. He could almost see this as home. "Do we know how large his army is?"

"My scouts say close to three thousand," Wurz answered gruffly.

"Three thousand! This is suicide," Mabane exclaimed.

Kavan swallowed the lump forming in his throat. "He's right. We can't possibly win against a force that size."

Pharanx flashed a grin. Brown teeth gleamed. "You'd be surprised."

"What do you have in mind?"

Kavan secretly hoped the Fist proved more capable against regular army soldiers than they did against a handful of Gaimosians. He passed Geblin a fleeting look. For his part, the Gnome accepted their circumstances remarkably well.

Encouraged by the sudden uplift of spirits, Pharanx explained. "This fortress is old, with strong roots. We've inspected the walls, and it will take much to bring them down. I have two engineers in my command who have been tasked with reinforcing the outer structure."

"That still doesn't give us much support for holding off an entire army," Aphere said.

Wurz scoffed. "We have a trick for that. Bastards will wish they never came against us."

"It'll take a dragon to beat them," Barum commented.

Pharanx stood. His bronze skin and scar-covered muscle frame dominated the center of the room. "Follow me. I need to show you something."

Geblin hopped down from his stool and fell in beside Kavan. He looked up and muttered, "If it's a dragon, I'm going home."

The Gaimosians stood with mouths agape, still unsure of what they were looking at. Pharanx and his commanders stood beside them looking smug.

"As you can see, formidable, but not quite a dragon."

Kavan found his voice first. "What are they? I've never seen such creatures."

"They are called dactyls. Remnants from an earlier age, or so I'm told."

The leathery creature nearest them craned an elongated head and studied them closely. It had large, intelligent eyes capable of seeing in almost a full circle. Three clawed fingers flexed at the ends of enormous wings.

"Where do they come from?" Aphere asked.

Pharanx caught her look, that impulsive desire to reach out and touch the orange tinged scales. He smiled as he reached out to stroke the dactyl's neck. "They only bite if they think you're food. But, alas, there is no place on these shores for them. They come from across the sea, on the island of Chrysrar. A tribe of men called Tamers raise and breed them within a dormant volcano."

Aphere followed his lead and tentatively stretched her hand out. The dactyl squawked and twisted its head. "How did you find them?"

"He likes you," Pharanx smiled. "I hired a trader to take us across the sea. A quality organization such as ours is always looking for new prospects. The price was steep, but it balanced out. They are invaluable in terms of aerial reconnaissance and attacks."

Kavan looked up sharply. "That would explain how you managed to track us so easily."

"Tricks of the trade. Mercenaries need every possible advantage."

"They are most certainly not tricks."

They looked past the dactyl to see a tall man, thin and gaunt, with skin the color of coal and long braids of hair. His accent was so thick, it was difficult to understand.

"Ah," Pharanx said. "This is M'kele. He is our Tamer expert. They wouldn't part with their precious beasts without a permanent presence among us. M'kele maintains them as best he can, given the circumstances."

"I do not approve your designs, Captain," M'kele snapped.

"Those being?" Kavan asked.

"Aside from the terror factor? My men can rain spears and arrows down on the enemy long before they approach the castle. We have twenty-four more dactyls awaiting my command in a makeshift camp a league east of here."

"It will take more than spears and arrows to break an army so large," Kavan replied. Skepticism overrode his growing sense of optimism.

Pharanx said, "Leave that to us. By the time our task is done, the enemy shall fear us until their dying day."

Kavan doubted that would be the case but knew when to keep his opinion to himself. He'd been around a long time but could still be caught by surprise occasionally. Besides, he had more important issues to deal with. The armies of Aradain were only half of the whole issue. Eglios could throw his forces against these ancient walls all he wanted, but as long as the ruins of Gessun Thune remained exposed, all of Malweir lay in danger.

Pharanx continued, "We have enough projectiles to hold them off, and my men are ready for payback. This will be a glorious battle sung for decades. And with a handful of Gaimosian Knights at our side, how can we lose?"

"We can't stay," Kavan told him. "I'd like to, but we've been set to task. This battle is the sideshow. We've got to reach the ruins and stop the greater evil."

"That is…regrettable. You've proven your skill and prowess to us on more than one occasion. The men would benefit from fighting alongside you."

"We'd be glad to do it. This kingdom has offered great insult. Eglios and his minister are like a plague upon the land. The oracle, however, was specific. We are the only ones who stand a chance at ending this turmoil."

The mercenary captain folded his arms and nodded gravely. "A harsh task, indeed. Whatever support you need from us is yours to ask."

Kavan felt some of the tension leave. Allies now, the Fist could divert Aradain's forces long enough to give the Gaimosians a fighting chance. Numbers were against them both, but the sliver of hope refused to fade.

"My thanks," he said.

"When do you plan on leaving?" Pharanx pressed.

Kavan exhaled a breath he'd forgotten he was holding. "Only four days remain before the eclipse. We must be in Gessun Thune before then."

"What then?"

Kavan stopped, the question catching him off guard. The oracle had told them to go to the ruins but never mentioned exactly how they were supposed to stop the enemy from releasing the dark gods. He doubted the task would be so simple as killing the man responsible. He admitted, "I don't know."

"Oracles are tricky business. Damned things can't come out and say what needs saying."

"Agreed," Aphere cut in. She alone bore the burden of the oracle's prophecy.

Clasping Kavan's shoulder, Pharanx said, "Trust the oracle. You may well be the hope of us all. Doesn't mean I wouldn't want to take a swipe at the bastard, though."

"That didn't turn out so well," Aphere added.

Kavan grinned at the memory. "We can't risk getting trapped here when Aradain arrives. We must leave as soon as possible."

"Tonight. Once the sun sets. How many men will you need?"

Kavan hadn't expected the offer but readily accepted. "Two or three should suffice."

"What?" Aphere exclaimed.

Pharanx laughed again. "You are mad, my friend."

Kavan defended himself. "No. It makes sense. We stand a better chance of slipping in undetected now that the hunt has begun. There's no call for drawing attention."

Wurz reluctantly grunted. "Makes sense."

Turning to Geblin, Kavan asked, "I'm afraid you're going to have to stay here. Eglios is look for a group traveling with a Gnome. We can't risk it. I'm sorry."

Geblin spat on the ground. "Just as well. I've grown tired of your company."

"I'll stay with him," Barum announced. "My bow is no good in a cavern. They need it more here. Besides, someone needs to keep an eye on Geblin."

"Bah!"

Aphere cast a sharp, concerned gaze to Barum. While she approved of the man he was becoming, she couldn't help but fret over his decision. Odds were decidedly not in their favor and he stood a fair chance of winding up dead. She tried, and failed, to ignore the pain deep in her heart.

"We're all crazy, you know that right?" Pharanx asked. "Chances are good we'll all be dead by the time tomorrow ends. But you never know. This just might work."

Kavan nodded. The notion of splitting forces sat ill with him, weighing heavily against the oracle's words. All were meant to play a part, but what that part was remained to be discovered. Kavan knew the others were meant to stay. It felt right. "It's settled. We leave at dusk. May the gods smile down on us all."

FORTY-NINE

Partings

"Why do you have to go?" Phirial asked through her sobs.

Kavan was suddenly uncomfortable. He'd never been in such a position and had no idea how to react accordingly. He felt warmth at the thought of having her close. Her smile never failed to dazzle. A host of answers went through his head. Deciding which was appropriate was elusive. Phirial was bright, enjoyable to be around. She wasn't a warrior. Her only exposure to violence had been the cowardly murder of her father.

He uneasily wrapped his arm around her shoulders and held her close. "Sometimes, a man's life is not his own."

"That's an escape, not an answer," she snapped back.

"What do you expect me to say?" he countered. "I have no land, no people, no kingdom. I have nothing but this sword."

Phirial looked up through tear-filled eyes. "You have a choice. All men have a choice."

"I wish that were true."

His voice trailed off to a whisper. Free will. He'd not had the luxury of such since Gaimos fell. The very genes in his blood demanded obedience to steel. His was a life of battle and discontent. Nothing that man nor woman said would ever change that. She clutched him even tighter, afraid that, if she let go, she'd lose him forever. It was at that moment that Kavan made up his mind. He maneuvered them over to the simple cot in the far side of the room and sat her on the edge. He almost lost himself looking into her deep, warm eyes.

"There are things about me you don't know. Things you wouldn't want to know."

Kavan took her silence as a sign to continue.

"Phirial, I've not lived a good life. When I think of all the men I've killed, all the families I've broken, I wonder how I've managed to live with myself for so long. This is not a friendly world. Evil and malice corrupt our souls. A greater truth has never been more evident. There was a saying amongst my people once, long ago. We called it the howl of the wolf. Have you heard this?"

She shook her head.

He continued, "It is a call to arms. An answer to wrongs committed. Every time Gaimos went to war or drew swords, we answered the howl of the wolf. So it is again. A terrible darkness threatens us all. This is not a battle any army can fight. Instead, a handful have been chosen.”

“You and the others,” she offered.

“Aye. Chosen by the Oracle of Wenx. Five of us were chosen to perform a deed none of us know. It seems the gods have deemed the sons of Gaimos have more to do.”

Phirial drew back. “You say five, but there are only four.”

Kavan felt a stab of pain in his heart. “We haven’t seen or heard from Pirneon since arriving in Rantis. I fear he has fallen.” He omitted telling her of the bond. Some matters were too private.

“Dead,” she gasped.

He closed his eyes in prayer. “Worse.”

Phirial couldn’t imagine a worse fate than being put in the ground early, but she knew when to let something drop. Instead, she asked he continue his tale. He did. At times, it was easy to tell, simple and straightforward. Other times, he choked on the words. Phirial did her best not to let emotions override reason. The more he spoke, the more she began to understand both his complex way of life and his charge from the oracle. The young blacksmith from Rantis fell more in love with the stranger from nowhere.

Surprisingly enough, Kavan felt better. He’d held almost nothing back, going to lengths to explain Gaimos’s plight and the sort of lives his people were reduced to living. The charge of the oracle was sacred. He didn’t care to think of the consequences of failure. Then again, if they did fail, none of them would be around to suffer the ramifications.

Phirial wiped the tears from the corners of her eyes. “Can you win?”

Her voice cracked, coming out timid.

“I honestly don’t know,” he replied softly.

That much alone was more than he was comfortable admitting. Doubt often led to fear, and defeat after that.

Mabane watched Kavan with a queer look. The one-armed drunk knew something was out of place but couldn’t put a finger on it. What he did know was that no sane man should be smiling and whistling hours from going to his death. *Or maybe I’ve got it all wrong. Maybe Lord Death wants us all to jump into his embrace with song and dance. What fools are we?*

Kavan finished strapping his pack to the saddle and faced Mabane. “What?”

“You,” was all he could say.

He shrugged. “What about me?”

Amazing. These Gaimosians are demons in flesh. "How can you be so calm in the face of what comes next?"

"There's not much point in being anything else," Kavan replied. "We all must die, but it's the measure of a man how he chooses to do so. You should be glad of this. Not every man is so fortunate."

The Gaimosian slapped him lightly on the shoulder and walked away. Mabane stared after him for a while. He started searching his soul, hoping to find the well of resolve. One question prevented it. When the time came, would he be able to stand up to his fears? He didn't know.

"You really shouldn't be going with them," a deep voice rumbled from behind.

Mabane turned to see the taciturn Dwarf lieutenant standing there. His thickly corded arms were casually folded. There was a hard look to him, much the same as every Dwarf Mabane had ever met.

Wurz spit and shook his head. "Doesn't make any sense. Not to me, at least. They're leaving a good man behind and taking a cripple. Don't get me wrong, lad, you've got courage, but you won't be much good in a hard fight against those monsters."

"I know," Mabane answered sadly.

Wurz spit again, and a wad of dark, chewed leaves went with it. "So why go back? Stay here and help with the wounded."

"I can't. I owe it to a friend."

"You slept with her, didn't you?" Aphere asked.

Kavan wasn't positive, but he thought he detected a glint of jealousy in her tone. He almost enjoyed it. "What makes you say that?"

Her eyes narrowed. "You damned well know what."

Kavan shrugged. "Not that it's any concern of yours, but yes."

"That was reckless, Kavan. I bet she hasn't stopped crying since we left," she scolded.

He let out a long breath, trying to prevent his anger from rising. "My business is my own. It is not the subject of casual conversation. Can we just leave it at that and focus on the task at hand?"

Aphere reined her horse in, forcing him to do the same. "Listen to me first. That girl just lost her father and her entire world. She's not right in her mind and you slept with her. You should not have taken advantage."

Kavan watched her ride off. He didn't know how to tell her that his own world had been upended as well, and his feelings for Phirial were growing. He wasn't certain but felt like he was falling love. Defending himself to a fellow Gaimosian would be a waste of time. Kavan kicked his horse forward, leaving two confused mercenaries following close behind.

Night was dark, intimidating without the light of the moon. The five riders inched across the unforgiving landscape towards an uncertain destiny. Of the group, only the Fist members had yet to bear witness to the pain and loss of Gessun Thune. Kavan almost felt sorry for them. Trained mercenaries weren't prepared for what came next.

Aphere decided to leave them alone until reaching the ruins. Each of the party had personal demons threatening to strangle them. It was as individuals that they must confront those demons. Her greatest concern was for Mabane. He was the least stable of the group. Past experiences haunted him to the point of ineffectiveness. She had little doubt this venture might drive him irreversibly over the edge. If it didn't kill him first.

Instead her mind stayed focused on that final glance at Barum. That singular moment keeping her motivated to push forward. His serene face helped calm her, for going to war and, in her mind, certain death was never an easy feat. No, Aphere ignored the others and remained focused on Barum.

Kavan had already gone ahead to scout. He felt the most as ease there, and after their earlier discussion, she was inclined to let him be. Maybe a little time alone would help him clear his head. She eased back and attempted to console Mabane.

"You're frightened," she said.

Mabane eyed her curiously. "I'd be a fool if I wasn't."

"I agree. This is not an easy task we attempt."

He snorted mockingly. "Why are we having this conversation? You and I both could have ridden off into the night and put this nightmare behind us. We're all doomed. I should never have gotten involved with you."

She empathized with his sorrow, though it was never one of her stronger characteristics. "We are not always in control of our destinies, as you would believe. You could run to the far ends of Malweir, and it wouldn't save you from what is coming."

"I don't believe you. I may not know much of this world, but I know we are all given choices," he told her.

"I wish we were. Mabane, there are forces working against us, even as we speak. Have you any idea of the magnitude of evil we are going up against? It may not seem like it to you, but this darkness threatens to consume the world. If we fail, everything we have ever known will devolve into horror. We're fighting for the lives of every single being on Malweir."

"You expect me to believe that you're all doing this out of sheer nobility?" he said. His voice bore hard edges. "I'm simple, not naïve. We all know the stories of your kingdom. Your people brought damnation down upon themselves. Is this supposed to be some sort of crusade for redemption or just another attempt at domination?"

Aphere sat up, shocked to hear his words. Having been born after the Fall, she'd never had the opportunity to know either her people or her culture. The ways of her homeland were as much mystery to her as the rest of the world. Her father did his best to instill a deep sense of values and core beliefs, always with the intent on making her the very best of people. She learned the legends, the names and history of the land long defeated. The world knew them as malevolent conquerors. No one bothered learning the truth. That they were hard working people, the same as in every other kingdom. That honor and loyalty were placed above all else, propelling them to be better than the previous generation. They could never understand that Gaimosians were no different from anyone else.

"You know not what you speak," she snarled.

"I've seen enough to know better."

Aphere felt an uneasy feeling spring to life. Old doubts resurfaced. They challenged her beliefs, giving her pause to wonder. Doubt on the battlefield kills more than wounds or disease. So she'd always been told. No Gaimosian ever feared taking up the sword. It was the rest of life they shied from. Aphere silently cursed Mabane, letting her anger manifest in his words. Then she noticed his empty sleeve billowing in the slight breeze. Mabane knew suffering at depths few others could comprehend. That pain bled out into daily life. He was bitter, broken. Alcohol became his prison, leaving him a gnarled shell.

Aphere sighed. Perhaps, just perhaps, he was right. Loath as she was to admit it, she had to open her mind to the possibilities of a past she was equally unaware of. "One way or another, it really doesn't matter."

Mabane coughed, his lungs breathing fire. "How so?"

"In the end, we either live or we die."

"Now you're a poet as well?" he snapped.

Aphere laughed. "No, half man. I am a warrior. We are about to enter the storm, and those are the only two ways out. How do you plan on greeting death?"

"At the bottom of a bottle back in Rantis."

Nothing else needed saying.

The first indication they had stumbled upon the hunt were the hundreds of vultures dotting the sky. Their violent red heads and broad black bodies were visible almost a league away. The moon was out now, directly overhead. The near horizon threatened the sky with shades of orange, yellow, and red from the heat of hundreds of licking flames.

Kavan smiled grimly as he halted. This was campaign. He had always felt more at home among armies of battle brothers eager for the fight than at any other time in his life. All the training and personal hardships led up to this one perfect moment on the eve of battle. Blood, suffering, and unthinkable horrors lay ahead. But here, now, the world was perfect.

"No sign of the army," Aphere said coming alongside him.

Kavan tilted his head. "Is that good or bad?"

She didn't know. "How do we do this?"

Kavan rolled a kink from his shoulders and laughed. "We ride down into camp like we belong and pray to our gods that there is still time."

FIFTY

The Hunt

Typical of civilians pretending to be soldiers, the campaign base for the hunt was a rowdy mess. Order and discipline were lacking. Already, the smell of urine and excrement was strong enough to suggest latrines hadn't been dug properly. Horses were everywhere instead of in kraals. Kavan frowned in disgust. He was already planning on disengaging from this rabble.

True to his instincts, the mixed group of Fist and Gaimosians wandered into camp without being questioned. Few, in fact, bothered to look up as they passed. Only Mabane betrayed emotion. The drunk was ill at ease with being this close to the ruins again — so much so that Kavan slipped back to growl his own brand of encouragement.

"If you give us away, I swear I'll gut you," he threatened in a low voice.

Mabane's eyes widened. "We'll be caught and captured!"

"If you keep acting like a fool, indeed. Calm yourself and relax. After tomorrow, this will all be a bad dream."

Kavan left him before his natural urges took over and he crushed the fool. He was quickly at wits end with the man, a trait he found increasingly common the more companions he was forced to take on. His thoughts naturally turned to Pirneon, wondering if he had suffered similar indignities en route to Aradain. Setting those thoughts aside, Kavan dismounted when he found an unoccupied spot large enough for all five of them.

Aphere turned to the mercenaries. "Set up the tents. I'll start a fire."

The Fist nodded and went to work. Mabane fidgeted nearby, the only question she had left. Like Kavan, she grew concerned about his anxious behavior. Worse still, none of them fully understood what was expected of them now that they were here. Frustrations compounded.

"I'm going to scout some. There's the possibility someone knows what's really going on," Kavan told her.

"What about Pirneon?" she asked, regretting it immediately.

"If I happen to run across him," was his reply.

Clearly, neither was interested in stopping the quest to search for the missing Knight Marshal. Both wanted answers as well as a small measure of retribution, but the mission remained paramount.

She smiled, cruel and wicked. "Try not to run a dagger through him before I do."

Kavan suddenly felt uneasy. Being abandoned was almost acceptable. After all, it was the Gaimosian way. But to turn traitor and harbor thoughts of harming one of your own blood was inexcusable. He feared the Gaimosians were reaching a new point, unavoidable and forever damning, in the sad tale of their bloodlines. Whatever happened, nothing was ever going to be the same again.

"He was my mentor, Aphere," he told her in low tones. "I cannot do what you would suggest." *Not yet, at any rate.*

"Clear your mind. We are alone now. For all we know, he has gone over to the enemy. You saw his thirst for power. The hunger always lurked behind his eyes. He hasn't been the man you knew, not since we learned of our task from the oracle."

Kavan turned his back on her, refusing to listen to more slander. The animosity between Aphere and Pirneon had grown since leaving the Kergland Spine, a fact Kavan wasn't unaware of, though he failed to know the reasoning behind it. Pirneon was the oldest living Gaimosian, standing for all their culture represented. He alone had been the mountain in the wind since the Fall, a beacon for the young to rally behind.

"Listen to me, Kavan," Aphere pressed. "He is dangerous. You must force yourself to look past old allegiances and see the truth. Either confront him or avoid him for as long as you can. You can't run from him forever."

He slowly faced her. "If the gods will it, then so shall it be. Just know this: I cannot and will not be the first to raise arms against my own blood. If Pirneon has changed as you suggest, we shall all find out soon enough."

He left her standing in a whirlwind of emotions.

"Madness," Mabane muttered from the burned tree stump he'd claimed as a stool. "Madness."

Malweir, though never welcoming or friendly, was not the world it had once been. Shadows had crept in. They drove men to new heights of barbarism and despair. Kavan felt those urges swell at times. They threatened the depths of his soul, seeking the foundations of who he was. Was this what made Pirneon abandon his principles? The question incensed him.

It was on the slopes of Skaag Mountain, their most sacred training grounds, that he had met Pirneon for the first time. Pirneon was already an old man, Kavan a lad of no more than ten. He recalled staring wide-eyed at the venerable legend. Every boy growing up had known of the deeds of Pirneon. He had been a source of wonder and awe for the young. Gaimosians were taught from a young age the glory of his sword.

So it was the day Kavan's father had taken him to the hallowed grounds to turn his only son over to the Knight Marshal. Pirneon had taken a child made of the softest clay and transformed him into a warrior, a knight, and a man. Years of teachings ingrained in young Kavan what it truly meant to live up to the virtues expected of him. Above all, he now recalled that final lesson. Smiling fondly, he could still hear Pirneon's voice that day on the slopes of the Skaag.

You have learned your lessons well. Pride was our greatest crime. We let it consume us, sway us just enough to let the dam break. Never give in to pride, for it shall be your undoing.

Kavan frowned. Pride was, indeed, a terrible force. Kavan laughed to himself. "Where is your pride now, Pirneon? Did it finally claim you?"

He stopped in front of a large gathering in the camp center. Two women dressed only in translucent colored scarves danced provocatively against each other. Soft winds whipped their hair, the tails of the scarves chasing. One had skin the color of darkest night while the other was pale and lightly freckled. An old man whose eyes had been cut out beat an entrancing song on a pair of drums. The women danced faster, rubbing their sweat covered bodies against each other as the scarves slipped away. Naked, both leaned forward to kiss deeply. Men hooted and cheered, all the while tossing hard-earned coin at the women.

Kavan's thoughts turned from Pirneon to Phirial. Inside, he felt nothing but conflict. She proved an admirable distraction; one he could ill afford.

Kavan didn't expect to live past the eclipse. None of them did. That was no secret, but he had found reluctance admitting as much to Phirial as they lay trying to catch their breath. He tried putting a positive spin on events lest she break down entirely. The combination of losing her father and her life had almost been too much. She was on the brink of collapse. Her proclaimed love for him was the only thread keeping her together.

And now he was gone from her as well. Kavan let thoughts of what another life might be like creep through the minor cracks in his mental armor. He could leave now and never look back — take Phirial and build a small cabin to the east, raise children. Kavan laughed at the idea. If the gods wanted to make him a farmer, they would have already done so. At best, he could only give back to the fallen sons of Gaimos and move on.

He chastised himself for having such weakness at this late hour. Doubts remained. Phirial was a special woman deserving of more than his sworn life offered. His heart occasionally won through, and he longed to return to her loving embrace, to be the man he'd never known existed. Torn between the demons in his soul and love, Kavan headed back to Aphere.

One of the Fist was already asleep, snoring softly from the depths of his tent. Aphere and the other sat talking quietly on events to come as Kavan walked up.

She glanced at her fellow Gaimosian. "I was explaining the layout of the area around the cavern mouth. They haven't been this far yet."

Kavan nodded. "That should prove our easiest task."

"How do you figure?" asked a flaxen haired youth named Tym.

"We are surrounded by hundreds of eager men and women seeking glory. Getting into the ruins won't be an issue. It's what's inside that worries me."

Tym offered a blank stare. Clearly, the two Fist hadn't been warned of the nightmares burrowed deep beneath the earth.

Kavan crouched down in from of Tym and gestured towards Gessun Thune. "There are monsters there, lad. Spit from the deepest pits of the underworld."

Tym blanched.

"Your captain should have told you at least that much."

"Stop trying to frighten him," Aphere admonished.

"I merely speak the truth."

Aphere added, "Tym, when we go inside that cavern, we will be beset by werebeasts, monsters the likes of which you've never imagined. You must trust in us. That is the only hope we have for victory. Faith and steel, my friend."

Tym crawled into his tent, his face a twisted mess of emotions. The knights watched him before continuing.

"You undermine our task," she scolded.

Kavan held up his hands. He hadn't returned seeking a fight. "I told him the truth. They deserve that much."

"That doesn't mean we need to change his mind. What's to keep them from leaving in the middle of the night?"

"Aphere, those men are mercenaries. Their loyalty is to money. Any man with an ounce of sense would leave."

She took a moment to calm down before responding. "I don't like this any more than you, but we've been given a task."

"Aye, and I pray we live long enough to come out of it," he said. "We're both tired. There's no point in bickering. Let us sleep and tackle the beast tomorrow."

Through it all, Mabane watched from his stump.

Corso stalked the empty chamber, lost in thought. Childish giddiness flowed through him. After so long, he was about to be released from his prison. Corso pressed a hand against the cracked granite slab. They were so close. He could feel his wicked masters pulsing from the other side of the veil. One thousand years of exile left them hungry. They thirsted to wreak havoc among the living. Corso delighted in the images of whole continents enslaved under his dark banner.

Very soon, the last hunt would begin, and hundreds of fresh souls would be slaughtered upon this very slab. Their blood would open the keys to the prison. His only hope was that the blood of the Knight Marshal was strong enough to work. Thus far, his experiments had been a source of constant disappointment. Dozens of Gaimosians had died in his quest. His seduction and eventual transformation of Pirneon was his last hope. If that failed…. Corso shuddered. He dared not think of the suffering his masters would visit upon him. The sound of hot spittle striking stone disturbed him from his delusions. Corso slowly turned and faced his newest pet.

"Anxious, aren't you?"

Evil laced his words.

The Pirneon beast crouched on all fours and snarled. Slender fangs protruded from his elongated snout. Whatever creature was blended with him was lost to the dust-covered tomes of history.

"You'll get your opportunity soon enough. Please me, and I'll let you feast upon the flesh of your friends."

Pirneon salivated hungrily.

FIFTY-ONE

Siege

Pharanx Gorg had grown up a gambling man. His entire life was a series of well-gambled chances that had played out perfectly. He'd grown up a pickpocket on the streets of a city long forgotten. Every scrap of food and coin he had was fought for. That's where Alcha had found him. Tall and immensely powerful, the former master of the Fist had taken Pharanx in and cared for him like no father ever had. It quickly became evident that he was being groomed for command.

Pharanx had reveled in the chance to prove himself against his betters. He'd mastered any craft he could in the constant quest to prove his worth. Others had grown jealous, and more than once, he'd found himself the target of an ill-conceived assassination attempt. All who tried had been put in the ground. Pharanx had learned to become a ruthless killer and keen tactician. When Alcha had fallen in battle, Pharanx had assumed command and never stopped. His first task had been to cull those he couldn't trust. Some were dismissed, others disappeared. Yes, Pharanx considered himself a lucky man.

This morning, however, he almost believed that luck had run out. A runner came to him in the predawn hours. Out of breath and visibly shaken, the boy explained that Wurz needed him on the wall at once. Pharanx swung out of bed and strapped on his weapons. The pair made their way back to the aged walls in silence. The Fist prepared for battle all around. Pharanx gave them all the look of approval. He was inherently proud.

"What goes?" he asked his lieutenant.

Wurz gestured over his shoulder. His axe was already in hand. "They're here."

Pharanx stared into the brightening dawn. Moncrieff's army had, indeed, arrived. They marched out of the darkness in great waves of crimson and black. The creak and groan of heavy wheels accompanied crisp sounds of thousands of marching boots striking the ground. Siege machines.

"I'd almost hoped they weren't that smart," he breathed.

The Dwarf snorted. "They're not taking chances."

"I guess we angered the king."

"If he truly is one. Listening to the Gaimosians leads me to believe he's just a puppet."

Pharanx stared sharply at the Dwarf. Through all their trials, he remained constant, a stalwart companion who never shied from speaking his mind. Pharanx needed that.

"King or not, Eglios is our enemy now," he said. "He's spilled enough of our blood. Vengeance, my friend. When hope fades, we must look to vengeance to keep us warm. Perhaps the Gaimosians have the right of it."

Hundreds of soldiers marched into place.

"We might not get the chance to find out," Wurz grumbled.

Pharanx agreed. "All we have to do is hold them long enough for Kavan to get to this Gessun Thune and do what needs doing."

"I'd rather be here than with Kavan. They're not going to have an easy time of it."

"There wouldn't be much fun otherwise. Moncrieff will spend most of the day getting into position. His soldiers will be tired from marching through the night."

"It's not the soldiers that worry me. We have to do something about those engines."

The bulky shapes of catapults and scaling towers rumbled into view. Pharanx suspected Moncrieff wasn't willing to waste lives in the assault, making him cautious.

"Let us see if our brother Gaimosian has any ideas for dealing with those machines," he offered.

Together, they turned their backs on the approaching storm. They found Barum and Geblin at the armory, fletching arrows. Hundreds already filled quivers with many more bundles scattered on the ground.

"They are here?" Barum asked, seeing the two Fist commanders approach.

"Every damned one of them, by the looks of it," Wurz answered.

Geblin rolled his eyes.

Barum slapped his knuckles against the Gnome's chest. "How much siege equipment do they have?"

"Enough. About a half dozen catapults, three scaling towers, and hundreds of ladders. They'll make quick work of our defenses unless we act first."

Barum set his half-finished arrow down. "How many flying beasts did you say we have?"

"Two dozen."

"I say we use them while Moncrieff is still marching. Take him off guard and reduce his assault capability."

Pharanx gestured him to continue. "I'm listening."

Confidence bolstered, Barum explained, "Circle around behind them and dive. They won't be expecting an assault from the rear. Firebomb their machines and they lose momentum and, hopefully, some of their will to fight."

"We also lose that singular advantage."

Pharanx was loath to invest his greatest asset so early in the fight, even if meant being pummeled by the siege engines. Then again, there was the chance, small as it was, that his dactyls would be enough to break the enemy's will. Cut off the head, and the snake dies. "It might work."

"We have nothing to lose."

"It will be light soon," Wurz said.

Barum looked up. "Do we have enough time?"

"Aye. I'd say yes. Let's go give these bastards exactly what they want," Pharanx grinned, broken teeth gleaming in the torchlight.

"What do you say, Geblin?" Barum asked.

"I'll stand the wall, but you haven't a prayer of getting me on the back of one of those beasts. Gnomes belong on the ground, not flying like some fancy bird."

Pharanx barked a laugh.

"What's so funny?"

"Fancy birds are exactly what we shall become, little Gnome. Birds of death and fury."

Regret. That singular emotion threatened to take control of his thoughts and push him to the point of distraction. Pharanx battled his mind as he clenched his thighs around the slender neck of his pet and companion. The cool predawn air felt good to both. It had been too long since they'd taken to the skies. Up here, lost among the clouds, was the only time he truly felt at peace.

Pharanx's regrets stemmed from various sources. He regretted taking Corso's contract, thus jeopardizing the lives of five hundred. He'd no idea how evil Corso was. He regretted wasting lives recklessly hunting the Gaimosians. Too many had died for no reason. The Fist had sorely underestimated their enemies and paid dearly for it. He regretted staying in Aradain after Corso turned on them. How many more need to pay for his arrogance? Too many at the least.

His final regret came from deciding to stand and fight in the abandoned fortress of Kalad Tol. The illusions were gone by now. They were all going to die. There it was, plain and simple. Every last one of his brave warriors was a dead man. Naturally, he hoped one or two might escape in the confusion, but the possibility was unlikely. No, the Fist would make its final stand at Kalad Tol and pray history looked back kindly.

Pharanx Gorg regretted it all.

He glanced about, ensuring the rest of his squadrons were in sleek V formations of six each. Each rider was grim faced with determination. Sacks of explosive powders some claimed were created by ancient sorcerers in the dark corners of the world draped from the dactyls. Pharanx wasn't interested in where they were discovered. All he needed to know was that they were highly potent and effective with devastating results. Moncrieff's army had no idea the nightmares it was about to undergo.

Pharanx tossed his head back and bellowed. His long black top knot trailed behind. Dawn was breaking, the red sun crisp against the dark horizon. The enemy army was fixed on the fortress, ignoring their rear and the sky. The Fist was about to make them pay for that error. Spying the massive scaling towers, Pharanx signaled for the attack. The army of Aradain was little more than one massive shadow in the fading night. Campfires illuminated the area enough to give the dactyls a target. Pharanx cracked a shallow smile. Corso and Moncrieff had played their hand too early.

The Fist dove.

Wings tucked back, the dactyls screamed down on the unsuspecting army. There was no air power in Malweir, giving the army no cause to look up before the explosive sacks rained down on the engineer site. A catapult burst into flames. Wood and metal shattered through tents and flesh. Men screamed. The ground trembled. Soldiers raced to extinguish the flames, but it was for naught. Two dozen more explosions ripped through the camp. Bodies and engines were torn apart without ceremony.

The sickly sweet smell of freshly spilled blood traced the air. Soldiers abandoned their posts in order to find cover, any cover. There was none. After the first pass, all the scaling towers were in flames and half of the catapults were destroyed. By the time the Fist were out of ammunition, only a single catapult remained. Acrid smoke poured into the sky in great funnels, blocking the withdrawing dactyls.

Moncrieff stalked through the wreckage of his army. His face burned the deepest crimson. Never had he been embarrassed so on the battlefield. The sheer weight of destruction here was unheard of. He knew of two things capable of doing this: dragons and elder sorcery. He carefully stepped over body parts and impact craters. He couldn't comprehend what had happened. Couldn't wrap his mind around the facts.

"General," his adjutant saluted. The man was out of breath and in disarray.

Moncrieff took the man in. Blood splattered the front of his tunic, though he appeared unharmed. "What?"

"I have initial casualty reports."

Some of his anger faded. "Give them to me."

The adjutant cleared his throat. He was more nervous now than during the attack. "More than four hundred are believed dead. Eight hundred more were wounded. The surgeons believe another hundred in that figure won't last the day. Most of the siege engines are inoperable. Our engineers are trying to piece together what they can but aren't having much luck."

Moncrieff held up a hand. "How soon will we be ready to lay siege to those scum in the fortress?"

"With minimal casualties to the infantry? No sooner than a day."

"Captain, this day has barely begun, and we've already lost almost a third of our combat power. You dare tell me all we can do is build campfires and stare at the enemy? Unacceptable."

The adjutant stammered, "B…but sir, we're in no position to lay siege!"

Moncrieff raged, "Damn the siege! I want every last man inside that fortress dead! Do you hear me? No one walks out of there alive."

"Sir, there might be unarmed combatants inside."

The general paused as brief conflict trembled his face. He swallowed hard, and it was with great personal regret that he replied, "Not anymore there aren't."

He resumed his march through the carnage. Every corpse was personal. A friend. Son. Father. Those godless mercenaries had casually ended their lives without honor. A sick feeling spread through his stomach. Moncrieff wasn't prone to thoughts of vengeance, but today was different. He cursed the king for being so weak and Corso for being greedy. Whoever won this battle, the day would end badly for both sides. He knew what he had to do but was reluctant.

"Your orders, sir?"

Moncrieff almost smiled. His adjutant had been around him long enough to recognize his moods. "Summon Jestis. I have a mission for his commando squads."

"Yes, General."

Moncrieff stood alone again on the crowded battlefield. Surrounded by frantic men and havoc, he'd never felt this isolated in his life. He hoped it wasn't a sign of things to come.

FIFTY-TWO

Gessun Thune

"It's time."

Kavan heard the horns blaring from the southern end of the encampment. He climbed out of his sleeping bag and stretched off the stiffness from the night. Muscles hardened from decades of battle flushed the sleep away. He felt tired, despite all his experiences. A lingering sense of dread hung in the back of his mind like a miasmatic cloud. He'd never felt so desperate before. The oracle's words were strong yet left him with grave doubts.

He wasn't a leader. He knew that. A solitary man, Kavan couldn't help but wonder if he was up to the task. Aphere was more than capable, confident in her abilities. She, out of them all, felt the oracle's inspiration. He envied her. She had a brand of faith he would never possess. Perhaps it was the mutation of her blood bond. Pirneon certainly seemed convinced. His anger and disapproval had slowly fed into an undercurrent of hatred towards her. Kavan scoffed. If faith kept her going, who was he to argue against it?

Aphere emerged from her tent, yawning. "What's happening?"

Her eyes were bloodshot. Kavan regarded her in new light. He respected her more. He also knew that he needed her more than either of them could guess.

"I think the hunt is beginning," he replied.

Mabane had heard the horns in his sleep. The sounds produced volatile memories. He awoke in cold sweat. The Vengeance Knights watched him closely. If he was going to break and run, now was the time.

"Are you all right?" she asked.

His shoulders trembled. "Those horns."

"Yes. An official party comes," Kavan replied.

"I know."

It suddenly dawned on Kavan that they'd been forgetting the one important piece of the puzzle: Mabane. Kavan moved beside the one arm man.

"Mabane, listen to me," he began. "We have sorely underestimated you. I have personally. For that, I apologize."

"What are you talking about?"

"You've been the key to this quest the entire time, and only now do I realize it. You've done all of this before. The hunt, I mean. We should have been seeking your guidance from the start."

Humorless laughter tainted his voice.

"How could we have missed that?" Aphere asked, the idea suddenly dawning on her.

Mabane wanted to cry. The last thing he expected was a confession of ignorance from two venerable warriors. Old fears tormented him, more so now that he was sober. He lacked personal courage necessary to enter this fight. His nerve was gone. A coward maybe, though not by his own choosing, Mabane knew it would take more than fanciful accolades to change his mind. Yet still....

"Yes," he said after calming down. "I've been here before. It's all the same. All I see are dead men."

"Dead men?"

He barked derisive laughter. "Every last one of us. Dead. All dead."

"It doesn't have to end this way. We can still find victory," Aphere tried to sooth.

"How so?"

It was a tired conversation. The Gaimosians seemed to have a deep-rooted need to know they were doing the right thing, which he failed to understand. They'd become an insistent lot focused only on goals meeting their needs. In his mind, they were also naïve.

"Do you have any idea what's going to happen next?"

Kavan struggled to contain his irritation. "We already know about the werebeasts in the pit. What we need to know is how to get in without being noticed. Tell us what happens in camp. How does the hunt begin?"

Mabane took a steadying breath. He was reluctant to speak of such things, despite being under their protection. Further argument was pointless. The best course of action was to tell them and hope for absolution in his own words. "All right. Those horns are Corso's own party. King Eglios always sends his minister to oversee the event."

Aphere and Kavan exchanged a knowing glance, not lost on Mabane.

"Corso will take his place at the head of the camp on a great stage. He'll give a rousing speech appealing to our egos and then send the hunters in."

"How does he determine who goes first?" Aphere asked. Suspicions awakened. She decided Corso was a figure needing a closer look.

"There's no order, if that's what you mean. Guards start a line and send in twenty at a time. The caverns are huge. A man could get lost forever in there. The groups are staggered every half hour or so. They claim it is to give us time to find our glory."

"That word gets used often in this kingdom," Kavan frowned. The more he thought on it, the more he didn't like Eglios or Aradain. A rot consumed the souls of this kingdom, and they were all too blind to see it. He questioned how a man like Corso managed such power.

"There's no glory here," Mabane replied coldly. "Only pain and suffering. Hundreds of men and women, Dwarf and Elf have died down there. Their blood stains the ground red. You lose track of time. It seemed like we walked forever without seeing another soul. How deep and how many miles, I don't know. Then the killing starts."

Not the words I wanted to hear. Kavan asked, "Does this Corso keep count of who goes in?"

"I'm sure there are administrators. We didn't pay attention to that. Our blood was aflame in the moment. We surged into the caverns in search of fame. Fools all."

Aphere asked, "Did you notice if Corso remained throughout the duration of the hunt?"

Mabane thought. "Long enough, I suppose. Come to think of it, he seemed to show interest in what we did. I remember getting an ill feeling from him when he visited me in the hospital tents."

Kavan turned to Aphere. "Corso is the one we've been looking for."

She agreed, arriving at the same conclusion. "Will this end if we kill him?"

"Possibly, but it might already be too late. The dark gods are close to breaching the veil."

"Dark gods?" Mabane asked.

Kavan cracked a wry smile. "You didn't think this would be easy, did you?"

"You can't fight a god!"

"Watch us," Kavan challenged.

Mabane backed down. Quite frankly, he was tired of fighting.

"How much longer before Corso gives his speech?"

Mabane shrugged. "Not long. Most of the hunters are eager to begin. They already had their downtime in Rantis."

Strapping his sword across his back, Kavan rose. "Let's go see what the man has to say."

They eased into the gathering crowd. Armed guards shimmering in black livery marched up the wind-worn stairs leading to a wide stone platform. Fresh flowers of every color lay heaped upon the mantle. Twenty feet above the plain, the stone chwas a natural platform for speakers. Sloping ground added to the effect. The guards filed up and took rehearsed positions one meter apart across the width of the stage. Hunters crowed around the base, hungry for Corso to deliver his benediction.

Kavan led his group to a spot in the middle of the crowd. He figured Corso knew who they were and that they were here, making the decision to blend in with the crowd easy. None of the hunters bothered with them, each having his own agenda. Drums began to beat, thick, monotonous. Electricity sparked throughout the crowd. People tensed as the booming echoed. The guards drew swords as one and began slamming them on obsidian shields. *Boom. Boom.* Several hunters followed suit. Kavan didn't doubt they were plants to heighten the frenzy. A man like Corso would have multitudes of spies.

"Is this normal?" Tym asked Mabane.

He nodded softly. "Exactly the same as the last time I was here."

Corso appeared. He wasn't very tall or elegant to look upon, but he had a certain air of authority. Kavan could tell by looking at him the man had come from nothing. Dressed the same as the personal guard, Corso had an iron fist emblazoned on his tunic. A short sword, for ceremony no doubt, was belted to his waist. His eyes were narrow, pinched. He came to the edge of the platform and raised his arms to the applause of the gathered hunters.

"My friends!" he called. The crowd quietly. "Brothers in struggle. Heroes of Aradain. I welcome you to this glorious hunt."

A cheer broke out.

"You have all heard our king's words. Our land is under siege by creatures with no claim to this world. Monsters and worse plague our nights. They slink through the darkness to kill our people. Many like you have heard the call and found glory on these cursed grounds. Hundreds of the beasts have been slain by ordinary men and women like yourselves."

He swept his gaze over the assembly. "Now it is your turn. Hundreds have been slain, but more struggle up from the foul pits to murder our world. This is your day! Your first steps towards immortality! Heroes are not the men of legend we grew up learning about. There are no men doing impossible deeds during times we can't begin to dream of. True heroes are born from the sacrifice of the common man. Today is your chance to become heroes and, hopefully, expunge the heart of darkness nestled in Aradain."

Another vivacious cheer. Corso gestured for the drummer to begin anew. *Boom. Boom. Boom.*

"Go forth! Go now and seek your glory for the greater good of Humanity and our future. Kill for glory and live forever!"

A series of three horn blasts crashed over them. The crowd surged. Eager warriors funneled toward Corso's men. The hunt had officially begun.

"Quite the speaker," Aphere told Kavan.

He secretly agreed. "A lesser man might be swayed by fancy words. He is dangerous."

"Why not put a shaft through him?" Tym asked. His fellow Fist nodded agreement.

Kavan replied, "A man like that has dark powers surrounding him. He'll not be without protection wards. Any arrow would be wasted."

"How can we best such a man?"

The Gaimosian eyed him sternly. "With cold steel through the heart."

The day dragged slowly by. Kavan and the others returned to their campsite to await the thinning of the crowd. Two hundred warriors had already disappeared in Gessun Thune. None had returned. Acolytes roamed those who remained, quelling rising whispers of uncertainty. The caverns were enormous, they explained. It was perfectly natural for individual hunts to last many hours.

Kavan listened to one of them speak. His first instinct was to rip the man's throat out. Common sense prevailed however, and he kept his seat by the fire. Unseen by all, an acolyte stared hard at the Gaimosians. Shock and recognition twisted his face. He scurried back to his master before Kavan spied him. Everything Corso had predicted was coming true.

He found Corso resting on a cushioned couch, being fanned by a pair of female slaves. Corso's disinterested look faded when his acolyte kneeled.

"Speak."

"My lord, they are here."

Corso's eyes narrowed. "Impossible. My agents were to have killed them back in Rantis. You are mistaken."

The acolyte swallowed his rising fear. Corso was known to flay people for speaking falsely. "Sir, I saw the man and the woman. They are accompanied by a man with only one arm. I am certain it is the Gaimosians."

Corso rose swiftly. This close to the eclipse, he felt fresh power coursing through his veins. The dark gods were giving him strength.

"Why haven't I heard of this until now, if what you speak is true?" he snarled.

The man dropped his forehead to the ground. "I only speak of what I see."

Always these damned Gaimosians. He hated being forced to rely on incompetent help. One thousand years, and all he'd striven for was now in peril. Centuries of influence and subterfuge might be unraveled at the hands of two warriors and a cripple. He wanted to laugh. He was too close to fail. Victory must come at any cost, even if he had to slaughter every living soul assembled in the camp.

He turned to his captain. "How many have been converted thus far?"

"Near two hundred, my lord."

Two hundred fresh werebeasts. More than enough to deal with the remaining hunters. Of course, he'd lose most of his new pets, but it was of small consequence. Once the dark gods were released, he'd no longer have need of them.

"There will be no more entering the ruins today," he said quickly. "I have something special planned."

The captain bowed and went to issue orders.

FIFTY-THREE

Old Friends

Most of the encampment had already quieted down and gone to bed. The main excitement of the day was gone, drained away to nervousness and boredom. All the best had already gone on the hunt. The others were forced to wait for the dawn in what was considered an unprecedented move.

"Our turn didn't come until well into the night," Mabane offered. "I've never heard of this happening."

"Corso is making his move," Aphere whispered.

He shrugged. "Call it what you will but know this is unnatural."

"Mabane, you may not realize this, but you are caught up in the middle of a terrible war. That man, Corso, is probably the most dangerous you will ever encounter. He is the puppet master we've been searching for. Kill him, and we might just stop the enemy from succeeding."

"You're a very bleak people," Mabane replied.

Kavan snorted. "I've been called worse, my friend."

"Now that we've got that settled, what is Corso up to? Do you think he knows we're here?" Aphere asked.

"It's possible. Those black robed fools are just fancy spies."

The two Fist looked suddenly nervous.

Kavan took note but continued. "One thing bothers me about this operation. Assuming Corso knows everything about us, why hasn't he stopped us yet? Clearly, he's willing to sacrifice everyone who gets in his way. The Fist, the Gnomes, and the people of Aradain. Why, though?"

"What do you mean?" she asked.

"Why does he want us dead? What about us drives his hatred?"

Aphere didn't have the answer. How could she? She hadn't thought much about the figure who became Corso until now. "We're clearly a threat."

Not good enough. "Why? None of you have ever been to Aradain before. There are fell powers at work here, obviously seeking our demise," Kavan replied.

An uneasy silence settled over them. Not even Kavan was sure where that answer had come from. They sat in muted silence until fatigue crept in. Kavan started the night watch and allowed the others to bed down. Thieves and petty criminals ran rampant in gatherings like this. It wouldn't do to awake the next dawn and find their horses and gear missing. He took up a seat beside their small fire and listened to the sounds of the night.

"I never thought to find your sorry ass in a place like this," rumbled a deep voice.

Kavan reached for his weapons before looking at the speaker. He was a burly man dressed in dark brown leathers. Tufts of white hair poked form the v cut in his jerkin. Twin scars crisscrossed one of his thick forearms. Both his beard and hair were pure grey, the color of old snow. Time had wrinkled his skin, but his eyes remained sharp, clear — much like the huge double-headed battle axe across his back.

Kavan snarled. "I don't really give a damn what you think."

"Insolent whelp. I ought to have my man put you over his knee and take a strap to your hide."

"You'd do it yourself if you were half a man."

Then the big man smiled. "Well met, Kavan."

"Dag, good to see you again. I didn't think you'd be staying."

Aphere, who hadn't made it into her tent yet, tried to conceal her surprise. "You two know each other?"

"Aye, lass. Since before you were a gleam in your papi's eyes, I'd wager," Dag answered.

"Careful, Dag. She's one of my blood," Kavan cautioned.

Dag seemed genuinely impressed. "I can't say as I ever met a female Gaimosian. Always figured you guys was created, not born. Allow me to introduce my humble self. I am Dag of Souderlik Keep, and it is my immense pleasure to meet you."

Aphere took his hand, a rosy tinge kissing her cheeks. "As well as mine, though I doubt you've ever been called humble by anyone but yourself."

Dag winked at Kavan. "I like her. Got spunk."

"She has her moments," he agreed. "What brings you here? And with men at arms. You're a long way from home, old friend."

"My lads and I heard there was trouble brewing in these parts, and we come to put an end to it."

Kavan arched an eyebrow. He gestured for them to sit. "I think you made a mistake in coming here."

"Nonsense. You know me, lad. I've never run from a fight and don't see reason to begin now."

"You don't understand. This place is evil. I don't think any of us are going to walk away," Kavan insisted.

Dag's curiosity peaked. "What are you going on about, Kavan? We've fought together a dozen times. Never been defeated. Get to the point. Riddles don't suit you."

Kavan gave him the short version of their tale, leaving out pieces irrelevant to Dag and his men. The moon was rising by the time he finished. Several of Dag's men had lost the color in their faces as Kavan spoke. Clearly, none had come to Aradain expecting to fight gods or monsters. Only Dag betrayed no emotion.

"If I didn't know you, I wouldn't believe a word you said. Gods and demons. What's this world coming to?"

"An end unless we can stop it."

Dag rubbed his kneecap. "I'm staying. My boys, too. We came to fight, and we're not going home unblooded."

"There'll be plenty of blood for all of us," Kavan said.

"And none of you know why this Corso fella wants you dead?"

"Not a clue. He's been after us, we believe, since we crossed over the Kergland Spine," Kavan replied. "It doesn't matter anymore. This is the final hour. It all ends during the coming eclipse."

"Desperate situation."

Kavan lowered his voice to a bare whisper. "I've never felt so helpless."

"What's the plan? I can't let you stand alone. What can I help with?"

Dag was a born warrior. He'd spent most of his six decades in the middle of one war or the next. Determination forced his loyalty.

"I wish I had a thousand more like you at our side," Kavan finally admitted. "Aphere, Mabane and I need to get inside the ruins. We have to find this nexus and stop Corso from freeing his dark gods."

"Us as well," Tym spoke up. None of the group had gone to bed, having returned to the fire to hear Kavan and Dag. "We gave our word to Pharanx Gorg. Our swords will not leave your side."

Dag glanced sharply at the lad. "Pharanx Gorg? You travel in strange company these days."

"Wait until you meet the Gnome," Kavan grunted.

"Ha! All this talk of doom makes me thirsty. Lars, break out the mead," Dag called to a golden haired youth behind him.

Drinks were passed out, and the two groups merged into one cohesive unit. Only Mabane passed as the mead was passed around.

Aphere finished the warm honey mead and asked, "Dag, how did you two first meet?"

Dag waggled a finger at Kavan. "It must have been twenty years ago. This young fool was about to get thoroughly whooped by ten brigands at a card table in a cheap Antheneon whore house. Claimed they were the ones cheating."

Kavan held up his hands in defense. "There were only three of them, and I was managing just fine by myself."

"Only cause you didn't see the one coming at you from behind with that knife in his hands. It only seemed right we become friends after that. He traveled with me for a time, as you Gaimosians are wont to do. I never understood your whole good deeds for the weak concept. But I found Kavan to be a decent enough fella."

Dag stopped long enough to drain his mug. "He visited Souderlik over the years. Even came to help my father quell an insurrection. That's where I busted my right knee, and he saved my life."

"Someone needed to save you. Trouble finds you too easily."

Dag stiffened. "Who says I don't go looking for it? That's why I'm here."

"I still suggest you take your men and leave while you can."

"My mind is set, Kavan. Now, what's really happening here? Your tale was well and fine, but I want to know what to expect from here on."

"I don't know," Kavan replied. "I have a feeling we're being set up."

"Ambush?"

"Looks like it, but we don't know when or where."

Dag nodded once. "This man really wants you dead. Don't you worry, lad. Me and the boys will do our part. We'll make this damned sorcerer wish he'd never come here."

Kavan hoped Dag was right, else they'd be the ones wishing.

"You should be asleep," Aphere said, walking up behind Kavan.

He gave her a half-hearted smile. "I can't sleep. It's no big deal. I get like this all the time before a fight. What are you still doing up?"

She eased down beside him. "I wanted to apologize before it was too late."

"For what?"

"Earlier. It wasn't right of me to speak of Pirneon so. He was your friend and mentor, and I disrespected you both," she forced the words out.

Kavan kept looking at the fire. "You spoke your mind. There's nothing to it."

"No, there is more," she added.

Kavan waited patiently for her to continue. He was the sort who tried to listen, though more times than not it came down to a sword in hand. Her apology was already more than enough, and unnecessary. She was a Gaimosian Knight. That was word enough.

"I saved Pirneon's life in the desert. We got along well enough at the time, but it didn't last. He found out about my unique abilities and started turning cold on me. I think he gradually came to hate what I represented."

"What you say makes no sense. Why would the Knight Marshal of Gaimos hate one of the few remaining knights?" Kavan countered.

He stopped himself, realizing he was already trying to defend Pirneon.

She fought down her rising ire. "Did you not see the look in his eyes when he spoke to me? The man avoided me as much as he could, but that's not what I have to say. It's the oracle."

"The oracle? We were told all we needed to know back in Hresh Werd. The oracle had no secrets, Aphere."

"Yes…it did," she confessed. "Right before I went to touch it, the oracle warned me about Pirneon. He said that Pirneon would turn on us, and one of us would have to fight him to the death."

Her words hung on the air, sour notes permeating their minds.

"Why would he do such a thing? Pirneon was the best of us. Hundreds of brothers and sisters trained under his hand. Any betrayal is abandonment of our principles. He is not capable of such," Kavan argued.

"I spent weeks trying to figure it out. He's changed, Kavan. He's not the same man we once knew."

He eyed her sharply. "We have all changed, Aphere. You have powers none of the rest of us possess or understand."

She stiffened. "What are you trying to say?"

"Just that we change."

"This isn't about you or me, Kavan." Her voice trembled as she tried to remain calm. "The oracle has spoken, and I have no reason not to listen. Everything else he foresaw has come to pass."

She fell silent, and an uneasy tension settled over them. Neither truly wanted to believe the oracle. His words were anathema to their core being. Pirneon was the shining son of all Gaimos once stood for. His deeds were legendary, his stature equally so. He was the domineering presence on every battlefield he'd ever fought on. To hear Aphere speak now, Kavan suddenly knew doubt. Doubt led to more deaths than the sword.

After much internal deliberation, Kavan asked, "What do we do?"

"One of us must fight him," she exhaled.

"Is he near?"

Aphere nodded.

"So be it."

Kavan left her alone. He had much to think on and would remain troubled until the final battle. He wondered if he had the strength to stand against his former mentor, let alone kill him. There was no doubt he was meant to face Pirneon. Fate was cruel that way. Kavan crawled into his sleeping bag and settled into an uneasy sleep. A few hours later, the screaming began. He reached for his sword.

FIFTY-FOUR

Corso Attacks

Mabane screamed at the top of his lungs. Old nightmares rushed back, driving the fractured man to the edge of sanity. The careful walls he'd erected around his subconscious were shredded in an instant by the braying werebeasts. Mabane cried. His life had finally reached its conclusion. Lord Death stalked the land this night.

The gods, it seemed, had turned their backs on the people of Malweir, condemning all to murderous villainy. Werebeasts poured from the bowels of the ruins. Scores of sleeping hunters died in the first few moments as Corso unleashed his weapons. Inspired by evil, the priest of the dark gods laughed into the winds. Aradain was about to crumble.

"We're all going to die!" Mabane wailed.

Men and women rushed by. All were armed, yet none knew what they were facing. Kavan glared down at the prostrate man, detesting Mabane's inherent weakness. Friend or not, Kavan recognized him for what he was. A coward. He prayed his own fate would not be so harsh.

"On your feet or die where you lay!" Kavan roared.

"By Hell, Kavan, what's all this about?" Dag bellowed from a few meters away. Blood stained his tunic, thick rivers dripping from his sword.

Kavan snarled. "Hell, indeed. Corso has unleashed his monsters. We'll not like the night like this."

"Let's give the bastards a war. Kill enough, and the rest will break and run."

Kavan had always admired Dag's singular mind. Only right now, he believed the man was addled. "There's no way. He'll have hundreds of them, and we're just a handful."

Aphere's crossbow thrummed.

"We've an army, lad!" Dag argued.

Kavan reluctantly conceded. "Organize the defense. Hopefully, we last the night."

"That's the spirit, lad!" Dag bellowed a deep laugh and turned to his men. "Start gathering as many survivors and weapons as you can. We can win this."

Whether it was truth or not, Kavan approved. Guttural roars temporarily drowned out the screaming. The iron rich smell of blood tainted the night air. What had been an orderly camp devolved into a charnel house. Limbs and organs littered the ground. An occasional werebeast corpse lay among the dead. The battle, what remained of it, was one suited for the Gaimosians: mean and dirty.

Kavan spotted a handful of beasts loping over the edge of Corso's stage and got an idea. "Dag! Send as many people as you can up to the stone platform. Give us the high ground, and we might hold them back."

"Aye!"

Dag raised his sword high, creating a rallying point for men. Tym and his Fist counterpart were among the first to arrive. They were eager for the chance to clear the Fist name. Dag let loose an old battle cry and charged. Close to forty hunters followed in his wake. They cut a fearsome path through the carnage. Men and monsters fell under the fury of steel and ripping claws and teeth. A scaled beast landed in front of Dag, knocking them both down. Dag clenched his sword and rolled into a battle stance.

"Go!" he cried to Tym. "Get up to that stone. This beastie is mine."

The werebeast bellowed. Strips of flesh hung from between jagged teeth. Coal black eyes glared sharply at the man before him. Jealous rage seethed from its very being. It saw Dag and remembered what it had been just that morning before the dark gods had perverted it. Dag and the beast charged simultaneously, meeting in a crash of flesh.

Dag reeled back as claws raked through his leather plate armor, tearing flesh from his chest. He grunted in pain. His sword slashed wildly in hopes of fending the beast off before it struck again. Dag could have sworn he heard the werebeast laugh. The beast attacked again. A lifetime of battle came alive and Dag moved. He dropped to a knee and cut up. The impact jarred him to the bone. Ropes of dark blood dropped around him. He quickly spun from the knee, lashing out to take the beast at the calf.

Grimacing in pain, Dag realized his wounds were deeper than he'd thought. "Come on, you ugly mother...."

Missing a hand and a foot, the werebeast crawled towards him. Coiling to leap, the werebeast became frantic. Dag sidestepped and slashed ferociously as the beast dove at him. His sword ripped downward and severed the beast's head in one clean stroke.

"Are you done playing?"

Dag looked up as Kavan jerked his sword from the dead heart of another beast.

"You and I can have a go when this is finished, lad," Dag roared through his pain.

He limped to his friend. The whirlwind around them had temporarily subsided.

"Bastards fight hard," he grunted.

Kavan nodded. A stiff breeze whipped his sweat-soaked hair around his head and shoulders. He knew all too well how hard they fought. His dark eyes caught trickles of blood running down Dag's chest.

"You're injured."

Dag snorted. "Just a scratch. I've lived through worse."

Aphere darted past. Her legs from the thigh down were drenched in blood. "Are you two going to stand around gabbing like old maids, or are we going to get back in the fight?"

Dag grinned, concealing his wince. "I really like her."

"Come on," Kavan said.

The trio headed towards the rendezvous point.

"One hundred and sixty," Lars reported.

Kavan grimaced. The numbers weren't good. He estimated there had been close to a thousand hunters and their retinues in camp. Now, they'd been reduced to a paltry two hundred. Hundreds of the werebeasts lay strewn amongst the corpses. Kavan didn't doubt that Corso had many more.

Dag asked, "Can we hold out?"

The sun was breaking. Kavan had never been so glad to see the sun. The atmosphere among the survivors rose sharply as the first rays of light kissed away the darkness and drove the enemy back into their lairs.

"We still have two more days before the eclipse," Aphere answered.

"Not good odds," Kavan said.

He stared over Dag's shoulder to Mabane. Against everything, the one-armed drunk had managed to survive the initial assault. Kavan felt the stirrings of hope. Gods were fickle that way.

"I've never known you to back down from a fight," Dag said wryly.

Kavan flashed a smile. "Set half the men to sleep. Keep a quarter on watch and have the rest gather weapons, food, and water."

"Now we're talking, lad."

Kavan faced Aphere. "Take a detail and clear the dead away from the base of the platform. We'll set watch fires every twenty-five meters to give us a clear field of fire when they return."

"That still leaves us with the problem of getting into the ruins," she said.

He agreed. Before Corso had played his hand, they'd had a chance at sneaking in unnoticed. "It certainly makes our task more difficult. Mabane is the key. As long as he lives, we have a way down to the nexus."

"A small chance," Tym said.

Kavan eyed the youth, reminded of his own days wandering the world aimlessly in search of fame and glory.

"Dag, I'm going to need you to take command of this rabble."

Dag's eyes narrowed. "Just where do you think you're going?"

"We're here for specific purpose," Kavan told him. "We need to get underground."

Aphere perked up. "You have a plan?"

"Tomorrow we sneak into the cavern and kill Corso."

It sounded simple in his mind. Break into a fortress, for all intents, and slay a being in possession of dark powers far beyond their understanding. Throw in a few hundred bloodthirsty monsters, and there was virtually no way for Kavan to win. Dag's blank stare confirmed that. Not even the aged veteran believed what he'd just heard.

"You've cooked up some wild schemes in your time, but this is crazy," Dag finally managed.

"I'm not left with much choice."

"You'll die down there."

"Down there or up here, it doesn't matter. We have to try or the whole world will suffer," Kavan said.

"So be it. We'll hold these bastards off long enough for you to do what you need doing. When are you going to make a run for it?"

The knights exchanged a dubious look. Neither wanted to answer the question. They'd risked their lives for a hundred causes, none their own. Now this. The risk of failure was overpowering. Kill Corso and close the nexus. It all sounded so simple.

Aphere finally answered. "If we go during the day, the caverns will be filled with werebeasts."

"Forcing us to fight through them to reach the nexus," Kavan finished. "There is no clear favorable choice. We must time it so that we enter the moment the werebeasts emerge. Pre-position by the cavern mouth and wait until dusk."

"Leaving the rest of us to slaughter," Dag murmured thoughtfully. "Sounds like your best option, lad. How many you taking in?"

"Myself, Aphere, the two Fist, and Mabane."

"Is that enough?"

Kavan could only guess. "We'll find out soon enough. Dag, listen to me. If we don't make it back, take as many survivors as you can and flee this kingdom."

"If what you say is true, there's no point in running. I'd rather die here then hiding in a hole. Damned, but this is a tight spot," he snarled.

Pride wouldn't allow him to retreat. Kavan couldn't think of anyone better to watch his back.

"Think you can keep them busy enough?" he asked with a grin.

"We'll soon find out. Those beasties fight hard but die good. It'll be a fight to remember."

"A good fight," Tym echoed.

The youth had a pall of defeat over him. The Fist seldom stayed to fight in such dire circumstances. That they'd chosen to remain spoke volumes of their tenacity. Kavan hoped Tym had enough left in him to survive the night. There'd be need of men like him in the future world.

"It's settled." Dag rose slowly. Pain racked his chest. His wounds threatened to put him down. Sheer bravado kept him going. Dag didn't think he was going to live past this battle anyway. "You get some sleep. Lars and I will see to this."

Kavan watched his friend limp away. He tried his best to hide the pain, but Kavan saw through the charade. Dag was hurting. They knew each other well enough to avoid the subject, but it hurt Kavan to see one of his closest friends so. The knight left his friend to go about readying for battle.

Dag ran a hand through his hair. He was tired, filthy. Blood stained his clothes. He was in a fight, no doubt about that. The burly veteran surveyed his chosen battlefield dispassionately. Most of the bodies had been cleared away from the platform. Lars and a few others had even gone so far as to begin burning them before disease set in. Water and rations lay piled in the center of the perimeter. Dag figured it was more than enough, especially considering the casualties he expected tonight.

Half of the men and women left were archers, but with only a few hundred shafts between them. *Not much at all. I reckon enough to hold off the first charge. After that, it don't matter none.* Great flocks of vultures were forming in the distance, hungrily awaiting the end.

"Not yet, you bastards," he whispered.

He caught Lars watching him and shook his head. "What is it, lad?"

"We're about as ready as can be," Lars said.

"But?"

Dag was no fool. He read doubt on the boy's face.

"Are you sure we're doing the right thing?"

"You're a good man, Lars," Dag told him. His stern gaze softened. "I hope one day you'll lead men of your own. This is a task far greater than me. I believe Kavan when he tells me this. Even if I wanted to leave, I think this fight would eventually catch up. Right or wrong, the gods have already decided for us."

Greater than ourselves. Lars felt deepening pride. "The men will do their part."

Dag placed a fatherly hand on his shoulder. "You've the makings of a fine leader. How about you and me go try to inspire the troops? We can all use a little encouragement."

Kill Pirneon. Raw emotions awoke in Kavan. A friend and mentor no longer, he was forced to view the Knight Marshal as the enemy. Doubts surfaced. He didn't know if he was capable of killing a friend. Kavan was good in a fight, but only because of Pirneon's teachings. His former mentor was a harsh man, not easily bested in combat.

The notion of fighting Pirneon twisted his stomach. He'd barely slept since he and Aphere had argued. Kavan looked around. Mabane snored softly. He envied the man. To have gone through so much and still live suggested much to the Gaimosian. He had no doubts Mabane was a vital player in this game, but to what end?

Both Fist were asleep as well. So, too, was Aphere. Only he found no rest from the demons lurking in the corners of his mind. Why? He'd been in comparable situations before. What made today so different? Kavan lay his head down on his pack and closed his eyes. Pirneon and monsters eased their way into shadows, wisps of imagination. Kavan soon found the beaming face of Phirial.

He smiled. There was a fact he'd been able to come to terms with. Love was still alien, never sticking around long enough to be ensnared. It was different with Phirial. She gave him balance, a reminder of what it meant to be Human. Kavan unexpectedly turned his thoughts to putting down his sword. Phirial's flowing red locks were the last thing he thought of when restless sleep finally came.

FIFTY-FIVE

The Battle of Kalad Tol

Like wraiths, the dark shadows crawled across the battlefield towards the ancient fortress. Moncrieff's commandos were dressed in black clothes, void of anything capable of producing noise. Ten men began their advance while the rest of the army was still moving into position. Exposed flesh was darkened with coal ash and mud. They moved in slow precision, a meter at a time. Moncrieff had arranged for a series of cavalry feints to give the commandos more cover.

The mission was simple. Infiltrate enemy defenses, kill the guards, and open the gates to allow the massed column of heavy infantry a chance at punching through the heart of the Fist before the enemy could regroup. They'd been crawling for seven hours. Most were dehydrated, angry. They wanted the fight. They wanted to avenge their fallen brothers and make the Fist pay.

Moncrieff collapsed his spyglass. All was going according to plan, leaving him with that nervous feeling in the pit of his stomach. Battle plans were perfect until contact was made. The sun was setting. His forces were able to deploy without any further aerial bombardment, further heightening his nerves.

"Commander," he barked.

A bald man eased to his side. "Sir?"

"Begin massing the assault column. I want one thousand men ready to attack within the hour."

"So many, sir? That's a great risk."

Moncrieff's eyes narrowed. "You dare to question?"

"Sir, you're asking to send the bulk of the army in one move," he said without backing down.

"Risks are part of war. The Fist must pay for what they did this morning. I'll have that fortress tonight."

The commander's face flushed. "Sir, do this for tactical reasons, not revenge. This will only result in the loss of more lives."

"My lives!" Moncrieff raged. "These are my men, and as commander of the armies I will proceed how I deem best. Either obey my orders or stand relieved."

Commander Jesterin snapped to attention, rebuked. He'd tried and failed. The only question remaining was how many lives were about to be wasted. "Sir, I request permission to lead the attack."

Moncrieff stood, speechless. Jesterin had invoked his ire — though, he forced himself to admit, his anger was misdirected. Perhaps, just perhaps, he was wrong. His blood was up, and honor demanded satisfaction. Moncrieff drew to his full height and eyed his commander for signs of treachery. Jesterin was one of his most valuable assets. Losing him was more than Moncrieff was willing to consider. Still, if the commandos did their part, a senior commander leading the troops might work.

He nodded. "Very well, Jesterin. Permission granted. You will advance as soon as you see the flare go up. Seize the gates and command center. I'll send the rest of the army in to keep the Fist from escaping. Bring honor to us, Jesterin."

Jesterin saluted and went to assume his post.

"Luck in battle," Moncrieff whispered.

One by one, the commandos rose and covered the last few steps to the base of the wall. The sergeant in charge wiped his brow and looked up. Ancient beyond recollection, the walls of Kalad Tol were strong. Rising twenty feet, they provided a daunting climb. He prayed they hadn't been spotted crossing the killing field.

None of the Fist appeared on the walls with crossbows. The sergeant relaxed slightly. Getting to the walls was the problematic part. His men quietly donned their climbing spikes while he inspected the gate. The wood was old, easy to burn. He hoped General Moncrieff saw that as a benefit should the commandos fail. The man beside him touched his arm and pointed upwards. The sergeant nodded and began to climb.

Pebbles and loose stone chipped away. The commandos froze in place each time it happened. They were dangerous but vulnerable. The climb resumed. Ten feet. Fifteen. When he reached the lip of the wall, the sergeant pulled his short sword from the sheath across his back. He whispered a quick prayer and rose just enough to get a look.

He smiled. There wasn't a guard in sight, and those Fist in the compound seemed to be going about normal business. Smells of stew and roasting meat filled the air. His stomach growled at the temptation. They'd caught the enemy unawares. If all was going according to plan; the army would be massing right now, waiting for his signal. He slipped over the wall and crouched in the natural shadows. One by one, his men followed until they were assembled.

A Fist guard emerged from the tower to his right, blindly heading their way. The sergeant set down his sword in favor of a throwing knife. His aim was true. The blade took the Fist in the throat. A commando darted out to catch the body before it fell. Three others rushed past to kill those remaining Fist in the tower.

"Go," the sergeant ordered. "Half and half on each side of the gate. I want it open in five minutes."

They nodded and filed down the aging steps.

Jesterin waited anxiously as night continued to deepen. He hated waiting almost more than any other single event revolving around a battle. It was both hated and necessary, the one moment every commander was forced to endure. Any one of a hundred things could go wrong. Tension and apprehension clashed in him. War was fickle, seldom predictable and run by raw emotions. Jesterin felt the unease rise among his men.

"Steady, lads, steady," he turned and said with all the poise of a veteran. "We've all been here before. You know this game. Once the gate is open, we rush in and kill them all. Nothing to it."

Jesterin hoped his captains and sergeants were doing the same throughout the ranks. The army was ready to attack, trusting in their leaders to do the right thing and keep them alive. He wished for their confidence. Moncrieff wasn't acting like himself lately, giving Jesterin pause. The senior commander was beginning to think Corso had gotten to the general.

Corso. He'd never liked the man, seeing him as a base coward who twisted others into doing his bidding. Jesterin doubted he'd ever gotten his hands dirty before. Yet for all that, Eglios trusted him implicitly. Corso all but ran the kingdom now. This campaign had been his creation. No one else in Aradain viewed a handful of mercenaries as much of a threat. Certainly not enough to send the bulk of the army with the commanding general in charge. Jesterin reckoned their current course of action was leading them all down an unrecoverable path.

"Why isn't the catapult firing?" one of the rankers asked.

Jesterin grimaced in the dark. "We don't want them to know we're coming, do we? You just worry about doing your job, trooper. That goes for all of you. Look after the men to your left and right, and you'll be fine. The enemy hides behind his walls hoping to break our morale. We'll put them to rights soon enough, never you worry about that. Get inside. Do your jobs. No prisoners. Come the dawn, we'll plant the king's colors on the highest tower."

Those nearest murmured approval. Fine words often were enough inspiration right before a fight. Jesterin knew this from experience, he just didn't know if they would be enough. Bright green light burst over the walls of Kalad Tol, shattering his thoughts. The sign. Jesterin's heart lurched. He drew his sword.

"Forward!"

The command echoed down the ranks. The army of Aradain committed to battle.

"March!"

One thousand heavy infantry surged forward under a symphony of grinding boots and jostling armor. Jesterin stepped out a quick pace, hoping to cover the five hundred meters as quickly as possible. The sooner he closed with the enemy, the less chance the Fist had to react, negating their air power. Grounded, the Fist were no better than his men.

Jesterin's legion moved faster. Concerns for stealth vanished. Speed became the key to success. The ten commandos inside the castle wouldn't last long without support. Soldiers surged behind as he broke into a jog. The flare burned supernaturally, reminding Jesterin of ghostly tales his father used to tell. He half-expected to see rotted corpses rising from the ground to pull them all down to the underworld. Jesterin shivered. They had less than one hundred meters to go. His pulse quickened. No matter what else happened, they wouldn't stop until either dead or victorious.

At fifty meters, he broke into a full sprint. The soldiers refrained from issuing battle cries. Jesterin burst through the open gates with his lead squads and froze. Moncrieff's commandos lay in front of them. Their bodies were torn and hacked. Jesterin lifted his gaze to find fifty archers and a hundred pike men leering back at them. Pharanx Gorg grinned savagely, blood staining his face. The Fist commander lowered his sword arm. Fifty bows thrummed.

"Fire!" Pharanx bellowed the command loud enough for the rest of the Fist concealed atop the walls to hear.

Two hundred men rose from cover and began peppering the advance ranks of infantry with well-placed fire. Having amassed so close, they were easy targets. Barum directed the assault from the center wall. He and those closest began targeting the rear ranks, driving the front closer to the false protection of the walls. Below came the sounds of clashing steel.

Pharanx Gorg attacked with reckless fury. He hadn't sought out this fight, but Corso had forced it nonetheless. He relished the surprise registering in the enemy commander's face right before an arrow cut him down. Geblin stood beside him, launching quarrel from his crossbow into the confused enemy. His wizened face was expressionless. The Gnome went about his work with dispassionate efficiency. Men died where he aimed, though he took no pleasure from it. There was no honor in this massacre.

"Check you fire, Gnome," Pharanx hissed. "I don't want one of your quarrels in my ass!"

Geblin ignored him. The Fist commander stepped into a slashing blow, slipping in a pool of blood while whipping his sword out. Steel crunched bone, and the enemy infantry dropped with a shout. One of Geblin's bolts pierced his forehead, driving through brain and out the back, cutting off his cry. A horn bellowed from outside the gates. Moncrieff's soldiers fell back in a disorganized rabble.

"They retreat!" Barum called from the wall.

Still on his back, Pharanx croaked, "Cease fire! They are broken."

Fist archers fell silent. Only now did they take stock of the carnage committed. More than three hundred bodies lay on the field. Most were dead, while a small handful tried to crawl away. The Fist had lost thirty with another ten out of the fight.

"Damnation," Geblin whispered.

Pharanx got to his feet, frowning at the blood coating his back. The acidic stench of so much death was overpowering.

"I've never seen the likes before," Geblin explained.

"Pray you never do again. No race should slaughter one another so readily."

Geblin slung his crossbow. "Will they retire?"

Pharanx lead his friend outside the gates. "No. Moncrieff will only try harder. We are still sorely outnumbered. He has the option of calling for reinforcements. We don't. Each of our dead hurts badly."

Wurz joined them. He was drenched in blood, some of it his. The Dwarf wore a surly look mixed with pain and exhaustion. "Bastards kept coming."

Pharanx looked his lieutenant up and down. "Get to the surgeon before you bleed to death on me."

"I can do my job just fine. There's worse in there than me," he argued back.

"That's an order, Lieutenant. I'm going to need you before this is finished."

Wurz grumbled something unintelligible and turned to leave. He collapsed first. Pharanx dropped to his side, fearful his friend was dead.

"Medic!" he cried.

Four men rushed to carry Wurz to the hospital. Barum walked up, shock in his eyes.

"What do we do now?" Pharanx asked him.

Barum wasn't sure. By rights, they should all be dead. If it hadn't been for Geblin spotting the commandos, the fortress would already have fallen. They owed the Gnome their lives.

FIFTY-SIX

Counterattack

The Fist counterattacked shortly before dawn, when the night was at its darkest and coldest. Fiery explosions raged throughout the Aradain camp. The price of slaughter was high. Men lay broken, screaming. Pharanx's riders targeted the camp center, hoping to cut off the command structure. They watched Moncrieff's tent burst into flames, along with a dozen more. Mission complete, the Fist riders headed back to their camp.

"That's the end of that," Pharanx said after taking his place on the wall. "We've got no more surprises."

Barum finished fletching the arrow in his hand. "They'll be wary at first."

"Only until they figure out we have no more tricks. If Moncrieff still lives, he'll hit us hard, nonstop."

"A hard fight," the knight agreed.

"Incoming!" shouted a sentry.

The Fist took cover moments before the first catapult round exploded against the wall. Gouts of flame licked up, catching any too slow. Black smoke curled into the sky. The smell of burnt flesh assault their senses.

"We won't last too long against that," Geblin commented, forgetting the enemy only had one functional catapult.

The Gnome appeared a decade older. His sarcasm was gone. The bitterness he'd had when the knight had rescued him had been replaced by the overwhelming need for survival. Most of all, Geblin had lost the urge to continue roaming Malweir. He wanted to go home. Gnomes weren't meant for war. Yet the only way home was getting through Moncrieff's army. Creidlewein had already been attacked once. He feared the worst was yet to come.

Barum asked, "I thought we took out their siege engines?"

"They had one remaining. Unless, of course, their engineers managed to piece together more."

"We need to take it down, fast. As long as Moncrieff has it, he owns the advantage. Time is our enemy as much as that army," Barum watched a second fireball scream towards them.

The projectile exploded against the crenellation of a guard tower, sending flame and rock everywhere. Men fell screaming. Others rushed to extinguish the flames. The barrage continued for another hour. Moncrieff clearly intended on pummeling them into submission and had the ammunition to do so.

By noon, the defenders were on edge. Gaping holes peppered the side of most of the buildings. Too many Fist had been wounded. Fortunately, only a handful had been killed. Surgeons treated the wounded, cursing as fresh patients continually arrived. Pharanx looked to the mass grave growing in the far corner of the main compound. The names of the dead were engraved in the stone walls of the old chapel. He wouldn't let those who died disappear into nameless history.

"We're already down to three hundred men," he told his council.

It was late at the end of the second day. Moncrieff's one catapult continued firing. The mercenaries had grown accustomed to it.

Barum scratched his chin. "They have to be hurting as much as we are."

"They can afford to. Moncrieff doesn't have to make a move. He can sit back and wait until we're reduced to nothing."

He had to admit Pharanx had a point. The Fist didn't have much left. "Do you think we can destroy the catapult? We need to negate that advantage."

Pharanx shrugged. "I don't see how. It has to be the most heavily guarded site in their camp. It would a suicide mission. Frankly, we can't afford to waste the manpower. You saw how well their raid worked out. Why should ours be any different?"

"We must do something," Barum insisted.

"We are just the diversion," Pharanx reminded.

"That doesn't mean I plan on dying here. Kavan can handle himself. What we —"

A cry from the wall cut him off. "Rider coming in!"

Pharanx and the others grabbed their weapons and rushed to the wall. One man on a chestnut mare rode casually within bow range. He bore a captain's rank and appeared just as haggard as the defenders. A small white flag hung limp from the end of a broken spear.

"That's far enough," Pharanx called down.

"General Moncrieff wishes to discuss a temporary truce," the captain said. The words were like acid on his tongue.

Pharanx felt a tremor of hope. "Speak your terms."

"We request amnesty to gather our wounded and dead from the field. General Moncrieff gives his word that we will not attack during that time, so long as you hold your fire."

"That's not really in my best interests."

"Time, Pharanx. They're giving us time," Barum whispered.

Clearly irritated, Pharanx submitted. "Very well, Captain. You have your two hours."

The mercenary leader left the wall. His thoughts were scrambled with trying to devise a trap for the enemy. Honor demanded otherwise. Were he a lesser man, he'd attack as soon as Moncrieff's men were distracted.

"What are your orders?" Barum asked.

Pharanx halted halfway down the stairs. "Let them have their dead. As you say, we need the time."

"You don't sound convinced."

"I'm not."

Barum caught the glimmer in his eye. "You're scheming."

"As long as he has that damned catapult, our position remains untenable. I'm going to lead a group and destroy it."

Barum balked.

"Take command here. The men will follow you," Pharanx told him. He enjoyed how Barum's mouth dropped. "I know what it is you have to say, Gaimosian. Save your words. My mind is decided. May fortune favor you. I have had my fill of fighting."

Moncrieff climbed into his saddle. Stretcher bearers and wagon masters readied around him. A platoon of fifty cavalry waited in columns of two. Moncrieff didn't suspect any treachery but couldn't leave it to chance. Mercenaries seldom were honorable, and, from what he'd been told, Pharanx Gorg was no exception.

"Sir, we are prepared to move," the chief surgeon announced.

"Very well, sound the advance," Moncrieff replied.

He still smarted from the loss of Jesterin. Regrets echoed. He shouldn't have let his most senior advisor lead the first assault, but anger had reduced his capacity for reason. Slaughter was the result. And in a day when a third of his army was diminished, he sorely felt the loss. The siege was taking longer than he wanted. Aradain was all but undefended while he wasted away at Kalad Tol.

He toyed with the idea of betraying the truce and ending it all now. The Fist certainly deserved as much. That band of misfits was making a habit of embarrassing him. His commando's failure cut almost as deep as Jesterin. With most of his tactical options shattered, he was left with the old-fashioned infantry assault with scaling ladders. The loss of life would be tremendous.

Moncrieff had proven capable on numerous battlefields. The Fist presented him with a unique dilemma. He'd never been attacked from the sky. It was unheard of, cowardly. It was also highly effective. His men spent more time watching the skies than on the forces in Kalad Tol. Both attacks thus far had taken heavy tolls. The men of Aradain were losing confidence.

His sole purpose in leading the recovery column was to get a glimpse at the man who had stymied his army. Good generals led from the front. He needed not only for Pharanx to see that but also for his men to understand that he cared. He offered encouragement here and there as they passed through the front lines.

Moncrieff studied the shattered front walls of Kalad Tol. They would have already crumbled if he'd still had use of his engines. The gates were old, probably shored up from within. Dozens of mercenaries watched from the ramparts. Their impassive stares told him all he needed. Naturally, they were no more impressed with him than he was with them. Moncrieff spied the distinctive features of a Gnome among them and tensed. Corso's Gaimosians were said to be travelling with one of the small folk. His stomach began to churn. His men weren't prepared to battle Vengeance Knights. He checked the men around him to see if any had noticed the same thing.

For their part, none cared about the defenders. They went about the grim task of gathering the wounded and dead. Surgeons acted desperately to save what lives they could. Others pointed out corpses to cloth-faced litter bearers. The dead were stack unceremoniously in the wagon beds. Once one was full, the driver headed back to camp.

"General, over here."

Moncrieff saw where the ranker was pointing and gradually slid from his horse. He removed his helmet, allowing nearby soldiers to witness the grief etched in his face. He knew who the ranker was point at. Drawing heavy breath, the general of Aradain's army knelt beside Jesterin's broken corpse.

A lifetime of warfare, and he still hadn't gotten used to how pale and waxen the dead looked. Especially when it was a friend. He laid a tender hand on Jesterin's chest beside a gaping wound. Whoever had killed him had done so instantly, a small mercy.

"Put him on the back of my horse," Moncrieff ordered. "He's to receive full military honors. He died a hero of the kingdom."

"Yes, sir."

Moncrieff stayed with the body until two more soldiers retrieved it and then walked behind them, eyes lowered to the ground. He'd made an unforgivable mistake, and it had cost Aradain many loyal sons. It would be many years before he managed to forgive his error. Moncrieff vowed to erect a monument to Jesterin and all the others upon his return to Rantis. He didn't speak again until rejoining the lines.

"Captain, where do we stand?"

"All of the siege equipment is ready. We've pieced together another functional catapult. The line units all know who will be in the main assault tomorrow."

Moncrieff nodded. "Very good. See that Jesterin's body is prepared for travel back to the capital."

"Yes, sir."

Moncrieff drained his mug of water. "I want every man not involved in the assault to attend the funerals. Order those two catapults to resume firing. Let's give the Fist scum a long night, shall we?"

"I'll send a runner immediately, sir."

Moncrieff watched him go, suddenly feeling tired. His senior commander was dead, his troops demoralized. He needed a victory, any victory, but was at a loss for ideas. Perhaps observing the funeral rites would ease his troubled mind.

"Sir, we're under attack!" shouted his captain from just outside the tent flap.

Moncrieff exploded from his cot. The initial daze and confusion bled away with the touch of familiar leather straps on his sword hilt.

"Where?"

Flames rose above the rear of the camp, dangerously close to his supply lines. Cold dread crept upon him. The catapults. Moncrieff scanned the semi-dark skies for signs of those damnable flying beasts. Squads of soldiers ran in various directions, taking positions on the perimeter.

Moncrieff grabbed the captain by the collar. "How did this happen? I ordered triple guard."

"The guards were all killed," the captain struggled.

"Impossible. That would mean the enemy has found a path into our camp."

"Yes, sir, that is what we believe."

Moncrieff shoved the man away, cursing them both for being fools. His mind raced through scenarios to discover the truth. Then it dawned on him. The dead. He had never bothered checking to ensure all the bodies had been his men. Now, the worst of all scenarios was playing out. Enemy assassins roamed his camp freely.

"Gather my personal guard," he barked.

The captain protested, "Sir, it's much too dangerous. If you fall...."

"I'm aware of the risks, Captain," he snapped. "Now, do your job. I want their heads before dawn."

"We could spend hours trying to find them. They may have already gone," he protested.

Moncrieff's face darkened. "No. They are still here. Get ready, Captain. I think they have come to kill me."

"Based on what?"

"That's the only move that makes sense. Pharanx Gorg knows we can pummel him down until they're no longer mission capable. He must attack now, try and break us when we least expect it." Smoke caressed his nostrils. "Send the attack."

His adjutant stared back in disbelief. "At night, sir?"

Moncrieff's eyes were ablaze. "Yes, damn it! Now! Form ranks and attack."

He threw a crisp if undecided salute and marched off barking orders. Moncrieff fought down a smile. Assaulting Kalad Tol wasn't his main objective, though he hoped it would flush out the mercenaries in his ranks. Moncrieff wanted the fight. Wanted to be done with this bloody affair.

The veteran general stalked through his camp, ringed in personal guards. He bellowed encouragement to the forces marshalling for the assault.

"For the glory of Aradain," he roared, sword raised high.

Weary men found their pride renewed and cheered both their leader and their kingdom. His blood up, Moncrieff authorized the advance. The siege of Kalad Tol had entered the final stage. By dawn, the battle would be done.

Moncrieff and his ring of steel marched past dozens of shadows. His focus was on exposing enemy infiltrators, to lure them out. What better temptation than the general of the army? His first two guards went down with arrows in their chests. The rest halted, constricting around Moncrieff. None had seen where the shots came from. Moncrieff snarled. Three more guards fell dead, all from different angles in the circle.

"Cowards!" Moncrieff shouted. "Face me and die like men!"

"Not much incentive to fight," a voice shouted back.

The last three guards fell. Blood ran in small streams under Moncrieff's heels. He gripped his sword tighter, fully expecting to be riddled with arrows. A slender figure emerged from the night, and he instantly knew it was Pharanx Gorg.

The mercenary commander bowed elegantly. "I've come for your head and to end this."

Moncrieff snorted a laugh. "You'll find that tougher than you think, unless you plan on using your cowards to finish me."

"No. I've already sent them off. This is just you and me."

"Your mistake," Moncrieff said.

He charged. Steel clashed with sparks. He was the older of the pair, more experienced. Moncrieff carved downward slashes from left and right before dropping back. Sword poised in high guard, he awaited the inevitable counter.

Pharanx barely raised his sword in time to block Moncrieff's assault. Vibrations echoed down his arms. He smiled grimly, momentarily letting arrogance show. He knew he was faster, stronger, and better than the old man. Pharanx wanted to get inside his head. It began by stealing confidence. The mercenary recognized that killing Moncrieff was the only way to give his meager force half a chance.

Soldiers began to ring in around them.

"Do not interfere!" Moncrieff ordered. "This is my fight. Let us be."

Pharanx accepted that he wasn't going to leave alive. All he could hope for was victory in this duel. *Funny, I never figured I'd die by suicide.* He lunged. Golden sparks showered his gloved hands. Slack. Parry. Hack. They spun and whirled. Bodies twisted in the dance of death. Breathing became heavy. Muscles ached from the sheer strain. Soldiers cheered their general with each move.

Moncrieff landed the first telling blow. Pharanx stumbled after blocking a brutal riposte. Moncrieff saw the opening and twisted out. His blade ripped across the top of a thigh. The Fist groaned, hot blood washing down his leg. He lashed out in reply, tapping the cutting blade away. Men roared approval. Pharanx Gorg felt the balance shift. Empty defeat became a very real possibility.

Moncrieff sensed victory. The blood running down his sword was bright in the light of a hundred torches. The very sight pushed him harder. He fought with reckless abandon, knowing the moment he slowed, Pharanx would rip him apart. Moncrieff hefted his sword and charged back into the fight for kingdom and glory.

Pain lanced through Pharanx's thigh. His window of opportunity was closing. In a daring move, he feigned letting the pain take control. Through the sweat dripping down his brow, he saw the bloodlust dominating Moncrieff's mind. Pharanx flexed, dropping to a knee. The deception worked. Moncrieff bore down on him.

The Fist used every ounce of will not to move in the face of the almost blinding attack. His opponent made a crucial mistake, however. The fury of his attack left him exposed. Pharanx stabbed up, taking Moncrieff at the base of the throat. Dark blood sprayed over both men. Moncrieff let out a gurgled cry and the blade punched through the spine and then out the back of his neck. His sword dropped. A stunned silence fell over the makeshift arena. Pharanx twisted his blade before ripping it out the side. Aradain's greatest general fell, dead before he hit the ground.

Struggling to his feet, Pharanx looked around. More than a hundred soldiers surrounded him. He offered a wry smile, fingers flexing on his sword.

"Come on, then, you bastards," he snarled.

The ring closed. Swords rose, and Pharanx Gorg fell.

"They're coming over the wall!"

Barum snapped his head around to the sound of the voice. Enemy soldiers were trickling over the ramparts, slowly swallowing the defenders. The night assault had taken the Fist by surprise. Aradainian soldiers swarmed up ladders. Arrows whizzed everywhere as the Fist struggled to rally.

Barum looked across the battleground with the aid of the pale moonlight and despaired. Hundreds of enemy soldiers were attacking. Moncrieff had sent his entire host. That could only mean Pharanx had failed. Barum watched the last flames from the catapults rage. It was a small condolence. The bombardments might be finished, but at the cost of the Fist leader. Barum knew once the others learned they were leaderless the defense would crumble. He had to act before all was lost.

"Geblin!"

The Gnome jerked his blade from the ribcage of a fallen foe and hobbled over. "This is hopeless. We've lost too many men. The enemy is fighting hard for the gates. Barum, if they get the gates open…."

He let it drop; no point in stating the obvious.

"It's worse," Barum said. "The eclipse has begun."

"Damnation. Do you think the others have succeeded?"

"I don't know.

Geblin nodded in grim understanding. There was nothing for it. "Then we defend the gates for as long as possible and hope for the best."

"I'll rally from here. Help the others. I think Pharanx is dead. We must hold. Kill enough, and the rest will break," Barum said.

Geblin nodded and slipped down the blood-slickened stairs as the first rays of sunlight crept into the night. Barum frowned, for the dawn was spoiled with an unclean taint. He cursed their foul fortunes. The oracle had never said what time of day the eclipse was supposed to be. They'd naturally assumed it would be late in the day; that it rode the dawn cast dread over his heart.

He prayed Kavan and the others were well about their task; otherwise…. Barum drew an arrow. There was little else he could do. The fate of Malweir was no longer in his hands. He'd done all he could to aid the quest, but now his part was drawing to a close. All he had left was the remnants of the Fist. He knew better than to think they'd survive.

The dawn grew dimmer. Bodies stacked around him. The ground grew soggy from blood and offal. The siege of Kalad Tol was almost at its resolve, and unless Kavan was successful, it would end badly.

FIFTY-SEVEN

Into the Ruins

Heartbeats sounded as thunder to Kavan as they crept into position near the cavern mouth. He felt as if this was his first campaign. Aphere and the others moved in single file behind him. Kavan seethed inside, building intensity in order to accomplish his task. Yet between Corso's mischief and Pirneon's abandonment, he felt insecure. Subterfuge wasn't a trait amongst Gaimosians.

The day was dying, casting a pall over the slaughter fields. Very soon, the enemy would attempt to retake the field. Dag and the survivors would be hard pressed to survive the night. Added defenses and preparations greatly improved their chances of success along with giving Kavan much needed time.

"There," he whispered, pointing to a shallow depression in the rock face.

Aphere slipped ahead, her lithe form nimbly climbing the handful of meters to where he pointed in a matter of seconds. The rest paused until she gave them the all clear. Mabane was helped up by Tym, the others following soon after.

The cavern mouth beckoned. Foul temptations leaked from the blackness, whispered promises of unbridled power, raw and wicked. He felt small. Doom, they whispered in a chorus of wails. Doom awaited the enemies of the dark gods. Doom to all the world. His mind clouded. The voices sought to gain control. His very soul felt threatened.

Kavan shook his head. A new voice, thin, entered his thoughts. *You shall not fall*. Kavan took heart.

"What was that?" Aphere asked, suspicion aroused by his queer actions.

"Later," he replied.

Her eyes narrowed with mistrust. She'd felt those same temptations, though not as distinctly. A golden presence surrounded her, driving away the darkness. It was nothing explainable yet was utterly familiar. She was only discovering her newfound powers. Perhaps they kept her safe from the darkness. Whatever her protections, Kavan had none but his strength of character. She decided to watch him carefully. Pirneon's betrayal stung enough to place a measure of mistrust deep in her core.

She pressed the issue, "I know what you felt just now."

"I said later," he shot back.

"No, Kavan. There is no later. Now is not the time for selfish pride. The allure of this place is strong. I've felt it since we first came here." She laid a hand tenderly on his forearm. "You must remain wary. The dark gods seek to spoil our minds with empty promise. Stay strong."

Golden light poured into his veins from her slightest touch. His faith and hope were restored. Kavan felt invigorated. The immense feeling took him to the brink of tears. When she withdrew her hand, the warmth remained. He at last felt ready to take on the host of the enemy.

"Thank you," he whispered.

She smiled.

"What happens now?" Tym asked, having heard none of their conversation.

Kavan answered, "We wait."

The sun continued to drop, letting the curtain of twilight advance over the horizon.

"They will come soon."

Tym asked, "Will they pass us by?"

"Who can say? These beasts are cunning, almost as if they know the ways of men." Kavan frowned at the last thought.

The enemy was savage, void of reason or emotion. Still, they betrayed an almost human intelligence. That made him uneasy. Kavan was already weary of fighting them. He longed for the open plain and massing armies.

Mabane watched the Gaimosians closely. His heart told him they were all going to die. No amount of well wishing or cheery thoughts of optimism would make a difference. He also knew when to keep his mouth shut. He'd foresworn any notion of survival the day he turned sober. The Gaimosians were self-destructive people. He now understood why their kingdom had been so easily destroyed.

Aphere said, "Relax. We stick to the plan, and all with be fine."

She didn't believe her own words. All their efforts hung on their bet that Corso was their foe. Any moment the sun would disappear and hordes of werebeasts would emerge. The odds that they would empty the caverns were slim at best. How many untold numbers would the small band be forced to fight through in order to achieve victory? She didn't want to know.

Kavan sensed her doubts and leaned close. "Is your power going to help us like it did in the Uelg?"

"I don't know, Kavan," she hushed. "I have no idea how it works."

"You may be our best shot at victory."

She offered a weak smile. "Corso had best watch out."

Kavan sighed. The board was set. All that remained was the opening move. His thoughts turned towards fighting Pirneon. All his earlier doubts were gone. He felt Pirneon nearby, confirming the Knight Marshal's treachery. Shadows grew deeper. A noticeable chill dropped. Night had rushed upon them, almost as if it wanted the coming battle to take place. As the world teetered on the edge of destruction, Kavan wasn't sure if it wanted to be saved. He sensed the sudden tremor in the ground. The time had come. Tomorrow, the eclipse would taint the sky and, unless he and his companions won the night, all Malweir would be enslaved for eternity. The dark gods laughed from their icy tombs.

"They're coming," Kavan said. "We move on my signal."

Crouching, willing themselves to blend with the shadows, they waited as rock and dirt poured down around them. Dust choked the air. What started as a low growl deep in the bowels of the earth evolved into a terrible roar. Hundreds of werebeasts burst from the opening in a mass of gnashing teeth. The smell of rot spurred them on.

Kavan gave up trying to count after one hundred. More and more issued forth. Corso had sent his entire force against the last of the hunters. Kavan offered a fast prayer for Dag, hoping they'd both survive long enough to share a mug of ale. The thick smell of urine assaulted his nostrils. He didn't need to look to know that the horror had already gotten to Mabane.

Sounds of battle filled the night sky, and still the enemy came on.

Screams followed cries of rage. Kavan held his team until well after the last of the werebeasts was gone. Now was not the time for carelessness. When he was finally satisfied, he slid down the rope and beckoned. Only the wind stirred in reply.

Hefting his sword, Kavan advanced into the gloom. The werebeast burst from the darkness with mouth open and arms extended. The attack was so sudden that Kavan couldn't react. All he saw was long teeth glistening with saliva and blood. Aphere's arrow took the beast in the mouth, punching through the back of the skull. Blood and brain matter sprayed against the rock face. Aphere dropped into position beside Kavan and reloaded. If this was any indication of what was to come, they were in for a long night.

"Fire!"

Dag's command was all but drowned out over the roar of the enemy. Bloodthirsty werebeasts pushed and clawed their way towards the stone platform for the chance to kill again. Dozens died in the first volley. A second round dropped more. Then the werebeasts were upon the defenders. Man and beast fell. Blood flowed freely across the scarred rock, but the line held. Some men broke and ran, only to be run down almost immediately.

The fighting was brutal, furious. A hulking monstrosity with the mane of a lion climbed over the backs of others to attack Dag. The big man hefted a long wooden spear and stabbed. The blunt tip pierced through the beast's wide chest and out the back. Gathering what strength it had left, the beast lunged. Dag clung to the spear, knowing he was dead if he let go.

The beast was strong, too strong for any mortal being. Impossibly long fingers dug deep into Dag's shoulders. Pain exploded. The beast squeezed harder, intent on crushing the life from his victim. Dag finally abandoned the spear to wrap his own hands, meaty from decades of labor, around the beast's throat. Both warriors stood locked in violent contest. Blackness crept into the corners of Dag's vision. He was no match for the sheer volume of hatred driving him down to his knees. The pain was excruciating. Dag squeezed harder. Desperation sank in.

Lars appeared from nowhere, driving his sword across the werebeast's hamstring. Dag dropped. Trapped on the spear, the werebeast could only bellow in frustration as both Dag and Lars stabbed it to death. Lars helped the old man up, careful not to mention the wince of pain in his lord's face. No man liked to be reminded of weakness.

"Thank you, lad."

Lars nodded and returned to the battle. Dag smiled fondly. He liked the boy, enough that he had misgivings about bringing him here to die. Frustrations pointless, he retrieved his spear and charged the snarling monster crawling over the lip of the platform. He stabbed with all his remaining strength. The blade sliced neatly through the beast's shoulders before shattering on the rock. The beast roar in agony, and Dag crushed his boot down through its skull.

A second bolted over the dead to tackle Dag. Dust roiled up around them from the force of collision. Man and beast grappled for the advantage. They punched and twisted, each trying to kill the other. Dag alternated blows against the exposed ribs until dark blood seeped through the diseased flesh. His knuckles were raw, sore. A bloody mess.

He'd never been in such a fight. The very limits of his strength were tested beyond measure. Dag's blows fell with the ferocity of hammers. Hot saliva drooled onto his cheek, stinging flesh. He looked up into the nearing maw. Strips of flesh were stuck between the long fangs. Bone fragments caked the tongue, dropping with each breath.

The beast targeted Dag's wounds. Claws dug into the holes already rent and ripped. Dag screamed from pain, hammering the beast harder. There was a sharp crack, and the beast reeled. One of the cheekbones was broken.

Ivory shards ripped through the flesh. Dag's blood boiled. He stepped up the attack. Strain and exertion were taxing him to the end. He was already at his limits. Dag gathered his strength for a final blow and was rewarded with the sickening crunch of the windpipe crushing.

Dag crawled away. The beast gasped, writhing on the ground in death throes. Dag slammed his dagger down to kill the beast. He nearly paused, finding recognition in the beast's eyes; it was almost as if it was pleading for the end. The beast died with a satisfied look. Dag sheathed his dagger and retreated before the next beast could succeed where the others failed.

FIFTY-EIGHT

Gessun Thune

The tunnel mouth was the most comfortable part of their journey, if such a thing could be said. The darkness constricting the passageway was almost pure. Though the way was rank from filth and decay, the tiny band proceeded unmolested. The beast Aphere killed in the opening had been the only sign of enemy activity they'd seen thus far. Kavan knew better than to think it would last.

Mabane was never more than a step behind — whether to point the way or out of fear, Kavan didn't know. What mattered was that he didn't break and run when given the opportunity. Kavan approved. The man was broken and certainly demoralized but managed to regain a measure of inner strength. He led them down into the caverns, edging closer to the ruins buried within.

None of them, not even Mabane, knew what to expect within the forgotten city. Myths and legends were few. The agents of the dark gods looked to secrecy to keep curious adventurers from getting too close. Those foolish enough to come anyway disappeared. Kavan and the others figured Corso had manipulated the peoples of Aradain and, to an extent, all Malweir to believe that the dark gods were gone, locked away in their ethereal prison.

That didn't matter to Kavan. His thoughts swirled around combating Pirneon and ending this nightmare. The prophecy must be fulfilled. He marched with squared shoulders and head high into the darkness. Some moments were shaped by an entire lifetime of struggle. Kavan was destined for this moment.

"Wait," Mabane whispered in his ear.

Kavan dropped into a fighting stance. He'd been embarrassed at being caught off guard once and was determined not to let it happen again. He felt Mabane shuffle closer.

"This is the entrance to the dead city."

Kavan narrowed his eyes. "Dead city?"

"Yes. Just ahead are dozens of ruined buildings. This was once a great city, long before Aradain became a kingdom."

"I don't like this. We are at too much of a disadvantage here," Kavan said. "Which way now?"

"The ruins are directly ahead, but from there, I know not. I can't help without knowing what we're looking for," Mabane replied.

"I can't help with that. We'll find out together," Kavan admitted. "Come on."

They slipped into the ruins, dangerous people intent on removing an ancient evil. Kavan displayed methodical precision. He led with flawless ability despite lacking a clear destination. The ground was smooth from the constant trample of boots and moccasins. Vision adapting, Kavan made out the edges of buildings. Ruined temples and homes filled the massive cavern. An entire civilization lay destroyed. Bones littered the ground at random intervals. Some were old, others not so much. Kavan had just stepped over a skeleton when Aphere hissed warning.

"Wait."

He froze. "Where?"

Aphere crept closer. "Pirneon. I can feel him."

Kavan's heart slowed. His mouth went dry. "Are you certain?"

She nodded vigorously. "Yes, but it…feels different. I can't explain it, but it's almost as if it is no longer the Pirneon we knew."

Fearful of her predictions, Kavan tensed. "How is that possible? He was our strongest."

The rational part of his mind refused to accept such a travesty could occur. Admittedly, Gaimosians were far from perfect, having their share of villains and fallen heroes, but Pirneon had been the pillar of their order for a very long time. The future of their bloodlines depended on men like Pirneon. For him to have fallen signified foul times approaching.

Aphere gripped his arm. "I don't know, but beware. I can feel the evil in this place. Gessun Thune thirsts. I can hear it calling. The dark gods are close. Kavan, the eclipse is nearly upon us."

"I thought the eclipse was late tomorrow?"

Her revelations changed everything. Precious little time remained for them to accomplish their task. Kavan felt new weight crushing him down.

"Look!" Mabane squeaked.

A haunting glow flamed to life in the cavern center. Pale green waves swept over the ruins like a thunderhead on a cool summer evening. The natural humidity of the subterranean chamber evaporated, leaving all with an eerie chill. Wails from a thousand broken souls rose from the ground. All had been murdered in this foul place and forever trapped by the eldritch powers desperately clinging to life. Centuries of pain suddenly erupted in undisguised glory. Promises of devastation entered the knights' minds.

Kavan sickened at the thought of wasting damnation as the green glow washed over them. The force was staggering. Pressure built in their heart and heads. Arteries swelled, threatening to burst. Blood trickled from ear and nose. Mabane fell to the ground, an unconscious waste. Tym screamed. His mind was no match for the influence being exerted over them. They watched the desiccation of their flesh, the brutal flaying of their souls. There was no hope. No future. Only misery awaited.

Then it was over. Aphere knelt in their midst. Her eyes screwed tightly while she combated the enemy influences. Ever so slowly, the horrors of the underworld receded until, at last, the beleaguered group was able to breathe. The intense pressure vanished. Whispers and screams faded to moans. Aphere opened her eyes to find the others staring at her. Only Kavan knew the truth.

"How?" Tym asked in awe. "I've never seen the like."

Kavan deflected him. "Do not question what we cannot understand. I think we figured out which way to go."

"The nexus is in the light," she confirmed. "They are so powerful, Kavan. It's almost seductive. I can feel their strength."

He tightened the grip on his sword, making the internal promise that none would fall under the dark gods' sway.

The slight glaze that had slipped into her eyes faded. "They know we are here. We must hurry. Corso will be quick to try and stop us."

"Right," Kavan agreed and turned to the others. "Kill everything that gets in our way. Leave the sorcerer to Aphere. The rest of us provide cover. We move now."

He took a step before remembering Mabane. Kavan knelt to shake his shoulder. The one-armed man didn't stir. Fearing the worst, Kavan rolled the body over to check for a pulse. There was none. Mabane's eyes were opaque. The irises had disappeared. Spittle trickled from his slack mouth. Blood dried around his nose and ears. Kavan whispered a prayer for the man.

He'd never understood Mabane. His very nature had perplexed Kavan greatly. One moment a craven coward, the next impossibly brave, his worth to their quest had been immeasurable. Mabane had offered hope where none existed. Now he was dead.

"Be at peace, my friend," Kavan whispered. He rose, his resolve that much stronger. "The power of the dark gods was too much for him. His heart and mind gave out."

"We'll bury him on the way out. He deserves that much." She reached down to close his eyes. "Kavan, time is gone. I fear Corso is already beginning the ritual."

He asked, "The green glow?"

She nodded. "We must hurry."

"At least there is no doubt which way we must go. Let us put an end to this nightmare."

Kavan sheathed his sword, favoring the close-quarters style of the crossbow. Loading a round, Kavan took point, darting through the ruins. The specialized crossbow Phirial's father had forged felt odd in his hands. He'd never excelled as a bowman. Aphere and Barum were far better, though he could hold his own when it came down to it. Still, his confidence was bolstered having Aphere a quick step behind.

Heavy footsteps made him duck against a sloping wall. The glow continued to strengthen. Aphere's dire look told him they had reached the nexus. Kavan drew a deep breath that exited his nostrils in icy plumes. Shivering, he readied to meet his fate. The cold edged down into his core. An ethereal hum vibrated the ground. Brackish mist pulsed out from the core of the nexus.

Kavan edged closer. His grip tightened around the crossbow's stock. Fingers danced lightly over the trigger. The tiniest inkling of fear awoke. Latent images of what the dark gods might actually be mocked him each time he blinked. He braved a look around the corner and froze. Both beautiful and bewitching, Kavan found himself gazing into the gateway to another dimension.

Grey light pulsed from a giant hole in the ground. Enormous blocks of marble ringed the pit, lending an air of majesty to the scene. Sparks danced from the light like so many butterflies. For a moment, Kavan was tempted to forget the nightmares visited upon the world so that he might bear witness with greater appreciation. The moment passed when he spied shackled hands protruding from the tops of the marble.

There were ten in all. Ten victims sacrificed so that the dark gods might return to the world. Kavan was sickened at the sight. Each had been flayed alive, ragged bits of flesh still dangled from bone and muscle. Each was gutted. An enormous altar upon which the organs had been laid out like a ghoulish feast dominated the center of the marble. Kavan finally realized just how wrong they'd been in assuming Corso was a man. No man could have committed such filth.

Rage filled his heart, forcing him to grab the wall to stop himself from charging in. Kavan tried clearing his thoughts, tried looking past the desiccated bodies. Four werebeasts protected the shrine. Spaced far enough apart to give any attackers time for one quick strike, they appeared enthralled. Kavan snarled. They'd be easy targets for the speed and brutality of the Gaimosian assault. Of Corso, there was no sign. Kavan took the information for what it was and slipped back around the corner.

"There are four guards, all posted on cardinal points. I didn't see Corso or anyone else," he reported.

"Sounds like a trap," Aphere said. "Corso wouldn't just let us walk in. He wants us to make a mistake."

"What choice do we have?" he asked. "For too long, we've been hounded by his foul craft. This must end, Aphere. We kill the guards before he returns and then figure out how to stop the ritual."

She let out a cool breath. Her feminine features appeared haunting in the pale glow. She prayed it was not a sign of things to come. Reluctantly, she agreed. The four survivors readied themselves. One way or another, their long quest was about to end.

FIFTY-NINE

Confrontation

They stealthily entered the chamber. Kavan being the closest, he dropped and fired. His bolt took the nearest werebeast clean through the throat. The beast died without a sound, warped body dropping lifelessly into the pit. Grey light enveloped the body, devouring flesh and bone with ravenous appetite. A haunting laugh danced across the walls. Kavan reloaded.

Aphere's arrow flew true as well. The beast died and was pitched into oblivion. Again the laugh resounded, for the dark gods were hungry. The Gaimosians moved swiftly, finishing off the remaining beasts before they could escape back into the cavern and sound the alarm. Tym and his Fist counterpart proved their worth by felling the other two.

"Keep watch," Aphere cautioned.

Her senses told her that Corso was close, as well as Pirneon. The oracle's predictions were coming to pass. She had feared the worst since leaving the Uelg; those fears were now being realized. She had no doubt that Pirneon was converted to the will of the dark gods. Her heart wept not only for Pirneon but for Kavan, too. It was no easy task to kill a mentor.

Satisfied for the moment, Kavan moved into the open. Curiosity took hold, making him want to see what the face of true evil looked like. He slung his crossbow in favor of his sword and moved closer to the nexus. He was amazed at how such a seemingly small thing like a hole in the ground could hold the fate of the entire world in the balance. The grey light was alluring, almost hypnotizing. He felt the raw power, the luring promises of glory.

"Tempting, isn't it?"

Kavan shook his head, slowly regaining his senses. His hand was almost touching the nearest blood-stained marble.

"Kavan, behind you!"

He turned and finally came face to face with the obsession of his recent past. Hidden beneath robes the color of blackest night, Corso emerged from the shadows at a measured pace. Kavan figured his frame was small, neither muscular nor fat. He judged the man insignificant save for the power at his command.

"You may touch the light, though I suspect you already know how the power will embrace you," Corso taunted.

Aphere and the Fist ducked down on either side.

"Show yourself," Kavan ordered.

Corso laughed at him. "What purpose would that serve? You already know who I am, leastwise you suspect so."

Tym fired off a quick shot aimed at Corso's heart. Corso didn't flinch as the bolt splintered a foot in front of him and fell to the ground.

"Did you truly expect that to work?" Corso asked. "I've lived more than a thousand years and you seek to slay me with one arrow? The oracle should have prepared you better, Gaimosians. I cannot be killed by mortal weapons."

Kavan stepped forward. "Lower your hood so we can see your face. I want to look into your eyes before I kill you."

"Ah yes, the fabled aggression of the Gaimosians. Save it. I've heard it all before, and from greater men. You are all that's left of a once noble bloodline. I should have you kneel for that arrogance."

Kavan raised his sword. "How is it you know so much about us? Who are you?"

Fragile hands reached up to slowly lower the thick, wool hood. His face, already sallow, appeared wraith-like in the glow. Centuries of corruption bled through his skin. Aphere saw the malice under his flesh. Her senses recoiled. The stain surrounding Corso pushed outward, attempting to ensnare her. She fought back, taxing her strength just to keep his power at bay.

Corso's eyes flashed hungrily. "Ah, you have such power. If only you understood your worth to the world. I've been watching your blood for centuries."

"Enough riddles," Kavan barked.

Lightning crackled between his fingers. Corso's face darkened. "Very well, the truth then. We have time yet, and my masters want you to learn the truth of your demise. This is a tale millennia in the making. When the world was still young, there was a race of beings. Our primitive minds termed them gods. How they scoff at such words. Imagine a race of immortal beings who controlled every facet of life.

"New races were born, entire species without the foresight to understand their roles in life. A schism occurred. Half of the gods discovered compassion, viewing the new races with sympathy and weakness. The stronger half, what you label as dark, grew enraged. They argued that the races had been created to serve as menial labor. They were the caretakers of the world so that the immortals could focus on larger agendas. It was man who tilted the scales."

He paused to clear his throat. "Man corrupted their minds, made them susceptible to weakness. The immortals shattered. A great war raged across Malweir. Thousands of immortals were killed, thus defying their very nature. Decay settled in. There is no possible way for you to comprehend what I am saying. The very fabric of creation was threatened, and it was all due to the simpering of the weak.

"The dark gods understood what needed to happen if their way of life had a chance of continuing. They renewed their war, fighting with ferocity that has yet to be seen again. The only way to victory was to eradicate the weak entirely. But they could not do so alone. So they swayed a tribe of men, tempting them with powers undreamed of.

"They fought long and did many foul things in the name of their new masters. For that, they were both hated and revered. The tide of war shifted against the dark gods, though, and they eventually became imprisoned in the vast nothingness of eternity. Can you imagine the torment they suffer in the void? Reduced from being masters of the world to mere prisoners of lesser beings. Deplorable," he spat.

Hostile intent glittered in his dark eyes. "But my masters had planned for such an event. They created agents to do their bidding. Some actively assisted them while others had no clue. I've been doing their work for a thousand years. But you, you don't even know it. The tribe of men they subverted were the ancestors of Gaimos. Your forbearers fought and died in the name of the dark gods. In return, they were given the keys to unlocking the prison. Your blood was endowed with the strength to open the gateway.

"You must see the irony in this," he taunted. "That damnable oracle knew the truth and still chose to send you here. The servants of the dark gods now come to destroy them. Surely, you can see there is no way for you to succeed. The very nature of your blood commands obedience. Poor fools. Even now, at the end, you fail to realize. Your precious blood is the keystone to my task."

A hulking shadow moved anxiously behind Corso. Kavan felt his body tense.

Corso sensed his eagerness to join battle and continued taunting. "It stings, doesn't it? Knowing your life is a lie. End your quest now and join your rightful place at my side. It's been long since I had a worthy slave to do my bidding."

Weeks of anger resurfaced. All the injustice they'd been forced to endure danced before him. Kavan found difficulty comprehending what it was Corso bragged to them. There was no way his people had been created to serve evil. He refused to believe his purpose in life was so base. Animalistic urges threatened to override his common sense. He would gladly sacrifice his life to keep Corso from succeeding.

"You dare shame our honor," Kavan snarled. The tip of his sword pointed towards Corso's face.

"Honor!" Corso raged. "What honor is left to a ruined land? What's left of mighty Gaimos has taken to slinking in the shadowed places of the world, scraping a meager living while their memories are forgotten. The guilty have no honor. Gaimos fell from false pride and recklessness. Your ancestors failed in their anointed task, betraying all they once stood for. All that you've known was destroyed through the manipulations of my kind, the true servants. It took many long centuries, but we finally achieved revenge."

"Your argument for us joining you isn't working. End this now, Corso. We don't have to do this," Aphere reasoned.

She wanted the fight as badly as Kavan, but Corso's power was…consuming. She didn't think she could best him.

"I'll get to you later. Your powers were born from the night, but you have no mastery of them. Your blood is the only thing special."

"Why our blood?" Aphere asked.

Corso gave a toothy grin. "No more talk. My masters hunger to breathe the fresh air again. I'm afraid you are quite mistaken. It's not your specific blood I need. The sole purpose of the hunts was to lure in those of your breed. Dozens of Gaimosians came in their self-endowed sense of righteousness. But their blood was weak, a watered-down blend of better times. All of them died, until the last.

"Finally, I have found once of the purest that could open the nexus and allow me to accomplish my task." His smirk slowly grew into a full-blown smile. "You know of whom I speak."

"No," Kavan gasped.

"Perhaps it is time I reacquainted you. Master and pupil again. But no more. The future of your relationship is victim and victor."

The werebeast emerged from the shadows. Easily larger than any of the others they'd encountered, the Pirneon-beast was a mass of muscle and hatred. Pure malice glowed from the backs of his transformed eyes. Gone was any trace of the man he once was. All that remained was a twisted waste of flesh created for the sole purpose of murder.

"Monster," Kavan hissed. "You'll pay for this blasphemy."

"Blasphemy? I've taken an impure being and perfected it. You should be so lucky to be remade so," Corso snapped back. "Bah! None of you have the foresight to appreciate the coming atrocities. When my masters come, they will teach you the meaning of your ignorance."

He turned to Pirneon and said, "Kill them."

The Fist reacted first. A pair of arrows whistled past each side of Kavan's head to strike Pirneon in the shoulders. He screamed in rage and charged. Larger than a pony, Pirneon was covered with ragged patches of black fur. Long claws dug into the broken stone as his barreled towards his enemy. Corso cackled in delight. Violent power swirled around him in a host of colors.

The ground began to tremble. Centuries-old rock and dirt crumbled from the ceiling. Clouds of dust rose from the floor to choke the heroes. An old doom resurfaced. The artificial humming grew louder, threatening to burst eardrums. Screams rose from a thousand skeletons littering the cavern floor. From the depths of the pit, the grey light turned green.

In the fading night sky, the moon slowly reached out to eat the sun. The dark times had finally returned.

SIXTY

Fear Betrayed

Kavan leapt at his former mentor. The intense stench of anger wafted off Pirneon, sickening him. Kavan failed to understand how the greatest knight in Gaimosian history had so willingly turned to embrace evil. Corso's words were just words, empty phrases cast out to lure them into darkness. Kavan didn't believe for a moment that his people had been bred for such foul purpose.

He roared back at his new enemy and slashed downward with the intent of ripping his chest open. The Pirneon-beast recognized the stance, flashbacks of his previous life driving him on, and reacted. He leapt over the committed Gaimosian. Sheer force drove both Fist to the ground. Tym rolled away, slivers of his broken bow still in his grasp.

"No!" he shouted.

Even then, he knew it was too late. The Pirneon-beast punched a great clawed hand into the second Fist's chest and through the back. Blood and tissue dripped from elongated fingers. Spinal fluids leaked from the wounds. The Fist's eyes rolled back in a moment of disbelief before he died. Howling perverted delight, the Pirneon-beast raised the corpse and ripped it's head off. Chewing sounds echoed disgustingly across the area.

Tym clenched his eyes, fighting back tears. He'd seen more than his share of men die, but none so viciously. Worse, he knew his fate would be the same. Paralyzed with fear, he waited for the end. Warm urine ran down his leg.

"Monster! It's me you want!" Kavan bellowed.

The diversion saved Tym's life. The Pirneon-beast paused his attack to face his new threat. Recognition flashed. He spat out the broken remains of the Fist's skull and crouched low to the ground. His mind played a hundred memories. Every strength and weakness Kavan possessed filtered through. His muscles flexed, ready to pounce on his former student.

Pure, unadulterated evil lay within his heart now, so wholeheartedly had he devoted his life to the dark gods and their powers. All his old allegiances and loyalties were gone. Corso was his master now. The man who had been Pirneon was dead. Murdering Tamblin had been the defining moment. That minor sliver of his conscience still human had been eager to repay her betrayal by ripping her throat out. He had relished devouring every scrap of her flesh.

Kavan continued his taunting, hoping to give Tym enough time to get to cover. This wasn't his fight. Pirneon had been a friend, teaching Kavan every style of combat he knew. Master and apprentice. That relationship left them on equal footing.

"You had my loyalties, Pirneon," he said. "I believed in you, your vision, and the hopes of our people. You betrayed us all. The oracle was right. We all have a role to play in this game."

The Pirneon-beast snarled. Spittle drooled from his elongated jaw.

"Yours is to die," Kavan whispered.

Kavan spit, knowing what was left of Pirneon would recognize the challenge. Ancient Gaimosian custom demanded a duel of honor for such foulness. Kavan waited. Each heartbeat was the sound of a mighty drum pounding. A single bead of sweat dripped from his hair, over his forehead, and into his right eye. The salt stung, reminding him of the host of hardships overcome to reach this moment.

"Come on," he said.

As much as he wanted the beast to attack, he didn't see any chance of victory.

The Pirneon-beast eased Kavan's hesitations by charging. Kavan waited until the beast was almost on top of him before dropping to a knee and punching his sword up. The Pirneon-beast jerked aside, preventing fatal damage. Kavan's sword caught it in the back of its right arm. Dark blood sprayed from the wound, burning the ground. An arrow thrummed over his head, lodging deep in the base of the beast's neck. Kavan glanced up to see Tym draw and fire again.

"Run!" Kavan shouted.

Both men fled the battleground. Kavan's last sight of the nexus was of Aphere facing down Corso.

He wished her better success than he was having before forcing her from his mind. Aphere was on her own. He had his own troubles to deal with. Both Fist and knight ran as hard as they could to put distance between them and the werebeast. Kavan felt pangs of regret from not believing Aphere when she'd tried so hard to convince him. That ignorance might well be the end of them all.

Neither thought escape was possible. Their best hope lay in confusing the Pirneon-beast enough to ambush it and, hopefully, slay it. Kavan wished he'd thought about such things on their route into the ruins, but he'd been arrogant.

He listened to Tym's breathing as they ran. Gessun Thune seemed to grow around them. The ruins cast no shadows in the pale light, which Kavan

"Leave their dead and drag the wounded away. Let Moncrieff come to get them. Hopefully, that will buy us more time."

Pharanx kicked one of the corpses, staring deep into the dead man's eyes. A cold chill ran down his spine. "Perhaps. But how much time do you think that will really buy us?"

"There's only two more days until the eclipse," Barum answered.

Pharanx Gorg nodded. They'd given a good account so far, but he wondered if they had enough left to last two more days.

noticed had gone from pale grey to pale green, though their sheer size dominated the surroundings. Kavan snatched Tym by the shoulder and pulled him into an empty doorway where both men collapsed. Pirneon howled in the distance.

"We can't beat that," Tym gasped.

Kavan shook his head. "No."

Tym looked hard at his companion. "How do you know that thing?"

Fighting to get his breathing back under control, Kavan swallowed before explaining, "He was my mentor. Everything I know I learned from him."

The Fist cursed. "Corso spoke true."

"Yes."

"I knew you people were dangerous. You killed my best friend at the swamp edge." He paused, jaw twisting thoughtfully, as if deciding whether Kavan was his enemy or not. "Fine, let's kill him or die trying. I've lost the will to run any further."

They caught heavy footsteps approaching.

"How many arrows do you have?"

Tym checked and was dismayed. His quiver was empty. Not that it mattered much since his bow had been shattered. Picking up the second had been sheer luck. Kavan still had his crossbow, but only two bolts. All the rest had fallen out during their retreat. Swords and daggers weren't going to be enough.

Kavan shoved the crossbow and bolts at Tym. "Here, take them."

"What are you going to do?"

Offering a sarcastic smile, Kavan said, "I'm going to lure him in, and you're going to shoot him. Get up high and aim for the heart. I'll keep him busy down here. If he kills me, do what you can to get back to the surface."

"That's your plan?"

"I'm all ears if you have a better one," he replied as he walked away.

Tym cursed again and began to climb. He'd already learned that once a Gaimosian got it in his head to do something there was no turning back. The Fist crouched down behind a broken pillar on what used to be the second floor. He carefully selected his field of fire and waited. Werebeasts were difficult to kill in the best situations, and here he was trying to kill the strongest. He suddenly regretted volunteering.

Kavan slipped back into the street. "Pirneon!"

The beast roared in response. Heightened senses told him where Kavan was. He charged through the ruins. His bulk crashed through already broken buildings. Hate spurred him on, hate and the three arrows driven deep in his flesh. Blood splashed down his ruined form. His muscles were hideously gnarled. Pustules and lesions covered his body. The Pirneon-beast rounded the corner and saw Kavan's diminutive figure waiting. Another challenge. He attacked, all the while hoping Kavan remained still so he could relish in the slaughter.

Kavan held his ground. Pirneon's arrogance had transcended into his new form. That would work to his disadvantage. He hoped Tym was ready; otherwise, it was going to be a violent death. Kavan broke and ran. The Pirneon-beast followed.

"Come on, you bastard," he taunted through clenched teeth.

The glow in the caverns grew stronger as if unchallenged powers were being funneled into the nexus. He ignored it, focusing instead on the five hundred pound monster chasing him. That minor distraction was enough that he failed to see the rock. He fell and rolled. Sharp pain lanced through an ankle. The sprain might as well have been an amputation. There was no way he could continue running. Hobbling, he made his way back through the doorway.

"Wait for your shot," he warned the Fist. "Don't worry about me."

Tym swallowed and raised his weapon. Too many images crowded his mind, desperately trying to be noticed before the end. Concentration wasn't easy. Nerves made him tremble. The weapon wavered. Common sense said to break and flee. The Gaimosians could kill each other. If what Corso said was true, the world might be a better place without them.

Tym wiped his palm across his trousers and tried to swallow. His mouth was parched. He couldn't stop sweating. Further thought fled when the werebeast crashed through the building's exterior. Great chunks of the ceiling crashed down.

The building rocked from a second and third impact before the Pirneon-beast managed to break free. The beast howled fierce enough to make his ears bleed. Wicked eyes scanned the unnatural darkness. Kavan had made it too easy. The fist-sized rock caught Pirneon in the jaw, shattering one of the upper fangs. Kavan pitched another rock, this one catching the beast in the throat. Pirneon reared back, exposing his upper body.

"Now!" Kavan shouted.

Tym whispered a quick prayer and fired. He reloaded and fired again. Both shots took Pirneon in the chest, close to the heart but not enough to kill. The werebeast staggered under the blows. Kavan struck. Stabbing as hard as he could, he found brief resistance followed by the sound of steel ripping through flesh and organs. Hot blood gushed forth, and Kavan slipped. The Pirneon-beast lashed out and caught Kavan in the chest, spiraling him backwards.

Rising to full, terrifying height, the Pirneon-beast was a vision of nightmares. Tym stared in astonishment. Kavan groaned and rolled over to his knees. Bright red blood drooled from his lips. Sharp pain spread across his chest with each breath. He looked up at his enemy, knowing there was only one shot. Waiting until Pirneon was over top of him, Kavan used every ounce of his strength to reach forth and grab his sword, still buried in Pirneon's chest. He twisted, ripped. Blade and heart flew from the body as the Pirneon-beast lashed out one final time. The mighty nightmare collapsed in a lifeless heap. Pirneon, Knight Marshal of Gaimos, was dead.

Kavan limped next to the broken body. Tears struggled to win free. He looked down on his former mentor and clove through Pirneon's neck. The head rolled away.

"I am sorry," Kavan whispered.

SIXTY-ONE

Power Unrestrained

Aphere narrowly avoided being decapitated as the Pirneon-beast launched at them. Her enhanced reflexes were the only difference between life and death. She flattened herself as the massive creature hurtled over. Whatever foul powers had transformed Pirneon had succeeded in making a monstrosity. Already consumed with the deadly combination of jealousy and suspicion, Pirneon's mind practically welcomed the change. A stifled scream and the iron smell of fresh blood told her one of her companions was dead. The battle joined behind her and quickly moved away.

Alone, Aphere rose and prepared to battle Corso. Her only hope lay in his underestimating her. Aphere was ultimately unprepared to do battle with the powers arrayed before her.

Corso, for his part, waited patiently with his hands lost in the sleeves of his robe. He leered at her. "Pretty thing. You have no idea what you've gotten yourself into, do you?"

"I know enough," she fired back. Having grown up in a world of harsh men, Aphere was undaunted.

Corso snorted. "I doubt that. The oracle has no power over the world of men and gods. He's led you to your death, only you're too blind to see it."

"This isn't about the oracle," she countered. "I won't let you open the nexus. Your dreams end tonight."

His laughter echoed over the humming sound. "Obstinate fool. The dawn is already upon us. You lose! Soon, the eclipse begins, and my masters will be set free."

Aphere clenched her jaw. "You're wrong, Corso. I'm going to stop you and end this for good."

"Pirneon thought the same. Look at him now, my willing servant devoted to hunting down his own kind."

Doubt flickered behind her eyes. He noticed and pressed the advantage. "Do you have any idea how easily he converted to my will? It took but a hint of a whisper, and he was lured in. Of course, the promise of a beautiful girl didn't hurt. Your Knight Marshal came too willingly to my side."

She refused to believe, for doing so would shatter the foundations of her strength. Pirneon had been filled with anger, frustration. She wondered what seductions could possibly have changed their greatest champion.

"I see the same doubt gnaws upon you," Corso cooed. His words were measured with hypnotic cadence. "You don't have to die here. Join me, and I can give you the treasures of immortality."

"And become a slave like Pirneon?" she spat. "I'll take my chances with the underworld."

Corso's eyes narrowed angrily. Harsh flames shot from his fingertips. He flung his hands at her, gouts of flames shooting forth. Aphere instinctively raised her arms to protect herself. Corso's power exploded against an invisible wall a meter from her. The force of the impact was enough to stagger her back a step. Acrid smoke curled up against the invisible wall, shimmering like ripples in a pond. Aphere watched in awe.

Corso snarled. "Impressive, but it won't avail you. Why can't you understand? Your entire, pathetic race was bred to achieve their will! Others once thought they could stand against the rising tide. They all either died or became your so-called werebeasts. Pah! Superstitious filth. You should never have been gifted by their truth."

Corso sent another devastating blast at her. Again, she was driven back. Aphere realized that the sheer strength of Corso's power was enough to destroy her a thousand times over. Nothing in Kistan's teachings was remotely capable of deflecting such ferocity. She was dead if she didn't act fast.

"Too late, you begin to realize," he soothed. "Kneel, and live. Stand, and die."

Aphere shook her head with what resolve she had left. "No. You're going to have to kill me."

He smiled, savage and filled with malice. "A hero's fate."

Corso adjusted his aim, blasting at her feet. The impact lifted her off the ground. He cackled with delight. She was far too easy a target. Her body flew backwards along with a hail of dirt and rock. Killing her was going to be more than easy; it was going to be thoroughly enjoyable. He was almost disappointed. Corso checked his ego. The Gaimosian was an easy target, but he had more important matters to see too. The hour of the eclipse was at hand. He must open the nexus. His masters were eager to resume their reign of destruction upon the peoples of Malweir.

Dust settled over Aphere's prone body. She felt a hammer pounding deep in her head. Her body ached. Corso was more powerful than she had imagined. Truthfully, Aphere hadn't a clue what to expect. Any use of her powers thus far had been more accident than intent. She'd helped them survive the lich of the Uelg out of sheer desperation to survive.

Aphere groaned quietly as she rolled over. Rocks and sediment dribbled from her. She was relieved to see Corso's attention already diverted. She grimaced, pushing up to all fours. Another blast caught her off guard.

"Stay down, bitch," Corso barked at her. "I'll return to you later."

He turned back to the pillar of green light pulsing up from the bowels of the world. Hot enough to melt flesh, Corso was protected by ancient wards. The legs of the closest dead werebeast caught fire. The smell of cooked flesh joined that of the rotting corpses.

Aphere's vision swam. Through the haze, she managed to distinguish miscellaneous body parts. Corso's masters had brought back some of their victims from the initial attack on the surface. Stark horror punched her in the stomach. She'd been blown into a feeding area. The ground was permanently stained with blood. Flies and maggots were everywhere. Was this a sign of things to come?

She searched for Corso. The sorcerer had returned to the marble ring. The glow was almost blinding. She could only guess, but the moon must already be eating the sun. A chime sounded throughout the farthest reaches of Malweir. The hour of doom had fallen upon them. Aphere swallowed her disgust and crawled through the filth towards her crossbow.

Corso was oblivious to her now that the ritual had begun. A thousand years of waiting had finally ended. Long years of torment among the lesser races had nearly done him in. His will often lagged. More than once, he had considered suicide. His masters wouldn't allow it. Each time he suffered a moment of doubt he was punished severely. It took years to recover from the pain of each punishment. Each was a subtle reminder of his task yet to come and the horrors the dark gods would visit upon him should he fail.

He moved forward to the lip of the hole. Green light reflected in his normally hollow eyes. Corso felt the power dancing over his robes. Their electric touch was inviting, reminding him of a greater time. He spread his arms wide to accept their embrace and began to chant. Corso spoke the old tongue, words unheard on Malweir for centuries. The dark disciple spoke the hastening of the end of the world. His voice picked up strength, booming from the artificial walls. A dark circle opened at the base of the pit. *At last. The prison opens.* The dark gods surged towards their long-awaited freedom. Steam poured up from the bowels of the world.

Aphere swore as figures emerged from the steam, shadows of beings both beautiful and grotesque. She fought back the torments trying to enter her mind, knowing that if she succumbed now, it was finished. Her mind lacked the strength to ward off the powers of the ancient beings. Fingers curled around the handle of her crossbow. Calling on her power, Aphere took aim and depressed the trigger.

The bolt exploded across the protective shields in the middle of Corso's back. The impact pushed him forward, perilously close to falling into the pit. Aphere suddenly got an idea. She reloaded quickly.

Corso spun on her. "Still alive? No matter. I'm going to burn the soul out of your very corpse."

He fired twin blasts of condensed energy. Aphere pitched forward, letting the main force hum past to explode in the ruins. A large chunk of rock landed on her right calf. She cried out. Fearing her leg was broken, Aphere took aim and fired again. The second bolt exploded as the first had, again pushing him to the very edge of oblivion. She reloaded as fast as she could. Firing her last bolt, she flung her crossbow away.

"Why won't you die?" she croaked from a parched throat.

Corso laughed bitterly. "I am death! Come close and see the full fury of the dark gods."

She gasped as unseen hands lifted her from the ground. Her body moved against her will. Aphere drifted towards the waiting sorcerer, arms and legs dangling uselessly beneath. She decided not to struggle, knowing this would be her only shot at killing Corso. Patience was required. She gazed at her captor and felt incredible terror ice her veins. Corso's eyes were ablaze with madness. She wondered what nightmares consumed him as the powers of the dark gods filtered into his mind and body.

"All of your nightmares, your pain and suffering. It all belongs to them now," he raved. "This is the fate of the world. You never stood a chance at stopping me. I was preordained centuries before you were conceived. At long last, this is my hour. Every perversion you ever imagined is about to manifest into reality. Pretty bitch, before this night is done, you will beg me for release."

Corso laughed.

"Aphere!"

They both snapped their heads at the sudden call. She wanted to smile but knew better. Kavan leaned heavily against Tym, both looking battered and near broken. Corso's eyes crossed sharply. Their presence could only mean Pirneon was dead. Whatever pleasures he might normally have taken, Corso needed the monster for the final phase of his plan. There had to be fresh sacrifice in order to release his masters. Corso summoned his last reserves of strength to throw Aphere down into the nexus.

He forgot about Kavan and the Fist. No matter what else happened, he must complete his task. Corso shuddered at the thought of what would happen if he failed and moved faster. Aphere's body was less than twenty meters away. So close. Ten meters. Corso's pulse quickened. He drew the sacrificial dagger from his robes. The weapon that would finally free his soul from the failure of generations. This was everything he'd been dreaming of. At five meters, his dreams dissolved.

Aphere waited until she was too close for him to react. She raised her arms and directed all her energy at Corso. The blast shredded his shields, already weakened, and struck him full in the chest. Corso screamed. His hold on her broke, and she fell. The power of her blast shoved him back. His heels slipped over the edge. Realization turned to fear. Aphere continued her assault. Corso realized he was going to die. Aphere pushed harder until she watched him slip over the edge.

He fell screaming into the waiting mouth of the nexus. The dark gods howled wails of panic. Corso's blood was of no use. His dark energies were released when his body struck the nexus. Both exploded. The green glow flickered, losing brightness. The ground trembled. With the nexus destroyed, the world became unstable. One by one, the marble blocks slid into the pit.

Kavan's eyes went wide with the understanding of what was happening. "Run!"

The wounded warriors hobbled their way back towards the mouth. They slipped past Mabane's corpse, saddened at not being able to fulfill promises as the ruins collapsed around them. Kavan looked up as the roof began to drop. The three survivors were trapped but continued to run.

SIXTY-TWO

Many Partings

Dag watched the sun emerge from behind the moon. The moment of their doom had passed, and his band of survivors still lived. Sounds of battle faded almost immediately. Dag looked around in disbelief. Werebeasts dropped dead where they stood. Some tried to escape once they recognized the threat. They burst into flames or simply dissolved where they stood.

The older man clapped his hands and barked a laugh. Kavan and the others had succeeded! Malweir was saved from the dark gods. Only then did Dag take account of his surroundings. Lars was dead, as were most of the others. Dag lamented their sacrifice, necessary as it had been. After a series of devastating quakes, the world returned to calm. Dag, wounded and barely on his feet, was ready to collapse.

The Gaimosians emerged from the destruction of Gessun Thune and dropped. Men rushed to their aid. None had believed that any could have survived the battle underground. Dag glanced up at the commotion and wormed his way towards them.

"Clear away! Let me through, damn it."

Dag regretted yelling. All of them were exhausted beyond belief. All were wounded. Some wouldn't last the day. His real regret stemmed from not knowing the names of the men, and those few women, who had died. They deserved better than to become a lonely pyre in the middle of nowhere.

He knelt beside Kavan's fallen form. "By the gods, lad. You did it."

Kavan groaned. "Remind me not to do that again."

Dag and those around him broke out in laughter. The battle of Gessun Thune was over.

Kavan's eyes fluttered open. He tried to move, but his body argued otherwise. Every muscle ached. After long minutes of trying, he finally rose high enough to examine himself. His chest was heavily bandaged, confirming more broken ribs. His eyes were bruised, swollen. Two teeth were missing. Candles lit the small tent enough for him to see he wasn't alone. His eyes gradually focused on Phirial's trembling figure.

"How?" he asked weakly.

Tears streamed down her face. "We arrived this afternoon. They told me you were still alive. Oh, Kaven."

He tried to smile, but it hurt too much. Instead, he dropped back onto the cot. "I feel dead."

"You look horrible," she joked.

His eyes softened. "Thanks for confirming it. What happened at Kalad Tol?"

Phirial sat down softly beside him, careful not to bump him. "We won, though I don't know how. One minute, they were coming over the wall, and the next, they were in full retreat. I didn't see much of it, though. Barum and Pharanx kept me the furthest from the fighting, under guard the whole time."

Kavan smiled genuinely. He knew his friends wouldn't let him down. "Where are they now? I'd like to speak with them."

She hesitated. "Barum is with Aphere; so is Geblin."

"What of Pharanx?"

Phirial lowered her eyes. "He's dead."

She went on to explain how he had led a suicide mission behind enemy lines and never returned. She told him how Barum had stepped up and led the brave Fist to repel wave after wave of Aradainian soldiers. Kavan could see the events play out in his mind. The attack was working, almost to the point of swarming the defenses and opening the gates. The battle paused during the eclipse. Once it passed, the enemy lost their will to fight. They broke contact and left the battlefield.

"No one knows why," she finished. "At first, we thought it was a trap, but after an hour, it was clear they had retired. They even left their wounded behind. Kavan, all of those men died, and for what?"

"That's war, my love," he told her.

A new shine filled her eyes upon hearing him call her that.

"What happened next?"

Phirial reached out to take his hand. "Barum took command. Wurz was too badly injured. We left half of the Fist behind to see to the wounded and then hurried here. Geblin was the most insistent. The rest, you know. Is it truly over?"

He sighed. "Yes. I believe it is."

Fresh tears broke loose. "Kavan, I love you." Her voice was timid, but the words were loud in his ears. His heart felt alive for the first time.

Kavan looked at her dark, red hair and soft, blue eyes. "I love you too."

They stayed in Gessun Thune for the remainder of the night and most of the next day. Dag and Barum shared command of the ragtag bunch. They piled the dead and burned the bodies with honor. Kavan insisted on leaving as soon as possible. The fighting may have ended, but he continued to feel ill at ease in the shadows of such an evil place. Thoughts of the men he'd left behind tormented him. Mabane. Pirneon. Once the last fire burned out, the survivors loaded the wounded into wagons, and the small train headed back to Kalad Tol. Phirial never left Kavan's side. Neither did Barum stray too far from Aphere.

Much changed in the kingdom of Aradain the day the dark gods resumed their exile. None of the heroes were foolish enough to believe that war was finished. Another thousand years would pass before the fate of the world again hung in the balance, this time in the foul land of Gren. But that is a tale for another time.

Their army routed, commanding general dead, the people of Aradain braced for the worst. A subsonic wave washed over Rantis in the exact moment the nexus closed. A high-ranking official rushed to the royal chambers to inform the king. When there was no answer, the guards broke the doors down. What they saw sickened them.

Eglios, king of Aradain, lay dead in a gathering pool of blood and bodily secretions. No one would ever learn the truth, never knowing that Corso's power over him was so strong Eglios's mind couldn't withstand the pressure of being relieved so quickly. He'd died in terrible agony while his city slept. So it was the influence of the dark gods passed from Aradain. Life was given the opportunity to return to normal. But it would be long before the wounds healed. Many had died in the name of evil. The kingdom carried a stain with it until the day it fell into decay and was no more.

A month passed before Kavan and the others were healed enough to take their leave of the Fist. Wurz, the taciturn Dwarf, placed Tym in command until he fully recovered from his wounds. The mercenary unit was equally crippled. Less than one hundred remained out of their original five. Dag and his band of survivors remained at the old fortress. The big man and Dwarf hit it off immediately. It was that one drunken night they agreed to an alliance.

Every man was given the option to stay with the group or strike out on his own. Some left, but most stayed. Eventually, the Fist abandoned Kalad Tol and headed east. They fought in occasional conflicts along the way before running into Aphere again. She invited them to travel with her. The Fist slowly faded into legend. Their deeds and exploits became the talk of barrooms and taverns.

Of Corso's black tower, there was no word. Men stayed away from that forest. It was rumored that an apparition dressed in black robes stalked the trees at night. Those who strayed into the wood were often never seen again. Many centuries later, during the great age of Mages, a brash young man named Sidian would undertake a mission to rid the world of that spook. His exploits would be well known by every living soul in Malweir.

A crisp winter wind blew across the ancient mountain. A ring of torches lent color to the otherwise pale moonlight. Two figures, a man and woman, stood with hands clasped before them. Their identities were carefully concealed from the onlookers. Several others lined a stone path rising from the valley floor.

Pine trees and firs lined the clearing, with juniper bushes marking the path. A broken stone lay before the man and woman. It was the ancient symbol of a forgotten time. Tens of thousands of warriors once stood on this very spot in the hopes of becoming more than themselves.

It hadn't been used in generations. All the mystique and power laced deep in this small acre of land slowly faded beyond memory. Long had it been since Man knew the glory of such. This was Skaag Mountain, and here ordinary Gaimosians became knights.

A chime echoed from deep in the woods.

The man announced, "Let the supplicant come forward."

Dressed in robes of purest white, the supplicant marched with deliberate intent. His heart beat just that extra bit more. All the long years of training and dedication had paid off. At long last, he was going to join his ancestors. Their glory and valor was now his own. Barum had never been prouder. He stopped before the broken stone.

"Kneel out of obedience to your dedication," the woman commanded.

Barum knelt. The midnight moon was directly overhead, the sky bright and cloudless. Dag, Geblin, Wurz, and more fell in behind. They'd all been instructed in their parts.

Aphere spoke from beneath her hood. "From the dawn of the world, select men and women have come forward in times of peril and unrest. All readily accept the burden of sacrifice, dedicating their entire lives to the pursuit of justice."

Kavan continued, "The weak shall be protected, the wicked punished. The road will be long and unforgiving. Often, decisions must be made for the greater good rather than personal interest. Can you discharge these duties faithfully and without pause?"

"Yes," Barum said, bowing his forehead to the stone.

"Will you sacrifice yourself in order that justice be done?" Aphere asked.

"Yes," he repeated the gesture.

Aphere and Kavan raised their arms high into the night sky. The chime rang again. Both drew their swords and carefully laid the blades on Barum's shoulders.

"Rise, Barum of the House Keidi. Shed your former life, and arise a knight of ancient Gaimos," Aphere instructed.

Barum rose slowly.

Aphere smiled from beneath her hood. "Welcome to the fold."

The gathering held its collective breath as the chime sang three times. As the echoes of the third faded, they broke into applause. Barum was officially a Vengeance Knight. They rushed to embrace him. Each offered congratulations. Aphere and Kavan lowered their hoods. They'd been waiting for this moment since the Kergland Spine, and now, almost a year later, Barum was rewarded. As was tradition, Barum led them all to a large pyre constructed on the far side of the clearing. He lit it in honor of all the fallen. It was only after the fires burned out the celebration began.

The order of Gaimosian Knights continued.

Kavan lost the urge to fight. He and Phirial took their oaths to each other and left the world behind. That night on Skaag Mountain became his last official act as a knight. They settled down in a quiet part of the world. Phirial gave him three sons and a daughter with fiery red hair like her mother.

For her love, Kavan built a nice sized cabin just south of the great Relin Werd. Eventually, others would come, and a village would spring up around him. Men came to call the village Fel Darrins. Centuries later, Kavan's descendants would give birth to a baby boy and lovingly name him Delin.

"I love you," Barum told Aphere.

She blushed much the same as she always did when he told her. "I love you more."

He smiled. The years of knighthood had been kind. He and Aphere had married a few years after his induction ceremony. She had gone on to become one of Kistan's greatest students. Without powers of his own, Barum had become the captain of the guard. At first, others protested having a military arm in their community, but recent events in Gessun Thune calmed their ire. The Fist, and Dag, comprised the rest of the guard.

The community along the shores of Thuil Lake steadily grew. The great castle was erected and fast became the focus of knowledge and learning for all Malweir. Aphere and Barum sat looking down on Ipn Shal, though they only had eyes for each other. She reached out to take his hand. Together, they walked back down the hill to enjoy a new day in a brand new world.

A Foul Night

High-pitched screams pierced the wood and stone halls of Chadra Keep. Badron, the liege lord of Delranan, sprang from his ancient throne at the sound, his band of favored captains and counselors doing the same. His pale blue eyes boiled from shock to feral rage as he quickly registered what was happening. Screams could only mean one thing: his very family was under attack in what was supposed to be the most secure place in his kingdom. More screams and blood-choked cries mixed with the sound of clashing steel. Badron snarled grimly. The house guard, his guard, was locked in brutal struggle somewhere deep within the wooden halls of the Keep.

Badron drew his trusted sword and stormed off in search of the battle. The senior most lords and captains of Delranan followed him. Eight in all, they comprised a most lethal band of warriors. Their deeds had forged the kingdom from a pack of warring tribes and clans into a singular monarchy that quickly became the strongest of the northern kingdoms. They wordlessly chased at the wolf skin cloak of their king as he headed towards the royal sleeping chambers.

Fear drove Badron. Long red hair, now streaked through with gray, flowed angrily down broad shoulders. His normally pale blue eyes seethed red with rage. Wrath commanded him, wrath so strong it could threaten the foundations of his hard-fought kingdom and make the old gods of Malweir tremble in fear. Muscles bunched under his jerkin. His bulk filled the doorway. Badron felt the old energies flow into him. His was a warrior's life and this night but an extension of it. The sound of glass breaking drew his attention. Badron bellowed and charged, heedless of any lurking dangers.

Fleeting visions of battle appeared through the flickering torchlight. The flash of a sword. A spray of blood. The ruins of a body lay in the middle of the hall, a crumpled mass of flesh. Badron knelt beside the corpse. The smell of blood kissed the stagnant air. Deep cuts and gashes immolated the young house guard. Badron tried to close the eyes, if for no other reason than to avoid staring down into the pure agony. A feathered spear, broken at the hilt, was embedded in the lad's throat.

"Pell Darga," growled Jarrik. He rubbed his bald head and spat.

The king brought his gaze up to his friend and captain. "Rouse whatever watch remains, Jarrik. I want these monsters run down and skinned alive. The rest of you with me."

Badron led them further into the Keep. The inner doors to the royal chambers were smashed to ruins. One lay in splinters across the hall while what was left of the second hung in shreds by a single hinge. Smoke curled up from the chamber, running down the ceiling. Fresh blood stained the floor and walls in ragged patterns. More bodies. Badron grimaced. From the looks of it all of his private guard had been caught unaware and slain. Their furs and spiked helmets lay stained in growing pools of blood. Badron splashed his way past.

At last they came unto the king's chambers. The doors were similarly smashed, leaving a gaping maw, dark and uninviting. Shadows leaked into the hall. Unknown fears danced around the men and threatened their resolve. Preparing his mind for the worst, Badron bunched his shoulders and surged forward. Nothing in this world meant so much to him as the memory of his late wife Rialla and the children he'd sired.

Rough hands snatched at his collar and jerked him back. "No my lord, we cannot afford to lose you," Argis whispered. Harsh tones ground from his throat.

He gestured with his head and two of the largest guards crept forward to flank the doors. Satisfied the king wasn't going to do anything rash, Argis released him and tossed his torch to the nearest man. Inion snatched it and gave his battle brother an awkward look. A hint of smile, no more than the slight curve of his lips, caressed his face. It had been too long since they'd last gone to war. Inion hefted his tulwar and threw the torch into the bedchamber. He charged in after, Argis immediately following with a litany of battle cries. Berserker strength churned inside them.

Badron impatiently waited. Sounds came back to him, making the hairs on his neck stand. The breaking of furniture. A crash in the dark. He forced himself to stand by and wait while others rushed to defend his honor. The idea pained him, but he must be king before warrior. That was the price for the gift he'd usurped from his brother long ago. Inion reappeared a heartbeat later. Disbelief stained his naturally dark eyes. He mouthed words that were incoherent babble.

Badron pushed forward, forgetting all restraint. "Speak man, what of my family?'

The stunned captain could only point back at the broken door.

"Is she?" he whispered.

Inion could not bear to look his king and friend in the eye. "I don't know, sire. There are traces of blood but no bodies. It is clear that there was a struggle."

Emotions collided in a mass of confusion. Badron was beyond enraged and on the verge of breaking down. He'd never truthfully cared much for his daughter. In fact he constantly blamed her for the death of his precious Rialla during childbirth. But Maleela was still his flesh and blood. He punched a massive fist into the nearest wall.

"Find my daughter or I'll have your heads on pikes by dawn. No one sleeps until the Pell Darga are found and killed. And bring me my son."

One by one they bowed and deployed throughout Chadra Keep. Only Harnin One Eye stood fast. Oldest and most loyal of the eight, Harnin watched his king with concern through his remaining eye.

"My lord, your daughter…" he whispered.

Badron shot him a cross look. "Do not remind me of what I know all too well. We shall deal with this when the time comes."

The bloodied halls of Chadra Keep felt surprisingly empty despite the flurry of activity. What remained of the decimated house guard began a room-by-room search for the royal family. Bodies were taken away and prepared for burial while servants scrubbed the blood from the walls and floor as best as they could. Many believed this night of terror was already finished. Badron knew it was only the beginning. Whatever evil the Pell had in mind would spark his final designs and begin a long anticipated war. Badron stormed through his Keep barking orders.

It was then that he came upon the body of his only son.

The young prince's head sharply drooped to the side. Pell Darga spears riddled his body. Blood wept from dozens of wounds. His sword was sheathed in blood. Badron's heart lurched. Clearly his boy had put up a good fight. Then he spied it. The gentle rise and fall of the chest. His son was not yet dead. Badron quickly dropped down and cradled his son to him.

"My son," he choked.

"They…came in….through the…windo…." Blood spit through his broken lips as he talked. Soon he would journey to the halls of his ancestors, no longer a pawn to the vagaries of life. "Took… Maleela…"

A last gasp made his body shake gently. The heir to the throne of Delranan was dead, at peace. Badron shook uncontrollably. Humbled and belittled, Badron could only stop and stare. He wanted to drop down and cradle the lad one last time, to let his tears flow free. But he was king, and kings do not do such things.

"He died honorably, sire," Harnin soothed. "We should all hope for such."

Badron spun on his friend. "Honorably? He died at the hands of cowards and assassins! Do not speak to me of honor!"

"Lord Badron!"

Jarrik strode purposefully down the hallway. "Lookouts spied men on horseback riding east. They claim to have caught the wisp of a woman's gown among the riders."

Anger's edge diminished, if only slightly. The desire for revenge grew.

"How many?" he asked.

"Between thirty and forty near as they could tell."

A cold gleam twisted Badron's eyes. "Reform the council. I want blood."

Badron reentered the throne room, his unfocused eyes streaked with red. The throne seemed less. The hearth fire was cold. It was only late summer and already winter's reach struggled to find purchase. The brightest of the summer sun had already faded. It wouldn't be much longer before the snow blew in from the cruel Northern Ocean. None of that mattered of course. Badron could see only despair in the near future. The threat of winter held no danger for him. His dreams, his very life, had come crashing down this night. All of the hard work he and his kind had done in building a mighty kingdom might well have died with his son. Delranan had no heir. None that is, except his unwanted daughter Maleela. Badron snarled.

His captains entered in somber procession. Each was armed and geared for campaign. Whatever they were now, they had all been among the very best warriors in the north countries. Now was the time for sharpened steel. Words and posturing didn't belong in the future Badron envisioned for his kingdom.

"The house of the king is ruined," Badron drawled. "The Pell Darga have shamed us all this night. My son is murdered and my *daughter* taken. How can this have happened under our noses? Chadra Keep is supposed to be the most secure building in Delranan."

His words dripped venom. All at once a chorus of rage echoed across the chamber. The call for war lifted their spirits. Frightened talk fell in hushed tones at the mention of the Pell though. Ancient hatred and superstitions cloaked the mountain dwellers. Some claimed they were nothing more than myth; one told to children to keep them in line during the long winter nights when mischief was prone to spark. No one living had ever seen one. Legend said they came from the Murdes Mountains far to the east, the Mountains of Death. No sane man volunteered to travel those dark paths.

"The Pell Darga do not exist. Surely we are missing some vital clue in all of this," Jarrik cautioned. For all of his great strengths, strategy was not one.

Harnin rose and cast down a blood-stained short spear. "Truly? Then explain this! Taken from the body of the king's own son as he lay dying. Mind your tongue, Jarrik. The Pell exist and it is time we confronted them."

The old man glowered at his rival, but said nothing else.

"How is it they managed to sneak past our guard and slay half of the house with us unaware?" Skaning, a burly man with coal black hair man, asked.

Badron grunted. "How do giants shape the mountains or the gods make war? You ask questions only a sorcerer might answer. This I tell you all. We have but two choices. Either we ignore this night's foul deeds." Chaotic roars swept through those assembled. Badron held his hands up for quiet, "Or we raise the Wolfsreik and march to war. To the very heart of the Murdes Mountains if need be."

"Sire, it will take a month or more to raise the full strength of the Wolfsreik," Harnin cautioned.

Ten thousand fully armed men complete with supplies and kit was no easy feat.

Badron had a familiar twinkle in his eyes. "Six weeks and we can march."

"On who exactly? The Pell Darga are not a nation. By rights we would be invading Rogscroft," Argis said.

Skaning stood. "Such an action would surely jeopardize your family more. If our goal is to retrieve the princess alive we need speed and secrecy, not the strength of arms."

"What would suggest then?" Badron asked sharply.

Clearing his throat, Skaning continued. "Send men to scour the inns and taverns. Find a stalwart band of mercenaries and adventurers willing to become heroes for a small price."

Harnin spat. "Not even a drunken fool would risk facing the Pell on their own territory. We must raise the army."

"I agree with Skaning," Jarrik seconded. "These are troubled times. Money can be a powerful motivator and the types of man we will attract are expendable at best."

"Battle against Man is one thing, but these are demons from the Old Times. I for one will not waste my life so recklessly," Harnin fell silent.

"Not even at the behest of your king?" Badron asked. "We are all led to a place of dark thought. Evil must be used to combat evil if we are to succeed."

No one noticed the sudden guarded look in Harnin's eye. "My apologies sire. I have forgotten my place. But the question remains. What fool would dare enter such a realm and risk certain death?"

"Every man has a price," Argis chipped in. "All we need do is find the right ones."

Badron thoughtfully rubbed the gray stubble on his chin. "This might work. Stouds has more than enough men of lesser quality for what we need. One Eye, since you so willingly champion this idea I place you in charge. You have two days to collect the men you deem necessary. After that I sound the muster and the Wolfsreik marches."

Harnin's smile was sharp, wicked. "Yes, sire."

The king pushed away from the table. He had heard enough. He paused in the doorway to look back over his shoulder and reiterate, "You have two days."

Chadra Keep's familiar shadows offered no comfort to the lone warrior marching through. Soft winds kissed the torch in his hand. Fractured darkness covered the windows. The first hint of dawn seeped through the cold grey night. Funeral pyres were already being erected in the main courtyard. Soon the bodies would be sent to their ancestors. Servants scurried about in an almost vain attempt to return the Keep to its former glory.

He ignored it all. Gaining the top of the stair, he quickly headed down to the cellars. He eased past the dungeons and food stores. His destination was perhaps the biggest secret in the Keep. Unknown to most, there was a secret tunnel leading out into the surrounding forest, but he knew. After all, he was the one who had left the exit unsecure and allowed the attackers inside in the first place. And it was the only way he was going to be able to elude the guard without questions.

He slowly pushed the ancient door open. The sky continued to brighten. It was now a muted shade of grey; still dark but light enough for him to see where he was going. He knew that Delranan, and perhaps all Malweir, was now locked in a season of change. It was a time for myths. Trolls and Goblins, dragons and wizards. It was a season for treachery and betrayal.

He took his first step towards freedom and was met by the touch of cold steel at his throat.

DREAMS
OF
WINTER
A FORGOTTEN GODS TALE
CHRISTIAN WARREN FREED

It is a troubled time, for the old gods are returning and they want the universe back…

Under the rigid guidance of the Conclave, the seven hundred known worlds carve out a new empire with the compassion and wisdom the gods once offered. But a terrible secret, known only to the most powerful, threatens to undo three millennia of progress. The gods are not dead at all. They merely sleep. And they are being hunted.

Senior Inquisitor Tolde Breed is sent to the planet Crimeat to investigate the escape of one of the deadliest beings in the history of the universe: Amongeratix, one of the fabled THREE, sons of the god-king. Tolde arrives on a world where heresy breeds insurrection and war is only a matter of time. Aided by Sister Abigail of the Order of Blood Witches, and a company of Prekhauten Guards, Tolde hurries to find Amongeratix and return him to Conclave custody before he can restart his reign of terror.

What he doesn't know is that the Three are already operating on Crimeat.

ARMIES
of the
SILVER MAGE
CHRISTIAN WARREN
FREED

Malweir was once governed by the order of Mages, bringers of peace and light. Centuries past and the lands prospered. But all was not well. Unknown to most, one mage desired power above all else. He turned his will to the banished Dark Gods and brought war to the free lands. Only a handful of mages survived the betrayal and the Silver Mage was left free to twist the darker races to his bidding. The only thing he needs to complete his plan and rule the world forever are the four shards of the crystal of Tol Shere.

Having spent most of their lives dreaming about leaving their sleepy village and travelling the world, Delin Kerny and Fennic Attleford never thought that one day they would be forced to flee their town to save their lives. Everything changes when they discover the fabled Star Silver sword and learn that there are some who want the weapon for themselves. Hunted by a ruthless mercenary, the boys run from Fel Darrins and are forced into the adventure they only dreamed about.

Ever ashamed of the horrors his kind let loose on the world the last mage, Dakeb, lives his life in shadows. The only thing keeping him alive is his quest to stop the Silver Mage from reassembling the crystal. His chance finally comes through the hearts and wills of Delin and Fennic. Dakeb bestows upon them the crystal shard, entrusting them with the one thing capable of restoring peace to Malweir.

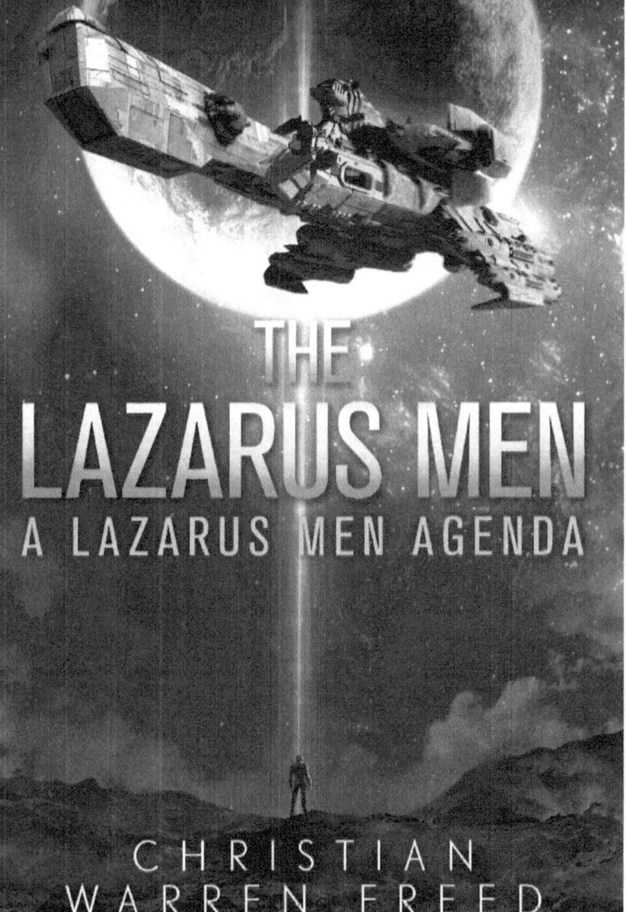

THE
LAZARUS MEN
A LAZARUS MEN AGENDA
CHRISTIAN
WARREN FREED

It is the 23rd century. Humankind has reached the stars, building a tentative empire across a score of worlds. Earth's central government rules weakly as several worlds continue their efforts toward independence. Shadow organizations hide in the midst of the political infighting. Their manifestations of power and influence are beholden only to the highest bidder. The most powerful/insidious/secret of these, The Lazarus Men, has existed for decades, always working outside of morality's constraints. Led by the enigmatic Mr. Shine, their agents are hand selected from the worst humanity has to offer and available for the right price.

Gerald LaPlant lives an ordinary life on Old Earth. That life is thrown into turmoil on the night he stumbles upon the murder of what appears to be a street thief. Fleeing into the night, Gerald finds himself hunted by agents of Roland McMasters, an extremely powerful man dissatisfied with the current regime and with designs on ruling his own empire. In order to do so, McMasters needs the fabled Eye of Karakzaheim, a map leading to immeasurable wealth. Unknown to either man, Mr. Shine has deployed agents in search of the same artifact and will stop at nothing to obtain it.

Running for his life, Gerald quickly becomes embroiled in a conspiracy reaching deep into levels of government that he never imagined existed. His every move is hounded by McMasters' agents and the Lazarus Men. His adventures take him away from the relative safety of Old Earth across the stars and into the heart of McMasters' fledgling empire. The future of the Earth Alliance at stake. If Gerald has any hope of surviving and helping save the alliance he must rely on his wits and awakened instincts while foregoing the one thing that could get him killed more quickly than the rest: trust.

BIO

Christian W. Freed was born in Buffalo, N.Y. more years ago than he would like to remember. After spending more than 20 years in the active duty US Army he has turned his talents to writing. Since retiring, he has gone on to publish more than 20 science fiction and fantasy novels as well as his combat memoirs from his time in Iraq and Afghanistan. His first book, Hammers in the Wind, has been the #1 free book on Kindle 4 times and he holds a fancy certificate from the L Ron Hubbard Writers of the Future Contest.

Passionate about history, he combines his knowledge of the past with modern military tactics to create an engaging, quasi-realistic world for the readers. He graduated from Campbell University with a degree in history and a Masters of Arts degree in Digital Communications from the University of North Carolina at Chapel Hill. He currently lives outside of Raleigh, N.C. and devotes his time to writing, his family, and their two Bernese Mountain Dogs. If you drive by you might just find him on the porch with a cigar in one hand and a pen in the other.